## IT WAS GOING TO BE
## A WICKED SUMMER. . . .

She saw him lying there, stretched out on his surfboard in the early morning sunlight. She wanted to walk casually over and say hello, to reach out and touch that smooth dark skin glistening with moisture and tell him that he was the most beautiful man she had ever seen. But, of course, she wouldn't. She couldn't.

He was not completely naked, although he might as well have been, since the tight red nylon brief he wore did little to conceal his straining manhood.

Slowing her steps as she came down the path through the dunes, she could not seem to take her eyes off the young man with the beautiful body. He was standing on the hard, wet sand near the water's edge, staring off toward the line of surf breaking just offshore.

Then the beautiful stranger carried his surfboard out into the shallows and bent to wax the gleaming fiberglass surface. She watched him, noting the muscular shoulders rippling in the early light. She marveled at his powerful arms, wondering what it would be like to feel them holding her close.

Her pulse began to quicken with every move he made, and she felt sensual tremors that seemed to ignite a warm, tingling excitement in her groin. His long, lean body stretched and twisted over the length of the board. He waxed it to perfection as if he were caressing a lover. . . . It was the beginning of a day, a new summer. Would it be wicked, or wonderful?

*These two would be the least wicked of all the people who'd come to The Hamptons this summer. And, with luck, love might even break through to bless them, should they be among the survivors.*

by Charles Rigdon

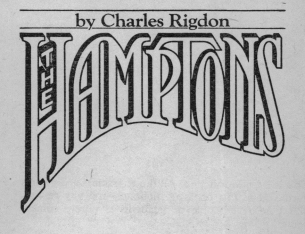
# THE HAMPTONS

PINNACLE BOOKS          LOS ANGELES

This is a work of fiction. All the characters and events portrayed in this book are fictional, and any resemblance to real people or incidents is purely coincidental.

THE HAMPTONS

*Copyright © 1979 by Charles Rigdon*

All rights reserved, including the right to reproduce this book or portions thereof in any form.

An original Pinnacle Books edition, published for the first time anywhere.

First printing, May 1979

ISBN: 0-523-40232-5

Cover illustration by John Solie

*Printed in the United States of America*

PINNACLE BOOKS, INC.
2029 Century Park East
Los Angeles, California 90067

This book is dedicated to my mother, Mary Somerhouse, and in loving memory of Bhagawan Nityananda.

"There are only diamonds in all the world. Diamonds, and perhaps the gift of disillusionment."

—F. Scott Fitzgerald

# AUTHOR'S NOTE

All characters in this novel are purely inventions and should in no way be mistaken for persons either living or dead. The events described are equally fictitious, being merely fragments heard or seen. This is a montage of incidents taken from life and stitched together in composite form, in order to convey something of the dramatic and vivid background against which this very special breed of people play out their lives every summer of the year. They are the rich, the beautiful, and the restless, who inhabit a jet-pleasured world of revolving sex, glamorous celebrity-studded parties, magical drugs, and secret Swiss bank accounts.

For the Hamptons do indeed exist as perhaps the most fascinating, beautiful, compelling, and exclusive resort area in the world today. And while the characters whose lives span a single Hampton season within the pages of this novel are merely literary inventions, they existed at least in my imagination for one glorious, golden, and all-too-brief summer of my life.

# PROLOGUE

The Hamptons lie like a broken strand of glittering gem-stones along the south shore of Long Island: Southampton, Bridgehampton, and Easthampton—jeweled playthings scattered along the seemingly endless summer sands.

Late spring is the sea's wild season along the Hampton shoreline. Dangerous riptides gather far out and hurl their storm-tossed mass against the land, as if washing the beaches clean for the invasion that inevitably comes with the first clear and balmy golden days of early June.

Located just 90 miles due east of the Hudson River, at the end of the Sunrise Highway, the Hamptons are no more than two hours by car from the throbbing central nervous system of the western world. Yet in many ways, they remain light years away—a world set apart with its own rules, rituals, and codes of acceptable conduct.

Manhattan was the jumping-off place, the exuberant Sodom and Gomorrah of the platinum-plated 1970s. It was a brutal monolith of concrete and stone, where escape was akin to survival. A city pulsing with feral energies, its towers and spires rose to dominate the western skyline like a mythical kingdom emerging from a futuristic dream.

At that point in time, it was the axis on which the world turned. And the Hamptons were the seaside playground that drew all comers the way a highly polarized magnet attracts the filings of baser metals.

Mecca, Kismet, and Shangri La. The ultimate triad of resorts, founded and nurtured by the dynamic dollar dynasties of the Irish-Catholic super-rich.

Perfectly preserved from the turn of the century, the Hamptons have survived as enclaves of wealth and privilege. It was there, at the very margins of the lusty and brawling American continent, that baronial castles came to nestle amidst topiary gardens surrounded by putting-green lawns. These were the feudal preserves of tycoons, robber barons, and captains of industry, whose lineal and spiritual descendants continued to return, to spawn, and to perpetuate themselves each summer during the "Hampton season."

They were rich, rebellious, egocentric, and potentially explosive—the restless, footloose siblings of the old guard, coupled with the grand designers who dictated fashion to the world with the imperious wave of a conjurer's wand. They were flamboyant Madison Avenue ad execs and the young genius decorators who shaped and molded the taste and style of an entire culture gone mad with its own creative exuberance.

Together, they reflected the clamor and disparate ingredients of a new, nomadic international elite, a high-powered and disputatious society, whose members were as selfish and disdainful of one another as they were rich and highly mobile. A galaxy of stars singularly burning with a hard, brilliant light.

These were the pace-setters of the trendy, whirlwind seventies: the brilliant, the talented, and the merely beautiful, who hit the Hampton beaches like sailors on liberty, demanding to be fed, fucked, frolicked, and satiated until their psychedelic senses had been drugged into ultimate submission.

With their primal, animal natures aprowl and their egos stripped to the buff, they were the hedonistic *wunderkinder* of a gilded space age—mystical children

2

with golden tans who divided the world between *us* and *them*.

It was summer. The season was upon them, and the Hamptons were the only place to be.

# Roxanne

It was a day filled with sunlight. Beyond the windows of Roxanne's chauffeured white Rolls, Fifth Avenue was a moving, weaving stream of sparkling kaleidoscopic color as brilliantly varied as the shop windows spanning the boulevard. It was a day for light summer dresses, browsing through boutiques, and lunching with friends at the Plaza's Palm Court, and yet Roxanne could scarcely wait to put the city behind her.

In a country with no real tradition of royalty, Roxanne Ryan Aristos had long reigned as virtual queen of the tabloids—a raven-haired American beauty whose aristocratic features automatically would cause the sales figures of any magazine to double in a given month if her face graced its cover.

Roxanne was a deeply ambitious and extremely resourceful woman who, more than anything else, had fully mastered the art of celebrity. First and foremost, she was *the* star among all lesser luminaries. She conveyed a sense of untouchable elegance wherever she went, and in previous marital incarnations had been the wholly owned subsidiary of three of the world's richest, most powerful, and celebrated men.

Roxanne, however, remained a sovereign figure in her own right, and to the public at large, she was imbued with some indefinable magnetism that succeeded in seizing the imagination of large numbers of people. She was a highly social, impeccably groomed aristocrat who collected important diamonds, and was in the habit of

4

marrying rich men the way other women changed their underwear.

In a word, she had charisma—a certain burnished incandescence that went far beyond the famous jewels, the expensive and exquisitely tasteful designer clothes, or even the unshakable self-confidence born of habitual wealth and generations of carefully selective breeding.

Her presence was magnetic and commanding, while the blood running in her veins was of the bluest certified blue. The way she carried herself, however, spoke of both an overriding ego and a sense of relentless self-discipline.

Roxanne was forever smiling and graciously aloof. And she was a diet-conscious food faddist who didn't smoke and never touched alcohol, other than the very finest vintage champagne. Invariably she rose with the birds, and she loved to speak French and ride to the hunt, although she had no real intimates. She herself had created the image that deliberately set her apart, and she jealously guarded her own celebrity with a canny social intelligence that somehow seemed to seal her within a sphere of crystal glass.

Everything about Roxanne reeked of wealth and affluence. She knew everyone of importance, and her celebrity was such that it cut across social barriers the way a laser burns its way through tempered steel. She was rich, highly intelligent, and at the peak of her beauty. Yet for Roxanne there was no such thing as having enough of anything.

Her primary mission in life was marrying rich men. In fact, Roxanne simply could not conceive of herself in any terms other than as the showcase wife of some wealthy and powerful figure of international stature.

In the world in which she traveled, it was money and power that counted, and Roxanne had a practical enough turn of mind to realize that what she was merchandising was depreciating at an alarming rate. The wear and tear incumbent in wedding, bedding, and

5

burying three husbands in 18 years had inevitably taken its psychic toll, although she had numbered among her conquests a Spanish marquis, an English viscount, and a flamboyant Greek shipping tycoon by the name of Stavros Aristos, who had been her latest and richest husband.

Their wedding five years earlier aboard his palatial yacht, the *Golden Hind,* had been considered the international merger of the decade. Roxanne and Stavros had been feted like uncrowned royalty wherever they went. And after their first 12 months of apparent marital bliss, the international press had billed their highly publicized union as "The $20 Million Honeymoon."

Roxanne had expected the honeymoon to go on forever, but soon they were screaming at each other like Greek fishwives in the very best restaurants. More than a few people had heard Stavros take violent exception to Roxanne's role as extravagant, super-consuming goddess of just about everything that money could buy. Before their third anniversary, the "match made in heaven" had become little more than a highly publicized travelogue, with each of its famous participants off and running in a different direction.

Without resolution of their marital difficulties, Stavros had died of a heart attack some 12 months before. But it wasn't until the reading of the will that Roxanne discovered, much to her dismay, that he had failed to leave her the richest widow in the world. Instead, she had been endowed with nothing more than a paltry trust fund, a pair of gold cufflinks, and a drawer full of canceled credit cards.

That final denunciation had come as a terrible shock to Roxanne. And during the long months of official mourning, she had engaged in endless litigation, which had resulted in nothing more than a lot of ugly publicity and revelations of almost obsessive philandering on the part of her late husband.

Throughout it all, the trappings of great wealth in the

6

royal sense had somehow managed to elude her grasp. Roxanne missed the private planes, the $7 million yacht, and the houses and apartments around the world, just waiting for occupancy. Yet perhaps more than anything else, she missed being Mrs. Roxanne Ryan *somebody or other,* and she had absolutely no intention of remaining a widow for long.

As an objective realist, Roxanne realized only too well that there were few miracles after 45 years of age, and she was practically down to her last million.

The coming summer season in the Hamptons was likely to be her last time out on a very fast and slippery track, Roxanne thought, as the Rolls sped through the midtown tunnel. And she had absolutely no intention of letting anyone or anything stand in the way of her acquisitive instincts on the prowl.

Roxanne was out to score—and this time, she was out to score bigger than ever before.

# Kim

Kim Merriweather was a tall, blade-thin California blonde on the run—a disillusioned young cinematographer who had been driving east for two days in a bright red Ford Pinto, when she stopped to pick up a darkly brooding young hitchhiker on the road.

Fleeing the stifling emptiness of her life in Hollywood, Kim had jumped at the chance to work with Franco de Roma, an exuberantly lecherous Italian director of international repute, whose ferocious satire invariably captured images of contemporary society spinning at the vortex of social breakdown.

When Kim received Franco's unexpected cable outlining their collaboration on a BBC documentary about the American rich at play, both her talent and photographic equipment had been gathering dust for over a year. The rent was three months overdue on her small West Hollywood apartment, her unemployment had long since run out, and her live-in actor boyfriend had just walked out, taking the TV and stereo, and leaving Kim with little more than a bruised ego and a stack of unpaid bills.

Kim had never been lucky with men, and she always kept a bail-out bag packed for just such emergencies. She was broke and sick to death of Southern California smog, freeways, and meaningless one-night stands. Twenty-four hours after receiving de Roma's lengthy cable from Paris asking her to join him in the Hamptons, Kim was on her way east.

It was a journey made almost entirely in the fast lane, to resume a relationship broken off over two years before. It had been a relationship she had never wanted in the first place—only this time Kim was no longer willing to compromise her talents by screwing in order to work. She was older now and, she hoped, wiser.

Then, just outside of St. Louis, she picked up Jaime Rodriquez—a beautiful and hardened young drifter who was hitchhiking across the country, with visions of easy money and rich women on the make who would be willing to pay for the only thing he had to sell.

That was it. A brief and highly erotic sexual encounter on the road, between two total strangers in transit. Yet for the first time in both of their short, fast lives, each of them actually felt something stronger than his own obsessive desire to survive in a world where youth and sex were the coins of the realm.

# Jason and Helene

The cockpit of the Tri-Star Executive jet was bathed in a rosy red glow against the vast immensity of night. There had been some turbulence crossing the Carolinas, but Jason had slept right through. Now, as the Tri-Star approached Myrtle Beach, the moonlit Atlantic appeared beyond the left wingtip, with tufts of gossamer cloud punctuating the clear midnight sky.

"Tri Star Bravo Six enroute from Acapulco to Easthampton," Helene radioed the tower. "Presently I'm at fifteen thousand feet, two-six-five compass degrees north by northeast. Please advise on weather conditions —over."

There was a crackling of static; then a deeply male voice reported the weather in a lazy Southern drawl. "It's all clear for smooth sailing all the way to Easthampton," the tower operator radioed. "And by the way, sexy lady—why not drop on down and pay us a visit here in Myrtle Beach? Me and the boys here in the tower would like to have a look at the equipment that goes along with that sexy voice of yours."

The woman poised at the controls of the Tri-Star smiled enigmatically. "I'll take a rain check," she breathed in her husky, slightly baritone voice. "In the meantime, boys, just keep 'em flying. Tri Star Bravo Six—over and out."

The man seated next to Helene in the cockpit stirred, then jerked abruptly upward in his seat, opening a pair of incredibly blue and very bloodshot eyes. "Where the hell are we?" he demanded.

"Relax, darling," Helene responded. "We'll be landing in Easthampton in a little over an hour."

Jason turned to stare at her, and his jaw muscles tightened. "You conniving bitch," he grated out between clenched teeth. "You only came down to Acapulco to get me wasted, so I couldn't drive in the Mazatlan 500. Isn't that the way it was, Helene?"

Helene glanced down at her Cartier watch and smiled thinly. "The race started an hour ago, Acapulco time. And, yes, you're right. I had no intention of seeing you smash yourself up again on some bloody stupid obstacle course somewhere between Acapulco and the asshole of the world. I had your Lotus sent air freight, and if I have anything to say about it, you'll never race again, my darling, so you might as well get that through the steel plate in that thick Germanic skull of yours."

Jason slumped back with his head against the seat, removed a platinum cigarette case from his inside coat pocket, and lit a Salem filter with shaking hands. "You're up to something, aren't you, Helene? I can always tell when you've caught the scent of fresh blood and are moving in for the kill."

"Andrea's coming," Helene responded blandly. "I've invited her to spend the summer with us at Miramar."

She glanced over at the handsome, bronzed man she had married five years before. His lean and leonine features were a great deal more dissipated now. His mouth was a little harder, with the charming, slightly European manner worn a bit thin. The accident had crushed his nerve, Helene thought to herself. It was only the drugs that animated him now, endowing his beautiful, broken body with life.

Jason had closed his eyes, and the narrow scar running from his cheekbone to his chin appeared livid against his pallor. For a moment, Helene thought he was asleep, but then he spoke in a voice from somewhere deep within. "Lay off Andrea, Helene. I'm giving you fair warning that my half-sister and my father's fortune are definitely off limits."

The Baron and Baroness Von Bismark were the couple with everything—the newest jet set darlings of the high-powered social elite who commuted with the regularity of migratory birds between Manhattan, Acapulco, and the Hamptons. By almost anyone's measure, Jason and Helene were a striking duet with just the right combination of title, charm, and good looks overlaid with a veneer of almost casual decadence.

The title was derived from Jason's aristocratic Austrian mother. Helene herself had sprung from far humbler origins, but she seemed to know instinctively everything there was to know about making money. Both claimed to be in their early thirties, although Helene was, in truth, at least eight years older than her handsome and titled husband.

Jason had been graced with the kind of blond Aryan good looks one saw on the skiing slopes at Kitzbuel or St. Anton during the winter season. He had been, in fact, a passionate skier, ardent bicyclist, and racer of fast cars from his early teens on.

There had been a time, not too many years before, when the dashing and recklessly rich Baron Jason Von Bismark Aristos had been clocked as one of the fastest men on the glamorous international racing circuit. But that had been before the spectacular multicar smash-up that had ultimately taken 16 lives and precipitously ended Jason's short, fast career as a professional racing car driver.

Helene was taller than her young husband and was a striking woman with Middle Eastern eyes, flame-colored hair and extraordinary breasts. She had always turned men on like flashing neon, and then just as quickly turned them off again, once they had outlived their usefulness.

12

As the Tri-Star passed over Cape May at 20,000 feet, Helene removed a small cellophane packet from the pocket of her smartly styled pantsuit and handed it across to Jason. "I smuggled a little something through the customs at Nogales, to tide you over, my sweet. But if you don't ease up, you're going to wake up one of these mornings with the *coke horrors* and find that you've got bugs crawling underneath your skin."

Jason did not look at her as he poured a small mound of white powder on his thumbnail and quickly applied it first to one nostril and then the other. Then he licked the sparkling white crystal from his thumbnail, sniffed twice, and blinked hard as crystalline waves began to wash over him and the pain began to ease.

Jason smiled, but it failed to reach his eyes. "You think of everything, don't you, Helene? You're always baiting the hook."

"A girl has to stay on her toes," Helene laughed. "After all, Jason my love, it's no secret that there are sharks in these waters."

# Andrea and Sarah

Monte Carlo was a sprawling white city wilting in the brilliant Mediterranean sunlight. Summer bloomed and blazed, and a moneyed international elite jammed the hotels, filled fine restaurants along the boulevards, and kept the nightclubs, cabarets, and gambling casinos ablaze until dawn.

In the executive board room high atop the towering glass, chrome, and marble Aristos Building, a young woman dressed in deepest mourning was addressing the gathered board members. It had been 12 months since the death of her father, Stavros, and Andrea Aristos sat at the head of the conference table, in the same high-backed leather chair from which he had ruled his maritime empire for over 40 years.

Behind her, the floor-to-ceiling windows provided a magnificent panoramic view of Monaco. Seated at a discreet distance, Sarah Dane, Andrea's friend, advisor, and chief administrative assistant took notes on a steno-type machine, the keys clacking away beneath her prac-ticed fingers, as she recorded every word spoken during Andrea's initial meeting with her board of directors.

"In bringing this meeting to a close," Andrea an-nounced, "I feel it is only fair to advise each of you that there are going to be extensive changes made, now that I am president of Aristos Shipping. I'm sure that all of you are aware that I never had the slightest ambi-tion to fill this seat. But I am very much my father's daughter, and I fully intend to carry out my responsibilities to the very best of my abilities.

"As you know, gentlemen, for the past six months, I have had a prestigious American consulting firm monitoring every phase of Aristos Shipping, as well as the operations of its subidiary companies around the globe. And while each of you has been actively involved in making this company what it is today, I shall not hesitate to dismiss any member of this board who is either unwilling or unable to serve me with the same dedication with which you served my father."

The board room was very silent, and the ten top Aristos executives who sat listening to Andrea around the gleaming conference table gave away nothing of their private thoughts. Several were idly doodling on the thick yellow pads of paper set before each place, while one or two occasionally jotted down notes, figures, or specific memoranda. Most of them, however, sat listening with conspicuously blank expressions, as Andrea confirmed what they all had been dreading for months.

"Now," Andrea said in conclusion, "I will ask my administrative assistant, Mrs. Dane, to present each of you with a brief outline of the changes I have decided to implement. Each of you is to study the proposals at your leisure, and then sign to indicate your willingness to cooperate with the various audits I have instituted throughout the company. The proposals are then to be returned to Monsieur Henri Trouville, who will be acting as chief operating officer during the months of my absence."

Sarah rose and walked around the table, presenting each of the board members present with a leather-bound portfolio entitled "Reorganization Performa—Aristos Shipping."

"I'm sure that you can count on the full support of every man in this board room," Henri Trouville put in smoothly. "And on behalf of my colleagues, I want to wish you both a pleasant journey and safe return to Monaco. Rest assured, Miss Aristos, that we are all totally committed to serving your interests, even as we were dedicated to the service of your father. The company—*your* company—is in the very best of hands."

One hour later, Henri Trouville stood staring out the windows of the executive suite on the twenty-second floor of the Aristos Building. His expression was grim, and his gaze was fixed on the harbor below, where a magnificent white yacht was, at that moment, just starting to sail away.

Gleaming white and pristine in the sunlight, the *Golden Hind* dominated the harbor the way the Aristos building dominated the spectacular Monte Carlo skyline. The yacht, sailing out through the breakwater toward the azure sea beyond, was a breathtaking sight, and Henri Trouville stood watching with narrowed eyes, until he finally was interrupted by a soft buzzing sound.

Tall, silver-haired, and patrician of feature, Henri Trouville was immaculately dressed in an exquisitely tailored double-breasted pinstriped suit. There was a white carnation in his lapel, and he stubbed out his long, thin Monte Cristo cigar before crossing to his desk and pressing a button on the intercom. "Yes, what is it?" he questioned sharply.

"I have your call to the Baroness Von Bismark in New York," a disembodied female voice informed him.

Trouville visibly seemed to relax, and he smiled as he smoothed his luxuriant mustache with an unconscious preening gesture. "Helene, my dear," Henri said, as he picked up the phone. "I've been trying to reach you ever since the board of directors' meeting this afternoon, but your secretary said that you had flown to Acapulco."

Henri listened for a moment and then laughed deep in his throat. "You'd better be careful," he warned.

16

"The overseas operator might be listening in, and get the idea that this is an obscene phone call."

For all his arrogant self-assurance, Henri Trouville was feeling far from secure in his position as executive vice-president of the vast Aristos maritime empire. With Stavros dead and his daughter, Andrea, presently at the helm, changes were taking place fast, and his own base of power was quickly slipping away.

Acting contrary to his advice, Andrea only that morning had advised him of her decision to invest in the construction of a new supertanker despite a shaky world market. It was to be named after her beloved father. But in Henri's personal view, it was more likely to end up as a very costly monument to his passing rather than a viable commercial venture.

But there was far more to it than that. Acting, Henri was convinced, on the advice of Sarah Dane, her administrative assistant and closest friend, Andrea had also announced her intention to broaden the ranks of the aging board of directors, to include younger and more versatile executives brought in from the other side of the Atlantic.

It was, Henri realized, far too early in the game to even begin to assess Andrea's performance as the new operating head of Aristos Shipping. But beyond any question, she had begun making decisions that could very well jeopardize his own vaulted ambitions, even as Helene had predicted some 12 months before.

The king was dead, and the heiress apparent appeared to have some very definite ideas of her own.

"I've missed you terribly, darling," Henri said in a lower and more intimate voice. "But we must move carefully and with great dispatch. The *Golden Hind* has just set sail for America, so it looks as if Andrea is playing directly into our hands."

Henri smiled, listening intently as his eyes swept through the spacious executive suite and came to rest once again on the *Golden Hind,* which now had begun to shrink away upon the sea. "Don't worry about anything on this end, *ma belle* Helene. Just make sure that you gain Andrea's trust, and I'll take care of the rest."

Henri listened a moment and then laughed, flicking a speck of lint from his immaculate cuff. "It's a risky business, I'll grant you, Helene, my love. But then, we are, after all, talking about two billion dollars that is up for grabs."

# Franco de Roma

*"Dans vingt minutes nous allons arrivée à l'aeroport Kennedy. Nous vous remercions d'avoir choisi Air France et esperons de vous retrouver prochainement sur nos lignes."*

The lilting voice of the Air France stewardess completed the monologue in French and then slid easily into English, repeating the same message and adding, "Be sure, please, to take with you your hand baggage, and *merci beaucoup* for flying Air France."

As the girl moved down the aisle of the first-class compartment, checking to see if everyone had fastened his seat belt, Franco de Roma extended his arm slightly on the seat rest so that he deliberately brushed against her most extraordinary *derrière*.

The girl turned in response, but by that time, de Roma was staring out at the endless cloudscape stretching away toward the horizon. He had withdrawn his hand into his lap, and the stewardess's eyes widened as she saw that he was stroking a very sizable hard-on.

De Roma stretched as the girl passed on down the aisle, wiggled his toes in his sharp-pointed Italian shoes, and continued mentally to ravish Kim Merriweather's long, slender stalk of a body. He recalled the exquisitely small buds of her breasts, the long wheat-colored hair, and the glowing amber-flecked eyes that reminded him of nothing so much as the eyes of a hunting tigress.

Even the thought of her caused a familiar electric warmth to circulate upward from his groin and suffuse

19

his entire body with sensual, expectant feelings. Franco closed his eyes and recalled their lovemaking. He could almost taste the sweet tartness of her, wetting his lips with his tongue as if he were outlining the silken cleft between her thighs.

He sighed softly, even as the stewardess passed in the aisle, maintaining a wary and respectable distance between them.

De Roma had always been turned on by tall American types. To his thinking, they had the symmetry and statuesque proportions of skyscrapers, and he was very much looking forward to exploring the structural composition of Kim's magnificent contours during the months to come.

He wanted to move over her body like an explorer—climbing its heights, sinking into its niches, and searching out all its secret crevices. In that moment, flying at 30,000 feet above the Atlantic, at speeds beyond imagining, Franco de Roma felt like Columbus about to discover America.

Ever since their brief affair two years before in Rome, Kim had remained an enigma that both troubled and amazed him. *La California,* as he had fondly labeled her, was quite different from the kind of women Franco was used to—usually, aspiring European actresses he could have any time and any place, for the price of a meal and the vague promise of a part in some future film.

No, most definitely, La California was different—a sorceress who had cast an enchantment, a piece of ripe fruit only waiting to be plucked. She was also a distinct challenge to his Italian ego, but she was a challenge that de Roma fully intended to conquer. De Roma licked his lips in anticipation and whispered her name like a sigh.

The saints had smiled. Fired up by the prospect of filming the American rich in their own natural habitat, and with abundant funds at his disposal, Franco fully intended to make use of Kim's considerable talents as well as gradually break down her defenses. By the end of the summer, La California would be passionately in love with him. This time, however, it would be de Roma himself who would ultimately shout *"Basta,"* and walk out the door.

"I'm concerned about the American girl you've hired to assist with the filming," a querulous voice whispered from the seat next to him. "As you know, your work in the Hamptons must appear to be a perfectly legitimate documentary. No one must discover that I am in any way connected with the project, and the entire affair has to be handled with the strictest security measures in effect at all times. Just how much do you know about this girl and her background?"

De Roma turned to bestow his traveling companion with a wolfish smile, exposing an expanse of slightly yellowed dentures. The man slumped in the seat next to him had a "barf" bag clutched tightly between his hands, and he almost appeared to have been reading Franco's mind. His narrow, aesthetic features were ashen behind a pair of oversize dark glasses, and there was a beret pulled down low over his brow, in an obvious attempt to mask his identity.

"You just leave everything to me," de Roma assured him. "The girl is a first-class technician and very talented as a cinematographer. She is also madly in love with me and will do exactly as I tell her."

De Roma belched softly and made an expressive gesture with both hands. "Trust me, my friend. For the kind of money you are paying me for this project, I would gladly film the devil himself ravishing nuns in the Sistine Chapel. Don't concern yourself further. Everything is going to go exactly as planned. You have the word of Franco de Roma on that."

The heavy whine of the jet engines muted to a distant scream as the French Concorde dropped down out of an enveloping cloud mass and circled in a perfect approach pattern to Kennedy Airport, after the brief three-hour flight from Paris. "Rest assured," de Roma said, smiling, while his heavily pouched eyes gleamed with a hard dull light. "By the time I have completed my film, the Hamptons will never be the same."

# Kamal

Several hours after de Roma's Concorde flight had landed at Kennedy Airport, a bulletproof Caddy limousine preceded by a motorcycle escort with sirens wailing cruised down Forty-third Street in Manhattan and drew up at the curb in front of the Pan American Building.

Attracted by the police escort, low-digit license plates, and golden falcon flags fluttering at the fenders, strollers along the sidewalk quickly coalesced into a loose, curious knot, eagerly crowding forward to peer in through the tinted glass windows for a glimpse of the shadowy figure inside.

Then, as the crowd was rudely elbowed aside by a flying wedge of swarthy-complexioned bodyguards, Kamal Ali Reza, the Midas-rich Middle Eastern mystery man, stepped out of his limousine and was swiftly ushered inside the building.

Ali Reza was robed entirely in white, with the traditional kaffiyeh draped about his handsome, lightly bearded Byzantine face. He wore dark glasses as well, but unlike his attendants, with their fierce eyes that flashed with a primitive vitality, Kamal Ali Reza's expression was one of smiling, almost spiritual, repose.

The flight deck elevator had already been cordoned off, and as soon as Kamal and his entourage stepped inside, it rose with a sibilant whisper to the roof of the Pan Am Building within a matter of seconds.

Everyone had a different story to tell about Kamal

Ali Reza, and the stories for the most part were based at least partially on fact. He was usually said to be the bastard half-brother of a Saudi Arabian prince and was a man who had parlayed a seemingly unbeatable combination of charm, mercurial brilliance, moviestar good looks, and relentless opportunism into an Arabian Nights saga of unparalleled success.

Reputed to be worth uncounted billions, Kamal's name was seldom seen in print, and yet it was also said that not a single barrel of crude petroleum reached the west without Ali Reza cutting himself in on the take by one means or another.

For the most part, Kamal moved about the world aboard his fleet of private planes, helicopters, yachts, and limousines, scarcely stirring the air. And yet as evidence of his influence and wide-ranging connections in governments around the world he always received VIP treatment wherever he went.

Whatever the truth about Kamal Ali Reza, he was without question very smooth, very rich, and very, very powerful. The Pan Am heliport had been closed to regular helicopter traffic that afternoon in anticipation of his arrival, and upon emerging from the flight deck elevator, Ali Reza was met by a tall, spare man named Darnell Hanlan—a grim and dour figure of decidedly avian countenance, who in spite of the 87-degree temperature, was dressed entirely in leather.

In contrast to Kamal's smiling face, Hanlan had intensely brooding, saturnine features. The two men shook hands, engaged in several moments of brief and animated conversation, and then climbed aboard Kamal's 16-passenger helicopter emblazoned with twin golden falcons on the fuselage.

After Ali Reza's heavily armed bodyguards had scrambled aboard, the chopper lifted effortlessly into the air above midtown Manhattan and fluttered skyward across the East River, glinting silver in the bright June sunlight.

The original Darnell Hanlan had come to the American continent in 1654 with a British expeditionary force. And shortly thereafter, he had purchased the lush and richly fertile Sagaponak Island from the Montauk Indians. The price: ten bolts of calico cloth, some trinkets of little value, one large and very old St. Bernard dog, and three bottles of rum.

The island had remained in the Hanlan family ever since. Yet now, during their brief flight eastward toward Montauk Point, a deal was consummated in which Kamal Ali Reza agreed to purchase all rights to Hanlan's island for a considerably larger amount.

The final papers were signed in flight. A black Moroccan leather attaché case exchanged hands, and Darnell smiled narrowly—and for the first time. Then he snapped open the lid to feast his eyes greedily on $5 million in neatly banded and crisp, tax-free $50,000 bills.

It was enough money, he thought, to destroy them all, one by one. He would have his revenge and then some, on all those who had sought to rob him of his ancestral heritage.

After dropping his passenger at the Easthampton airport, Kamal took over the controls of the helicopter and skimmed low over stately mansions, exclusive country clubs, a half-dozen of the world's best golf courses, and seemingly endless miles of dazzling white sandy beaches.

It was a seductive panorama of white sails and azure sun-sparkled waters. And off on the horizon, the island he had purchased from Darnell Hanlan had become clearly visible. It looked lush, green, and inviting in the distance, with softly curling hills peaking up like a woman's breasts to gently caress a clear and cloudless sky.

There was no other island like it in the entire world, Kamal thought to himself, no other place like the fabled Hamptons. He laughed, savoring the challenge that sent adrenalin shooting through his veins. Within three months, Kamal vowed, he would rule there like a king, surrounded by a slavishly fawning court of the rich, the celebrated, and the beautiful.

Kamal Ali Reza played only for very high stakes, and he always played to win.

# Claire

Claire Ryan Spencer poured herself the first Bloody Mary of the morning and then retired to the deck behind the house on Georgica Road. The house was in the estate section of Easthampton, but by Claire's own estimation, it was far from being an estate, and there wasn't even a pool.

It was merely a comfortable three-bedroom home on a single landscaped acre, surrounded by trees and a rose garden that Claire carefully and lovingly tended herself even though the gardener came twice a week. There was a maid's room as well, but there was only a three-day-a-week cleaning woman who did most of the heavy housework, since Claire's husband, Clayton, was "too fucking cheap" to pay for live-in help.

Claire stretched out on a padded lounger and swallowed some of her drink. Then, setting the glass aside, she reached for the Bain de Soleil and began smoothing a thin layer over her face and shoulders.

She lay back with her face lifted to the sun and willed the mind-blowing hangover she had awakened with that morning simply to go away.

According to Krishna Ram, her yoga teacher, Claire's body belonged to her, but in reality, she was *not* her body, and through the power of her mind, she could will it to do anything she wished. All very well and good if you just happened to be an Indian swami, Claire thought to herself. But what if you just wanted to be able to have an orgasm like every other woman she knew, or get rid of the hangover that was at that moment making her life miserable?

Her head was splitting, and for the moment, Claire was relatively sure that she didn't really want clear title to any of her anatomy, since all of it seemed to be betraying her in one way or another.

Claire was queen of the nocturnals—flying high every night of the week on diet pills, liquor, and the desire to escape the all-too-predictable boredom of being married to a man she found dull in bed, intellectually stuffy, and sexually uninspiring.

There could never be a moment of dead air or solitude in Claire's life—no space that wasn't filled with people who were as pretty, bright, and amusing as herself. She was always reaching for that second-strike capability that made everything seem better than it was, the psychic jolt of booze or pills that carried her beyond tired feet, tight pantyhose, utter boredom, and on into the shimmery, kaleidoscopic glitter-world of the "forever young."

Claire always had to be functioning at full throttle just to stay even, for if she ever dared to slow down for even a moment's quiet introspection, her anguish would swiftly begin to overtake her, and the game would very likely be called on account of incipient menopause.

Her sister, Roxanne, had phoned about 20 minutes before, to say that she was driving out to Easthampton and bringing with her some gowns she had tired of over the winter. It seemed to Claire on that particular morning that, more often than not, she always ended up making do with Roxanne's discards—not just the clothes her sister bought by the warehouse lot, or the amusing costume jewelry that had ceased to amuse, but the people Roxanne discarded as well.

In fact, Claire's own circle of friends was virtually littered with Roxanne's mistakes, those social faux pas of one persuasion or another, whom the imperious

Roxanne had banished from her circle for just not measuring up.

Even Claire's husband, Clayton, was one of her sister's cast-off beaux, from their early debutante days. But like almost everything else in Claire's life, Clayton had turned out to be a flop. A mildly innocuous country doctor at heart, he had been driven by his wife's relentless ambition to be "somebody" and had ended up as a plastic surgeon in attendance to some of high society's most distinguished aging faces, sagging breasts, and fallen buttocks.

He was far better known, however, for jacking up his celebrated clientele with booster rockets loaded with B-12 and a liberal quantity of speed. Of course, when everything began to go at once, there was always the promise of a total overhaul when one checked into Clayton's Golden Portals beauty farm, for two full weeks of placental injections, rigorous exercise, and a quick nip and tuck around the eyes.

Claire hadn't slept with Clayton for more years than she dared to admit, even to herself. There had, of course, been a variety of casual flings along the way, but Clayton had, thankfully, kept his own council in that regard, even though he must have known that she played around.

Gossip traveled faster than the speed of light in the Hamptons, and it was by now common knowledge that she and Clayton shared little beyond a Manhattan *pied à terre,* the Easthampton beach house, and *His* and *Hers* cabanas at the Maidstone Club.

Having inhabited the body that belonged to her but was not really hers for over four decades, Claire realized with poignant clarity that she wanted far more out of life than she had been getting. Deep in her heart, she had always believed that she deserved Winston jewels, clothes by Valentino, Dom Perignon every night of the week, and a dashing and romantic lover with a nine-inch cock.

29

Yet invariably, Claire ended up settling for paste copies, off-the-rack fashions, sparkling burgundy, and a limp handful, since most of the men she slept with usually were far too inebriated to even get it up.

Claire tried to relax, holding herself very still and willing the sun to do its work, to gloss her flesh with the illusion of youthfulness for a least one more summer season.

Throughout the long, sun-drenched summer days, wives of the Hampton summer colony, like Claire, could be found sprawled beside gelid aquamarine swimming pools, tossing off Bloody Marys and stuffed to the eyelashes on diet pills. They gossiped endlessly about hairdressers, face and body lifts, and who was currently sleeping with whom, in the ongoing game of musical beds.

While the womenfolk of the Hamptons were condemned to idleness and the pursuit of any well-hung male who happened to remain at large, it was quite a different story for their husbands. At least as far as logistics were concerned.

The Hamptons were, in fact, the culmination of a wild steeplechase ride across Long Island, beginning in the trenches of Grand Central Station. Hot, frenzied, and flying high on shakers of martinis, they all gathered together like lemmings each evening at the various *salles d'armes,* awaiting their pleasure among a gilded international elite—stylish foreigners oozing cachet and with enough loot stashed away in Swiss banks to allow them to live outside their countries of origin, most of which were galloping toward Communism by way of skyrocketing inflation.

The Hamptons were a world away from all that, and the disco-dancing scene was most definitely where it was at that season. It was all programmed by pied pipers of rock music, who gradually upgraded the frenzy quotient from within tinted plastic bubbles high above the dance floor. Through the drifting lavender smoke haze, Gucci- and Pucci-clad swingers could be seen hurling themselves at the mirrored walls like so many insects smashing heedlessly into onrushing headlights.

Everybody was out to get laid, and they all went at it with the single-minded intensity of shipwrecked sailors marooned on a desert island. Claire had observed, over the course of many summers, that no one seemed to be the least bit particular, and the various sexual couplings appeared to be merely a continuation of overriding acquisitive instincts—those same competitive drives that paid the tab for all those jacked-up booze and grocery bills, outrageously overpriced beach pads, and the inevitable influx of freeloading weekend guests, who descended like a horde of locusts every Friday evening.

*Action* was the watchword and Orgy was where much of it was heading—the ritual laying-on of hands and coupling of limbs, *la dolce vita* American style, fueled by an apothecary's grab-bag of drugs, and driven ever onward and upward by the compelling beat of disco music pounding away until dawn.

The fabled rites of summer were being led that particular season by trendy bisexual types—sybaritic switch-hitters who simply loved to see people get off amidst the chic accoutrements of a big hash and coke bash, one very likely to feature $1,000 worth of sparkling, magic crystals that simply everybody was snorting that summer.

It was all instant F. Scott Fitzgerald, seventies style, where the name of the game was "Choose Your Own Poison"—booze or drugs. And always there was sex—good old carnal knowledge, in whatever color, size, frequency, and kinkiness one might desire.

Claire herself had always been a one-man woman, she speculated idly, while rubbing on another layer of golden tanning oil—one man at a time, that was, and there had been plenty over the years. Still, none of them had ever measured up to her latest lover. He was simply incredible. Every time Claire went back over their meeting in her mind, she could scarcely believe it had actually happened to her.

Several evenings before, she had been dining with friends at Regine's in Manhattan when she saw him sitting there alone, at the most important table in the house. He was dark, devastatingly handsome, discreetly shadowed by bodyguards, and unquestionably the most intriguing man she had ever seen.

Their eyes met, locked, and held. Then he smiled in a way that made Claire go weak in the knees.

By midnight, Claire had found herself in the huge circular bed of Kamal Ali Reza's permanent Plaza suite. There was a mirrored ceiling overhead, and a host of erotic playthings had been readily available for instant amusement.

It all got pretty hazy as the evening wore on and the champagne continued to flow. Claire recalled the look of his dark body moving over hers in the mirrored ceiling, like some alien being from another world. The heady, musky scent of him made her dizzy, and the strange, shivery sensation she had experienced at his caress was like an electric shock.

Claire tried not to think of the things to which Kamal had forced her to submit during their night of sensual abandon. Everyone knew, after all, that rich Arabs were kinky as hell and went in for all sorts of highly exotic amusements.

All that simply didn't matter. It was enough that Claire had found herself in bed with a man her sister Roxanne would gladly give ten years of her life to have bagged on her own. Kamal was charming, rich, as handsome as Omar Sharif, and Claire was desperately hoping that she would hear from him again.

To belong to a man like that, she decided, there could be no price that was too high to pay.

# ═══CHAPTER 1═══

Abbey saw him lying there stretched out on his surfboard in the early morning sunlight.

He was beautiful, she thought, and she wanted to walk casually over and say hello, to reach out and touch that smooth, dark skin glistening with moisture and tell him that he was the most beautiful man she had ever seen. But of course, she wouldn't. She couldn't.

He was not completely naked, although he might as well have been, since the tight red nylon brief he wore did little to conceal his straining manhood.

Abbey often came out to Montauk Beach in the early morning to sketch or search for shells and bits of colored beach glass washed up by the outgoing tide. During the summer months, it was far less crowded than the Hampton public beaches, and she had a special place among the dunes, where she could watch without being seen.

The Montauk Peninsula jutting out into the pounding waters of the Atlantic was in itself a spectacular sight. There were thousands of woodland acres, stark cliffs, high dunes, and seemingly endless miles of wide white sandy beaches. There was always an offshore wind blowing through the golden sea grass, and on that particular morning, streamers of yellow, mauve, and ocher stained the sky like translucent watercolors spread on a vast canvas.

Slowing her steps as she came down the path through

the dunes, Abbey could not seem to take her eyes off the young man with the beautiful body. He had by now risen from his surfboard and was standing on the hard, wet sand near the water's edge, staring off toward the line of surf breaking just offshore.

Between them, the dunes leveled out into a wide white beach where a cluster of bright umbrellas dotted the sand and a variety of anonymous legs stuck out from under them. Some teenage girls she recognized from Easthampton were lying on a blanket nearby. Beneath her feet the sand was very warm, and it looked newly washed as it gathered the light from the sea.

Abbey finally dropped down on the sand and quickly opened her sketching pad upon her knees. She could feel the sun burning through her blouse, and the blue jeans she wore had turned pleasantly warm against her flesh.

The beautiful stranger by now had carried his board out into the shallows and bent to wax the gleaming fiberglass surface. Abbey began sketching with swift, sure strokes, recording the muscular shoulders rippling in the early light. She marveled at the powerful arms as she worked, wondering what it would be like to feel them holding her close.

His legs were long and well-defined and his waist slim and hard, with black hair curling crisply upward over his flat belly to blanket his chest like the opulent pelt on some male animal.

Abbey's pulse began to quicken as she continued to sketch. With every move he made, she felt sensual tremors that seemed to ignite a warm, tingling excitement in her groin. His long, lean body stretched and twisted over the entire length of the board. He waxed it to perfection as if he were caressing a lover.

Although it was only shortly before ten o'clock in the morning, the sun already was very warm. Perspiration glistened against his bronze-toned skin, and the mass of wavy dark hair curled damply at the back of his neck. Then he shoved his board out into deeper water, leaped on top of it, and began paddling swiftly away from shore.

Abbey continued sketching him for some time, with total concentration. Finally, however, she closed her sketching pad, spread out her towel, and slid her blue jeans down over her legs. Underneath, she was wearing a one-piece fishnet bathing suit, by now many seasons out of fashion.

Her mother, Annabel, had always insisted on helping Abbey shop for her clothes, pointing out what was "too flashy, immodest, or simply inappropriate, for a girl of her breeding and social position."

Nice girls simply didn't show everything they had, according to Annabel Randolph—not unless they wanted to start a lot of loose talk and be classed with those fast types, who wore "scads of makeup and dressed with a total lack of modesty."

Sprawled languidly on a blanket farther down the beach were two of the very types her mother was always warning Abbey to avoid. They were the twin teenage daughters of a prominent Easthampton stockbroker, and their white-blonde manes hung to their shoulders as straight as corn silk.

Both of them had perfect tennis tans and pouting, spoiled faces. Abbey had heard that they were a pretty wild pair. Nothing was too far out for them, and gossip had it that they took their sexual pleasure wherever they found it and with whomever happened along.

The Bailey twins were the offshoots of the indifferent parentage whom Annabel Randolph held largely responsible for turning the summer Hamptons into a mecca for permissive sex, all manner of drug abuse, and trouble in general.

Sex, beyond the most mundane and mechanical de-

35

tails had simply never been considered a matter worthy of discussion within the Randolph family. And yet Abbey herself thought of little else.

Men were constantly on her mind—beautiful young men like the lifeguards she saw along the beaches during the summer months, golden youths with strong, well-muscled bodies, and shaggy hair curling about their handsome faces. At times, Abbey felt that she was possessed by men's crotches. She was utterly appalled by her own wanton desires, yet remained totally incapable of doing anything about them.

Abbey had never really dated, at least not with any one she really wanted to go out with. Her various suitors had all been carefully selected by her mother and few of them had ever bothered to call for a second date.

She had lived in the Hamptons all her life and was only too aware that all those nice young girls from the very best families were out fucking like rabbits, apparently without being terribly particular about who their sex partners were and without experiencing the slightest twinge of guilt or shame.

Guilt and shame were the two emotions most prominent in Abbey's psyche—with the possible exception of envy. She couldn't help but envy the lax and gilded Hampton youth, with their perfect teeth, sun-streaked hair, and smooth, even tans. With the heavy influx of a wild new summer crowd during the past few seasons, they invariably glided early into the highly erotic disco-dancing crotch, tits and ass scene, while their secretly alcoholic parents were fully preoccupied with getting blitzed at the Maidstone or the Southampton Yacht and Tennis Club.

They were the emergent *demimonde* who crashed like waves against all those miles of golden shoreline, whacked out of their skulls all summer long on mescaline, grass, and coke, which, Abbey had heard, was the very latest "with it" drug that season. Coke was supposed to be the ultimate sensual high, preferred by the free-wheeling Hampton drug culture with its coterie of millionaire rock stars, cleverly amusing gays, and one-of-a-kind ethnics.

Abbey sighed, opened her sketch pad to stare for a moment at the drawings she had done, and then turned over on her stomach to allow the warmth of the sand to penetrate her flesh. Who was he? she wondered, staring off toward the figure in the red bathing suit. What was his name? And what was it about him that engendered the desperate longing she felt to love and to be loved?

He had paddled far out by now and was sitting upon his board, waiting for just the right wave. He leaned back with his face lifted to the sun and his long legs dangling in the water in an attitude of perfect, watchful repose.

Abbey closed her eyes and pressed her body against the warm sand. What would it be like, she wondered, to feel him pulsing hard inside her, to taste his mouth on hers, to have him flood her with his orgasm and whisper endearments as she writhed and clung to him in an ecstasy of sexual liberation?

Even after the imperious Annabel Randolph had engaged their family doctor to explain and define the broad generalities of sex to her only daughter, Abbey could never really imagine her mother actually doing it.

She had been born to her parents in their middle age, and her earliest and most treasured memories were of riding horseback with her father along that very same stretch of beach. Abbey couldn't have been more than five or six at the time, and yet she vividly recalled pressing her body against her father and feeling the warmth and security of being firmly encircled by strong masculine arms.

Brewster Randolph was long dead and buried now, and yet Abbey vividly remembered her father as a handsome, laughing man full of sparkling Irish humor and warm, generous gestures. What he had ever seen in her mother, she couldn't possibly imagine, for Annabel Randolph was the very epitome of coldly repressed sexuality, lacking the slightest modicum of warmth or sensitivity.

At her mother's insistence, Abbey had attended private Catholic girls' schools all her life, where she had always been considered a loner, a dreamer of distant dreams who wanted more than anything else to be a ballet dancer and was utterly terrified of the nuns, who always reminded her of black bats with pale, semihuman faces.

The other girls, secure in the safety of their own cliques, often cruelly ridiculed Abbey for her bookish attitudes and gangly awkwardness in sports. During the long years when she was forced to wear braces on her teeth and skirts well below her knees, Abbey had donned an armor of indifference, which she wore as a shield to keep anyone from knowing the depth of her pain and loneliness.

Her father, really her only link to reality, had drunk himself to death by the time Abbey was 14, and her body had begun to show the promise of ripening young womanhood. She had, in fact, gotten her first period on the very day they buried him in the Easthampton cemetery.

Annabel, for her part, had treated her daughter's approaching fertility as something requiring exorcism. Bishop Quinlan had been called in, and after a stern lecture on the evils of promiscuity, Abbey had been locked in her room as if somehow she had been cursed by God.

After that, when Abbey got "her monthly," she would often stand nude in front of the mirror, examining herself for hours on end. She hated her body. Her hair was the color of church mice, and the solemn gray eyes staring back from her reflection had the look of something trapped, something searching desperately for a means of escape.

Perhaps she wasn't really all that ugly, Abbey admitted a bit reluctantly. But on the other hand, no one was ever going to scale the walls of Bramwell Acres to free her from the imprisonment of her mother's steely will.

More than anything else in the world, Abbey wanted to fall hopelessly in love. She needed desperately to mean something to someone very special, and that need filled her with fierce and urgent longings.

By the middle of her sophomore year at St. Mary's of the "Immaculate Contraception" (as the other girls called it), Abbey was convinced that she was probably the only virgin in the entire school. Sex seemed to be the single topic of conversation, and it was openly discussed in the classrooms, washrooms, and cafeteria during lunch break.

Abbey was both shocked and fascinated by the frankness of the whispered conversations she heard going on around her. They were vulgar and disgusting, and yet she didn't want to miss a single word of what was being said. The sexual exploits of her schoolmates, however, were ultimately little more than exercises in masochism. With desperate longing, Abbey dreamed of having a boy make wild, passionate love to her, until sex was literally all she thought of. She attended all the local wrestling matches and swimming meets, avidly watching the straining muscles and utterly fascinated by the sweating, entangled limbs and bulging jock straps that drew her eyes like a magnet.

Sex seemed to surround and envelop her, blaring its seductive message from every TV commercial and billboard and leaping out at her from magazine racks where she nervously purchased copies of *Viva, Playgirl,* and *Penthouse Forum.* Abbey even went so far as to send for a nifty little package called The Love Kit,

39

which was said to contain "a thousand and one nights of purest ecstasy." Fruit-flavored lubricant, a seven-inch vibrator with batteries, and 100 Vitamin E capsules were included in the offering, as well as a musky fragrance called Jungle Love.

Everything that Abbey saw, heard, or read seemed to be utterly saturated with sex, continually pounding home the message that all you really needed to get laid was to have minty breath, an herbal essence crotch, a free-form panty girdle, and some kind of cold power laundry soap in your washer.

Throughout the spring, Abbey had virtually haunted a small art theater in Bridgehampton that was showing a sudden rush of badly dubbed vintage Italian movies. They were lavishly costumed spectacles presenting heroic beefcake gladiators stripped to the waist in hand-to-hand combat, battling each other to the death for the love of some melon-breasted Italian actress with slumberous lynx eyes; wide, sex-cushioning hips; and flowing dark tresses.

Abbey had seen them all at least twice, and her nightly fantasies had become richer and her sexual needs ever more compelling with the advent of summer. By June, her lusty phantom lovers had begun to take the form of rebellious slaves, youthful swim stars, and wrestling duos, all of whom paid nightly visits to her crinoline-canopied bed.

Even though the Catholic girls' school jumpers, white blouses, and saddle shoes were gone, her hymen was still very much intact. Beneath Annabel's ever-vigilant eyes, Abbey had never smoked a cigarette or touched a drop of alcohol, nor had she been touched intimately by a male hand.

The temptation was there, of course, to simply follow the example set by her classmates. But Abbey was afraid, since her mother's penetrating gray gaze was easily the equivalent of a combination lie-detector test and vaginal exam rolled into one.

At 28 years of age, Abbey Randolph looked sweet 16 going on lost horizons. While plain of feature, she had about her an elusive fragile quality, and she had always been so very breakable. She was not at all bright, glamorous, or socially aggressive like Roxanne and Claire.

The two sisters were her maternal cousins, and it had always seemed to Abbey that their hearts and emotions had come equipped with steel buttressing and Farberware safety valves.

Abbey was growing desperate. And it had begun to appear that her mother's single compelling mission in life was to keep her hymen intact until she could somehow manage to marry her off to some very rich, very socially acceptable, and very boring man of her own choosing—a second or third cousin, perhaps, who would most likely be paunchy, middle-aged, and highly unlikely in any case to miraculously restore the sorely depleted Randolph family fortunes, for the truth of the matter was that Bramwell Acres was in hock right up to the hilt, even though Annabel was far too proud to let anyone know that they were living on borrowed time.

Abbey sat up and looked around. She must have dozed, she realized. The young man she had been sketching earlier had come in from the water and now was walking up the beach, his surfboard slung casually under one arm.

As he drew closer, Abbey saw that the twins had taken off their bathing suit tops to expose their breasts to the burning rays of the sun. Their faces wore the regulation bored and disinterested look of the young, smart set, but it was clear to Abbey that they were anything but that.

"How's the surf?" one of the girls called out with a white, wide, inviting smile. Abbey wasn't sure which of them it was who had spoken, since they were absolutely identical, but she did know that she hated her for having the nerve to make such an obvious approach, while Abbey herself could only remain utterly mute.

The bronzed young stranger nodded and smiled. "Not bad," he replied in a surprisingly soft baritone. "But I've seen better."

Without another word, he continued on up the beach to where he had left his clothing neatly folded on a driftwood log. Then, with a total lack of self-consciousness, the young man, whom Abbey assumed to be somewhere in his early twenties, stripped out of his wet swim suit and proceeded to dry each part of his body carefully and thoroughly—face, neck, arms, chest, and finally his legs.

He used short, rough strokes and all the while he kept his eyes trained on the surf, which by now was piling in without pause. They were the largest waves of the morning, and after breaking in the shallows, they came hissing up the sand in a foaming rush and swirl of weed-strewn seawater.

Abbey began to feel sexual panic as the bronzed youth turned suddenly to stare directly at her, flashing a devastating white smile. Then, with the twins turning to watch, he snapped his towel out to its full length and quickly slipped it between his legs, pulling it back and forth in a seesaw motion against his crotch. His sex was hanging full and slightly tumescent, exposed with casual disregard to the sun and the day.

"Well, get a load of Hungry Hannah," one of the twins laughed. "She acts as if she's never seen a man's prick before."

Abbey could have died on the spot. But already the twins were gathering up their beach things to sidle over and engage the young surfer in conversation as he finished dressing. She couldn't hear what was said between them, but several minutes later, the newly formed threesome left the beach and went speeding off toward town in the twins' white Mercedes convertible.

Abbey just sat there among the dunes, remembering

42

his smile. Somehow, she felt that they had made contact, and her heart was pounding wildly in her breast as hot tears of frustration brimmed and spilled down her cheeks.

# ═══CHAPTER 2═══

Ever since Precambrian times, the Hamptons had been a place of sweet summers, lush vegetation, numerous clear-water ponds, and broad meadows covered with wildflowers.

The wind seemed to have been blowing there since the beginning of time. And the thunder of the surf was always gently underlaid with the whisper of golden sea grass, waving like Kansas wheat across the dunes.

Jaime had walked for over a mile up the beach that day, and by the time he reached the cliffs at Montauk, he was breathing hard. Pausing to catch his breath, he shook a joint from the back of his cigarette pack, shielded the match flame from the wind as he lit it, and inhaled the raw cannabis deep into his lungs.

Far in the distance, thunderheads had begun to gather and darken on the horizon, while sunlight flashed through layers of cumulus clouds to throw translucent patches of light on the sea below. There was a storm on the way, and Jaime estimated that he would just about have time to catch the early edge of it before the heavy seas became too treacherous to maneuver.

In surf like that, a simple miscalculation could easily reduce a board to kindling. Jamie, however, was used to living very close to the edge, and his day-to-day survival had always been a challenge to be met without question—like the weather, or being born in the first place.

The grass was beginning to work on his head. Tasting the clean salt air, Jaime allowed his eyes to drink in the rugged majesty of the coastline. There was something lonely and vast about the Atlantic, he thought—so different from the normally placid Gulf coast of Texas, where he had surfed and swam throughout his youth. He had always surfed the Gulf when it was announced that there was a hurricane roaring in.

Pitting himself against the elements was like a very potent aphrodisiac to Jaime, and he had climbed the cliffs that day to check out an almost inaccessible surfing spot called Suicide Alley.

Far below his perch on the face of the dun-colored palisades, huge combers battered the rugged shoreline with a deep, thundering roar. They were hollow—timeless—barreling into shore with a sound like the rumbling of great stones rolling together far in the primeval depths.

The tube at Suicide Alley, Jaime decided, was a killer all right. But some day, he promised himself, he'd come back to surf it. On that particular afternoon, he still had the entire summer stretching ahead of him like a yellow brick road, and he was in no mood to play Russian roulette with sea.

Jaime Rodriquez had spent his entire life in transit. He was, perhaps more than anything else, a drifter possessed by a dream—a very special place to which he could always withdraw in his imagination when the world started closing in on him.

In spite of all the detours he had been forced to take along the way, Jaime had been heading for Rio de Janeiro for as long as he could remember. It seemed to shimmer there in his mind's eye, a travel poster vision of a lush tropical landscape with white crystalline beaches and a sugarloaf mountain standing sentinel like a lofty and benevolent deity.

The surfing there was said to be the best in the world; the women were beautiful; and the seasons had

45

been combined into one long and endless summer.

To get there would cost money, and Jaime had left New Orleans in late spring after hearing fantastic stories about the streets of New York City. They were said to be paved with crisp green currency of large denominations, and money was exactly what Jaime needed to make his South American getaway a reality.

The coin of the realm was sex. And the product being merchandised was half Mexican, a dash of Apache Indian, and a lot of inter-*Americano* cross-breeding. Jaime had been born in Brownsville, Texas, where his mother had been a teenage prostitute. He'd never really known too much about her, other than the fact that she'd been pretty, and there had been a younger sister who had somehow gotten lost in a series of foster homes along the way.

Jaime never looked back and had learned from experience to live strictly within the moment. He had always been a street-tough loner whose past was like a trapdoor opening into a bottomless abyss.

With his dark, handsome features and pale green eyes that spoke of sea and distance, he'd never had any trouble getting along. His body was his fortune, and he had worked out over the years to develop his physique into a compact muscular mechanism of seduction. Jaime had been selling his sex for as long as he could remember.

With no more than five dollars in his jeans, his board slung under his arm, and a knapsack slung across his shoulder, Jaime had started hitchhiking north late in the spring. His ultimate destination was New York City's Forty-second Street, where he intended to hustle. But that was before he met Kim Merriweather.

After she picked him up on the highway, everything in Jaime's life began to change, and he wasn't even sure why. Kim was totally unlike any other girl that Jaime had ever encountered. There was an easy, earth-mother quality about her. And after making love that first night in a field of new-mown clover, he had found himself speeding east behind the wheel of her red Ford Pinto, heading for a place he had never even heard of, called the Hamptons.

Jaime hadn't seen Kim since the day of their arrival, although he liked her far more than he was willing to admit, even to himself.

But there was just no place for a girl like that in Jaime's life, and their relationship had ended very much as it had begun.

Upon arriving in Easthampton, Kim had stopped the car to go into a drug store for cigarettes. When she came out, Jaime was gone. He had simply taken his belongings and disappeared.

As it turned out, the Hamptons exceeded anything that Jaime might have imagined. And like a stray dog suddenly finding himself in a strange neighborhood, he had spent his first week making a careful reconnaissance of the territory.

South- and Easthampton were elegant, exclusive resorts for the very rich, with opulent estates, vast sandy white beaches, and beautiful yachts dotting the harbors. Westhampton and Bridgehampton, on the other hand, seemed to be somewhat more Bohemian in character, and they appeared to attract a wide cross-section of famous writers, painters, and theatrical personalities, with a smattering of millionaire rock stars—those essentially sybaritic types, whose summer pleasure domes were set upon exquisitely leveled stages among the dunes like illuminated display cases.

There seemed to be attractive people everywhere—lithe and golden women with ageless bodies, streaked hair, and stylishly contoured breasts. Their faces seemed to wear a look of almost terminal boredom, and yet their smiles had a way of conveying some kind of mysterious sensual promise.

They moved with a languid, easy grace, as if totally unaware of their beauty or the allure of their perpetually tanned bodies. They had searching huntress eyes, and up until the time of his arrival, Jaime had not even been aware that such creatures existed outside the pages of glossy fashion magazines.

Like their female counterparts, the men of the Hamptons appeared to be somehow suspended in time— eternally youthful, with lean, well-proportioned bodies and a swinging, confident stride. Their faces were firm and purposeful. They were men used to success, who tanned evenly and seemed equally willing to share their beds with either sex.

It was a whole new world for Jaime Rodriquez, and it was populated by the most extraordinary breed of people he had ever encountered. He was, of course, aware of the curiosity his presence created among them. But, then, Jaime had always been aware of his sensual appeal to both men and women alike. There was something about his eyes, his smile, and the way he carried himself. He had a highly potent sexuality that he took very much for granted.

Wearing his tight, faded jeans, T-shirt, and sandals like a second skin, he could feel their eyes upon him as he walked down the street. Women would turn to stare, and the men would smile and nod with the promise of something left unsaid.

The storm was building now, and Jaime finished his joint and started down the steep path toward the beach. The twins he had met the day before had been voracious. The three of them had dropped acid together, and the effects of the drug were still with him.

After getting it on in the pool house of their parents' pad, they had taken him to dinner at Squire's, and then on to a discotheque called Shazam.

It had been a wild scene, and Jaime had ended up spending every cent that he had. What he needed now was to score—a fast, easy make, like the girl he had seen sketching on the beach the day before.

* * *

48

Annabel Randolph was a magnificent-looking woman. Her perfectly coiffed hair was bone white and pulled high on her head in a coronet. The severity of style had never varied for as long as Abbey could remember, and with the imposing forehead and straight, aquiline nose, her mother's profile reminded her of an ancient Medea.

Both Abbey and her mother had long since been passed over by their more affluent relations, left like relics from a bygone age to guard the family feuds, endure the endless boredom, and nurse all manner of idiosyncrasies common to those of high breeding, impeccable moral standards, and sadly fallen financial status.

The morning fog so common at that time of year pressed close with soft, spongy fingers against the library windows. There was a wide covered porch encircling the lower floor of the old gabled mansion at the end of Lily Pad Lane, and the catalpa trees lining the long drive leading up to the house were still shrouded in mist.

White is for purity, Abbey thought to herself, as she stared vacantly out the library windows. But it wasn't really a color—merely the absence of any color at all. Like her life.

She lifted her gaze to stare past the gazebo to where the Randolph property dropped steeply away to the sand dunes above the beach. No one who had not sat alone watching the fog play among the dunes could truly understand the meaning of loneliness, Abbey mused. It seemed to roll in from the sea in wave after white, amorphous wave, taking on bizarre shapes as fog horns droned eerily from offshore buoys.

Abbey knew what it was like to be out there in the fog on such a day, and she had known the loneliness as well, for as many summer seasons as she could remember.

"You're not listening to me, Abigale!" It was her

mother's voice, breaking into Abbey's reverie and bringing her abruptly back to the moment.

Annabel stood in front of the paneled fireplace with her customary rigid dignity. Because of her arthritis, she had begun walking with a silver-headed cane. And now, as she stood warming herself before the crackling fire, she fixed her cold gray gaze on Abbey.

"You're a selfish and indulgent young woman," she went on to accuse. "You fritter your time away, mooning over trashy literature and longing to pursue trivial hedonistic pleasures. I have often suspected that, in your heart, you're no better than the rest of the flotsam and jetsam that washes up on the beach every summer, and I hesitate to think of what's going to happen to you once I'm gone."

It was a well-worn argument between the two women that inevitably degenerated into a seemingly endless diatribe detailing the evils of smoking, drinking, immodest behavior, and the perils of promiscuous sex—a running monologue during which Annabel rose dramatically to her favorite subject to rail, rebuke, and condemn the "utterly debased behavior" of the Hampton summer people in particular and the lax moral standards of the time in general.

Suddenly Annabel paused in her nonstop recitation and allowed an accusing silence to fill the room. The air seemed to be full of unspoken accusations, veiled guilt, and well-formulated hatreds.

"This brings us to you," Annabel pronounced finally, breaking the uneasy stillness. She moved to the desk, opened the top drawer, and removed Abbey's sketching pad.

"You might as well know that I found these disgusting drawings in your room, Abigale. Along with some other items that I can't even bring myself to discuss. Quite frankly, I'm utterly appalled by your behavior, and I've decided that it's time you performed your God-given duty to me and to the Randolph family name."

Abbey stood watching helplessly as her mother returned to the fireplace, crumpled the drawings of Jaime one by one, and fed them into the flames.

"What duty?" Abbey questioned.

Annabel turned and fixed her with an accusing look. "The answer to that question should be obvious. But if you insist on being obtuse, I shall endeavor to explain it to you. Tomorrow, the *Hampton Reporter* will announce your engagement to Kelly De Witte. You are going to be married before the summer is out."

Abbey's face went the color of ashes. "But how could you?" she gasped. "Not Kelly De Witte? You wouldn't really try and force me to marry that filthy old man. I've heard terrible stories about him, and so have you."

Annabel brushed this aside with an imperious wave of her hand. "Nothing but ugly rumors," she responded. "In any case, all the arrangements have already been made. Fortunately for you, it's become incumbent upon Kelly to produce an heir. We've discussed the matter of your betrothal at length, and to be quite frank, Abigale, your only outstanding qualifications are the fact that you're Kelly's third cousin on your father's side, still a virgin, and of child-bearing age."

Abbey fled the house in utter panic. And within a matter of minutes, she was driving out toward Montauk Point, with Annabel's words chasing round and round in her brain like frantic mice trapped in an endless maze.

She was literally being sold into bondage to a man she both feared and despised. There was only one way out for her, and there was no longer any question in Abbey's mind as to what she would have to do in order to free herself forever from Annabel's domination.

51

# CHAPTER 3

Easthampton had always been considered by many to be the only real Hampton, for it was there that the remnants of the Old Guard still reigned, out beyond the endless acres of Long Island's split-level housing developments.

The commuter era of prefab living had not yet penetrated this enclave of elegant nineteenth-century mansions that still belonged to the descendants of the early industrial ruling class. And one of the most impressive of these baronial estates belonged to Patrick Dodsworth De Witte.

For over four decades, Kelly, as he preferred to be called, had managed to maintain his position as playboy extraordinaire, pillar of the Catholic Church, ardent supporter of numerous charities, and principal relic of a social elite that used to be referred to as "The Four Hundred."

An iron-willed mother similar in temperament and social standing to Annabel Randolph had barely rescued him and the family honor when, during his teens, Kelly was caught performing perverted acts in the lavatory of an exclusive school for boys.

Because of his youth and the school's receipt of a generous endowment, the matter was summarily dropped. But the incident had resulted in a strict set of ground rules that Kelly continued to observe well into his sixtieth decade, at the risk of being disinherited from the vast De Witte fortune.

First and foremost among these rules, which had been set down by the dowager Mrs. De Witte, was the position of Kelly's official fiancée. And over the ensuing years, there had been a long procession of overage debutantes, titled women of no particular wealth and, during the fifties and sixties, a series of Broadway showgirls of no particular talent.

The responsibilities incumbent upon Kelly's betrothed were to appear with him at social functions, take up residence at the De Witte estate, monitor his daily liquor ration, and dole out the proper number of Seconals at bed time and the various amphetamines he took during the course of the day.

Her other duty was to totally ignore the endless parade of service men, hairdressers, male models, and common street hustlers who were a necessary part of Kelly's entourage.

Kelly bored quickly and easily, and as his tastes continually grew more demanding and bizarre, the tenure for his official in-house fiancées had shortened considerably. Yet even so, if they handled themselves well, they were still able to bank a small fortune, provide for impoverished families, and acquire jewelry and clothes worth several hundred thousand dollars.

Kelly's overt sadism and predilection for young male bodies had become one of the worst-kept secrets in the Hamptons. And Abbey herself was well aware that relatively few of Kelly's chosen had survived the experience with mind, body, and soul intact.

Several were reported to have been permanently exiled to mental institutions, and at least two of his intended had died under mysterious circumstances. Most of them, however, just seemed to disappear from the face of the earth, never to be seen or heard of again.

Now it seemed that Abbey was to be next in line, and the very thought was enough to chill the blood running in her veins.

There was, to be sure, a rather large and impressive

homosexual stratum included within the layered make-up of the Hampton social scene. A very rich woman needed at least one gay intimate to make her feel special—someone bright and clever, with whom she could exchange the latest gossip and trade tales of various sexual exploits.

Still, the Hampton gays were a far different breed from the ticky-tacky meat-rack mentality of those on Fire Island and Cherry Grove. The homos inhabiting the more rarified climes of Long Island's northern shore had the look and life-style of people who obviously had made it—a lavender elite of fantastically preserved middle-aged men who, for the most part, were extremely sophisticated about their sexuality and had extraordinary creative capabilities.

They seemed to exist within a charmed circle of delightfully regulated and orderly lives that were impressively redolent with pleasure and sensual gratification. In fact, they were said by many to comprise a society within society, with its own strict rules regarding what one could and could not do, say, or wear.

Somehow, they seemed to lack that frantic quality that so epitomized the Fire Islands gays. They usually confined their cruising to a little casual flirtation at tea time. They wore the latest fashions, held chic parties and *Thé dansants* aboard their sleek yachts, and usually went off to Morocco immediately after Labor Day, led by Kelly De Witte and his current entourage.

By the time Abbey reached the beach at Montauk, the horizon was enveloped by masses of dark clouds scudding ominously across the sky. Lightning flared and crashed, rending the atmosphere as massive waves humped up offshore to churn, foaming and thundering, into the shallows.

The last-ditch holdouts along the beach had finally begun to fold their blankets hurriedly and scatter toward the line of cars parked along the highway. Yet as the sky continued to darken, Abbey parked the car and searched the roiling seascape for some sign of the lone surfer she had watched the day before.

Then she saw him, outlined against the horizon as he sped down the face of a giant comber, with the wind whipping plumes of spray from the tail of his surfboard. He was like a young god, Abbey thought, challenging the elements as he deftly manipulated his body into the curl of the wave and then crouched down, only to be overcome by a massive churning tunnel of roaring white water.

Abbey's heart was in her throat. It was a vision of man against nature, pure and primitive in its simplicity. There was no applauding gallery of spectators and no glory, beyond the knowledge of one's own ability to survive against stupendous odds.

She held her breath until the surfer appeared once again, riding his board toward shore before a solid wall of rain sweeping in from the sea.

About ten minutes later, she saw him coming up the path through the dunes, and she honked the horn as he reached the highway. His white cotton T-shirt was already soaked through, and he was carrying his board on his head, to ward off the pelting drops of rain.

"Want a lift?" Abbey called, as he jogged across the road toward where she sat poised behind the wheel of her mother's vintage La Salle. Then, almost unbelievably, he swung open the opposite door and stowed his surfboard across the back of the seat.

"Where you headed?" Jaime questioned, as he slid into the seat beside her.

His sudden closeness was almost unbearably disconcerting, and the smile on Abbey's face felt stiff and unnatural. "I saw you out surfing and thought you might need a ride back to town," she managed. "It's probably not very easy hitchhiking with a surfboard."

"Somebody always comes along," Jaime smiled. "I never have to wait long for a ride."

Abbey started the car, and they drove along the

highway, with the windshield wipers slapping monotonously back and forth across the streaming windows. "It looks like we're going to have quite a storm," she commented, desperately searching for some topic of conversation.

"Yeah, it kind of blows the whole day, doesn't it?" he said, turning to regard her more closely. "Didn't I see you yesterday on the beach?"

Abbey swallowed hard. "I come out here a lot— ever since I was a child, really. My father used to take me horseback riding all the way out to Montauk Point."

"Then you must live around here," Jaime said.

"In Easthampton. It's the old house on the beach that looks like a museum. If you haven't got anything planned," she hurried on to say, "why don't you come home with me? You really ought to see Bramwell Acres. A lot of people still call it one of the old showplaces of Easthampton. President McKinley even stayed there once."

Abbey had simply blurted out the words and was utterly amazed when Jaime gave her one of those wide, white smiles of his and nodded agreement. "Why not?" he said. "I've got nothing better to do with my time."

The storm had worsened considerably by the time they pulled into the drive at Bramwell Acres, and the rain by now was lashing the windows of the car with great thumping splashes. "You were right," Jaime observed, with a low, appraising whistle. "It does look like a museum—or something out of a horror movie."

The drive leading up to the house was narrow and unkempt, with a bower of trees forming a dark, cathedrallike vault overhead. The mansion itself was only occasionally visible through the trees and pelting rain. It was a rambling two-story Victorian structure with time-mellowed shingles, crowned by turrets and towers. The windows stared out like vacant eyes on what had once been formal box-hedge gardens, and overall, there was a feeling of time, disuse, and disrepair.

As they reached the circle drive before the front veranda, Jaime looked up to catch no more than a fleeting glimpse of a pale face at the dormer windows on the second floor. Then the heavy drapes fell back into place, and he almost wondered if his eyes had been playing tricks on him.

"Do you live here with your family?" he questioned.

"Only my mother, but she's away for the afternoon." Abbey responded carefully.

By now she had driven around to the back of the house and pulled the car into the garage. The engine was switched off, the windshield wipers fell silent, and suddenly they were alone together, with only the sound of the rain thumping against the shingled roof.

"Why don't we go inside the gardener's cottage," Abbey suggested, with a lot more confidence than she felt.

They both climbed out of the car, and Jaime removed his board from the back seat before circling around to where Abbey was waiting for him.

Then, taking her completely by surprise, he pulled her hard against his chest and bruised her mouth with his lips. "This suits me just fine," he said, as Abbey shivered and felt herself melting against him.

The garage was damp, musty and very dim. And almost before Abbey realized what was happening, Jaime had pulled her into the back seat of the car and slipped his arm around her shoulders. His right hand was instantly on her knee and then it shot up between her legs as a small, tortured sound escaped her lips.

"No," Abbey moaned. "Not like this . . . not here."

By now Jaime's hand was deftly slipping beneath the elastic band of her panties, his fingers rubbing and probing the place that only Abbey's own hand had known before. "I saw you watching me yesterday on the beach," he grunted against her neck. "I knew what you wanted."

"Oh, God," Abbey cried, her legs opening to accomodate his hand. Jaime was unbuttoning his jeans now, freeing himself for action as he deftly slid her silk underthings down her legs with a thoroughly practiced motion.

"Ya see this?" he demanded, holding his prick in his hand like an offering. "This is what you wanted, isn't it? You may be a high-class broad and live in a big house, but you're really no different than the rest of them, are you?"

Jaime was in full, hard erection by now, and Abbey was startled by the size of him. "I wanted to touch your body," she pleaded. "I didn't mean for it to be like this. I wanted you to make love to me."

"You're gonna get exactly what you wanted," he said, shoving her roughly back against the seat. Then Jaime was wedging himself between her legs, and Abbey forgot everything except what was happening to her. Her entire consciousness was focused on that one part of her body.

She could feel him probing and trying to enter her, hard and pulsing, forcing himself in with an instant of sharp, unexpected pain. There was a sudden rush of wetness between her legs, and then he was sliding deftly in and out, moving faster and deeper as Abbey spasmodically thrust herself upward against his groin with a hard, punishing motion.

"Are you ready?" Jaime gasped, as his breathing began to quicken to a ragged, racing tempo.

Abbey didn't know exactly what it was that she was supposed to be ready for, but she sought desperately to gain and match his pounding rhythm, sobbing and twisting her head from side to side while her face contorted into a mask, somewhere between pain and ecstasy.

"Oh, yes," she cried, clawing at his back with clutching fingers. "Fuck me . . . use me. I want your mouth and your body. I want your sperm shooting up inside me. Oh . . . oh . . . oh . . . oh . . ."

By now, Abbey was almost delirious with the waves of pure pleasure that rose to engulf her mind and body. At last it was happening, and nothing else seemed to matter beyond the exquisite agony of Jaime thrusting deep inside her, pulsing and throbbing with each penetration, each ragged, gasping breath.

Then there was a startling crash against the roof of the car. Abbey's eyes shuttered open to see her mother's face staring in at them, with a look of utter horror. Again and again her silver-topped cane struck the roof of the car, until suddenly Annabel staggered backward, clutching at her heart.

# CHAPTER 4

It was nearly dawn when Abbey awoke, her hair wet and her body clammy with perspiration. She felt sick and she was trembling with fear.

It was the day of Annabel's funeral, and the dream from which Abbey had just awakened had a ghastly reality about it—as if she had actually been there, alone in a glacial cathedral brilliantly alight with a ghostly, eerie glitter.

His features glittering with hoarfrost, Kelly De Witte had been waiting for her in front of the altar. He beckoned her forward with a spectral hand, and Abbey found herself moving toward him, wearing her mother's long white lace wedding dress, with a ragged bunch of funeral flowers cradled in her arms.

Abbey's body was aching with the terrible cold, and a chill, briny mist swirled up to envelop her legs so that she could scarcely move. Then she found herself standing before her mother's open coffin, and the dirfting vapors rose to entwine themselves around her with icy tendrils, filling her nose and her mouth and choking her like poisonous cobwebs until Abbey was gasping for breath.

With an occult flair, the corpse began lifting upward; the arms reaching out to clutch her in a deadly embrace. "No," Abbey had screamed, trying both to free herself and to shove her mother's body back into the white satin-lined coffin. "No—you're dead. I saw you die and I'm glad, do you hear me? I'm glad you're dead!"

Kelly's obscene laughter was echoing in the vault of the cathedral, while half in and half out of the coffin, Abbey was struggling desperately as Annabel's steely fingers bit into her flesh like icy talons.

No matter how she tried to free herself, there seemed to be no escape. Kelly was slowly closing the lid down over her. And in that instant, Abbey knew that she was going to be sealed up forever with the mother she loathed, in that suffocating, lifeless box.

It was her own scream of pure animal terror that had awakened Abbey, and for a long time she simply lay there trying to still the wild pounding of her heart. In the garden below her bedroom window, a pair of red squirrels scolded the dawn, fluffing their tails against the chill, as sickly yellow streaks of light began to lace the eastern horizon over the sea.

Today was going to be the start of a whole new life, Abbey reminded herself as she lay there in the dimness. Annabel was dead, and she felt not the slightest trace of remorse. Now there was only Jaime, and the thought of him alone was enough to bathe her chilled limbs in a warm glow of fulfillment. No longer did she have to be afraid or alone.

Suddenly, all the dissatisfactions of her past life were forgotten. All the fears and failures faded away into a vision of the future that appeared limitlessly bright with promise.

Snuggling down under the covers, Abbey daydreamed of the life that could now be hers—of browsing in Bailly-Heubner, window-shopping in all those clever Easthampton boutiques and cluttered mews, or antiquing at Balassa's on Sunday afternoons.

Slim and chic, with golden-braceleted arms, she would stroll to a leisurely beat beneath the century-old trees along Main Street. She would wear a silk floral print dress and a big floppy-brimmed hat and there would be admiring glances from the men she passed along the way, but Abbey's secret smile was for someone else.

At around five—the official Hampton teatime—she'd stop off for a tall, cool gin and tonic on the tree-shaded terrace of the Old American Hotel. Jaime would be waiting for her there when she arrived, and without a word he would hold her chair and bend to kiss the back of her neck with tender intimacy.

Later there would be a leisurely candlelit dinner for two at Squire's, and then disco dancing at Shazam until the first gray light of dawn.

Abbey didn't know any of the new dances, and yet she could vividly imagine her and Jaime's deeply bronzed bodies undulating sensuously against the silver mirrored walls. Jaime, looking darkly handsome and very smooth on his feet, had eyes for her alone, while Abbey swayed beneath the brightly colored lights, with long blonde-streaked hair falling in shimmering waves about her swaying shoulders.

The horror of the dream was completely gone now, and Abbey felt drowsy and langorous. Lifting her arms, she stretched her body against the coolness of the sheets and wondered at the heady sense of arousal that caused her limbs to tingle expectantly.

Ever since her encounter with Jaime in the back of her mother's car, dark and sensual currents had been stirring within her. Somehow the rest of it—the part about Annabel's death from a massive coronary—had been shut away as if it hadn't really happened. At least not then and there.

Abbey closed her eyes, and her fingers moved down to slip beneath her nightgown. The curling mound of silky auburn hair was soft to the touch. She breathed deeply and slowly began to caress the velvet crease of her sex, marveling at the incredible heat and the moist, tingling sensation generated by her gently stroking fingers.

Abbey recalled Jaime's hands—heavily veined and strong, the fingers surprisingly long and blunt. She squeezed her eyelids tightly shut and envisioned those hands moving over her nude body, the long, supple fingers slipping between her thighs as if there were something there that belonged solely to him.

Her breathing began to quicken, and a soft sighing sound trickled from her lips. "Oh yes," she whispered. "I'd do anything, Jaime . . . anything at all . . . only love me . . . please love me."

Awareness stabbed at Claire. Vague fingers of nausea probed at her stomach, and her head throbbed with a heavy, dull insistence. What had happened to her? Where was she?

Lifting herself slowly against the pillows, Claire allowed her eyes to travel about the room. It was a beautiful room, luxurious, and feminine—the mirrored room of a sensuous and indulgent woman. Then Claire realized that it was her own room in the beach house on Georgica Road.

Her body felt sore and abused, and she could not seem to fill the empty void in her mind. Last night's cocktail dress and her silk underthings were strewn about the white fur rug. Her nude body felt feverish against the cool satin sheets; and then she remembered being with Kamal.

Still, the previous evening remained a series of fragments—elusive bits and pieces leading up to a total blank, which filled Claire with a sense of growing desperation. What had happened to her, and why couldn't she remember?

Claire slid her legs over the side of the bed, wiggled her feet into her slippers and reached for her dressing gown. It was almost eleven o'clock according to the softly glowing digital clock at her bedside, and she knew that she had to pull herself together fast.

She slid from bed only to experience a sudden rush of dizziness as she rose to her feet. Last night's booze was still with her, and she managed to save herself from falling only by clutching the back of a chair.

Finally, Claire managed to make her way into the bathroom. Switching on the light, she winced at the sudden flood of brightness. Then she deliberately averted her eyes from the mirrored walls and concentrated on adjusting the shower to the proper temperature and wrapping her long ash-blonde hair up in a towel.

With the water finally just as hot as she could possibly stand, Claire plunged into the shower and began soaping her body with a big, soft sponge.

Claire knew that she had a drinking problem, but she had never really thought of herself as an alcoholic. By spacing her drinks throughout the day and consuming them slowly, she somehow always managed to reach the cocktail hour in pretty fair shape for the evening to come. With the help of a couple of diet-ups and a few more drinks, she was still flying high well into the wee hours.

The night before, however, the whole thing had gone *kaflooie*. Claire felt as if she had crashed and burned from 20,000 feet.

Kamal had called her upon his arrival in the Hamptons the week before, and they had planned a rendezvous at an out-of-the-way motel. All during the hours separating planning from realization, Claire had dreamed of their embrace, savoring the sensual images of pleasure and intimacy.

Then, after spending the entire day in preparation with a hairdresser and masseuse, the magic hour had arrived. Kamal had sent a curtained limousine to whisk her away to their clandestine rendezvous, where they dined sumptuously and drank a bottle of vintage champagne. But that was just about as much as Claire remembered.

By the time they finally got into bed, Claire had passed into an alcoholic stupor, and the rest of the evening was almost a total blank.

Claire climbed from the shower and whipped the towel from her head, allowing her hair to tumble about her shoulders. Then she began drying herself before the mirrored walls, only to meet her own reflection with a look of shocked surprise.

Her back and buttocks were criss-crossed with angry red welts, and there were several large, purplish bruises on her arms and thighs. Claire was aghast, numb with shock and disbelief. How? Why? What on earth had Kamal done to her, and why couldn't she remember?

"Lovely day for a funeral," Claire suggested, sliding into the back seat of Roxanne's Rolls Royce. "It's a pity that Aunt Annabel won't be here to enjoy the festivities."

Roxanne gave her a sharp, disapproving look. "You never did like Annabel, did you?"

"I don't know anyone who really did," Claire responded. "She was a hard, cold, cynical, vicious old harridan who believed she had some God-given right to sit in judgment of everyone in this town."

"The Randolph name did mean something in Easthampton," Roxanne reminded her. "Like it or not, Annabel Randolph was a power to be reckoned with."

"Annabel and her breed are about to become as extinct as the woolly mammoth," Claire put in. "It's money that counts these days, and nobody really gives a good shit whether your ancestors came over on the *Mayflower* or not."

Roxanne chose to ignore the comment. "It is too bad that Annabel didn't live to see Abbey married off to Kelly De Witte," she commented. "God knows, she isn't going to do any better by waiting around."

Claire lifted a gloved hand to remove the pair of oversized sunglasses that partially obscured her face. "You can't possibly be serious, Roxanne. You know as well as I do that Kelly is an utterly depraved pervert who would have been hauled off to the lock-up long ago, if it weren't for all that De Witte loot."

"Abbey isn't exactly a prize," Roxanne commented dryly.

"Perhaps she is a little past first bloom," Claire said, shrugging. "Even a little strange. But I wouldn't wish Kelly De Witte on my worst enemy."

"He's just eccentric," Roxanne suggested.

"He's as gay as Chinese pajamas, and you know it."

"His tastes are merely a bit esoteric," Roxanne insisted. "Anyway, let's talk about something else. Abbey is officially engaged to Kelly, and as far as I'm concerned as executor of the Randolph estate, the marriage is a *fait accompli*. Kelly and I have discussed the matter at length, and now that Annabel's dead, he's agreed to move up the wedding to the end of this month."

"You're really pushing this, aren't you?"

"I'm not about to waste my summer playing nursemaid," Roxanne informed her tartly. "Abbey is simply impossible, and the sooner I can get her packed off to Kelly De Witte, the happier I'll be."

Claire had been waiting for precisely the right moment to drop a bit of gossip she had come by, and now she knew instinctively that her time had come. "I suppose you've already heard about Andrea?" she said almost too casually.

Roxanne turned to regard her with a cool, penetrating gaze. "I can always tell when you're baiting me, sister Claire. Just what is it you've heard?"

Claire removed her gloves to study her brightly lacquered nails. "Just that your ex-stepdaughter will be arriving shortly. She's been invited by Helene to spend the summer with the Von Bismarks."

"Andrea . . . coming here?" Roxanne exclaimed.

"You've got to be kidding! That little twit wouldn't dare set foot in the Hamptons. It has to be some kind of stupid rumor. Andrea hasn't even come out of mourning yet, and it's almost a year since Stavros died."

"*Au contraire,* sister dear," Claire drawled. "She's arriving next week aboard the *Golden Hind.* And you can just bet that with all those millions, this town is going to sit up and take notice of little Andrea."

"Don't be absurd. Even if she did come here, Andrea would be the laughingstock of the season. Why, she doesn't even shave her legs, and she's practically taken the veil already."

Claire's laughter was as brittle as breaking glass. "I'd like to make a prediction," she said. "Once Andrea gets a look at the local pussy brigade lined up and just dying to meet two billion dollars on the hoof, she'll learn to shave her legs fast enough, and a few other things as well."

# ====CHAPTER 5====

The funeral of Annabel Randolph was a disaster from the moment that Roxanne and Claire picked up Abbey in front of the mortuary.

Roxanne, having buried three husbands, knew all there was to know about staging funerals. And she had spared no expense in providing a fitting sendoff for the woman who had ruled over the Hampton Old Guard for half a century. Her aunt was, after all, a descendant of a signer of the Declaration of Independence, and the Randolph family tree had been traced back to the *Mayflower*.

In honor of her passing, flags were flying at half-mast from all the municipal buildings, and as the funeral procession moved slowly down Main Street beneath century-old trees, there was a considerable crowd gathered along the sidewalks.

Annabel had wanted a white funeral, and Roxanne had seen to it that her final wish was granted. She had been laid to rest in a white coffin covered with 500 white roses, and her body was transported to All Saints Church in a shiny white Cadillac hearse.

Abbey had set tongues wagging from the moment she arrived at the mortuary, driving an expensive new sports car. She had gotten herself up as if she were on her way to attend a garden party, in a bright yellow party dress, with white lace hat and matching gloves.

"You really should have let me help you shop for something more appropriate," Roxanne admonished her. "That outfit is far from the proper attire for your mother's funeral, but it's certainly too late to do anything about it now."

Abbey tried not to show her hurt at having incurred her beautiful cousin Roxanne's displeasure. She had always felt intimidated by her and had long since given up any hope of imitating her grace, sophistication, and exquisite taste in just about everything.

Roxanne was like a queen presiding over an elegant court full of fawning courtiers. And by comparison Abbey always felt badly dressed, hopelessly naive, and socially awkward. In fact, she had long since convinced herself that everyone wondered how she could possibly even be related to the fabulous Roxanne.

Her cousin had always been a collector of famous people, while Abbey herself was simply a poor relation. Roxanne collected ballet stars, Nobel prize winners of every stripe, painters of note, best-selling novelists, and even astronauts (but only if they had been to the moon).

As far as Roxanne's feelings about her cousin Abbey were concerned, she had never really paid much attention, since the girl was a good deal younger, and they had absolutely nothing in common. Also, there had always been something off-putting about her.

Abbey was like an accident about to happen, according to Roxanne's view—a hopelessly naive child-woman, always trying too hard and invariably ending up looking foolish and awkward.

Then too, although no one in the family really mentioned it, the assumption had always been that Abbey was just a little off—emotionally retarded somehow, and without question a potential embarrassment in any social situation.

"I'm sorry to seem hard on you at a difficult time," Roxanne went on to say in a voice that always reminded Abbey of tinkling silver bells. "I know, of course, that you're upset over the loss of your dear mother, but there are certain proprieties that simply must be observed. You simply have to start exhibiting some judgment now that you're on your own."

"I'm not really upset," Abbey heard herself saying. "In fact, I'm relieved that Mother's gone. She was a selfish and insensitive woman. It's no wonder my father drank himself to death. He was married to a woman who was frigid as a corpse even when she was alive, so nothing's really changed that much."

"Abbey," Roxanne gasped. "What a terrible thing to say."

"It's only the truth, and you know it," Claire put in. "You never could tolerate Annabel for more than twenty minutes at a time yourself. You only pretended to."

"That's not true," Roxanne protested. "I had only the greatest respect for my aunt Annabel. She stood for something in this town. Just look at all those people lined up along the curb. Annabel's funeral is going to be packed with mourners."

"I have absolutely no doubt but that it's going to be *the* funeral of the season," Claire shot back in acid tones. "But most of these people would attend a public execution if you invited them, since you really do give the very best funerals. Simply everyone knows that."

Roxanne was clearly anxious to change the subject. "I spoke with your fiancé this morning, Abbey dear. He'll be at the church waiting for you."

She opened her purse and extended a small velvet jeweler's box. "In fact," Roxanne went on to relate, "Kelly thought that under the circumstances, it might be best if you made your appearance at the church wearing this. He sent it over by messenger and asked me to deliver it to you."

Abbey opened the black velvet box to expose a large pear-shaped yellow-diamond engagement ring. "It's beautiful," Abbey said, "but I can't accept it. I have no intention of marrying Kelly. I never did. That was all Mother's idea."

Taking the ring from the box, Roxanne deftly slipped it over Abbey's finger. Then she lifted her hand so that the impressively large stone caught and sparkled with the light. "Rule number one, Abbey, is to never refuse expensive jewelry. Of course, I understand that you need time to get your thinking straightened out. But it just wouldn't look right to break off your engagement on the day of your mother's funeral. Those things simply aren't done in polite society."

By the time they arrived at the church, hundreds of curious onlookers had gathered out in front. The police had cordoned off the street. And as the three women emerged from Roxanne's limousine, a phalanx of reporters pressed forward, and flashbulbs popped on every side.

Patrick Dodsworth De Witte was there to embrace his bride-to-be with paternal benevolence, although Abbey was seen to shudder visibly as his lips brushed against her cheek.

Kelly De Witte was 55 years old and looked 80. His skin had a waxen, unhealthy pallor, and his watery eyes were the color of glue. They always seemed to be licking over someone as if searching for a soft or vulnerable spot. He was short and bloated from dissipation, while his head was massive, and its weight seemed to bear down on his narrow shoulders, endowing him with a slightly deformed appearance.

From within the church, the swelling chords of the *Piu Jesu* came rolling out in thundering waves of sound through the tall oaken doors. Franco de Roma and his pretty young cinematographer were on hand to film the processional, and as the mourners started up the church steps, there was no question that Roxanne herself was the star attraction at her aunt Annabel's funeral.

All Saints, on Three Mile Harbor Road, was the

church in which Annabel had worshipped all her life. She had also sung and played the organ there on high holy days. And as the procession stepped into the cool dimness with light streaming down through banks of stained glass windows, the dead woman's voice wafted eerily out of the loudspeaker system, singing "Abide With Me," in a high, operatic soprano.

The church was packed to capacity, filled for the most part with people for whom Easthampton appeared to have changed little with the passing decades. They were the old-money rich, those who could still afford to guard their elegant seclusion in the face of sky-rocketing property taxes and the influx of a whole new breed of summer resident.

For the most part, the mourners at Annabel Randolph's funeral had the look of people accustomed to receiving far more from life than they were willing to give. They appeared very sure of both themselves and their place in society, and they wore their jewels and expensive clothes with casual elegance.

After the coffin had been placed before the altar, amid banks of floral tributes, the lid was opened and the mourners passed before the bier.

In death, Annabel Randolph appeared very much the same as she had in life. She had the same perfectly coiffed coronet of bone-white hair, the same cold granite mask with parchmentlike skin drawn taut over her patrician bone structure. Abbey refused to look as she passed the coffin. She simply closed her eyes and shuddered, recalling the ghastly dream that had awakened her that morning before dawn.

The eulogy was given by Bishop Quinlan. He was an impressively rotund ecclesiastical figure, dressed in gorgeous gold and white vestments. As a former pastor of All Saints Church, he had been Annabel's bridge and canasta partner for the past 25 years. And perhaps more than anyone else present, he appeared to be genuinely bereft at her passing.

72

It had been largely through the bishop's efforts that Annabel had dedicated the massive "Randolph Crucifixion," a stained glass monstrosity that illuminated the altar with an aura of spectral roseate light. Abbey had always hated it, and she had never liked Bishop Quinlan very well either.

The bishop and her mother had spent every Friday evening together for as long as Abbey could remember. They shut themselves up together in the library at Bramwell Acres, and sherry was always served. After several hands of gin rummy, Annabel would play the piano and sing in a high, slightly off-key soprano, while the bishop kept time by tapping his scarlet silk slipper.

Bishop Quinlan's multiple chins quivered, his eyes teared, and his voice thundered as he spoke of "our dear departed sister—a fearless voice unafraid to speak out in order to preserve the time-tested morals of our founding fathers. She was a woman of dignity and great generosity, whose piety was known to all. She was a woman whose loss has dealt a blow to all those who revered the sanctity of the home in these trying times of deteriorating moral values, false prophets of easy virtue, the curse of drugs, and promiscuous behavior."

Abbey had been forced to listen to much the same sermon many times before, and she concentrated instead on the "Randolph Crucifixion"—the stained glass window that, more than anything else, was Annabel Randolph's revenge.

Although few seemed to be aware of it, Annabel herself had been pictured as the Virgin Mary, while the face of Mary Magdalene bore an uncanny resemblance to Abbey's cousin Claire. Roxanne's lovely chiseled features were clearly discernible on the face of a hovering winged deity, while cousin Darnell Hanlan appeared utterly diabolical in the role of Judas Iscariot.

I wonder if they know, Abbey thought to herself. She slid a glance first at Roxanne's serene profile beneath the folds of her black mourning veil, then turned to regard her cousin Claire's haggard countenance, hidden behind a pair of dark glasses. Neither face gave anything away.

"In closing," Bishop Quinlan intoned, "I would like to recite a poem by Edgar Allen Poe that was dear to the heart of our beloved Annabel Lee Randolph."

At this point, the bishop was forced to remove a white handkerchief from the pocket of his gown and dab at his eyes. Then he cleared his throat and began. "It was many and many a year ago in a kingdom by the sea . . that a fair maiden there lived whom you may know, by the name of . . . Annabel Lee."

That was as far as Bishop Quinlan got when the thundering roar of a motorcycle rose within the church to drown out his voice. People turned in their pews just as Darnell Hanlan roared through the open doors of the church on a Harley Davidson and came thundering down the center aisle, loudly gunning his engine.

"My God, it's Darnell," Roxanne gasped. "He must have gone completely mad to pull a crazy stunt like this."

Darnell skidded to a halt before the communion rail, and with everyone watching in stunned anticipation, he removed a .44-caliber revolver from one of his saddlebags. Then, taking careful aim with both hands, he blasted the "Randolph Crucifixion" into shards of brightly colored glass that shattered down upon the altar.

The six shots he fired off in rapid succession sent Bishop Quinlan and the attendant altar boys scrambling for cover, while the congregation remained utterly mute and frozen in their seats, staring in an attitude of shocked disbelief. The longstanding feud between the deceased and her quixotic nephew, Darnell, was known to everyone present. He was absolutely the last person expected to appear at her funeral, since the two of them had quite cordially loathed one another.

But then no one of any consequence really took

Darnell Hanlan all that seriously. For the most part, he was considered a colorful eccentric. And for 400 years, the Hanlan family themselves had never been popular with their mainland neighbors.

Dressed entirely in leather, Darnell was a spare, tallish figure possessed of a bearded, avian countenance, piercing dark eyes, and a decidedly barbed tongue. He had achieved fame of sorts as a novelist, and his literary style was characterized by urbanity, wit, elegance, polish and, more often than not, the venom of a scorpion.

His books, which sold in the millions, were clever cloak-and-dagger thrillers, written under the pseudonym Evan Kingsley. And they invariably were heavy with themes of isolation, rage, guilt, and macabre forms of sexual humiliation.

Still, no one could deny that for over four centuries, the Hanlan line had embodied much of the history of the Hamptons, and they were without question among the original founding fathers.

On a clear day, if one happened to be sitting on the terrace of the yacht marina, at Three Mile Harbor, it was often possible to make out the imposing outlines of Hanlan's Island, floating mistily on the horizon. And while the 27-mile-long Eden was easily accessible by boat, helicopter, or plane, that was just about as close a look as most people ever got.

To all but a chosen few, the island was totally off limits, and both the airstrip and private boat harbor were patrolled 24 hours a day by armed guards with German shepherds trained to kill. Treasure Cay, as it had come to be called, since the discovery of pirate treasure buried there, was Darnell Hanlan's own private domain, and no one intruded without a very personal invitation.

The truth was that everyone wanted a piece of Treasure Cay in one form or another. It was always out there, tantalizingly beautiful and just beyond reach.

And the fact that the acerbic and very antisocial Darnell Hanlan was pathologically committed to retaining the island's unspoiled wilderness as his own private hunting preserve had long been a situation that rankled a lot of the Hamptons' foremost citizenry.

Now, with the entire congregation held hostage to his incredible and dramatic entrance, Darnell gunned his engine several more times, then switched off the ignition and casually dismounted from the big, shiny black road bike.

The silence that followed was awesome. There wasn't a single sound among the hundreds of people. Everyone, in fact, seemed to be holding his breath, and there wasn't even a cough or whisper.

Darnell proceeded to prolong the suspense, the way a great dramatic actor holds his audience enthralled with faultless timing. Unstrapping his crash helmet and sweeping it off with a flourish, he slowly walked past the coffin and mounted the steps to the pulpit, where he stood staring out over the entire assemblage with maliciously glittering eyes.

"You have all gathered here today," he began, in a deep, almost oratorical voice, "to mourn the passing of one of Easthampton's leading citizens."

Darnell paused, allowing his gaze to lick like a whip over the upturned sea of faces. He looked haggard, utterly deranged, and driven by some kind of unbearable pain, some outrage that demanded satisfaction.

"I was not asked to deliver an oration on the occasion of my aunt's passing," he declared. "Nor was I even invited to attend this august gathering, even though I happen to be related to many of you through four gruesome centuries of gross miscegenation.

"Doubtless, you are all well aware that our beloved Annabel Lee—the deceased—quite frankly hated my guts. And her dearest wish, whether dead or alive, was to strip me of my ancestral heritage, to utterly destroy all that is mine to cherish and hold."

Darnell's voice crackled with force and vehemence through the loudspeaker system and echoed back and forth between the vaulted stone walls. "There is, at this very moment, a referendum before the town council on which you have all given an affirmative vote. If enacted into law, this same resolution would legally deprive me of the Hanlan historical heritage in lieu of back taxes that have been deliberately raised to drive me into ruin.

"You are all guilty of this infamy, even though the prime conspirator was my aunt Annabel, during her twenty-year tenure as president of the Hampton Historical Society—that same infamous organization that would like nothing better than to see Hanlan's Island turned into a nature preserve swarming with a lot of little no-neck monsters disguised as Boy and Girl Scouts."

There was a sudden flurry of movement as the congregation shifted uncomfortably in their pews. Then someone sneezed, and it was like a gunshot shattering the atmosphere of shocked expectancy. Darnell was pointing an accusing finger at all of them now. Then his eyes fell to where Roxanne sat next to Abbey, Claire, and Kelly De Witte in the front pew of the church.

"The end is near," he proclaimed, with his voice falling dramatically in pitch. "And who of you here today is without stain of sin?"

With that, Darnell stripped off one of his studded leather motorcycle gauntlets and flung it with a grand and disdainful flourish into Annabel's open coffin. "Beware," he hissed into the microphone. "Beware the apocalypse."

# CHAPTER 6

Andrea watched the sea birds fall away one by one and gradually recede with the last sight of land to tiny, worrisome specks fretting the sky with their shrill cries.

Her lips moved, whispering good-bye, for it was good-bye to the life she had known and the Greek Islands she loved.

"Did you say something?" Sarah questioned. She was reclining in a nearby deck chair, were a copy of *Paris Match* had fallen from her hands. "I must have dozed off for a few minutes."

"You've been asleep for over an hour," Andrea gently chided. "You're working much too hard, Sarah. I noticed that the light was still on in your cabin at three o'clock this morning."

Sarah cast a sharp, questioning glance in her friend's direction, only to discover that Andrea's features were entirely guileless. I'm getting jumpy as a cat, she thought. It's guilt that's doing it.

"I'm afraid I haven't been sleeping well of late," Sarah confessed. "I guess the thought that I'm finally going home after all this time is beginning to get to me."

"Why don't you just relax and let life happen to you?" Andrea said, smiling. "Isn't that what you're always telling me?"

"Yes, I guess it is," Sarah laughed. "But I make it a strict rule never to take my own advice. I've always seemed to prefer doing things the hard way."

Beneath them, the yacht's powerful diesel engines hummed as they propelled the *Golden Hind* steadily westward across the Atlantic. The sea had already begun to change as they left the coast of Portugal behind. The large glassy swells mounted up beneath them, only to fall away, as insubstantial as dreams in their frothy wake.

As the *Golden Hind* cruised toward North America on its first day out from Lisbon, a white-coated steward appeared on deck. Andrea stretched languidly and then pulled her robe more closely over her breasts as the steward bent to place a covered tray on a low table at her side. "How about some coffee?" she questioned Sarah. "I rang for the steward while you were sleeping."

"Sounds lovely," Sarah replied, propping herself up comfortably against the lounge cushions. She deliberately avoided the steward's eyes as she said, "Make mine black, will you please, Marko?"

There was something overly formal in the address; yet when their fingers touched as Marko handed Sarah a cup of steaming black Turkish coffee, she felt something stir deep within her.

The sensation was purely sexual, like an electric jolt that both troubled and amazed her, since Sarah had long doubted her ability to feel anything anymore. Her passion for the steward Marko, however, had become a labyrinth in which Sarah found herself inextricably enmeshed—a sensual maze into which she moved deeper and farther every time they made passionate, flesh-scalding love, as they had the night before.

"Signora Dane?" Marko addressed her. "You would perhaps care for something to eat?"

He proffered a plate of French croissants, but Sarah shook her head, deliberately avoiding his melting brown gaze. Marko really wasn't all that attractive, she tried to tell herself. But he had about him a primitive, sensual quality that drew her to him with magnetic certainty. His emotions were totally uncomplicated by any pretension to intellect, and once their clothes had been shed, they simply tore away at each other like animals.

There was a flash of uneven white teeth in Marko's swarthy face, compelling Sarah to glance his way. Then his tongue flicked out from beneath his heavy, dark mustache and slowly moistened his lips.

Oh Jesus, Sarah thought as her eyes slid quickly away. He's getting a hard-on right here in front of Andrea. Sarah knew only too well that glazed, volcanic look he got in his eyes. And all she needed now was for that donkey dick of his to poke out of his white shorts. Poor, naive Andrea with her convent upbringing would probably faint dead away.

Sarah drew a towel about her shoulders and deliberately arranged her body facing away from him. She reached for her Marlboros and then quickly turned her full attention to her friend, who was buttering a flaky French croissant. "I never have been able to tolerate the thought of food before twelve noon," she commented brightly. "All I ever want in the morning is coffee and cigarettes—my two minor vices."

"According to the nuns who educated me, there are no minor vices," Andrea commented with a little laugh. "It's simply a question of avoiding the occasions of sin."

Sarah smiled wanly and nodded, wishing that Marko would just finish his business on deck and get the hell back to the scullery. Occasions of sin indeed. What on earth would Andrea think of her if she were to discover the truth? Within the cloistered confines of Andrea's experience, one simply did not sleep around out of wedlock, and certainly not with the help.

"I think Marko's flirting with you," Andrea observed, as the figure of the steward disappeared down the deck. "If he bothers you in any way, Sarah, I want you to let me know. My father never tolerated that kind of behavior from the crew while he was alive, and I have no intention of doing so either."

"It's nothing at all," Sarah assured her. "I'm sure

he doesn't mean any disrespect. It's just that all southern European men think that American women are ... shall we say ... liberated."

Sarah fairly cringed at having lied to cover up her own shame, but she simply had no choice in the matter. "Well," she hurried on to say, "how do you feel now that you're on your way to America for the first time?"

Andrea sipped her coffee, smiling fondly at her. "You know you have my undying gratitude for coming with me, Sarah. I know it isn't easy for you to go back when you aren't really ready."

"Perhaps I'll never be ready," Sarah responded a bit grimly. "At least not until I find out one way or the other whether I'm a widow or not."

Andrea leaned forward, holding out her croissant for Sarah to take a bite. "I want you to tell me all about the Hamptons," she said, curling her legs beneath her. "I want to know everything."

"The feeding frenzy of sharks is not a pleasant sight to behold," Sarah informed her with mock severity. "But if you insist on knowing the truth, I have no choice but to tell it like it is.

"I grew up on the outskirts of the Hamptons," Sarah went on to relate. "And the truth about the American rich is that they are not really a very happy lot. Perhaps that's why they tend to take a lot of drugs, get divorced, engage in promiscuous sex, and often end up jumping out of windows or OD-ing with sleeping pills."

"Is everybody in the Hamptons rich?" Andrea questioned.

"No, but in order to tell the rich from the nonrich, you won't have to look very far for clues. The rich are most often characterized by terms like *grandiose, hypochondriacal and exhibitionistic*. Traditionally, they are very easily bored and tend to be extremely self-centered, easily angered, and exhibit a very limited awareness about themselves."

81

"Is that all that's wrong with them?" Andrea laughed, throwing up her hands in mock dismay.

"Not quite all. You really should be aware, as well, that their primary interests and the topics bound to be discussed at any dinner party are money, jewels, cars, clothes, and lovers, although not always in that precise order."

"You do have a way with words, Sarah Dane, but I just can't believe that it's all as superficial as the picture you paint. Surely, there must be some nice people around the Hamptons."

"I'm sure there are," Sarah assured her. "It's just that they tend to get trampled in the rush of parties, charity balls, and various and sundry sexual couplings that take place in the ongoing game of sleeping around with each other's husbands. It is the summer season, after all, and everybody's out to get his or hers while the getting's good."

Andrea shook her head in disbelief. "It's difficult for me to imagine a place like that. I was brought up so differently. The sensual things in life always seemed to be forbidden. I was taught to believe that it was a mortal sin to sleep with a man unless he was willing first to make me his wife. Frankly, Sarah, I don't really know how to act or even what to say to people like those you describe."

The apprehension so clearly evident in her friend's voice caused Sarah to relent immediately. "Don't worry about it, Andrea dear. You just be yourself. In any case, I'll be right there with you to point out the good guys from the bad. And if the going really gets rough, we can always pull up anchor and sail away to the Bahamas. There's a lovely tropical island I know of there that's totally uninhabited. Now that you're an heiress, you can simply buy it and we'll live happily ever after."

"I'd often like to do just that," Andrea said a bit

wistfully. "But my father left me a legacy for which I'm responsible. I simply can't betray that trust."

Andrea Aristos had never been considered pretty. Her features were far too strong, and her figure lacked the statuesque proportions extolled by current standards of feminine beauty. Rather, she had developed into a darkly handsome young woman of 23, possessed by the deep religious convictions of her Greek Orthodox faith.

Andrea had attended convent schools throughout her youth. And had it not been for the burden of great wealth and position so suddenly thrust upon her, she would very likely have gone on to become a nun, quietly taking her vows and living out the rest of her days in cloistered contemplation behind convent walls.

She had been shattered by her father's sudden death. And before the reading of his will, which made her his sole heir, Andrea's principal contact with the huge fleet of Aristos oil tankers plying the seven seas had been limited mainly to swinging champagne bottles against their bows.

Ever since childhood, Andrea had christened each new ship of the line. At least that was the way it had been up until the time of her father's disastrous marriage to *La Castrata*—the name by which Andrea always referred to her ex-stepmother, Roxanne.

Stavros Aristos had always loomed far larger than life to almost everyone, but to Andrea he had virtually been a god. He had always been careful to shelter her from the outside world, and since his death, she had been utterly bereft. There had simply been nothing to prepare her. Suddenly, without warning, Andrea was faced with the almost insurmountable task of taking control of the web of interlocking interests making up her father's vast maritime empire.

The superyacht, *Golden Hind,* had served as her father's highly mobile command center while he was still alive and roaming the world. It was a veritable floating palazzo with pink marble bathrooms, extensive communications equipment, and a multimillion-dollar collection of the very finest Renaissance art.

For Andrea, however, the *Golden Hind* had become a cloistered sanctuary. And ever since she had taken her father's body home to the island of Pandros for burial, she had remained in a state of deep and prolonged mourning. Even while she had reluctantly taken up the reins of command, Andrea had begun a desperate inner search for that diamond-bright hardness that would give her the strength to carry on in her beloved father's name.

Although the corporate headquarters of Aristos Shipping were located in the principality of Monaco, Andrea continued to oversee the company's day-to-day operation from aboard the *Golden Hind*.

Her roots were sunk deep in the seabed of the ancient Mediterranean trade routes, and Andrea, along with Sarah, had set out to sail among the Greek Isles, even as her ancestors had done for hundreds of years. Sarah acted as administrative assistant, and amphibious courier planes shuttled back and forth between Monte Carlo and the Aegean, bearing voluminous folders that contained pertinent statistical information, important documents requiring Andrea's signature, and the endless stream of directives through which she ran the company at a distance and sight unseen.

Andrea's basically practical instincts had enabled her to assume the burdens of command, and yet there was another side to her as well. Andrea had once again discovered the delicate swanlike beauty of Delos floating on an azure sea. She had seen Lesbos, thickly wooded and blanketed with olive trees that turned to a shimmering sea of quicksilver as the *Golden Hind* cruised offshore in the late afternoon breeze.

It was, more than anything else, a voyage of discovery.

Andrea had gone ashore at Kynthos, whose towering

mountain peaks were the color of bleached bones when viewed by moonlight. And she had climbed the high volcanic cone of Santorin as it turned fiery and golden with the approaching dawn. Finally, there among her own native Greek Islands, Andrea Aristos, heiress, had come to comprehend the truth about herself.

More than anything else in the world, she wanted to be free of the crushing burdens thrust upon her by her father's death.

The mantle of wealth and power was, after all, hers only by default. Jason, her half-brother, had been groomed since earliest childhood to assume the reins of power one day in direct line of descent.

Andrea had never really known the real reason for Stavros's sudden and violent repudiation of his only son. There had been some kind of sex scandal. But Andrea herself had been studying in Switzerland at the time and had remained totally sheltered from the knowledge of exactly what had caused the rift.

Nor had she set eyes on Jason since he had left Greece some five years before, to pursue a racing career in Europe and America. Jason had gotten married during the interim, and while Andrea had not heard from him directly, his wife, Helene, had remained in close and constant contact, through a lengthy and often fascinating correspondence.

Jason's wife had, in fact, managed to impress Andrea very much, and it had been Helene's last letter that had finally convinced her to set sail for America, to act as godmother to the Von Bismark twins.

After Andrea retired to the master's stateroom to handle various routine business matters, Sarah remained on deck, staring at the sea. She felt possessed by a cloying sense of time and loss. The peaceful vacancy of the past 12 months was slipping away with each nautical mile, to become as insubstantial as a pillar of smoke.

Sarah had not been entirely joking when she told Andrea about the uninhabited tropical island she knew of in the Bahamas. She had once spent an all-too-brief honeymoon there with a man she loved deeply.

But that, of course, had been part of another life in another time. Sarah knew in her heart that there was no going back. Not ever.

Sarah had been born Seraphina Carmella Bambaccio in a tall green-shuttered house overlooking the sea near Montauk Point. And whenever she remembered the colors, the sounds, and the smells of her youth, Sarah thought of the small fishing village of Montauk, from which her father operated his small fishing boat.

Her parents had been first-generation Italian immigrants, and following her father's death from cancer while Sarah was in her early teens, Mama Rosa and Sarah's four older brothers had opened a seafood restaurant on the fishing wharf at Montauk Station.

In both obvious and obscure ways, Sarah had never really felt that she belonged to the warm, sprawling, Italian family that considered her to be one of their own. Her brothers' progeny now numbered a good many nieces and nephews, and, according to her mother's frequent letters, Mama Rosa's restaurant had become exceedingly popular with the Hampton smart set, as the finest Italian seafood restaurant along the Atlantic seaboard.

All her life, Sarah had always wanted far more than the fishing village of Montauk, or even the adjacent Hampton summer beach colonies had been able to offer. At 19, she had accepted an art scholarship to Skidmore College. And after graduating with honors four years later, she had emigrated to Manhattan, to throw herself completely into the glamorous and challenging world of high fashion.

As one of Seventh Avenue's most promising young fashion editors and illustrators, her approach to the garment scene and its reigning personalities was as fresh and stimulating as an electric vibrator. Sarah could sense a new trend in fashion well before its birth on the market, and she delivered all her editorial commentaries in unique and unforgettable prose, with accompanying sketches of a very high quality.

Paris *Vogue* had hired her in 1968, and two years later, Sarah moved on to Rome to become a fashion coordinator for the ultraprestigious House of Fontana. Slim, darkly attractive, and utterly self-possessed, Sarah Dane had a real flair for fashion, and she felt utterly fulfilled in her work. She was a sleek, poised sophisticate, whose brilliance, talent, and charm quickly made her a natural ornament on the international fashion scene.

Returning finally to New York and a key editorial position with a glossy women's fashion magazine, Sarah was convinced that her star was on the rise. Then, shortly before her twenty-eighth birthday, she met Brian Patrick Dane, a man quite unlike any other she had ever known.

Brian was a handsome young Air Force pilot with a Harvard background, an Olympic gold medal in swimming to his credit, and a future that appeared fully as bright and promising as Sarah's own. He was someone whose quiet strength and firm moral values gave Sarah a certain sense of balance and security that her life and work had always lacked up until then.

It had all begun on a beautiful spring afternoon in the Plaza Hotel's Palm Court. Sarah had been lunching with an advertising client, when she glanced up to find the handsome uniformed figure of Brian Dane seated at a nearby table, in the company of a very attractive Manhattan model who was currently making the rounds.

Their eyes met, locked, and held. And for the first time in her life, Sarah was fully and deliriously in love.

Two weeks later, she and Brian were married in a small private ceremony at City Hall. Then, after a brief, ecstatic honeymoon in the Bahamas, spent almost entirely in one another's arms, Brian packed his bags and flew off to the Far East, to continue making bombing runs over North Vietnam.

Sarah continued with her career and tried to ignore the almost daily headlines about bombed-out hospitals, search-and-destroy missions, and napalmed villagers. After all, the war was becoming very unpopular and beginning to wind down. Brian was scheduled to return to New York within a matter of months. But more than anything else, Sarah just didn't want to think about it.

Then came word that his plane had been shot down during one of the final bombing raids of the war. Brian had been listed by the Air Force as missing in action. And for the next three years, Sarah was forced to endure the endless torture of simply not knowing whether or not he was dead or alive.

To occupy her mind and her time, Sarah became a work-aholic. And for almost 24 desperately frantic months, the ploy had been largely successful. Then, for no apparent reason beyond the death of a pet canary that Brian had given her, Sarah's world came crashing down around her shoulders.

She simply had no further reserves to fall back on, and ever since that time, Sarah Dane had been on the run, trying desperately to escape a world that she saw choking and drowning on its own excesses.

Sarah and Andrea had become friends in a graveyard on the Greek island of Pandros, where the grief-stricken Andrea had come to bury her father's body, and where Sarah herself had come simply to escape the blistering heat, in the shade of the trees.

There had been a peaceful sense of lonely desolation about the ancient church graveyard overlooking the sea. Sarah had been making stenciled reproductions of the crumbling marble and sandstone grave markers, which were overgrown with weeds and strewn with moldering wreaths.

Andrea had come to bid her father's grave a final farewell, and sitting there in the shade of the trees, the two young women had talked long into the afternoon. They both were women who had lost the men they loved. And while their individual stars and fortunes were very far apart, a bond instantly formed between them.

Something of their mutual grief had been shared on that blistering sun-drenched day some 12 months before. And had they been male and female, they might very well have sought comfort in one another's arms. But as it turned out, Andrea invited Sarah to join her odyssey aboard the *Golden Hind,* and they became fast and caring friends instead.

# =====CHAPTER 7=====

## THE SHINY SET
### by
### Cassandra

The rich and the beautiful are never happier than
when they're whooping it up in honor of some new
and celebrated face in town. And according to all
reliable reports, that is exactly what some of our
most notable notables were doing last night at
Miramar, the secluded Shinnecock Hills estate of
the Baron and Baroness Von Bismark.

Imagine, if you will, a lineup of limousines
stretching all the way to Wickapogue, with the
flow of party traffic being directed through the
gates of the Von Bismark estate like so many
demigods and goddesses climbing Mount Olympus.
A huge striped tent on a perfectly manicured lawn
the size of a football field. A live orchestra playing
for dancing, while men in black tie and women
in elaborate formal gowns danced into the wee
hours, following an elegant midnight supper served
around the Olympic-sized swimming pool.

Any Hampton hostess worth her salt will have
to go some to outshine this particular affair, which
was, by the way, filmed by Franco de Roma. In
case you didn't know, he's the noted Italian director who's in town making a BBC documentary
featuring all the beautiful people whooping it up
as if fun was going out of style.

This is not to say that all those chic international types were not very much in evidence. And foremost among their number was Andrea Aristos, the guest of honor, who also just happens to be the superheiress of the decade. Her arrival aboard the spectacular *Golden Hind* in Southampton Yacht Harbor has hit the Hamptons like a sonic boom.

Suddenly, the season has shifted into high gear, and the only notable name missing from the star-studded roster of guests last night at the Von Bismark soirée was that of Roxanne Ryan Aristos, long the undisputed queen of the truly beautiful beautifuls, in what passes for high-powered society here in the Hamptons. (She also just happens to be Andrea's ex-stepmother, but of course you already knew that.)

It was a simply splendiferous evening, and there are those who insist that Roxanne's failure to be invited to the Von Bismark affair signals a rift as wide as the Grand Canyon between her and her former stepdaughter. Furthermore, everyone with even the slightest cachet is said to be planning to honor the new arrival to our shores with a plethora of cocktail parties, dinners, and even a *thé dansant*. You know—that's one of those madly chi-chi affairs given by a certain eminently successful Seventh Avenue designer who is all the rage this season with the ladies who count.

Poor Roxanne. Can't you just imagine her twiddling her toes out at Ox Pasture Farm, counting her carats and wondering what happened to the good old days?

In the pit of her stomach, Roxanne felt the first faint, fluttering wings of panic—a surge of nausea and dizziness, which signaled the approach of one of her migraines.

She continued reading as Cassandra went on to give Andrea an absolute rave review on her introduction to the very *crème de la chic,* describing her as "pleasantly refreshing and, while no great beauty, about as demurely unaffected as one might expect of a girl who was sitting on $2 billion."

Angrily crumpling the morning paper, Roxanne threw it aside and deliberately turned her attention to the breakfast tray riding the tangle of pink satin sheets: two perfectly browned slices of diatetic wheat toast resting serenely on a Limoges plate set between heavy, crested silverware. A steaming pot of herbal tea and a container of low-fat yogurt only served to emphasize the sterility of the meager fare, while one perfect Pink Princess rose lifted its head from a slender bud vase.

Where had it all gotten her? Roxanne wondered bleakly—the years of endless weight-watching and careful counting of every calorie, the singleminded devotion she had always exercised in keeping her body elegantly trim with carefully programmed exercise, daily massage, and a yearly two-week stay at Golden Portals.

Roxanne had not only set the clock back ten years at least, but at 45 years of age, she appeared to have stopped it entirely. For purely cosmetic reasons, she had deliberately avoided having children by any of her three husbands. Even now, she engaged in sex only rarely and quite discreetly.

Roxanne set the breakfast tray aside untouched and swung her legs to the floor. How could they do this to her? she agonized. And yet even as she asked the question, Roxanne was painfully aware of the all-too-obvious answer.

It was all those Aristos millions—money that by all that was right should have been hers upon Stavros's death. God knows she had earned it, since her late husband had exhibited the sex drive of a Greek mountain goat. And just what did Andrea need the money for anyway? She was homely as sin, without the slightest modicum of sophistication, and she would have been perfectly satisfied to spend the rest of her life on her knees, in some dreary nunnery.

Yet, in spite of Andrea's naiveté, Roxanne by now was convinced that there was far more to her visit to the Hamptons than appeared on the surface. Like something out of a Greek tragedy, Andrea had come to seek revenge. She had always been blindly jealous of Roxanne, and in that subterranean Greek mind of hers, she just might be misguided enough to think that she could challenge her ex-stepmother on her own home turf.

Roxanne was possessed of a raw, almost chilling kind of courage that never wavered in the face of a threat. And yet now, for no reason she could clearly define, Andrea's presence in the Hamptons that season had begun to undermine her confidence. It was almost as if suddenly the tightrope upon which she had been so precariously balanced all these years, had been quietly loosened by some malignant and unseen hand.

Like a drowning person struggling upward toward air and light, Roxanne padded across the room to pull open the drapes and then moved to stand before a life-size portrait hanging above the fireplace in her ivory, gold, and rose velvet boudoir.

As her eyes lovingly caressed the familiar figure in the painting, Roxanne felt an immediate lessening of tension. The painting had been done some 20 years before, and in spite of the intervening years, there had been absolutely no visible change in her appearance.

She had been captured in a summer garden, wearing a gauzy yellow gown and a big, floppy-brimmed garden hat with trailing streamers. Neither young nor old, the portrait conveyed a timeless quality in which Roxanne seemed to remain suspended—lovely, aloof, smiling, and serene among the flowers, with a delicate tracery of sunlight filtering down to illuminate softly her lovely features.

That was the answer, Roxanne suddenly realized. She had remained frozen in aspic for over 20 years. Beyond the slightest shadow of a doubt, the time had come for a total change of image.

"What really happened between you and Father?" Andrea asked. "He never told me before he died, and I think it's important that I know the truth."

Jason didn't look up from the rubber raft bobbing on the surface of the pool. It was very hot, and Jason's head was beginning to ache. At that moment, he wanted nothing so much as to just roll over into the water and swim away, pretending that the question had never been asked.

Jason didn't move, however. He just lay very still, with his eyes closed against the merciless summer sun.

"Jason?" Andrea questioned softly from where she sat at the side of the pool, dangling her legs in the water. "I've had the feeling ever since my arrival that there's something terribly wrong. We've never been close, I know . . . but it doesn't have to be that way. I'm your sister. I want to understand."

Jason lifted his head from the pillow of his arms and glanced off toward where Helene stood laughing among a cluster of guests on the lawn. She had insisted on inviting several dozen people for luncheon that day, and the sounds of laughter and conversation drifted across the grass, to where white-coated waiters prepared an elaborate buffet beneath the trees.

"What do you really think of Helene?" Jason asked abruptly. "She is, after all, the one who convinced you to come here this summer. It wasn't my idea. I can assure you of that."

"Jason, why are you so embittered?" Andrea questioned with genuine concern in her voice. "I had my own reasons for coming, although I must admit that Helene was most persuasive. To tell you the truth, I like and admire her very much. I'm sure that Father

94

would have been greatly impressed if he had lived to meet your wife."

Andrea reached out to touch Jason's shoulder lightly with her fingertips. "Can't you see how very much I want you to be my brother again, Jason? Father's gone now, and no matter what kind of grudge you're nursing, I happen to know that he loved you dearly. I was never meant to be the head of Aristos Shipping, and I've only done what I had to do because I simply had no choice in the matter. It was always you who were meant to take over the company when Father died."

Jason refused to meet her eyes. "I get the feeling that you're trying to tell me something, Andrea."

"I am," she responded quietly, "which is why I really came to the Hamptons this summer. I'm trying very hard to convince you that we have to put the past behind us. We have a responsibility to preserve and sustain the empire that Father built. It belongs to us now . . . to you and to me. I mean to share it with you."

For a moment Jason stared into her eyes with a look as sharp as pain. Then he said, "I don't want any part of my father's legacy, Andrea. He disowned me— ordered me out of his life, as if I had suddenly ceased to exist. To be totally frank, little sister, I don't want any part of Stavros Aristos's fucking legacy."

With that Jason slipped from the float and dove toward the bottom of the pool, leaving scarcely a ripple in his wake.

Every Friday afternoon during the summer season, Roxanne maintained a standing appointment at Soli San Lorenzo's Southampton Salon. Now, as she slid from her car, hurried across the sidewalk, and swung breathlessly through the swinging glass doors, the foyer, with its beveled mirrors and Greco-Roman decor, was as familiar as her own living room.

She nodded to Fleur, Soli's receptionist, and then glanced nervously down at her watch to discover that she was not late, as she had feared, but rather several minutes early.

Soli San Lorenzo had the distinction of being one of the few people that Roxanne never kept waiting. He was, by her own estimation, an absolute cosmetic wizard, as well as a veritable fount of fascinating information. As part of his stock in trade, Soli prided himself on keeping in touch with absolutely all the latest gossip, and Roxanne could always count on him to reveal all the Hamptons' worst-kept secrets.

The ambiance of Soli's salon was consistently upbeat and entirely in keeping with the swinging, seasonal pace of the summer beach colony. Background music played against the hot rush of blow dryers, while the air was climate-controlled, and pleasantly perfumed with the scent of Ultra Magic setting lotion.

The establishment was as efficiently run as it was outrageously expensive, and Roxanne considered her weekly appointment to be one of the most relaxing and enjoyable hours of her busy schedule. Time, however, was never wasted, and Soli, who was currently all the rage, employed a dozen other hairdressers, as well as a back-up team of pretty young manicurists in lavender smocks, to smooth the various transitions with tiny watercress sandwiches and coffee in styrofoam cups.

"How's my beauty today?" Soli demanded as he made a sudden and dramatic appearance through a pair of mirrored double doors. He brushed her cheek lightly with his lips and then stood back, scowling, clasping both her hands in his own. "Tsk, tsk, tsk," he mouthed disapprovingly. "Do I detect some ugly frown lines around that beautiful mouth?"

Roxanne took a deep breath and willed her tense facial muscles to relax. Soli always seemed to sense her mood perfectly, and she knew only too well that nothing aged a person quite as fast as nervous tension. "Why, I haven't a care in the world," she said, smiling and reaching to brush a smudge of bright lipstick from Soli's cheek. "And by the way, darling, my brand of lipstick, as you know, is indelible. That must have come from one of your other ladies."

Roxanne's voice carried a note of disapproval that Soli totally ignored. "All part of a day's work," he laughed, leading her back through the mirrored doors with a sweeping stage bow. "After all, I live only to serve the rich and the beautiful. And in case you didn't already know, there is a certain breed of middle-aged woman who can get very physical when you're combing her out."

Soli mugged outrageously, doing a perfect imitation of one of the Hamptons' foremost hostesses. "Believe me," he went on to say, "in my business it never pays to make selfish libidos suffer too much, or you'll end up getting stiffed on the tip."

They laughed comfortably together, moving arm in arm down a wide, brightly lit corridor with curtained alcoves opening off on either side. Roxanne's weekly appointment with Soli was easily worth three times the price she paid. And in a sense, he was the only real confidant she had.

Beneath his very capable and extremely creative hands, Roxanne felt glamorous and recharged when she walked out the front door, after being pampered, coiffed, manicured, and ultimately reassured that she was indeed a very desirable woman. She was a star transcendent among the lesser luminaries, with whom she was reluctantly forced to share the talents of the Hamptons' foremost beautician.

In many ways, Soli replaced the psychiatrist so many women of her acquaintance found to be an absolute necessity. He had been doing Roxanne's hair and makeup for over five years. And during that period, their relationship had evolved to a point of such intimacy that Roxanne sometimes tended to disbelieve the stories about Soli's unquestioned preference for rough trade.

Occasionally over the years, Roxanne had invited Soli to escort her to important functions when her various husbands had been unavailable. He clearly enjoyed being part of her life, as well as gaining intro to the glittering social whirl that consistently orbited about her. Roxanne had, in fact, largely been responsible for making him famous, and she frankly had no idea how she could possibly get along without him.

They shared many interests in common, although Soli was younger than she by at least a good dozen years. He was slim as a snake, with roguish Italian good looks and a mass of chestnut curls framing his handsome features. Roxanne had realized from the very beginning, of course, that Soli was a natural-born hustler on the way up, and she had played upon that knowledge to gain her own ends. Soli always liked to play on the winning team, and in that regard they were very much alike.

Finally, he led her into a cubicle somewhat larger than the others, with mirrored walls and a boldly striped tented ceiling. Royanne settled herself in the comfortable padded chair, and Soli moved swiftly about, meticulously arranging the tools of his trade for easy access.

"Now, are you ready to tell me all about it?" he asked rather sternly. "I see something in those lovely eyes of yours that looks to me like a storm warning."

"Did you read the Cassandra column today in the *Hampton Reporter?*" Roxanne asked. She was clearly overwrought, and the huge 37-carat diamond worn on her slender hand sparkled in the light as she twisted it ceaselessly and without conscious thought. "It was a real hatchet job."

"Tsk, tsk, tsk," Soli scolded, running his long, supple fingers through her hair and gently tickling her scalp. "Don't tell me my beauty's allowing that little bit of tacky trivia to cause her to lose sleep. Andrea Aristos, after all, is only news because everybody wants to see what a billionairess looks like. She's really nothing but a side show freak . . . like a hermaphrodite, or a tattooed lady with three tits. Everyone in town wants to have a peek, but they'll be bored to stone by the end of the week. I talked to several of my ladies who attended Helene's party. And they all said that Andrea was plain as a mud fence and dressed as if she had fallen off the back of a Salvation Army van. She didn't say boo to anybody, dances as if she has two club feet, and scurried back aboard the *Golden Hind* before midnight, as if she was afraid she'd turn into a pumpkin."

Roxanne was not entirely reassured. "Andrea is doing this deliberately—I know she is. I've simply got to think of some way to put the little bitch in her place."

Soli dropped Roxanne's chair into a horizontal position, tipped her head back into the sink and, after lathering up a fragrant herbal shampoo, began to massage her scalp. "I've got an idea," he said. "Why don't you give a fabulous party, stock your swimming pool with hungry barracuda and then conveniently arrange to have some drunk push Andrea in? You could probably sell tickets if it were properly staged."

Roxanne was scarcely listening, and her dark gaze had drifted off into the endlessly reflecting mirrors, to linger in some haunted, solitary place. "What I need is a complete change," she informed him. "Something entirely new, exciting, and totally different. What I want to see in that mirror when I get ready to leave here today is a completely new me."

Soli chuckled softly. "In that case, my beauty, why don't you just close those lovely eyes and leave absolutely everything to me?"

Roxanne did exactly that, after taking a Valium as

99

Soli suggested. Within minutes, the perfumed atmosphere became dreamlike and filmy, and she felt as if she was slowly dissolving in it, succumbing luxuriously to the sense of peaceful relaxation that she inevitably experienced whenever she placed herself entirely in Soli's extremely capable hands.

Roxanne trusted him completely, and she gradually allowed herself to drift off into her regular weekly fantasy as he worked on her hair.

First, she imagined herself sitting like a queen in a large tub. It was constructed of fragrant wood, and she was immersed in a foamy bubble bath, nibbling on large purple grapes and sipping from a goblet of hot mulled apple cider. The setting was not any place in particular, although there were candles burning with a golden glow, and the air was perfumed with a heady floral incense.

Next, a pair of mirrored doors opened and a beautiful nude man with chestnut curls crossed the room to join her. It was Soli. His body was smooth, very tan, and almost entirely hairless, as he stepped into the tub to bathe her, feed her fruit, and cater to her every whim.

His genitals were innocently childlike in repose, and there was absolutely no sex involved. Roxanne was simply there to be adored and totally pampered without having to concern herself even slightly with what might be expected from her in return.

It was a leisurely fantasy. She was bathed, anointed with scented oils, and completely massaged and stroked, while having to do nothing but relax and enjoy a variety of pleasurable feelings. Then, after the long, luxurious bath, Soli wrapped her up in a large, warm towel, lifted her in his strong arms, and carried her to a massage table where she stretched langorously as he caressed her from head to foot with incredibly soft rabbit-fur mittens.

The fantasy ended abruptly as Soli switched on a

blow-dryer and began moving the rush of hot, dry air over her head. "I imagine you've already heard about Darnell Hanlan," he said, lifting his voice to be heard above the noise. "The story about his performance at City Hall this morning must be all over town by now."

Roxanne's interest was immediately galvanized. People had been talking of little but her cousin Darnell ever since the funeral, and she was almost afraid to know what his latest exploits might include. "I suppose you might as well tell me the worst," Roxanne replied with a deep sigh of resignation.

"Well," Soli went on, obviously relishing the opportunity to recount the tale. "Hang onto your seat for this one." By now, Soli was well on his way toward creating a totally new image for Roxanne. And as he talked, he turned her this way and that, while his scissors flashed and great swatches of her long, dark hair fell to the floor.

"Darnell has done it again," Soli announced. "This morning, he marched into a council meeting of the city fathers, dumped a million dollars in back taxes on the table, and informed them he had sold Treasure Cay to some Arab by the name of Kamal Ali Reza."

Roxanne stiffened. "Sold Treasure Cay," she repeated. "But that's impossible. There's a referendum before the city council at this very moment, turning the island into a federal nature preserve. It was my aunt Annabel's pet project before she died."

"Forget it," Soli advised her. "For some mysterious reason the Department of the Interior has dropped the entire project. It seems, from what I hear, that this Ali Reza has one hell of a lot of pull in Washington. Treasure Cay belongs to him now, although no one is really sure just what he intends to do with it."

# ════CHAPTER 8════

The interior of the Von Bismarks' Manhattan pent-house was a spacious, opulent, and purely undiluted modern statement with a grand sense of space and scale. It seemed to float high above the East River like a spectacular yacht freighted with treasures. The $2 million worth of contemporary art splashed dramatically across the stark eggshell-white walls not only provided a lavish backdrop, but had proven to be a very shrewd investment as well.

The art had been painted by Ian McVane, the Hamptons' foremost artist in residence. Helene Von Bismark had been among the first to recognize the potential value of his work. Helene was like that in everything she did—creative, inventive, daring, and ultimately ruthless. She was a hard-headed business-woman whose mind had often been compared to an IBM master computer.

Competition was in her blood, and the challenge and excitement of the marketplace was like a drug she couldn't live without. Winning was everything for Helene, and pitting her own keen intelligence against men in the business world acted like a highly potent aphrodisiac.

She had learned early on that men thought of women only as objects. It was a condition that most women seemed simply to accept by becoming glorified host-esses, while others assumed that it was all part of a sex war where a peace treaty was at least possible. Helene, however, was always prepared to barter anything and everything in order to win. She would use guile, intelligence, sex, or even feigned submission if that happened to be the card to turn the trick.

During one brief fling with psychoanalysis, her psychiatrist had accused her of being drawn to "the dangerous edges of life." She always climbed out on the narrowest precipice available, where it became incumbent upon her to negotiate each upward step of the way like an aerialist, spanning some terrible void through sheer guts and grim determination.

Even during the summer months, when the Von Bismarks were in residence at their Southampton estate, Helene spent five days a week in her midtown offices. Manhattan was the hub on which the world turned, and over the years, Helene had become addicted to the city's tremendous flow of creative energy, much in the same way that her husband Jason was addicted to drugs of every kind and sort.

Manhattan was a vast competitive arena that managed to be all things to all people—gaudy, bawdy, and yet incredibly sophisticated all at the same time. Yet for Helene, more than anything else it was a testing place, where the weak were quickly winnowed out in a championship game of winner-take-all.

Helene's success as a budding cosmetics tycoon over the past several years had, however, been little more than a net thrown over the abyss. Power was the magical and mystical wand that made things happen, the ability to accomplish that which had not been done before in order to confirm her own pre-eminent place in the overall scheme of things.

Had she been gifted with no more than the desire to have shown herself the equal of any man, Helene Von Bismark would have had every reason in the world to feel smugly satisfied with all that she had been able to accomplish. She was, after all, wife, mother, fashion-trend-setter, and president of her own corporation.

Helene was never satisfied with anything, however. And now, with the vast Aristos shipping empire literally up for grabs, she saw her ambition climb even higher, to the platinum-plated world of international finance. She viewed it as a form of manifest destiny— the exquisitely egotistical act of creating herself, along with a future of fulfilled dreams.

No matter what she had been able to accomplish up until that point in her life, the hunger was still there. The emptiness was still gnawing at her insides like an insatiable succubus demanding blood sacrifice.

Friday was the maid's day off, and the telephone was ringing for the tenth time when Helene stepped through the front door of the penthouse. She had been expecting Henri Trouville to call, and she hurried down the steps into the sunken living room to snatch the phone from its cradle.

"The Von Bismark residence," she recited in a slightly breathless voice. "Yes, operator. This is the baroness. Please put Monsieur Trouville on the line."

Kicking off her spike-heeled pumps, Helene curled up on the low, deep couch before the fireplace and hastily lit a cigarette as the overseas operator put the call through from the Aristos Shipping headquarters in Monte Carlo.

"Henri, darling," she said, smiling and exhaling a stream of smoke through her finely chiseled nostrils. "I dashed in from the office just in time. Yes . . . yes, of course I miss you terribly too. I'd give anything to be on the next flight to Monte Carlo, darling. But as you know, there's some rather important business to attend to here in New York."

Her voice dropping in pitch Helene went on to relate the details of the party she had given for An-

104

drea upon her arrival. "There are, of course, some rather major problems," she said carefully. "Two, in fact. Andrea and Jason. They act like complete strangers, and while I'm sure that Jason can be brought around, as far as Andrea is concerned, the situation is rather more complicated. She and her friend, Sarah Dane, are inseparable, and the Dane girl is nobody's fool. Andrea obviously relies upon her heavily for advice, and I'm going to have to figure out a way of getting rid of her without arousing Andrea's suspicion.

"Yes . . . yes, of course, darling. I understand completely, but it's going to take time. Just trust me, darling, and be patient. As soon as I have anything definite, I'll let you know. I think I've come up with a way to discredit Sarah Dane and bounce Andrea right off the wall and into our waiting arms.

"No, I can't give you any details over the phone, and I really have to hang up. Jason is expecting me for dinner out in Southampton, and I've still got a two-hour drive ahead of me."

Helene's voice dropped into a low purr as she whispered parting intimacies into the phone. Then, just as Henri signed off and she was about to replace the receiver in its cradle, she heard a soft click on the upstairs line. My God, she thought, someone must have been listening in.

She rose slowly to sweep the upper gallery with a questioning glance. It was the maid's day out, and the door to the master bedroom at the top of the spiral staircase was closed. Helene clearly remembered leaving it open when she left for work that morning, which could mean only one thing.

Jason had driven in from the Hamptons and was at that very minute in their upstairs bedroom. He must have heard everything.

Crossing slowly to the bar, Helene's hands were deliberately steady as she selected a heavy crystal tumbler and splashed it half full of Napoleon brandy. She drank it off neat, steeing herself against the inevitable confrontation.

As shaky as things were between them at this stage of the game, Helene was in a very tight spot. She'd have to keep a very cool head, or face the possibility of seeing all her carefully laid plans go down the drain like $2 billion worth of dirty bathwater.

Quickly, she opened her bag and applied fresh lipstick, using the mirror behind the bar. Then she sprayed on a whisper of scent and, with a few deft brush strokes, arranged her hair to curl softly about her face.

After slipping off the top of her exquisitely tailored black Chanel suit, she quickly unbuttoned her silk blouse and then poured herself another brandy. Now she was ready, and she moved across the room to drape herself languidly across the couch.

Helene had never been a true beauty, but it had always been fully within her powers to make people believe that she was anything she chose. Men had always come after her like a bitch in heat, and she had learned early in life how to use sex very much to her own advantage.

In reality, her face was an arresting configuration of unusual features in which the classic canons of beauty went largely unfulfilled. Her nose was a bit too sharp and prominent, her forehead was a shade too high, and her upper lip was a fraction of an inch too long.

Still, Helene had about her an illusive aura, an amalgam of glamor and strength—a fusion of both her masculine and feminine qualities into an arresting, seamless whole. Perhaps more than anything else, however, Helene was a consummate actress with an infinite repertoire of roles. Her features changed from moment to moment so that the classically high cheekbones, wide, sensual mouth, and widely spaced gray-green eyes could assume any dimension she chose.

From the gallery above came the sound of a door closing softly. Helene turned and threw back her head, looking up to find Jason standing at the upper landing and staring down at her. He had a trenchcoat slung carelessly across one shoulder, and in his hand he carried a single Vuitton suitcase.

"Would you like a drink?" she called up to him.

Without response, Jason began moving slowly down the steps, with the spectacular Manhattan cityscape hanging like a glittering scrim beyond the vast expanse of floor-to-ceiling windows.

"Is that it, Helene?" Jason questioned. "Just one more for the road?"

Helene shrugged. "I can only assume that you overheard my conversation with Henri. And as usual, your response is an entirely emotional one. Really, Jason, one of these days you are going to have to start growing up. Running away from home is strictly for juveniles."

"I'm not running away from home, Helene. I'm running away from you—and what you've become."

Jason dropped his suitcase like a weight that had suddenly become unbearably heavy. Then, slinging his trenchcoat across the back of a chair, he crossed to the bar to drop ice cubes into a glass. "Just for the record, Helene, how long have you been having your affair with Henri Trouville?"

"Henri is having an affair, Jason darling. For me, it's strictly business. I have no intention of seeing my children's rightful inheritance lost simply because their father is too gutless to demand what is rightfully theirs from the estate of his late, great father, Stavros Aristos."

Jason's laugh was harsh and entirely without mirth. "You know, Helene, you're really something. You knew that my father had disinherited me when we got married. I don't want any part of Aristos Shipping or my father's legacy. As far as I'm concerned, Andrea's welcome to the whole works. What you have to realize, Helene, is that I'm no longer my father's son. Don't you know what it means to be disinherited? The Aristos fortune doesn't belong to me . . . or to you . . . or to the children either, so you might as well face facts."

Helene fixed him with a piercing stare. "Tell me, Jason. Just what was it that your father found out about you that makes you hate him so much? You weren't yet an alcoholic or a drug addict when the split came, so it must have been something else— something that Stavros Aristos simply couldn't tolerate in his son and heir."

Jason's brooding sense of bitterness and resentment hit him forcefully, almost like a physical blow. "What does it matter now?" he flashed angrily. He finished his drink in a single swallow and quickly poured himself another. "Why don't we talk about you instead, Helene? I've known all about you and Henri Trouville for months—all about those intimate weekends in Paris and Rome. Tell me, Helene. Did you honestly think that I was so far gone that I didn't suspect what you were up to?"

"Henri means nothing to me," Helene informed him lightly. "I simply had to make sure that there was someone in Monte Carlo looking after our interests, since you seem totally incapable of looking after them yourself."

"Only whores use sex as a negotiable asset," Jason spat out.

Helene's features hardened into a smooth mask as coldly stylized as the face of a Dresden china doll. "Listen to me, Jason," she said. "And you had better listen well, because I'm going to give it to you straight. It's time you earned your keep, one way or another. You are a man with some very expensive habits for which I have been picking up the tab. All I'm asking is that you make yourself irresistible to Andrea, long enough for me . . ."

". . . to screw her out of two billion dollars," Jason cut in."

"Not exactly," Helene continued with exaggerated patience. "All I need is her power of attorney. She's got to trust me—at least for a while."

"What about Henri Trouville?"

"Henri is a very disposable commodity, and far too ambitious. Once I gain control, he'll be one of the first to go. Of course, Henri's a charming man, but merely the means to an end."

"And how do I know that I too am not an entirely disposable commodity? Once you have what you want, why should you keep me around? After all, Helene, isn't that why you married me in the first place? You've always known what you were after."

Helene laughed softly. "Somehow, my darling, the role of the neglected husband does not become you in the least. We're not children, Jason, and the real world is not always a pretty place. But then, since you walk around like a zombie in a drugged fog all the time, what could you possibly know about the real world? The truth is, Jason, you can't even support your cocaine habit, which is, by the way, running about a hundred dollars a day."

Jason shook his head with a dogged, weary motion and ran his fingers back through his wavy dark blond hair. "It's no good, Helene. I want a divorce. I want out."

Helene's large smoky eyes turned to cold slate, and the atmosphere in the room seemed to polarize into separate force fields, like mined terrain where one false step on either side could trigger an explosion of magnum force.

"Divorce?" she repeated, disbelieving. "What do you mean *divorce?*"

Jason's shoulders sagged, and his voice dropped to

little more than a whisper. "There's nothing left between us, Helene. I'm leaving here tonight, and I'm not coming back. I need time to think things through on my own. Time to decide just where I go from here."

"You're wrong, Jason," Helene said. "It isn't over between us. We just know each other a little better, that's all. Whatever I may or may not be," she breathed, rising to her feet, "I'm still your wife, still a woman. I need you, Jason. And whether you know it or not, you need me just as much."

In the next moment, Helene had crossed to where Jason stood and pressed herself against him. "Don't shut me out," she whispered. "Together, we can have it all."

Then she was going down on him, pulling his shirt away and allowing her tongue to slide across his bare chest, flicking it over his hard brown nipples, even as her hand slipped down to unzip the front of his pants.

"Don't," he said, one hand tightly clenching the glass he held. "This isn't going to change anything."

"I want you to use me," Helene said huskily, as she dropped to her knees and buried her face against his crotch. "Anyway you like . . . anything. You know I can be good to you, Jason. Please, my darling. Let me show you how good I can be."

Helene shuddered against him, stroking, fondling, and encouraging him, tasting and savoring his cock with her mouth, even as one of her hands slipped beneath her skirt to probe the moist, silken crease of her sex, caught between tightly squeezed thighs.

There was a resounding crash as his glass shattered against the fireplace. In the next instant, Jason had wrenched Helene's head back by the hair, and his closed fist exploded against her jaw to send her sprawling before the hearth.

It all happened so fast that Helene was taken completely by surprise. Stars seemed to explode in her head, and somehow she found herself staring up at

110

him from the floor, in shocked disbelief. Her eyes were wide and unblinking, her mouth a vivid crimson slash across her chalky face.

"You conniving she-bitch," he grunted, shoving his shirt back into his pants and zipping up his fly. "How many guys have you gone down on to get where you are, Helene? Do you even remember what it took to get to the top of the shit heap?"

# CHAPTER 9

Jaime swung his board around and glanced back over his shoulder at the approaching wave. It was a monster, humping up so high that it had already lost the deep-water blue of the ocean depths and taken on a pale green luminosity where the sun showed through.

Watching its approach with bated breath, Jaime felt the slow chill of fear circuit upward along his spine. At some point, the really big ones always did that to you. So awesome in their mass and power that for an instant, all you wanted to do was shoot your board out into safe water beyond the line of breaking surf.

Yet for Jaime, the moment of fear always passed and was immediately replaced by a grim kind of determination as he forced himself to hold his ground and he carefully positioned his board for take-off. Never in his life had he surfed the kinds of waves he had encountered along the north shore of Long Island, and there were days at Suicide Alley when he didn't even dare put his board in the water.

The monster wave had by now moved from the distance with a loud roar, drawing itself up into a towering cliff of sunlit water, cresting high above his head. Jaime felt the sea fall away beneath him as the huge wave swept him up and then continued to rise smooth, pure, and undiminished, without a trace of foam.

Ritualistically, Jaime grasped between his teeth the small gold cross he wore about his neck, sucked air deep into his lungs, and then gave a couple of powerful strokes with his arms. He felt as if he were stepping off some kind of cosmic escalator, with the world falling away beneath his feet.

Then he quickly stood up and dropped into the curl, as the great, green comber rushed shoreward with the deafening roar of an onrushing freight train. He was a solitary figure poised in that vast, moving aquatic world, crouching down low as the board gracefully skimmed down the face of the wave and then angled off into a hollow, foaming tunnel of rushing white water.

By now, the noise was deafening, as the wave crashed and foamed into the shallows. Thoughts rushed and careened through Jaime's mind, one piling incoherently upon another to form a kaleidoscope of impressions that somehow were all mixed up together with the taste of brine upon his lips and the avalanche of seawater thundering in his ears.

Arising unbidden, erotic images from the night before flashed before Jaime's eyes, as flying sea-spume stung his flesh like BB pellets. He saw the whip in his hand, rising and falling methodically, flailing the white flesh before him into an angry criss-cross pattern of raised welts. Once again he experienced the rushing, pulsing surge of his own orgasm, felt the incredible sense of power, and heard the ecstatic cries and pleas of the man groveling at his feet.

Finally, with the wave expiring beneath him, Jaime dropped back down on his board and began paddling toward shore. He simply didn't have any idea what to make of Darnell Hanlan or of the offer he had made the night before. Big money. A flashy new sports car, a wardrobe of expensive custom-tailored clothes, and a fantastic beach pad, with all expenses paid.

It seemed to Jaime like the chance of a lifetime, the really big-time score he had always been looking for. And yet, for some reason he remained wary and very much on his guard. It wasn't because of the masochistic sex, which was really only a question of playing a given role. If Hanlan was into a heavy bondage trip, that was his business. What bothered Jaime was something he sensed strongly—some diabolical and deformed quality in Darnell's character, an almost palpable evil.

Hanlan had picked him up at a raunchy roadhouse bar called the Zodiac, near Westhampton. It was a semigay, semistraight watering place that included among its clientele a host of local bikers, a few vagrant hustlers like himself, and a pretty good sampling of some of the foremost names on the Hampton Social Register.

Although they had spent a wild night together aboard Darnell's schooner, which was moored at Three Mile Harbor, the middle-aged writer remained very much an enigma.

Without question, he was a homo into a heavy sado-masochistic trip, while at the same time being in no way effete or even slightly gay. Darnell wore leather, rode a big Harley Davidson, and was obviously rolling in loot. He was a voluble, volatile personality who talked fast, persuasively, and with a kind of erratic energy sparking his eyes.

He was staying at Three Mile Harbor, on a 65-foot Chris-Craft called the El Diablo. And for his efforts the night before, Jaime had been amply rewarded with five crisp $100 bills, some coke, and an ounce of Colombian red.

A note written on lavender stationery and smelling strongly of perfume was waiting for Jaime when he got back to his Bridgehampton rooming house. It was from Abbey Randolph, inviting him to come for dinner that evening at Bramwell Acres.

Jaime really had nothing better to do with his time before meeting Darnell again at midnight, so he decided to accept.

He hadn't stuck around the afternoon of old lady Randolph's heart attack, but the following day, Jaime had read the story in the *Hampton Reporter*. No question about it, Abbey was one weird broad. And as strange and incomprehensible as it seemed, Jaime had the feeling that somehow, she just might have staged the whole thing, that she had used him.

On the same day, he had read of her engagement to some millionaire playboy by the name of Kelly De Witte. And when he found Abbey's invitation waiting for him, Jaime determined to go to Bramwell Acres and collect what he felt he had coming to him.

He took a taxi to the Randolph estate, paid off the driver at the gate, and then walked up the drive toward the house beneath a three-quarter moon. The evening was unusually warm and balmy, and the air was pungent with the smell of honeysuckle.

There was a brand new bright red Jaguar XKE sitting in the driveway before the house, with a gleaming chromium surfboard rack attached to the trunk. Jamie mounted the front steps, crossed the wide veranda, and rang the bell. Then he listened intently for sounds from within, but heard only the faintest distant chiming.

At last he was able to discern the sound of slowly approaching footsteps. Finally, the door opened partially to frame a tall, stooped figure dressed in funereal black. A fine tapestry of wrinkles traced the butler's dark face, and his shiny domed head was haloed by an electric fringe of stark white hair.

"Is there something you wish?" the old black houseman questioned, frowning out at him with pouched and rheumy eyes.

"I got a note from Miss Randolph asking me to come here," Jaime informed him, shifting uneasily from one foot to the other. "My name is Jaime. Jaime Rodriquez."

The man's milky old eyes widened, and there was

a faint tremor to the withered black hands. "So you're Miss Abbey's young man? If you'd be good enough to step inside, I'll see if she's ready to receive you."

The butler ushered Jaime inside the house and then left him there, shuffling away across the parquet flooring to disappear down a long corridor.

It was very dim and cool inside the house, and the lower floors of the mansion seemed to slumber in a musty, brooding silence. From high above Jaime's head, softly muted light filtered down through the dusty prisms of a massive crystal chandelier, bathing the walls and Corinthian columns in a ghostly, muted aura.

Everything about the place spoke of age and disuse, of things faded and having outlived their usefulness. The murky paintings hanging on the walls, the ornate Victorian furniture, the stained glass windows along the staircase, and the fading tapestries all conveyed a sense of another age.

Jaime had never in his life seen anything like it, and for some unknown reason, he found that his palms were sweating, and he was very ill at ease. He had no idea how to act in those surroundings, and the knowledge disturbed him greatly.

When he was finally shown into the dining room, where Abbey was arranging flowers as a centerpiece, Jaime could scarcely believe his eyes. She appeared totally transformed. She was flashy yet expensively dressed, with gold loop earrings and a vivid slash of lipstick. Her fingernails, as she put the finishing touches on a bowl of white chrysanthemums, were brightly enameled, while her soft, brown hair had been streaked with silver and hung in casual disarray about her thin shoulders.

Abbey had the look of all those stylishly bronzed and beautiful Hampton women Jaime saw in town, only something was missing. With Abbey, it just didn't quite work. She was trying hard to bring something

116

off but had only managed to make herself look slightly ridiculous.

"I'm so glad that you came," Abbey gushed, hurrying forward to take his hand. "I do hope you like chateaubriand and artichoke hearts in vinaigrette dressing. And I've even talked Simmons into making us some crêpes flambés for dessert!"

Jaime only barely grasped the essentials of what she was talking about, and he didn't really have any idea of how to respond. "I read about your mother's death in the papers," he said a bit lamely. "Sorry I didn't stick around that day . . . it just seemed best for me to split."

Abbey simply stared at him with that odd, spaced-out look of hers, and when she spoke, her voice was even more breathlessly animated. "Let's not talk about that. It's over and done with. You're here now, Jaime. That's all that really matters to me."

He allowed her to lead him to a baronial high-backed chair at the head of the table; then Abbey took her own place on his right. The long, gleaming dining table was set with silver, crystal, and fine china that caught and reflected the light from tall, multibranched candelabrum shimmering against the gold damask walls. A soft, warm breeze blew in through the open windows, billowing the white lace curtains and making a gentle sweep of the spacious room.

During dinner that evening, Abbey told Jaime about her life—about the father she had worshipped, and how proud he had been when she won a blue ribbon at the Bridgehampton horse show.

Abbey had smiled sadly when she told him about the time she had run away to Manhattan to study modern dance. Somehow, she had gotten an audition with Martha Graham, and she had lived for a week in the Barbizon Hotel for Women. It had been the most exciting week of her life, Abbey related—at least until Annabel had managed to discover where she was

117

staying and sent old Simmons to bring her home in a Cary limousine.

After that, Abbey confessed, she had simply stopped trying to be or to do anything, other than to make herself invisible. Abbey's rebellion during the years that followed had taken the form of strange fasts and long silences. She hid her uneaten food in cupboards throughout the house, and every chance she got, she slipped away to ride, swim, or spend hours sketching along the beach.

Abbey knew almost nothing of the outside world. And when guests did make rare appearances at Bramwell Acres, she would withdraw from the conversation slowly, as if a shade were being drawn over a window. Abbey did not like to be criticized, especially in front of others. Nor did she like what she considered to be Annabel's *grande dame* brand of charm, which she felt was strained, fake, and hypocritical.

As long as her mother had remained alive, Abbey confessed, she had known that there was simply no escape. She was utterly trapped.

Sitting there in that cavernous dining room, Abbey appeared fragile and infinitely vulnerable, in spite of her awkward appearance. Jaime scarcely spoke during the course of the meal, while Abbey rattled on continuously in short, tautly strung sentences. It was almost as if to pause for even an instant might completely shatter her control.

As far as Jaime was concerned, the entire evening was like a surrealistic dream. His usually healthy appetite had deserted him, and he merely picked at the food while consuming large quantities of wine.

By the time dessert was served, Abbey's unwavering gaze had begun to get on his nerves almost as much as the dour and disapproving air of Simmons. Moving slowly in and out of the room to deliver one course after another, the butler mumbled darkly to himself and on one occasion almost spilled the gravy in Jaime's lap.

Finally, after coffee and crêpes flambés, they adjourned to an upstairs sitting room, where Abbey served him brandy from a crystal decanter. She insisted that Jaime select a cigar from an ebony humidor, and after lighting it for him, she suddenly excused herself and disappeared into the next room.

Jaime took the opportunity to pour a small mound of white powder on his thumbnail, and applied it first to one nostril and then the other. He inhaled with several short snorts and then licked the coke from his thumbnail with a quick, practiced flick of his tongue. It was almost eleven o'clock, and he had promised to meet Darnell Hanlan at the Zodiac between twelve o'clock and twelve-thirty.

Jaime blinked hard as bright crystalline waves seemed to wash over him, penetrating his thoughts with their radiance. It was that extra dimension that he liked about coke, the way it spun your head around and made it possible to do things you really didn't want to do.

After 20 minutes of restless pacing, Jaime heard Abbey's voice calling to him from the next room. This was it, he thought. Time for the score, and then he'd be off and running, on to bigger and better things with a man who had promised to show him a way to make at least $20,000 by the summer's end.

Abbey lay on her back in the big canopied four-poster bed. She was propped up by a froth of lacy pillows and surrounded by a variety of dolls in all shapes and sizes.

Her nude body gleamed whitely beneath a gauzy peignoir, and once again her mood had shifted, as it had done all evening, rising and falling like the wind.

"Abbey?" Jaime questioned, as he pushed the door open and then closed it silently behind him.

She was waiting for him there in the dimness. But for a moment, Jaime stood transfixed in the middle of the room. His mind was a whirling vortex of confused impressions from the quantity of wine he had drunk with dinner. And now the coke was beginning to work on his head, with everything wavering and distorted.

"Come to me, my darling," Abbey called, stretching out her arms. "We're alone now . . . just the two of us. Just as it was always meant to be."

Moving as if in trance, Jaime crossed to the bed and slumped down upon it. Then Abbey was in his arms, pressing her warm, soft body close against his. She kissed him passionately, and her tongue was like a dancing flame. But there was something voracious about her mouth—almost as if she wanted to devour him, body and soul, to possess him totally in order to quell some kind of insatiable inner hunger.

He felt the swell of her belly rubbing against his groin. And he felt her hands massage the throbbing bulge at his crotch as she groped frantically for the zipper of his pants. Jaime hated the sounds she made and hated being there. But he allowed her to undress him, and moments later he was pushing Abbey back against the pillows and ranging himself between her legs. All he wanted was to get it over with and be on his way.

"Oh, Jaime," Abbey moaned, pulling on his erection with long, loving strokes. "It's so beautiful," she crooned.

For some reason, Jaime kept flashing on the face of Annabel Randolph as she peered in at them through the car window. "Easy, baby," he warned, in a voice that sounded far more sure of himself than he was. "Don't damage the merchandise."

Abbey was oblivious and seemed to be all over him at once, smothering him with her mouth, her hands, and her body. "This is the way I wanted it to be," she said huskily, suddenly thrusting herself hard against him and demanding penetration with every straining muscle of her body. "You don't know how long I've waited for this moment."

With a noncommital grunt, Jaime closed his eyes and buried himself between her thighs. Still envisioning the specter of Annabel Randolph, he just wanted to get it over with, and their bodies began plunging together in the dimness, two shadowy forms humping up in the faint light, accompanied by heavy breathing and the creaking complaint of old bedsprings.

Abbey's cries started with a low whimper and then rose steadily into a wildly spiraling shriek. She was clawing at his back now, and her demand for satisfaction seemed to gain in tempo with her wildly thrusting pelvis, as she squirmed and wallowed beneath him on the bed.

"Oh, oh, God," she cried out as their bodies arched up, slapping ruthlessly together. Jaime began to shudder and groan. Then he was flooding her with his orgasm, as Abbey rose to meet him again and again, thrusting and climbing with each bodily convulsion.

Finally it was over, and Abbey simply lay there on the bed amidst the crushed pillows and a half-dozen displaced dolls that seemed to be staring at Jaime with brightly fixed eyes. Wide and unblinking, they reminded him once again of Annabel Randolph.

Jaime rose from the bed, quickly gathered his clothes, and went into the bathroom, closing and locking the door behind him. He was disgusted by the whole scene, and he hated himself for what he was about to do, for what he had to do.

Jaime stood for a long time in the rushing hot water of the shower, as the steam clouded up about him. Then, as he finally felt the hard knot of muscles in his stomach begin to relax, he switched on the cold water and took almost brutal satisfaction in the sheer physical shock of the icy pelting spray.

Finally, after washing away all the self-doubt that

121

had come to possess him, he climbed from the shower and carefully dried himself with a towel. Jaime was calmer now but still aware of the tiny vein of fear throbbing somewhere deep within him. For reasons he could in no way fathom, his experience with Abbey had shaken him badly, and the worst was yet to come.

Jaime was fully dressed when he left the bathroom, and Abbey slipped from bed and came to crush her body against him. "You aren't going already?"

"I have to meet someone," Jaime informed her.

Abbey appeared crestfallen. "I need you, Jaime," she whispered. "I need you so very much to love me."

It was now or never, Jaime realized. The moment had come, and he steeled himself against the look of utter vulnerability he saw in her upturned face. Abbey seemed so painfully young in that moment, almost childlike in her nakedness.

"I just don't get you at all," he said in a flat, hard voice. "Aren't you supposed to be engaged to some guy named De Witte with a lot of loot? I read in the paper that you were going to marry him sometime in August."

"Kelly is a sick, degenerate old man," Abbey protested. "He means absolutely nothing to me. The engagement was all my mother's idea."

Jaime disengaged her arms from around his neck. "Let's you and me get something straight, Abbey. I'll screw you any time you want, but I expect you to make it worth my while. I've got plans, and I just can't afford to be giving away the only thing I got to sell. I wasn't born rich like you, in a big house with servants."

Jaime lifted her hands so that the huge diamond engagement ring she wore caught the faint light. "Now, you wouldn't want anybody to know the truth about how your mother kicked off, would you? I mean, in a town like this, that kind of talk could get around pretty fast."

Jaime dropped the cigarette he had been smoking onto the floor and deliberately ground it out on the

Oriental carpet. Then he stood searching her eyes, to make sure that Abbey understood.

Suddenly, however, she just didn't seem to be there anymore, and Jaime had the eerie sensation that Abbey had somehow slipped away, that the nude and defenseless figure standing before him with head bowed was no more real than the dolls strewn about the crumpled bed.

"I want you to have something," Abbey said in a flat, detached voice. It was a voice that carried a kind of hollow echo-chamber quality, as if coming from another dimension entirely.

Abbey slipped the diamond engagement ring from her finger and placed it in Jaime's hand. "Please take it, Jaime," she whispered. "I don't want to lose you."

# CHAPTER 10

"I love being spanked," said the neatly dressed young woman. "Sometimes, just to add a little something extra to our sex life, my husband ties me up with a rope and uses his leather belt on me."

It was shortly after 8:00 A.M., and the television studio audience was rapt and silent, hanging on her every word. There seemed to be a mutual conspiracy that not even a cough should interrupt the young woman's confession.

"Sometimes we invite other couples over," she continued. "You know, friends of ours from the country club, or people we meet with the same tastes. We play bridge or poker, and once a week we plan a special night. For instance, on women's night, the men strip us and do things like . . . ah . . . pour hot wax over our breasts, pinch us with clothespins—lots of bondage and discipline sorts of things."

The red eye of the television camera zoomed in on the handsome face of Cody Maxwell, the debonaire host of "The Hamptons: Live." He sat opposite the attractive young woman, in a comfortable executive chair. His virile features were composed, but there was a probing edge to his voice as he continued the questioning.

"You have already told us that there are literally hundreds of local couples who engage in what has commonly become known as wife swapping, swinging, or mix-and-match parties. But perhaps you might go into more detail in regard to these . . . weekly soirées. I can only assume that you engage in sexual relations with others present. Is that true?"

"Oh yes," she exclaimed, crossing her finely shaped legs with a whisper of nylon. "Let's face it, Mr. Maxwell, it gets very boring just making it with your own husband all the time. I mean, after all, isn't that what the sexual revolution is all about? The only difference is that women are now doing openly what they used to only fantasize. Sex is really only another form of social intercourse, so to speak."

"Might we generalize by saying that the married couples engaged in these . . . activities, do not experience what might normally be termed jealousy?" Maxwell pursued.

"I think you could say that," she agreed. "I mean, after all, what is sex but friction between two bodies? I think that the newly liberated female in urban society feels that having sex with the same person all the time is about as dull as masturba—" *Blip. Blip.*

The nervous squeak of the censor interrupted her explanation, and Cody Maxwell smiled benignly. "We all appreciate your candor, Mrs. Devane. But I must remind you that this program is going into thousands of homes on Long Island that may not be quite as liberated as your own. And while I'm sure that our television audience is extremely interested, if not fascinated, by your disclosures, I must ask you to be careful of your terminology."

The warning given, he leaned slightly forward and pursued his questioning. "Now, perhaps you can tell us some more about these group sex parties you mentioned previously."

The young woman immediately warmed to her subject. "Oh, they're lots of laughs. As I said, we have these special nights when we send the kids off to somebody's mother for the evening, and several couples will drop on over to our place for fun and games. For

125

instance, last week we had 'Key Night.' After having a few drinks, smoking a little pot, and watching some blue movies, the men all toss their keys into a dish. The wives are blindfolded and have to pick a key. Whoever the key belongs to is your partner for the night."

The program moderator cleared his throat. "Isn't there a chance that in such a situation you just might get paired off with someone whose sexual tastes are considerably different from your own?"

"Hmm . . . well . . . maybe, but then, most everyone in our group goes the whole route." She shrugged prettily. "And if they don't . . ." Her pause was pregnant with implication. "Well, that's all part of the bondage and discipline scene. Forcing someone to do something they haven't tried before . . . even against their will."

"I see," Maxwell murmured. "Now, this is perhaps a very personal sort of question, Mrs. Devane, but I hope you will be able to answer it, as I'm sure that many of our viewers and members of the studio audience are wondering the same thing. Is there something . . . some specific act that you do not like to participate in?"

Sandy Devane, mother of two, housewife, and PTA member nibbled on the end of one pink-enameled fingernail for a moment before answering. "Well . . . yes. There is one thing."

"Can you—bearing in mind the censor—tell us what that is?"

"I think so," she responded, squirming slightly in her chair. "I really don't like to have clothespins fastened onto my nipples. It just runs me right up the wall."

The studio audience exhaled a ragged breath in unison. The television studio had become electric with underlying tension, and even the usually unflappable

126

Cody Maxwell evidenced a slight patina of perspiration. "I think that we can all sympathize with that," he said, deftly closing off the questioning while the audience was still on the edge of their seats.

"But now, unfortunately, our time is running short, and so I'll have to end our most informative interview with Mrs. Sandy Devane of Bridgehampton with one final question. Everyone is interested in fashion these days. So perhaps you will be kind enough to tell us something about what you wear to these so-called swapping parties."

She pondered a moment, darting her tongue out to lick at the corner of her mouth. "Well, Mr. Maxwell, of course there are a lot of people into leather this season, but it really depends on what your bag is. You know, sadism, masochism, homo, hetero." Her laugh was low and intimately sparkling. "In any case, you can just bet that we all climb out of our clothes pretty quick once the party gets under way."

Then, almost as an afterthought she added, smiling, "Of course, we do have lots of props. Rubber hoses, leather lashes, dildos, and all that sort of thing. You know, the usual party gear."

Cody Maxwell swung around toward the audience and leaned backward in his chair. "Sorry to have to take you away at this very exciting moment, but we're going to have to have a word from our sponsor. After that, we'll be back for another candid and engrossing interview. Don't go away, folks, for next we're going to be talking to Mr. Franco de Roma, the noted Italian director. He's a man who is very much a part of the Hampton scene this summer, with the documentary he's filming on the superrich and their place in today's society."

The camera panned away, and the monitors were immediately animated by prancing containers of vaginal spray deodorant, tapping out a monotonous com-

127

mercial jingle. Then, Cody Maxwell was back with his second guest of the morning—a beaming Franco de Roma, comfortably ensconced in the deeply cushioned chair so recently vacated by Mrs. Sandy Devane.

With the advent of warmer weather, Franco de Roma had blossomed. He wore a white alpaca suit and had a florid, mobile face; a thick, stunted nose; and deeply hooded, pouched eyes. There was a smiling, ironic twist to the sensual lips, and in one pudgy hand he held a cigarette holder, which he waved continually like a conjuror's wand.

In spite of his mangled English, he was a voluble man, with expressive features and dramatic gestures that kept his arms, hands, and feet in continual motion.

In introducing him to the television audience, Cody Maxwell explained, "Mr. de Roma's movies are often difficult to explain in words. And yet once translated to the screen, they often deal compellingly with major social issues of the day. For instance, one of his principal themes is the disintegration of sex roles, and the breakdown of the urban way of life."

Maxwell turned to de Roma to address his first question. "Indeed, Mr. de Roma, you are regarded by many critics as a cinematic genius. And yet there are others who often decry your use of the excessive, the repulsive, and the downright sordid. Your latest films have, in fact, been described by one prominent American critic as 'ferocious satire that captures images of contemporary society on the verge of total apocalypse."

De Roma threw up his hands and rolled his eyes heavenward. *"Ecco bene.* These critics . . . they are, I think, intellectually constipated. In my films I only portray the truth of what I see happening around me. It is true that the values that once have existed in society are no longer serving their purpose. I am talking about the family, morals, and economic relationships between the people and the state, which is no longer able to govern. All is chaos in society," he pronounced emphatically.

"Perhaps, Mr. de Roma," Maxwell suggested, "You might give us some examples to illustrate your theory."

"Is no problem there," de Roma expounded. "Consider, for instance, New York City and the big blackout. The world's greatest city with its skyscrapers in darkness, while below in the streets of Manhattan there are bands of hoodlums, looting and pillaging. It is in many ways like the Middle Ages and the sacking of Rome by the vandals. You are all living in a society that you are told still works, but the truth is that it does not. The situation is ludicrous, no?"

"How would you reply to those who accuse you of using excesses in your films for the purpose of shock value alone?"

"What I show in my films is no bigger shock than you see in everyday living. In Europe we have already seen the writing on the wall, but you Americans are still treading water and pretending that the deluge is not yet upon you. What I have come to America to film is not the rich at play, but an entire civilization that is ready to self-destruct."

The white Rolls Royce Silver Cloud cruised along between the green, rolling, meticulously manicured fairways of the Hampton Bay Club, circled the eighteenth hole, and finally drew to a halt beneath the front portico.

The chauffeur, resplendent in a visored cap and immaculate dove-gray uniform, leaped out to swing open the rear door, and Roxanne stepped out of the car into the bright June sunlight. She was immediately ushered inside by the doorman, who informed her that the fashion show was about to start and that Jean-Pierre Fabian had been anxiously awaiting her arrival.

It was Roxanne's first opportunity to display the entirely new persona that had emerged beneath the imaginative hand of Soli San Lorenzo. And the new Roxanne did indeed look youthfully stunning for a woman only four years short of her first half-century.

Her new hairstyle was a perfectly sculpted cut that provided a totally different perspective from every angle. The slightest movement of her head was sufficient to unleash a smooth tawny flow that shaped, framed, and defined her handsome features to perfection.

It was just the right length to accentuate her elegantly slender neck and angular bone structure, while playing up widely spaced eyes beneath a thick fringe of mink lashes.

In her tailored white sharkskin pantsuit, with a Gucci bag slung over one shoulder, Roxanne was in a buoyant and expectant mood. She felt optimistic and expansive, and her life at that moment seemed to be totally open to the future. It was almost as if by changing her image, she had somehow been transported into a world governed solely by its newness.

Roxanne's appearance that day at the Southampton Bay Club had been carefully orchestrated and planned down to the last detail. And the two Dexamyl she had taken before leaving Ox Pasture Farm had endowed her with a luminous sweep of lucidity that imbued even the most mundane details with signs and portents of all that was to come.

In spite of the problems facing her that day, Roxanne was determined to prevail. And as she stepped out onto the wide flagstone terrace overlooking the bay, Michael, the maitre d', hurried up the steps to greet her. "Your sister has already arrived," he announced. "I've seated her at the table you requested, beside the pool."

Jean-Pierre Fabian's fall collection was being shown that day, and as Roxanne made her way down the steps toward the pool, the master of haute couture himself rushed forward to lift her slim hand, bearing the huge 37-carat ice cube diamond, to his lips.

"Sorry to be late," Roxanne apologized. "It was, I'm afraid, quite unavoidable."

Jean-Pierre brushed the apology aside and complimented her lavishly on her new hairstyle. Roxanne was always late when it served her purpose, and she was well aware that the fashion show would not have started without her in any case.

"I'm sure that you're going to be extremely pleased with the showing," Jean-Pierre assured her. "There are several items in the catalogue that I designed explicitly with you in mind. Casual, elegance personified, and I think perfect with your height, coloring, and marvelous new hairstyle."

Roxanne wished Jean-Pierre well and was ushered to her table amid a flurry of excited activity. Heads swiveled, bodies rotated, and every eye was upon her, amid a low murmur of voices punctuated by the tinkle of silver and glassware.

It was a brilliant summer day and pleasantly warm in the sun. The fashion show was being held around the pool, where fashionably dressed women and exquisitely tended men in gold chains and safari outfits had gathered for luncheon beneath striped umbrellas. Terra cotta pots spilled colorful cascades of summer annuals onto the flagstone deck, and a long, raised runway had been constructed to span the entire length of the Olympic-sized swimming pool.

They had all been invited there that day as devotees of style and elegance, while the proceeds of the showing were to be distributed among various Hampton charities. The affair, however, was already a half-hour late in starting, and Roxanne had been preceded only minutes before by a notorious duchess and a millionaire author who was the puckish pet of publisher and jet setter alike. A Hampton dowager displaying her sixth face lift had made a grand entrance amid a brace of white poodles and was cheered by a large

131

contingent of the Hampton gay set on hand for the festivities.

Like exotic hothouse blooms, the gay men were considered by local socialites to be prized adornments for formal dinners, the perfect escorts to all those boring charity balls, and the most exquisitely entertaining house guests when husbands were away and there wasn't an available man to be found between Quogue and Three Mile Harbor.

"Late as usual," Claire announced, presenting a well-tanned cheek for a whispery noncontact kiss. Roxanne took her seat, and Claire promptly placed a copy of the *Hampton Reporter* on the table in front of her, with a look of barely subdued triumph illuminating her features. "And just what do you think of that?" she questioned, pointing to the headline. It read:

### TREASURE CAY SLATED TO BECOME LAS VEGAS EAST

Representatives of Middle Eastern financier Kamal Ali Reza today unveiled his plans for a $50 million casino resort complex on historic Treasure Cay.

During an interview with the Easthampton city planning board, his lawyers outlined the project, which eventually will include a luxurious gambling casino, several gourmet restaurants, and a large dinner theater scheduled to present stars of international caliber and such shows as the Paris Lido Review and Folies Bergéres.

The representatives of Mr. Ali Reza indicated during the course of the meeting that he is presently in the process of negotiating with Inter-Continental Hotels to construct the lavish hotel-casino complex, while a bill has already been introduced into the state legislature to legalize gambling on Treasure Cay.

132

The article went on to describe Ali Reza as a man whose financial interests were inextricably woven throughout the economic fabric of dozens of countries, while very little factual information was known about the man himself.

What was known, however, was that Kamal was a man of endless, restless ambition who controlled great masses of money on the move, currency of every kind and sort skillfully deployed by dozens of lawyers, accountants, and cadres of highly placed investment bankers—money that flowed in endless directions and touched countless political and economic nerve centers throughout the world.

Ali Reza seldom allowed himself to be photographed, and yet the picture displayed on the front page of the *Hampton Reporter* was extremely flattering, and his volcanic dark eyes blazed with intelligence.

"Well, what do you think?" Claire questioned with something more than casual interest. "Isn't it exciting?"

Roxanne was quite frankly so stunned by the news that she really didn't know what to think. Treasure Cay had always had mystical, almost magical associations for her, ever since she was a child and used to go visit her mother's sister, who had married into the Hanlan family.

It was a lonely and yet magnificent spot, and in her youthful imagination, she had envisioned the French chateau that crowned the island's highest point as a miniature Versailles. Often, as a child, she had fantasized about reigning there as queen of her own island domain, with the great and the famous of the world begging admission to pay homage and fealty at her feet.

"It sounds to me like a spectacular Circus Maximus," Roxanne finally replied. "The Arabs have already bought up most of fashionable London, and now they think they can just walk in here with all that

133

filthy oil money and snatch up anything that takes their fancy."

"Don't be so stuffy," Claire admonished a bit defensively. "I think it sounds like a fascinating idea, and from what I hear, this Kamal Ali Reza is not exactly your run-of-the-mill Arab. He's dashing, handsome, oozing charm from every pore, and rich as Midas."

"He probably keeps a harem back home," Roxanne responded tartly. "Everybody knows those Arabs are horny as goats and have to have a different woman every night of the week."

Claire took up her menu and deliberately held her tongue. It was enough that Roxanne was so obviously outraged, and she simply didn't trust herself to comment further. Kamal was hers, and that was all that counted.

"I'll have my usual," she said, sitting back and extracting a cigarette from her case. She lit it with a flick of the platinum lighter that Kamal had given her, and then slipped it quickly back into her purse. Roxanne had an eye like a hawk for expensive gifts, and Claire realized that she would have to watch her step until Kamal was signed, sealed, and delivered—all the way to the altar.

"I must say you're looking smashing," Claire commented, deliberately leading the conversation away from Kamal. "But I am curious. Just what was it that made you decide to have a thorough overhaul? By cocktail hour tomorrow, half the women here will be on their way to Soli San Lorenzo's, demanding the same treatment, like social-climbing clones."

"I just felt like a change," Roxanne replied. "A whole new look for the party I'm giving for Andrea on the Fourth of July."

Claire did a fast double-take. "Party . . . for Andrea? Something seems to be wrong with my hearing. I just couldn't have heard you say what I thought I heard you say."

134

"I think I may have been a bit hard on the girl in the past," Roxanne related smoothly. "Of course the poor little thing was jealous when I married her father. Why shouldn't have been? Stavros was mad for me in the beginning, and Andrea has simply never forgiven me for it. I've decided the only decent thing for me to do is to put aside past animosity and give her a smashing welcome to the Hamptons."

"Good afternoon, ladies," the head waiter greeted them. "Would you care for something to drink before lunch?"

For a moment, Roxanne appeared to be a thousand miles away, but quickly recovered herself. "Yes, of course. Bring me a sherry, and we might as well order now as well, since the fashion show's about to start. We'll both have the filet mignon rare with the diet salad."

"Something more for you to drink, Mrs. Spencer?" the waiter questioned.

"Bring me another gin Bloody Mary, only make this one a double. No ice and easy on the bitters."

As soon as the waiter had departed with their order, Roxanne arched one finely penciled brow and waved away the smoke from her sister's cigarette. "Isn't it rather early in the day to be drinking doubles? You know how people love to gossip, Claire. I sometimes think you deliberately try to provide them with a target."

"So I'm a lush," Claire confirmed, eyeing Roxanne over the rim of her drink. "I don't give a damn what anyone thinks, and you know it. They aren't paying my bills, and I only do in public what most of them are doing in private. You know that half of these so-called *ladies* are stuffed to the eyelashes on quaaludes, and will be falling off their golf carts by teatime."

"There is such a thing as personal pride," Roxanne informed her. "How do you think poor Clayton must feel when he hears all these stories going around about your drunken exploits with men half your age?"

Claire exhaled a single perfect smoke ring and watched it billow out across the lapping waters of the pool. "The truth of the matter is that it's over between Clayton and me. *Finis*."

"What do you mean 'over'?" Roxanne questioned sharply.

Very slowly and deliberately, Claire tapped the ash off her cigarette. "I've decided to file for a divorce, Roxanne. I want a lot more out of life than Dr. Clayton Spencer has been able to give me."

Roxanne took a sip of her sherry and deliberately allowed her gaze to drift away. "Frankly, sister Claire, the picture of a 44-year-old alcoholic sleeping around and aging without grace is not an attractive one. I hope you'll give the matter some further thought before proceeding to make a complete public spectacle out of yourself."

"You mean like the spectacle you intend to make out of Andrea, at your gala Fourth of July party in her honor?" Claire laughed, knowing she had unmasked her sister's motivations. She had always been able to read her like a book, and with the whole town talking about the feud between them, it obviously hadn't taken Roxanne long to decide that her best defense would be a cleverly deployed offense.

"Since you seem to be able to read my mind," Roxanne suggested, "just what is it you think I'm planning to do?"

"Well, right off the top of my head, I suspect that your plan is simplicity itself. You simply can't afford to go around playing the role of the wicked stepmother to Andrea's Cinderella. So what could be smarter than throwing a lavish spectacular in her honor? You'll probably invite a rather impressive and amusing mix to generally intimidate her. Then, with sly-boots Roxanne writing the evening's script and strewing the poor innocent's path with cleverly disguised pratfalls, little Miss Got-Rocks won't stand a snowball's chance in Hell."

From her vantage point across the pool, Kim Merri-weather was having perhaps the worst day of her life, trying to film the fashion show at the Southampton Bay Club. She was so nervous that when she loaded the first roll of film into the super 16mm camera she was using because of the close shooting space, the camera sprung open, and yards of ruined film fell out to unwind about her ankles.

De Roma, who had been feeling her up at the moment the mishap occurred, glared, exploded briefly into guttural Italian, and then stalked away toward the outdoor bar, leaving Kim on the verge of tears.

She had gotten there over an hour early in order to get her equipment set up, but nothing seemed to be going right. The grips had failed to construct the small elevated platform Kim needed in order to angle her shots properly. And instead, she found herself hemmed in on every side by fashion correspondents with lethal tongues and hard lines around their mouths.

All of them seemed to be talking and writing at once, while directly behind where Kim had set up her camera were the wire-service photographers, surrounded by row upon row of gimlet-eyed buyers as dumpy and dowdy as truck dykes, all of them supposedly devotees of the fashion industry, while remaining totally devoid of any fashion sense themselves.

The center of all attention was the long, raised walkway stretching the length of the pool, neatly dividing the languidly lunching and elegantly turned-out Hampton fashionable elite from the working stiffs like Kim herself, who clung like crabs to the outer Siberia of the farther shore.

It was hot. The thermometer had reached 92 degrees

at twelve o'clock and threatened to climb even higher as the afternoon progressed. High overhead, the sun marched across a pure blue sky like a white-hot disk, burning through the material of Kim's light summer blouse, and covering her entire body with a moist glaze of perspiration.

In that moment, she utterly loathed Franco de Roma, despised the Hamptons, and wished more than anything else in the world that she was back in California, drawing unemployment. It was a futile dream, in any case, since Kim had sold everything she owned in order to raise the money to come east and work with a man she could cordially despise without any trouble at all.

The amiably annoying Franco de Roma she had known and barely tolerated in Italy two years before had become an unmitigated asshole, according to Kim's very best estimate. She had been stunned to discover, upon her arrival, that the rest of the film crew de Roma had promised to hire had never materialized. And other than two half-witted Sicilian grips who were never there when she needed them, Kim herself was forced to handle all the technical aspects of filming.

She had also discovered quite by chance that Franco had barely escaped Europe one step ahead of his creditors, who had slapped a legal injunction on his departure. It was rumored that his latest directorial venture had been confiscated by the Italian government, after being labeled by the Vatican press as "licentiousness incarnate."

The film was bound to be tied up for years in the Italian courts, and de Roma had escaped a possible jail term only by keeping one step ahead of the magistrate. The Catholic Church was up in arms, the American studio that had bankrolled the project was hysterical, and all Franco de Roma could think of was getting into Kim's pants.

Kim had made it very clear immediately upon her

arrival that she had no intention of sleeping with the aging and dissolute director, although she probably would have been a lot better off in the long run if she had simply given in. But she knew she was good at her job, and for once in her life, Kim was determined to put a price on her own professional integrity. And that meant she had come east to film a documentary, not give the director head just to keep the paychecks coming in.

As a result, the five-foot five-inch glob of petulant Italian manhood had been in a constant temper tantrum, and Kim had become his primary object of abuse and disdain. She was, after all, a woman in need of a job, in a man's profession. And without a track record, she was easy game.

The film being made was de Roma's first documentary, and upon finding himself without a cast of paid actors he could browbeat and tongue-lash into performing, he had clearly decided to make Kim's life utterly miserable. If she wouldn't sleep with him, de Roma was determined to make her hate him, and he was succeeding to an extraordinary degree.

"*Stupido*," he would shriek for everyone within hog-calling distance to hear. "How many times must I told you the reflections are hitting the lens? A millimeter to the left . . . no, no . . . *bastarda*. A fraction more *profilo* on the lady with the purple hair and diamonds like ducks' eggs. *Ecco bene*. Your both hands are like two club feet. Back a fraction. *Basta*. Okay. *Motore. Azione*."

Communication between them was no better than *così così*. Franco's only fluency, in fact, seemed to be with his hands, which were usually halfway up to Munchkinland by the time she could bite, kick, scratch, or slap them into submission. And then, it was only temporary, since de Roma appeared to be in the throes of some kind of terminal lechery.

To add insult to injury, the shooting schedule with

139

which Franco had presented her was absolutely mind-boggling. It seemed to Kim that they needed footage on every single aspect of life in the summer Hamptons —lawn parties, weddings, dinners, and even the funeral of old Annabel Randolph, which didn't really seem to make any sense. In fact, for some reason that Kim could not really determine, there was something strange going on.

But that was only for starters. Summer in the fabled Hamptons was expensive, exuberant, and very, very social, with spirits bubbling over well into the wee hours at the various restaurants and disco-dancing palaces. Kim was averaging no more than four hours of sleep a night, and she was beginning to show the strain.

The show was by now over an hour late in starting. Then suddenly there was a burst of music, and a disembodied voice began to chant the ritual praises of Jean-Pierre Fabian—*couturier par excellence* to rich and famous women the world over.

"Jean-Pierre Fabian is without question among the most influential fashion trend-setters in the world today. In the past, whenever he has presented his collections, either through inspiration or imitation, his ideas have gone on to affect the way women dress and the clothes that they wear all over the globe.

"Without question, with his fall collection being shown here today in the Hamptons, Jean-Pierre Fabian has proven himself to be the ultimate king of fashion. Especially for you, he has designed a fall couture collection that carries his dreams of fantasy even further than the romantic peasant look of last year.

"Today you will, for the first time, see clothes that echo the rich realms of the Orient, the exotic indolence of life in a harem and the lavish opulence of a Moroccan seraglio. Loose, sensuous and free flowing, this collection, with its brilliant multiplicity of styles and

140

ideas, has been designed with today's sophisticated urban woman in mind.

"She is the kind of woman the French call *farouche* —a word used to describe a woman of natural elegance and unusual appeal. A woman who has a sure sense of her own identity and the ability to express it. She is independent but not aggressive, strong but unimpeachably feminine. A woman capable always of doing the unexpected.

"Ladies and gentlemen—allow me to present Jean-Pierre Fabian's *farouche* woman of tomorrow."

Kim began filming as, one after another, the models began traipsing out along the runway over the pool like Helen on the ramparts of Troy. From then on, it was nonstop—a blur of skinny legs, gaunt cheekbones, flat chests, and slathers of garish makeup that looked as if it had been applied with a cement trowel. *Farouche,* my ass, she thought to herself.

For the next two hours, some of the strangest outfits Kim had ever seen were paraded along the runway by prancing mannequins of every exotic persuasion. Each individual creation was greeted by waves of ecstatic applause, and finally, as the gowns became so bizarre as to be totally impractical, with bravos and a standing ovation.

It was all gorgeous and utterly surrealistic. Provocative harem pants flowed like bubbling champagne out of tall suede boots. Capes of ostrich feathers and furs of at least a half-dozen endangered species were paraded, as on and on it went into the afternoon.

Kim herself was most comfortable in faded blue jeans and firmly hated even the idea of being in fashion. She was a child of the "back-to-nature" sixties, and she saw the whole incredible spectacle as something very much akin to the Versailles costume madness during the reign of Marie Antoinette.

141

It was all utterly insane, and yet millions of women were shrinking their bodies in order to get into skimpy little nothing dresses that cost an arm and a leg. But that was only the beginning. Once you were hooked, you might as well count on a life of diet salads, faggot hairdressers, and a weekly bout with a masseuse that quickly became as necessary as the oxygen you breathed.

Kim was convinced, at least in her own mind, that whatever time or energy or money you might have left after all that was spent on a glut of vaginal deodorants and cosmetics, so that you could paint yourself up like a cannibal king in drag.

No way, she thought. The formaldehyde look definitely was not for her. Makeup clogged her pores and the one and only time Kim had used a strawberry douche prior to an important date, she had broken out in a terrible rash and stained her blond-haired blue-eyed boyfriend's mustache a ghastly, shocking pink.

The fashion show ended with a *robe de mariage*— an indescribable bubbling white confection, with butterfly sleeves, acres of floating train, and a towering trellis of lace veiling that totally obscured the face of the bride.

Finally, Kim zoomed in for a close-up of the master of haute couture himself—Jean-Pierre Fabian emerging radiantly smiling from a bank of white lilies, bowing and throwing small kisses to the audience. The applause was deafening.

Beyond any question, the show had been an enormous success. Kim had shot a full mile of superb footage, for which she was being paid $250 a day plus expenses in one of America's most fabulous resorts, and she had never been more miserable in her life.

# =CHAPTER 11=

The dimly lit bar of the Southampton Bay Club was crowded when Kim arrived, and fairly bristling with the Hampton rich and their various hangers-on. It was one of the most popular local watering spots, and there was always a crowd at teatime, gathered to gossip over Pisco Sours and pick at the sumptuous buffet.

The background soundtrack was a sophisticated ripple of music from the piano bar, while beyond the tinted floor-to-ceiling windows there was a spectacular view of the yacht harbor and the sea ablaze with the setting sun.

"Make mine a double Scotch," Kim said to the bartender, as she placed her purse on the bar and wearily fished a cigarette from her pack.

Kim had been busy until almost five, filming the reception following the fashion show, and by the time she had packed up her equipment and stowed it in the van, she was ready to drop in her tracks. As she placed the cigarette between her lips, a gold Dupont lighter immediately was produced by a disembodied hand. Quite studiously, Kim decided to ignore the gesture and proceeded to light her own Doral menthol with a book of matches from the bar.

She was tired, discouraged, and lonely, but not yet desperate. Had she wanted the attentions of some dirty old man, all she needed to do was go back to the Spindrift Motel, where there was a good to excellent chance that Filthy Franco would be waiting for her, positively oozing lechery.

Kim had never really been very lucky in love and had always seemed to attract the wrong kind of man, which she could only explain as being some kind of rotten karma. According to her most recent horoscope, it all had something to do with her ascendant Virgo getting all screwed up in the tenth house of Uranus or some such garbage. And she had paid $50 for that kind of news?

God knows that she herself had suspected for some time that the signs were not all that auspicious when it came to finding her white knight, and she had come very close to throwing in the towel on that score.

Kim's childhood had passed like a dream or an enchantment, and her general orientation had been that of a clean-cut girl-next-door with tomboy tendencies—a situation that was fairly understandable when one considered the fact that she had been the youngest child and only girl among four athletic older brothers.

Still, she had been duly cherished by everyone concerned and went on to discover the joys of masturbation when in the fourth or fifth grade. Kim couldn't remember exactly which. But she clearly recalled accidentally losing her cherry while riding horseback around the age of 12.

In junior high school, she had begun petting early and smoking pot in the girls' restroom, while engaging in erotic fantasies about older men ranging from 18 upwards. An unwanted pregnancy followed, as well as a disastrous shotgun marriage to a boy named Ernie, with acne and one undescended testicle.

Kim had often wondered about the child she had borne and put out for adoption, a brown-eyed boy who by now would be five years old, and who didn't even know that she existed. He was out there somewhere— and today was his birthday.

Eventually, Kim had graduated from UCLA with a

B.A. in Film. She had always been good with a camera, and her technical skills were such that she had once totally dismantled the engine of her brother's 1959 Thunderbird and reassembled it, complete with a new transmission, all within 24 hours.

To date, she thought rather grimly, that had probably been her single most important achievement in life. Big deal.

More than anything else in the world, Kim had always wanted to write. But after a series of early successes in the photographic modeling game, she quickly managed to convince herself that she was going to make a fortune by shooting composites for promising young models in San Francisco. Yet after spending one very long, depressing, and nearly sexless winter alone in a big, strange city, Kim had come to realize that the most difficult problem confronting any new arrival to the commercial marketplace was simply survival.

Still, she had persevered, saved every penny she earned, and in the spring of 1975 had taken off for Europe in an attempt to see the world through the lens of her Hasselblad camera, which was never far from hand. Finally, she ended up in Italy, driving a fourth-hand Fiat and believing that every handsome Italian she met was sincere. She had never really dated handsome men before and was soon getting jilted on the average of once a month, because of the terrible habit she had of deflating their egos by laughing in bed.

It was utter madness, and Kim had loved every minute of it.

Rome, however, seemed to be flooded with aspiring photographers masquerading as paparazzi, and work was difficult to come by, especially if you just happened to be the only female in a male-dominated field, didn't speak Italian, and were able to make repairs on your own car. Then she met Franco de Roma at a party.

Franco was the archetypal dirty old man with a perpetual hard-on and in a froth of excitement over the pretty young girls who flocked to his office in hopes of winning a part in one of his movies. They all called him Count Dracula. And it was whispered among them that he would resort to any diabolical ruse in order to get a girl into bed with him.

Following their initial meeting, Kim immediately came up with the idea of shooting a magazine layout showing de Roma surrounded by a bevy of beautiful girls. It was a prospect that both flattered his ego and would likely be easy to sell to an American human interest magazine, since de Roma's films were all the rage in America and considered to be highly erotic fare.

De Roma was immediately intrigued by her proposal, and Kim made an appointment to see him in his office on the day following their first meeting. She had been so excited at the prospect of getting her first magazine clippings for her portfolio that she sat up most of the night, sketching the various shots she wanted to capture and writing the captions for the overall layout.

It was her first big chance to climb out of the minor leagues as a photographer, and she was determined to make the most of the opportunity. The following day, Franco still seemed to go for her idea, but he insisted that they discuss the project over dinner that evening. Oh shit, Kim thought. All the stories about de Roma's lechery were true. He was going to try and put the make on her.

She finally consoled herself, however, with the thought that by pretending to go along with the action but staying just out of reach, she'd be able to hold de Roma at bay. All she had to do was play it cool, shoot the layout, and then take a walk, with her professional ethics still pretty much intact.

As it turned out, however, nothing with Franco de Roma was quite that easy. After a romantic candlelit dinner, during which he insisted on playing footsie and kneesie under the table, he suggested that they go for a drink on the roof of the Excelsior Hotel, where there was a very swinging disco.

"It'll have to be a fast one," Kim informed him primly, and then went on to insist that she had to be up early for work the following day.

De Roma chose to ignore that, and once they reached the Excelsior, he went straight to the reception desk and picked up a key. Franco obviously was well known by the staff, and when they stepped into the elevator, he quite confidently pushed the button for the fifth floor instead of the Starlight Roof.

"I thought we were going to the discotheque," Kim reminded him sternly.

"Yes, yes, my pet," Franco replied with widely innocent eyes. "But first we stop and have some champagne in a room that I keep here for purposes of business. It is . . . how you say . . . a hospitality suite."

Kim protested all the way to the fifth floor, but when the elevator's doors glided open, Franco strutted out, and she had no choice but to follow him meekly down the hall, hoping that she had miraculously gotten her period two weeks early.

In spite of her resolve not to fuck for favors, Kim was taken aback by the brazenness of the aging director's approach. Yet at the same time, she was also determined to get her first photographic spread off the composition board and into a first-rate magazine, with proper credits. Any way she sliced it, de Roma, for all his repulsive qualities, was famous and powerful enough to help her break though all the doors that were presently closed again her.

Five minutes later, she found herself sitting stiffly on the edge of a king-size bed, while Franco poured chilled champagne and nipped at her ear lobe.

What the hell, she thought. I might as well give in and get it over as quickly as possible. Bracing herself against the inevitable, she squeezed her eyes tight when

147

he started kissing her neck. Within seconds, his hand was up her skirt and into her pants faster than you could say *"Ecco bene,"* which was exactly what he said.

With the lights out, it wasn't all that bad, however, and she ended up dating him more or less regularly for the next six months, as her career prospects soared. Ultimately, Franco de Roma taught her a great deal about film, about her work, and even about herself.

As if by some mysterious process Kim's thoughts had summoned the devil himself, she suddenly heard de Roma's voice raised in protest. He was seated at a banquette table just beyond an intervening wall of plastic ferns. He was with a man she failed to recognize, and there was quite obviously an argument in progress.

His companion was a tall, gaunt figure dressed entirely in leather, and sporting a single gold bangle in his right ear. There was something about the man that Kim found disturbing, some kind of malevolent intensity that she could not quite define, as the two men continued to converse in guarded but argumentative tones.

While shielded from view by a large planter at the end of the bar, Kim could easily overhear at least parts of their conversation.

"You idiot," the man with the earring was saying to de Roma. "You could have ruined everything by giving an interview like that."

*"Ecco bene,"* de Roma protested. "I speak only about my art. Everyone knows the kind of films de Roma makes. It is no great mystery to discover my view of the world. Why are you getting so excited? Is nothing, my friend."

"Bullshit," the man exploded. "Not one out of fifty people in the Hamptons could even name one of your films if somebody put a gun to their head. All they know is that you are *somebody*. It's the name that counts, and they don't give a good shit about your vision of the world."

148

The man lowered his voice suddenly, and Kim was forced to lean closer in order to hear. "Look, de Roma. I'm going to give it to you straight. Just keep the cameras rolling and continue to play yourself minus all the bullshit about society on the verge of apocalypse. That is, if you expect to collect the quarter-million dollars I'm paying you to make this film."

Kim was astounded at the figure, and as the two men rose to go their separate ways, she bowed her head low over her drink to avoid being seen. Beyond any shadow of a doubt, she knew now that something strange was going on, and whether she liked it or not, she was right at the center of the action.

After finishing her drink, she ordered another. She swished the liquor and ice around with her swizzle stick, while watching a snail creep with slow, inverted elegance across the glass of a large bubbling saltwater aquarium behind the bar.

*Jaime*. His name came unbidden into her thoughts even as she struggled to dismiss it, along with the pain his desertion had caused her. Normally, Kim was able to hang onto the relatively few men she was attracted to, for at least three to four weeks, but Jaime had skipped out within a matter of days.

All she wanted to do was forget all about him. And yet even as she tried, a sense of his presence kept stabbing at her like some kind of weird radar. She turned on her bar stool, as if summoned by forces beyond herself, and there he was, standing in the doorway and monitoring the crowded tables as if searching for someone.

For a moment, Kim wasn't exactly sure that it was in fact he. Jaime had changed greatly in the weeks since Kim had seen him last, yet there he stood, more devastatingly handsome than ever, and wearing a look of suave sophistication like a halo. He had grown a very becoming mustache in the interim, had his hair expertly styled with a razor cut, and was dressed expensively in a dark blue blazer, tailored gray slacks, loafers, and open-neck polo shirt.

It was a total transformation, and yet Jaime's own natural sense of self-assurance somehow put the whole new image together. Then, as she just sat there, wanting more than anything else simply to evaporate off the face of the earth, Jaime nodded, flashing that white movie star smile of his. Next, he was moving purposefully among the dimly lit lounge tables, toward a woman who had risen to greet him with all the enthusiasm of a beribboned French poodle in heat.

She was one of those slender, fortyish, bleached blondes, fashionably bronzed and casually braceleted with jangling gold bangles running halfway up her arms. The woman wore tawny gold lamé bell-bottoms with a drawstring pulled tightly about the hips, to expose the deep well of her navel beneath a figured silk halter.

Her breasts appeared girlishly small, and her sharply pretty features had been tanned and siliconed to glowing, waxen perfection. Kim loathed the bubbling whisky laugh, as the woman rose on tiptoe to kiss Jaime on the cheek. Then she was clinging to his arm and introducing him to everyone at the table, before finally snuggling into the banquette at his side, her hand resting intimately upon his knee.

Kim experienced a sudden hollow emptiness in the pit of her stomach, coupled with a sense of regret as sharp as pain. All too predictably, she had foolishly allowed herself to fall head over heels in love during the incredible three days and four nights they had spent together on the road.

Then, without so much as a "See you around," Jaime had simply disappeared between one moment and the next, walking out of her life forever, in the space of time it had taken Kim to dash into a drugstore to purchase a pack of cigarettes.

Her cheeks burned, and fearing a sudden hot rush of

tears, Kim turned back to her drink with brimming eyes. Kim's affair with Jaime was over now, nothing more than a remembrance of something past—like awakening from a beautiful dream of love to find yourself very much alone in an empty motel bed, as she did every morning.

In that moment, Kim knew that she simply could not return to the Spindrift Motel for her nightly tussle with a leering and determined Franco de Roma. She just couldn't face it, and she turned instead to glance at the man who had just taken the seat next to hers at the bar. "Tally ho the fox," he said, smiling. "What would you say to my offering to buy you a drink, so we can get better acquainted?"

The fox wore a yachting cap set at a jaunty angle. He was probably about 50, with rakish but fading good looks, a ruddy outdoor complexion, and watery blue eyes that seemed to focus somewhere between her cleavage and her crotch. His name was Gregory Bateson III, he informed her—his speech slurring slightly—and his game was clipping blue chip coupons.

Finishing her drink in a single gulp, Kim thought what the hell. She was alone, about half whacked, and had absolutely nothing better to do with her body that night than perhaps wash her hair and shave her legs. It was something short of an inspiring prospect, considering the kind of day she had already had.

Gregory Bateson's red-rimmed eyes were watchfully appraising. She was expecting him to make a move, and he did almost immediately, by placing his hand on her knee beneath the bar.

Kim responded by pushing her empty glass toward him, after which Gregory immediately summoned the bartender and ordered doubles for each of them.

"Do you have a name?" foxy Gregory asked as their drinks were placed before them.

"It's Kim," she said.

"Don't you have a last name?" he laughed. "Didn't

anyone ever give you one? I mean, it is the custom, you know . . . at least in better families."

"You aren't going to be needing it. I haven't got all that much time. I'm a working girl who's just passing through, on my way to absolutely nowhere."

Gregory's laugh was a boozy wheeze that immediately kicked off his cigarette cough. "All right, little lady," he said. "I'll lay it on the line. I'm rich, spoiled, and out to get laid. I have a forty-five foot cabin cruiser docked about ten minutes away from here, and my wife is not expecting me home for dinner."

His hand felt clammy as it slipped up beneath her skirt, but Kim was in no mood to exercise discretion. "It sounds like a proposition," she responded. "The first one I've had today."

"Fifty bucks is as high as I'll go, and I'm not going to make the offer twice," Gregory warned.

"Skip the money and you won't have to," Kim told him. "At the moment, I'm not really into being all that particular."

Gregory smiled a boozy wash of a smile. "You know what, Lady X, I must say that I like the cut of your sails. What say you we get the hell on over to my boat and get naked?"

Kim reached for her purse and swung around on the bar stool, only to come face to face with Jaime Rodriquez. "I'd like to talk to you," he said. "Outside."

"The little lady is already booked up for the evening," Bateson snarled. "So why don't you just stick to hustling rich middle-aged broads who are willing to pay the freight, sonny boy." His voice was loud and grating, and people immediately turned to stare.

"Jamie?" his lady friend called, twisting around in her seat. "Is there some problem?" By now, she was wearing a fading smile that looked to Kim like a light bulb slowly burning out.

"Well . . . is there a problem?" Jaime challenged, staring hard into Bateson's bleary-eyed countenance.

"Look, punk . . ." Bateson started, but that was as far as he got. With the split-second timing of the street fighter he was, Jaime landed a murderous right hook, and there was a sickening crunch of cartilage as Gregory Bateson III staggered backward to crash sprawling into a nearby table.

But by then Jaime had already grabbed Kim by the hand, and they were sprinting toward a curtained doorway marked "Exit," as all hell broke loose behind them.

It was almost midnight in the rented beach house at the end of Dune Road. Kim was asleep on the couch, and Jaime stood staring out the sliding glass doors toward the sea beyond. He was nude, a little drunk, and there was a bottle of wine hanging loosely in his left hand.

Jaime always felt better without his clothes on, and for a moment, he studied his tanned and muscular body as it was reflected in the glass. He looked like the same street-wise drifter who had hitchhiked east from New Orleans in late spring. But something had changed him completely, and it went far beyond the new mustache, the clothes, the buttercup yellow Ferrari, and the beach house that Darnell Hanlan had rented for him.

Jaime felt as if somehow a crack had opened in an impenetrable wall and, almost miraculously, he had been able to slip through. Now, on the other side at last, he realized that he would have to be totally ruthless in order not to be destroyed by the man who had brought this new Jaime into being—the same Jaime who made 500 bucks every time he scored successfully with one of the names on Darnell's Hampton blacklist.

And it wasn't even as if he had to do all the footwork himself. Darnell always set them up, and all Jaime had to do was to be in the right place at the right time, to move in on the action.

It had all begun the night he walked out on Abbey Randolph with a good-sized diamond ring burning a hole through his pocket. After meeting Darnell at the Zodiac, they had climbed onto his Harley Davidson and sped on out to Three Mile Harbor, where he kept his boat.

At Darnell's suggestion, Jaime had dropped a tab of window pane acid. And after that, everything tended to get a little hazy and confused. He must have finally passed out, and he didn't even remember the boat trip out to Gull Island, where Darnell had already stashed a two-week supply of food, drugs, and various necessities for a prolonged stay.

Although Jaime didn't know it when they went ashore in a dinghy in the dark hour before dawn, his total transformation into Darnell's instrument of vengeance had already begun.

What Darnell Hanlan needed to implement his vengeance was a decoy—someone with the necessary qualifications of youth, good looks, and ambidextrous sexuality, someone who could easily infiltrate the bedrooms of all those marked for retribution on his Hampton blacklist.

They were all fair game as far as Darnell was concerned, and Jaime Rodriquez could not have been more perfect to fulfill the role of Darnell's beautiful and sexually magnetic dark angel.

For the next two weeks, they remained totally isolated on Gull Island, with Darnell Hanlan taking total charge. It all seemed so easy to Jaime that there was really no point in resisting. Darnell, for whatever reasons, was willing to offer him everything he had ever dreamed of having, and all Jaime was required to do was to obey.

The relationship between them, however, was greatly changed. Now Darnell took the role of a firm but astute teacher, drilling Jaime for hours on end for the mission he was about to undertake.

Adapting quickly to his role of prize student, Jaime had proven himself to be a quick study, an untutored but highly receptive pupil who rapidly absorbed every-

154

thing that the middle-aged writer had to teach him about etiquette, the various social graces, personal grooming, and even elocution.

Darnell himself had rightly suspected from the very beginning that Jaime was a natural-born actor. And what was more, he had the looks, the body, and the sexual magnetism that would make him an obvious standout in any crowd. In fact, Jaime had so much going for him, as he moved from their first halting beginnings to self-assured mastery in just two short weeks, that Darnell realized only too well that he would have to take steps to keep his newfound protégé totally within his power.

Jaime Rodriquez belonged to him now, and Darnell had no intention of ever again allowing him his freedom.

Outside the beach house, the wind stalked the night. Jaime took a long pull on his wine bottle and continued to stand looking out at the waves rushing madly up on the sand. They reached out toward him with foam-crested tentacles, as the wind conversed mournfully among the trees, whipped the canvas awnings, and rattled the windows like china in an old cupboard.

Jaime heard a sound behind him and turned to find Kim stretching languidly. She was smiling softly at him, as if the taste of sweet dreams still lingered in her mind. "I still can't believe that I'm here," she said, sitting up and clasping her arms about her knees. "It's all so unreal. These sorts of things just don't happen to ordinary girls like me."

Kim was wearing Jaime's white terrycloth bathrobe, and her feet were bare, toes curled against the chill that had begun to pervade the house as the fire burned low in the grate.

"I don't find you ordinary at all," Jaime said.

He crossed the room and bent to kiss her tenderly on the forehead. Then he moved over to the stereo and placed a record on the turntable.

"You had no right to do what you did today," Kim said quietly. "You do know that, don't you?"

"I just couldn't sit there and watch you throwing yourself away on some asshole," he responded as the voice of Peggy Lee singing *Music For Lovers Only* began to spill out into the room.

"I've slept with plenty of assholes in my time," Kim informed him. "And what about your lady friend? Gregory called you a hustler, and he seemed to know what he was talking about."

Jaime knelt to put another log on the fire but said nothing.

"Why didn't you tell me you were a male whore when we first met?"

"Why didn't you tell me that you slept around with assholes?" Jaime countered. Then he pulled her down onto the white fur rug before the fire and poured her a glass of wine. "Look . . . Kim. I'm sorry I walked out on you. I didn't want to . . . I had to."

Kim sipped her wine but refused to meet his intense, melting brown gaze. "Not like that you didn't. Not as if I was something disposable that you could just use and then throw away."

Jaime tipped her chin upward with his hand and kissed the tears from her cheeks. "It wasn't like that at all. Believe me . . . it was different between you and me. I guess I just didn't know how to handle what I was beginning to feel."

"You aren't going to walk out on me again?" she whispered. "At least . . . not like before."

In answer, he bent to kiss her lips with exquisite tenderness, and their bodies melded into a single silhouette before the dancing firelight. They scarcely moved, rocking gently together until Kim's eyes were smoky with wanting him. Her body stirred against his, as she ran her long, articulate fingers through the dark hair curling thickly across his chest and belly.

Kim sighed and slid down along his body until her

156

lips were fluttering around his sex like butterfly wings, her hands lifting and weighing his testicles like ripe fruit. Her mouth was warm and passionately exploring, her lips and tongue moving with an erotic churning motion the sent tremors circuiting up from Jaime's groin.

He moaned softly and turned his head to press his face into the tawny silken V at the natural juncture between her legs. He kissed her sweetly, gently, then pressed further and deeper, tonguing her sex until he felt himself dissolving within billows of consuming warmth, his head pillowed within the soft, compelling vice of her thighs.

Kim cried out, expressing her hunger and her need. Faster now, their bodies moved together. Their senses were feverishly tuned as they both sought to release the imminent fluid movement that threatened to overtake and engulf them at any moment, aching, swelling, heaving up and down with a gentle flowing motion, until at last their voices mingled ecstatically in a rushing frenzy of mutual gratification.

Abbey parked her car at the end of Dune Road and slid from behind the wheel. The night was hermetic with darkness as she made her way down the driveway of the beach house where Jaime was living, and then cut off on the path leading to the beach.

Her footsteps on the gravel walk seemed to crunch loudly in her ears, and Abbey quickly scuttled into the shadow of the dense foliage surrounding the house, making her way toward the wide deck opening off the living room.

The beach in back of the house looked pure and pristine as the moon moved out from behind a bank of clouds. The gusty wind that had been blowing earlier had finally fallen away to a steady off-shore breeze that sifted through the boughs of the surrounding trees.

Abbey slipped off her shoes, mounted the steps, and

began to inch her way across the redwood deck toward the sliding glass doors. Then, pressing herself against the side of the house, she held her breath and leaned sideways to peer inside the sunken living room.

Two figures were clearly visible before the fireplace— a man and a woman whose bodies were painted with flickering golden light, as the flames leapt and danced in the grate. The girl was lying nude on a white fur rug, with Jaime buried between her straining thighs.

Their bodies were plunging together in the dimness, and their movements were punctuated by cries, groans, and rasping, agonized breathing.

"Oh, oh, oh," the girl moaned.

As she watched, Abbey suddenly found herself clammy with perspiration. Her muscles ached from the rigid posture she unconsciously had been holding as she crouched unseen beyond the glass.

A sickening sense of loss and dizziness swept over her, as the sounds rose with a steadily mounting beat that seemed to imprint itself upon Abbey's brain. She fought it, fearing that it would be there always as the soundtrack of her life without Jaime.

Abbey stood there with her hands clenched into tight fists, which she pressed hard into her groin as the steady sexual beat of flesh slapping on flesh became ever more fevered and insistent. Now she could hear the girl's voice, high-pitched and climbing as she cried, "Now, Jaime . . . oh, yes, now."

As if in answer, a violent, strangled sound escaped from Abbey's throat. Then she was off and running down the beach, with her scream rending the night like the cry of some mortally wounded animal.

# ══════CHAPTER 12══════

Patrick Dillon was a burly, florid-faced man with untidy sandy hair. His appearance was closer to that of a Midwestern college professor than to what one might expect of the finest private detective in New York City, an impression that was further supported by his bushy ginger beard, his tweedy sport coat with leather elbow patches, and the briar pipe clenched fiercely between his teeth.

After he was shown into Helene Von Bismark's office by her secretary, she remained standing in front of the windows for a moment before turning and motioning him to a chair. Helene was obviously on edge, and when she spoke there was a nagging impatience in her voice.

"Well, Dillon, what have you been able to find out?" she demanded. "You said on the phone that you had made some progress in your investigation."

"Almost more than I like to admit," Dillon suggested as he rifled through his battered leather briefcase. "I'm afraid, Baroness, you're not going to like hearing what I came here to tell you today."

"My personal likes and dislikes are none of your concern. I've simply hired you to perform a service, and I want results. Now let's skip the bullshit and get on with it, shall we?"

Dillon made no response as he produced a notebook from his briefcase and flipped it open on his knee. Then he cleared his throat and began reading, a slight

Irish brogue coloring his speech. "Subject Jason Von Bismark checked into the Hilton Hotel on Tuesday June 15 at ten o'clock P.M. He was carrying one suitcase."

Dillon paused to produce a box of matches from his coat pocket. He struck one on the sole of his heavy walking shoes and then puffed away on his pipe, while Helene impatiently drummed a set of brightly lacquered red nails on her desk.

"Now then," Dillon continued, settling comfortably back in the deep suede chair, his face wreathed in billows of aromatic smoke. "Within two hours after checking in, the subject left the hotel and proceeded by taxi to the St. Mark's Baths, where he rented a room and remained for the next twenty-four hours."

"Baths?" Helene questioned.

"Yes, ma'am. It's a rather notorious gathering place for homosexuals. According to the attendant who was on duty that night, your husband appeared to be in a severely drugged state upon his arrival. He occupied Room 328, and during the course of his stay, the subject was seen in the company of various homosexual men, although no specific sexual encounters were observed by the attendant."

"Are you absolutely sure about this?" Helene questioned sharply.

Dillon lifted his eyes to observe her with a level, penetrating gaze. "I can assure you, Baroness, there's been no mistake."

Dillon proceeded to shuffle through his papers for a moment and then handed her a registration card with Jason's signature scrawled almost illegibly across the bottom. "That is your husband's handwriting—is it not, Baroness?"

Helene nodded. "It's Jason all right. Please do go on."

"Now then," Dillon continued, turning the page of his notebook. "The subject returned to the Hilton on

160

the evening of June 16. According to the hotel records, he neither made nor received any calls and had dinner sent up to his room. The meal consisted of . . ."

"I don't give a damn about that," Helene exploded. "For Christ's sake, man, get on with it, will you? I'm a busy woman."

Dillon refused to be hurried and continued at his own pace. "On June 17, the subject paid his bill at the Hilton with an American Express credit card and had his car delivered to the front of the hotel."

Dillon looked up at Helene apologetically and closed the notebook. "That's about as far as we've been able to trace your husband so far, Baroness. I've still got two men on the job and will let you know as soon as I have anything further to report."

Just then they were interrupted by a soft buzzing sound from the intercom, and Helene swung around to press a button. "Yes, what is it, Rosella? I told you I wasn't to be disturbed."

"Your sister-in-law is on the line," her secretary informed her. "She's calling from aboard the *Golden Hind*. I was sure you'd want to be informed."

Helene bit her lip in exasperation. "Very well, Rosella. I'll speak to her."

Helene's features were instantly rearranged into a bland, noncommittal mask. "Andrea, darling," she exclaimed, removing one earring and placing the phone to her ear. "I'm so terribly sorry not to have called. But Jason's been down with some kind of virus and I've been up to my eyelashes in work. I'm afraid we won't be able to make it out to the Hamptons tonight for the showing at the Watermill Gallery. It's such a pity, too. I do adore Ian McVane's work and was hoping to pick up several of his newest canvases."

Absently, as she talked, Helene twisted the white phone cord into the form of a noose and then pulled it tight with a quick jerking motion. "I'll tell you what, Andrea darling. Why don't you and your friend Sarah

161

go along without us? I'm going to be stuck in town nursing Jason for at least a week or more, so why don't I just put the Bentley and my chauffeur at your disposal? You really ought to start getting out and around more, dear. You two are like a couple of old maid recluses on that boat of yours.

"Yes, of course, Andrea. I'll be glad to give Jason your best regards for a speedy recovery. It's really not all that serious at this point, but since the accident . . . well, as I've told you, his health hasn't been very good. I am concerned and I know you are too."

After hanging up the phone, Helene stood for a moment, staring up at the Jonathan Wainwright portrait of herself that hung behind her desk. It had something of a surrealistic quality to it, and Helene had been depicted as glacially poised and unsmiling, while her complexion appeared night-life white beneath flaming tresses that nature might envy but never duplicate.

Helene had never really decided whether she liked it or not, but she quickly dismissed the thought and turned once again to face the private detective. "Look, Mr. Dillon. A man like my husband does not simply disappear into thin air. Now I'm paying you a great deal of money, and I expect results."

Dillon rose and ran his fingers through his sandy hair. "It's a difficult sort of case, Baroness. You see, your husband doesn't appear to *want* to be found. It's going to take time to check out . . . the kinds of places he's likely to frequent."

Helene accompanied Dillon to the door. "I'm not in the least interested in excuses, Mr. Dillon. I only want results. I also want you to continue your surveillance of the *Golden Hind*. I want to be kept up to date on every move that Sarah Dane makes, and you're to inform me personally every time she leaves the ship. There's some important business I have to take care of aboard, and I must know in advance when she's going to be ashore for any length of time."

162

* * *

As the guests began to arrive at the Watermill Art Gallery that evening, more than anything else, the scene resembled a movie premiere. Hordes of curious onlookers were clustered about on the sidewalk, ogling the parade of famous faces as they stepped from their cars and were quickly ushered inside.

Even as Cassandra had predicted in her column the week before, the Hampton social whirl had undeniably slipped into high gear following Andrea's arrival aboard the *Golden Hind,* although as yet, both she and Sarah Dane left the yacht only on rare occasions.

With the climactic events of the summer season crowding one upon another in fast succession, it was generally agreed that this was the season not to miss. Very social types were flocking in from all over the world, and no one wanted to miss out on a single moment of the swiftly paced action.

The rich, the beautiful, and the celebrated had come to the Hamptons that summer as if drawn by some kind of irresistible urge to reaffirm their species. By night they jammed the restaurants, bars, and discos, and by day they lined the pools and beaches, willing themselves a rich, golden brown beneath a glorious summer sun. The hotels all were filled to capacity.

The weather was utterly spectacular throughout the month of June, with warm, golden days and balmy nights. On Shinnecock, Mecox, and Great Peconic Bays, water-skiers sliced white-water wakes behind sleek speedboats. Southampton Harbor was filled to capacity with luxurious yachts and multicolored sails dotted the seascape in sharp contrast to the cloudless cerulean blue of summer skies.

Action was exactly what that particular summer season was all about. And on the evening of July 1, the huge Watermill Art Gallery in Bridgehampton was where the action was—the place to *be* and to *be seen*.

Everyone with even the slightest modicum of social

cachet had been invited to preview a showing of the retrospective work of Ian McVane, artistic iconoclast, genius of creative imagination, and perhaps the most mercurial and talented of all the artists making up the so-called Hampton art colony—those sturdy and self-reliant souls who survived the summer exodus after Labor Day and the assault of the chilling northeastern winter on Long Island.

Still, Ian McVane was not really one of them. He stood apart from all. He was a man who belonged least of all to himself.

The roster of some 400 formally attired, radiant luminaries of one wattage or another had been drawn to the showing that evening at the Watermill partly because it was *the* place to be, but more specifically, in response to the story that had been circulating about how Ian McVane had publicly tried to execute himself some ten days earlier.

The incident had taken place at a shabby artists' hangout by the name of Friendlie's Tavern—a shoddy and roistering local gin mill on the outskirts of Easthampton. It was a place of no particular distinction beyond the fact that it was the place where Big Mac hung out when he was on the sauce, a not infrequent circumstance according to the local grapevine.

McVane was, in fact, the only painter around that summer who had really made it big. He painted huge, expressionistic canvases and was a large, bearlike man with an intense face, well-developed torso, powerful arms, and some strange kind of magnetic energy emanating from his surprisingly steady, clearwater-blue eyes.

McVane was like a magnet the night of "the incident," compelling everyone's attention as he walked through the front door of Friendlie's and slowly approached the bar. His presence there among them quickly traveled the room like an electric current.

Ian was one helluva a nice guy. Everybody said

164

so—those who bought his paintings, the sleek society women he bedded and even other less-successful artists, who talked with him about painting far into the night, over bottles of Dago Red in the kitchen of his Deerfield Road farmhouse.

He was generally considered to be a soft touch. Nearly everybody in the Hamptons, in fact, was looking for a piece of Ian McVane, some small spark of his soul and his talent, the deeply rooted strength that seemed to radiate from him like a powerful aura, setting up a magnetic force field that gradually extended to encompass everyone in his general vicinity.

Yet Ian's charisma did not stop at any social perimeters, and he was equally revered among the rich who collected his paintings as blue chip investments. In spite of his often boorish behavior and antisocial attitudes, Ian was liberally showered with invitations to their extravagant parties and sumptuous homes.

Ian, however, looked tired that evening at Friendlie's. His whole large, raw-boned body sagged against the bar as he ordered a double Jack Daniels and drank it down neat. For several months, he had not been able to paint anything he himself considered to be of artistic merit, and he had become convinced that his talent had deserted him.

His hand shook as he carefully replaced the heavy shot glass on the bar and then slowly ground out his cigarette in an ashtray at his elbow.

No one seemed to notice the terrible stillness of his features, as people began to crowd forward to slap him on the back and order him more drinks than he possibly could have consumed.

Finally, without a word to anyone, Ian quietly removed a Colt Python .357 magnum handgun from his jacket pocket. It was a big, heavy gun that Ian referred to as his "bulldozer." And for a moment, he simply stood there as if weighing the weapon in his hand.

Next, Ian methodically proceeded to slip a single large shell into the chamber. He twirled the gun once Western style, and then, placing the barrel squarely against his right temple, Ian McVane pulled the trigger.

The metallic crack of the hammer registered on the stunned silence amid gasps of shock and surprise, but nothing happened. Ian had simply tested the fates one more time, in a private game of Russian roulette.

Ian McVane already knew in his heart what everyone else had come to suspect. That ultimately there could be only one outcome.

Sarah and Andrea arrived at the Watermill Gallery well after the showing was into full swing. Sarah had, in fact, not really wanted to come. She would have preferred instead to remain secluded aboard the *Golden Hind,* pretending that there was absolutely nothing wrong with her when she knew it simply wasn't true.

Ever since her return to America, Sarah had been increasingly unable to sleep, and her thoughts were continually racing. Even in the most ordinary situations, she would suddenly be swept by paralyzing terror—in an elevator, walking along the street, or even shopping with Andrea in a Hampton boutique.

The simplest tasks, like painting her nails or even ordering breakfast over the phone, had to be negotiated as carefully as if she were walking a high-wire. She felt tense, moody, and was often deeply depressed.

Of course, she really knew the cause, even if there was no available cure. The months and years during which she had been left to twist slowly in the wind without resolution of Brian's ultimate fate had finally begun to take their full toll.

Sarah was neither wife nor widow, with a husband who was neither alive nor dead. The Vietnam war was long over. Fifty thousand American boys were dead and forgotten except by those who had been left behind. Hundreds of thousands had been maimed for life, and hundreds more were still missing in action, yet nobody really seemed to give a damn.

Sarah's jangled emotions, mixed with her sense of guilt, loss, and frustration, had become a web too complicated to negotiate anywhere but in bed. And her violent sexual relationship with Marko the cabin steward had begun to approach a point where something simply had to detonate.

Sarah's luxurious stateroom aboard the *Golden Hind* had become a sensual arena, where she and Marko tore away at one another with appalling wantonness until they both were totally drained, until that moment of total surrender when Sarah Dane—successful career woman, globe-trotting sophisticate, and M.I.A. wife—was finally subjugated by the simple mechanism of a man's cock being planted firmly inside her like the trunk of a tall tree.

By the night of Ian McVane's showing at the Watermill, Sarah was well aware that she had entered into some kind of psychological netherworld and probably needed help. She simply couldn't bear to be around all those superficially indifferent people, and perhaps even more she dreaded the distinct chance of running into friends who had known her before she had dropped off the edge of the world following Brian's disappearance.

Sarah went finally because of Andrea. There had been something brooding and distant about her friend ever since their arrival in the Hamptons. Obviously she was feeling frightened and unsure of herself in the face of her mounting celebrity. Finally, Sarah felt she had no other alternative but to pull herself together and set off for an evening of fun and games among the Hamptons' gilded social elite.

At the very least, it took a whole new outfit, since Sarah had been living in Europe, and her clothes were seasons out of date. She finally ended up blowing $500 on a whirlwind Easthampton shopping spree, and when they arrived at the Watermill that evening, Sarah managed in spite of everything to look absolutely smashing in a low-cut geranium chiffon, with handkerchief hem and floating sleeves.

Andrea herself had never had even the remotest interest in fashion and was gowned as usual in a simple black dress with a string of heirloom pearls as her only adornment. At 23 years of age, she appeared to be at least several years older. Her hair was thick, dark, and lustrous, and she habitually wore it drawn severely back from her face with an absolute minimum of makeup or artifice of any kind.

From earliest childhood, however, Andrea had been blessed with a flawless complexion and on that particular evening, Sarah had been able to prevail upon her to wear the faintest hint of lip gloss and a minimum of mascara to accentuate her huge wounded-looking dark eyes beneath their thick, naturally arched brows.

The improvement was considerable, and as they braved the crush upon entering the gallery, there were some admiring glances in Andrea's direction instead of the usual, glassy-eyed $2 billion response. It couldn't be easy for Andrea, Sarah realized, to live up to that kind of advance billing, and she shuddered to think of what must be running through her friend's sensitive mind.

Then, suddenly, Sarah was confronted by the sensual and stirring reality of Ian McVane's paintings, and all else was forgotten.

She had always loved his earlier work, but these were simply astonishing, firm and full, with thick, flowing colors. The paint was thickly or thinly laid out on the canvas, according to some exquisitely rare sense of vibratory response. The execution was free, soaring, supple, and often daring, never wild and yet never insignificant.

There was in Ian's paintings a spontaneous feeling

very nature and substance of things, a sense of proportion that never erred. He had mastered the art of being precise without explaining too much, of making the viewer understand everything with a single stroke, of omitting nothing, while taking the unnecessary and the obvious utterly for granted.

Sarah was utterly astounded, moved, and thrilled to the very depths of her being. Never, she thought, has anyone painted better . . . nor likely ever will. If Ian McVane could only manage to survive his own notoriety and success, he could very possibly turn out to be the finest painter of the decade.

After viewing the paintings in silence, they allowed the natural momentum of the party to carry them on through the gallery and out into a spacious sculpture garden at the rear of the building. It was a warm and balmy night, with the smell of jasmine heady in the air. The garden was a forested Eden of tropical fern trees, colored spotlights, and hundreds of tiny lights twinkling among the foliage like galaxies of stars.

All about them, the rich and the celebrated milled, gossiped, and swilled champagne amid an impressive array of starkly modern steel and aluminum sculpture. It was an elegantly futuristic backdrop for the glittering array of beautifully gowned and bejeweled women and formally attired men in black tie and dinner clothes.

With Sarah deftly providing both of them with a glass of champagne from a passing tray, the two young women deliberately skirted the broad converging currents of social intercourse that seemed to be sweeping and eddying around them.

"I've been wanting to talk to you about something," Andrea confessed, upon reaching a relatively secluded corner. "I don't know why it's been so difficult for me to discuss what I'm feeling. But I've come to see things very differently since my arrival in the Hamptons. Until this summer, I never before realized that there was a whole, wide world out there just waiting for me.

169

"At first I thought it was just Roxanne who ̶ made me feel socially inadequate and totally lacking in the kind of poise and charm that she seems to possess in such abundance. But now I know that my father's unhappy compulsion is not entirely to blame. I was always jealous of her, of course, since she was a rather formidable barrier thrown up between myself and the father I utterly adored."

"And now?" Sarah prompted as Andrea's eyes fell away and she bit her lip uncertainly.

"Now I see that I was just a very naive and provincial little girl who was terrified of the unknown—of the world that existed beyond the golden circle of money that protected me from the real world outside. Of course, my father was very much a part of that world, as was my brother Jason. But I remained the cloistered princess shut up not in an ivory tower but a convent on a small Greek island, where very little had changed in the past hundred years."

"Is it the party that Roxanne is giving for you that has you worried?" Sarah questioned softly.

Andrea nodded. "I just hate the idea of showing up and having Roxanne look down her nose at me in front of all those glamorous people. Oh, Sarah, you know how I loathe any kind of ostentation. But for just one night of my life, I'd give anything to be suddenly transformed into some ravishingly lovely and captivating creature, to have men look at me because I was beautiful and not just the richest heiress in the world. I want to be someone special . . . on my own."

Sarah was deeply touched, and in spite of her own problems, her heart went out to her friend. "Dearest Andrea," she said, squeezing her hand. "You already are someone special. Someone very, very special indeed. But your time of mourning is past. You're a woman now, and your father's daughter. It's time to come out of the closet."

It was true—for while Andrea's plainness, her simple

taste in clothes, and contemplative manner would not have drawn more than a passing glance from most men, she had about her a shy, almost incandescent quality that gave her a positive glow.

If you happened to come upon her sitting quietly somewhere, it was simply impossible not to stare, for Andrea's serenity and quiet strength of character had a captivating quality that somehow translated itself through an inner radiance.

"Help me, Sarah," Andrea pleaded. "I'll do anything you say. But I just can't go to that party and bring shame upon my father's name. He always adored beautiful woman, and on that particular night, I want so much to be beautiful for him."

"Sarah?" a voice called. "Can that be Sarah Dane?"

Sarah turned to see a smiling and familiar face making its way toward them through the crowd. It was Soli San Lorenzo, who was not only an old friend of long standing, but the talented young stylist who had done Sarah's hair and makeup when she was still very much a part of the upwardly mobile New York fashion scene.

"Don't look now," she said to Andrea, bursting into a big welcoming smile. "But I think your fairy god-father has just arrived to wave his magic wand."

Ian McVane was already three sheets to the wind when he arrived at the Watermill, and he walked in on a scene that was very close to controlled bedlam.

No one really seemed to mind the crush, the smoke, and the noise, however. In fact, most of the participants seemed to be enjoying all the close body contact. Social intercourse, after all, was often likely to lead to intercourse of quite another sort, which was ultimately what much of the Hampton social scene was all about.

Beyond the slightest shadow of a doubt, McVane's showing was a huge success that evening, but mostly as a backdrop against which all those pretty glass-, silk-, and satin-rustling people could troop their colors, display their newest gowns and jewels, and say the most outrageous things about each other. All of them gaily awash in an expensive and heady brew of intoxicating perfume, flashing strobe lights, and the hard, pounding beat of a blaring disco band.

Surrounded by a coterie of admirers, Ian stood at the bar for a while, fueling his outrage with boilermakers, until reaching some kind of flashpoint. Then suddenly, his face contorted with rage, and a violent, strangled cry was torn from his throat.

Everything that happened after that had a wildly surrealistic quality about it, with events piling one upon the other in fast and furious succession. A woman's piercing scream unleashed a hysterical tide of mass panic, as McVane suddenly grabbed up a fire axe and began sweeping through the gallery, destroying everything in his path.

Burglar alarms wailed, windows shattered out onto the sidewalk, and a trampling rush of bodies spilled out onto the street, in a headlong dash for safety. None of it made any difference to Ian, however, and he continued his rampage, chopping, hacking, splintering, and defacing, until the interior of the gallery had been reduced to a state of mindless destruction.

It finally took a half-dozen crash-helmeted policemen to disarm him and another half-dozen to subdue him, by clubbing Ian McVane into a state of blessed oblivion.

# CHAPTER 13

Kamal's arrival at Roxanne's Fourth of July party had been as carefully timed for maximum effect as had his transformation from white-robed desert sheik to immaculately tailored and suavely sophisticated man of affairs.

He arrived at Ox Pasture Farm in his curtained limousine, and he had just been shown into the marble foyer by a maid, when Roxanne chose to make her own entrance.

"I bid you welcome, Mr. Ali Reza."

Kamal turned to glance up the gracefully curving staircase and saw Roxanne moving down the steps toward him. She wore a sheer white and gold caftan and seemed to float down the stairs with a fortune in emeralds shimmering at her ears and throat. She was slender, elegant and, by Kamal's own estimation, far lovelier than her photographs revealed.

"I'm so very glad you were able to make it this evening," Roxanne announced, as she reached the bottom of the staircase. "Everyone here is simply dying to meet the very handsome and mysterious Mr. Ali Reza, so I couldn't resist inviting you to my little gathering."

Kamal lifted her slender hand to his lips, and his dazzling white smile flashed in his dark face. "I wouldn't have missed the opportunity of meeting you for anything," he said, with only the slightest trace of an accent. "Receiving your invitation was more important to me than . . ." Kamal hesitated and spread his hands helplessly, as if totally at a loss for words.

Roxanne's laugh was low, sparkling, and amused, as her eyes met and held his volcanic dark gaze. "More important perhaps, than owning another supertanker, Mr. Ali Reza?"

"More important than owning another fleet of supertankers, my dear Mrs. Aristos."

*"Touché,* Kamal. And please, do call me Roxanne," she said. "All my most intimate friends do."

"I would be honored," Kamal responded with the merest hint of a courtly bow. "I do so very much hope, my dear Roxanne, that we're going to be the very best of friends."


Dr. Clayton Spencer parked the Buick Ranch Wagon at the bottom of the drive at Ox Pasture Farm. Then he climbed out, circled the car, and opened the door for his wife, Claire.

In spite of the heavy makeup and loose hairstyle partially obscuring her face, Claire's right cheek looked puffy and badly discolored. In a further effort at concealment, she had donned a pair of lavender-tinted sunglasses with oversize curved lenses.

"Well, we're here," Clayton informed her. "Aren't you getting out?"

Claire remained staring toward the mansion for a moment longer, then slid reluctantly from the car with a flash of lovely long legs. Without a glance or a touch, the two of them began walking up the drive toward Roxanne's sprawling Palladian manor house, which she always referred to as simply, 'the cottage.' It was surrounded by neatly barbered lawns, tennis courts, and a swimming pool, with 60 acres of woodlands fanning out on every side.

Ox Pasture Farm had come into being during Roxanne's four-year marriage to Viscount Burnley, Her Royal Majesty's Ambassador to Washington, and later, the Secretary-General of the United Nations. Roxanne herself had been the undisputed toast of the diplomatic set in those days, and she decided she needed an *au naturel* country place with antiques, where her guests could ride to the hunt and spend long, pastoral weekends.

Twelve months, several million dollars, and seven decorators later, Ox Pasture Farm became a *fait accompli,* complete with stables, an English rose garden, and servants who had all been in service at Buckingham Palace at one time or another. But all that had taken place during her English period, during which Roxanne even developed just the slightest trace of a Mayfair accent.

The long, winding gravel drive was lined with expensive cars—Facel Vegas, Maseratis, Bentleys and Rollses, which had been snaking through the imposing gateway and nosing in to park wherever space was available. Now, as they neared the house, Claire's steps faltered, slowed, and then stopped abruptly.

"What is it?" Clayton asked. "What the hell's wrong with you tonight? You're jumpy as a cat."

"I don't know. It's just that suddenly I don't think I can face all those people. Not with my face like this."

"Are you ready to tell me what really happened?" Clayton asked patiently. "The truth?"

"I already told you. I got dizzy and fell in the bathroom. There's no point in making a federal case out of it."

Clayton placed his hands gently on his wife's shoulders. "Look, Claire. No matter what you may think or feel about me, I'm your husband, and I love you very, very much. These accidents have been happening a lot lately. You're just not the same woman you used to be. Your drinking has become a serious problem, and I'm concerned about you. Honey, look— there's just no use in pretending anymore. Stop shutting me out. Let me help you."

175

Claire pulled away from his touch, and her complexion colored with an ugly, blotchy swiftness. "You're beginning to sound like a broken record, *Doctor*. But why don't you just save that patronizing bedside manner of yours for your rich-bitch patients? I'm frankly good and tired of hearing about my fucking 'drinking problem.' "

"All right, all right, whatever you say. But maybe we'd better go home," he suggested. "I'll give you a sedative, and after a good night's rest, you're going to be feeling a lot better. Face it, Claire, you're in no shape to be attending your sister's Fourth of July party."

He was right, of course, and perhaps it was because he was so very right that Claire decided that nothing was going to stop her from attending. "You do what you damn please," she said, starting for the house. "I'm going in."

Clayton sighed and turned to follow her across the grass, shaking his head with a weary, dogged motion. He knew that his wife was a sick woman undergoing intense psychic trauma. But there seemed to be no way to break through that brittle exterior wall she had erected between them.

Dr. Clayton Spencer had the perfect physical appearance for what he was—the resident Dr. Feelgood to the Hampton smart set. He was a patient, mild-mannered man with a mane of silvery hair and a firm handshake. The rich trusted him to see to their rather specialized needs, and they flocked to his Golden Portals sanitarium in droves.

By the time Claire and Clayton reached the front door, a few warning drops of rain had begun to fall. A hurricane watch had been announced earlier in the day. But during the drive over, the car radio had said there was a good possibility that the storm would miss the Hamptons entirely and pass harmlessly out to sea.

On entering the house, they were greeted by a smiling

black maid who ushered them inside and took their coats. "Miss Roxanne was just asking whether or not you had arrived," she informed them. "There's someone she wants you to meet."

The Spencers moved on through several lavishly decorated reception rooms, nodding and smiling to those they knew, while a rich brew of tobacco, perfume, and conversation ebbed and flowed about them.

Mostly, people were talking about the approaching hurricane. But no one really seemed to take it all that seriously, even though during a storm in the early twenties, a tidal wave had swept clear across Long Island, leaving a tragic trail of death and destruction in its wake.

Even now, there was a solid wall of rain moving in off the Atlantic Ocean, driven before a white-splintered crash of summer lightning that was scarcely even audible above the laughter, voices, and music.

Claire felt wretched, but she was doing her best to catch the expectant, upbeat mood of the party. She had been with Kamal the night before, and of course had had far too much to drink. By midnight, she had blacked out entirely and remembered absolutely nothing of what had taken place.

It was all a ghastly blank until she had awakened that morning alone in an empty motel room, with a hangover to end all hangovers, a black eye, and cigarette burns on her breasts, buttocks, and inner thighs.

"Claire, darling," Roxanne called out, as she broke away from a cluster of guests and hurried toward them. She embraced her sister lightly and then offered her cheek to Clayton, while taking both their hands with jewel-encrusted fingers.

"I always like to have a doctor present at my parties," she laughed. "You never can tell when someone is going to have a coronary arrest on the dance floor."

Roxanne was in rare high spirits, and when neither of them even smiled at the jest, she realized immediatedly that all was not well with Claire and her brother-in-law. "I was afraid that you weren't coming," she said, staring openly at Claire's swollen face. "The party started over an hour ago."

"I had kind of a nasty accident," Claire responded. "It was in the tub."

One of Roxanne's finely penciled brows shot skeptically upward, and she gave a short, mirthless laugh. "What was it filled with, sister dear? Gin and tonics or Bloody Marys?"

Claire was immediately on the defensive. "You aren't going to start on that, are you? Because I'm going to warn both of you that I'm just about ready to start screaming if I hear one more word about my 'drinking problem.' So let's just drop it."

Roxanne took the warning at face value and immediately flashed one of her beaming, searchlight smiles. "I think we've all heard far more than we really want to hear about your drinking problem, Claire dear. So why don't we all just put on a happy face and join the others? No fights and no drunken scenes, *s'il vous plaît*. We're all going to act like the civilized and sophisticated people we are, with no problems for at least one evening. I'm utterly determined that this is going to be the most talked-about party of the season, and I will personally strangle anyone who does anything at all to screw it up for me. Now that we understand the ground rules, there's someone I want both of you to meet."

Claire looked up at that very moment to see Kamal Ali Reza coming toward them, bearing two glasses of champagne with floating strawberries. "Here comes my mystery guest now," Roxanne exclaimed with a radiant smile.

She slipped her arm intimately through Kamal's and accepted one of the glasses from his hand. "Kamal, darling, I want to introduce you to my sister, Claire, and her husband Dr. Clayton Spencer. Like everyone else in town, they've been just dying to meet you."

Kamal was smiling broadly as well, and he looked brilliantly handsome in a white Cardin suit. He nodded, shaking Clayton's hand, and then turned to acknowledge Claire with a slight, very formal bow. His volcanic dark eyes seemed to look right through her, as if she had suddenly ceased to exist, and for a moment Claire had the feeling that this could not really be happening, especially not after last night and the terrible things he had done to her.

Then, almost before she had time to catch her breath, Roxanne was sweeping her conquest away to greet some new arrivals, and Claire was left standing there with her world crashing down about her. Kamal had cut her dead, and from the look on Roxanne's face, Claire had not the slightest doubt in the world that her sister had found the perfect prospect for husband number four.

At the stroke of ten, Andrea arrived—although her appearance was so dramatically transformed that at first Roxanne simply stood and stared, totally unable to believe that it was she.

Andrea was wearing red—an off-the-shoulder Grecian-style gown with spirals of matching ostrich feathers. The color served to dramatically accentuate the pale ivory of her complexion, and the gown was extremely flattering as it clung and flowed about her.

Andrea's dark hair curled softly about her face in the very latest style, and the daringly extravagant use of makeup, highlighting her almond eyes and high cheekbones, gave her face a decidedly Oriental cast that was utterly captivating.

Sarah, with Soli San Lorenzo at her side, remained deliberately in the background as Andrea made her grand entrance. And as word of her arrival began to flash through the party like wildfire, heads began to swivel, while bodies twisted, turned, and rotated for better vantage.

Roxanne's party by now was well under way beneath a candy-striped tent that had been erected over a spacious marble terrace. Crystal chandeliers had been hung from the tented ceiling overhead. The walls were liquid with silver vinyl, and the shimmering reflected light seemed to melt and pour over couples dancing to the music of a 12-piece orchestra.

In that moment, however, Andrea herself was the focus of all attention. "Who is that young woman who just arrived?" Kamal questioned as the music came to a halt, and he and Roxanne moved slowly from the dance floor.

Roxanne blanched visibly. She could scarcely believe her eyes. "It's Andrea . . . my ex-stepdaughter. She's the guest of honor this evening."

As Roxanne and Kamal moved toward her, Andrea appeared to be slightly bewildered at the stir her arrival was causing. The atmosphere was charged and electric as the two women exchanged whispery kisses on each cheek without actually touching. Roxanne's face was a lovely mask, totally devoid of expression, all glacial poise and steely self-assurance, in contrast to Andrea's youthful radiance and appealing vulnerability.

"I want to thank you for giving me such a lovely party," Andrea said after all the introductions had been made. "I certainly wasn't expecting anything quite so lavish."

Whatever Roxanne's feelings might have been at that moment, her smoothly lacquered features gave absolutely nothing away. "Why, it was Soli himself who came up with the idea of throwing you a fabulous party," Roxanne informed her with a steely razor's edge to her voice. "And I can only assume that we have Soli to thank as well for transforming you into such a vision of loveliness."

180

"Soli's been a dear," Andrea said, smiling sweetly. "I only hope I can convince him to sail back to Europe on the *Golden Hind,* when I return to Monte Carlo in early September. I don't know what I'd do without him now."

"Andrea's made me a most generous offer," Soli put in a bit defensively. "She's interested in financing a chain of San Lorenzo salons in Paris, Rome, and Monte Carlo."

"I'm sure you're going to do very well indeed," Roxanne responded in a bright, brittle voice. "But now I know that everyone's just dying to meet the guest of honor, so I really think that we should circulate."

"I have a better idea," Kamal said, smiling into Andrea's eyes. "May I have the privilege of being the first to dance with the guest of honor?"

"Why . . . yes, I'd love to dance," Andrea responded with sparkling eyes. Then she was moving away on Kamal's arm, while Roxanne stared, speechless, after them.

Andrea's arrival seemed to spark the party into a blaze. The noise level rose, the Moët Chandon flowed, and the orchestra seemed to play with renewed enthusiasm, as Andrea and Kamal danced through set after set, locked in one another's arms.

Sarah was thrilled with her friend's success, and for a while at least, her own problems were eclipsed in the rosy glow of knowing she had somehow completed a very successful mission. Even so, Sarah was amazed that the transformation had gone far beyond the beautiful new gown, the added height afforded by her first pair of heels, or even Soli San Lorenzo's unquestioned cosmetic wizardry.

Somehow, Andrea had gotten a new vision of herself—the essential female mystique that every woman believed to be buried deep within the heart, waiting only to be liberated.

Roxanne wasn't sure just where it had all begun

to go wrong. But by midnight, there was no question left in her mind that her fabulous Fourth of July party was the ultimate disaster.

No sooner had she performed the introduction between Andrea and Kamal, than she sensed that she had made a tactical error of tremendous proportion. She felt slightly numbed by all the champagne she had put away, and she was furious with herself although why, she wasn't exactly sure.

The immediate and intense sexual chemistry between the handsome Arab and her ex-stepdaughter had been clearly evident to anyone with the eyes to see. And who, after all, had not been present to witness her humiliation?

Even her carefully planned party was by now totally beyond her own control. Andrea and Kamal had long since gone off together in his limousine, while her cousin, Abbey, had without a doubt become the unchallenged star of the dance floor.

Soaring her own private skies on God knows what combination of liquor, pills, and general emotional disorientation, Abbey had arrived at Ox Pasture Farm that evening, looking as if she had been made up by a gay undertaker. Her party dress was a garishly beaded and fringed creation that appeared to have been snatched off the rack at Goodwyn's Thrift Shop, and she had streaked her hair until it looked like a fright wig on a skunk.

Her intended, Kelly De Witte, had been on the verge of a stroke all evening. And after shamelessly vamping her way around the dance floor, thrusting her pelvis against any man she could manage to beg, borrow, or steal, Abbey had finally gone into total orbit.

Roxanne would gladly have throttled her on the spot, but it was already too late, for Abbey's own peculiar brand of madness seemed to have infected the entire party like a virus, and all about her Roxanne was surrounded by bedlam.

The orchestra had lost its schmaltzy Lester Lanin sound and was belting out hard rock music with almost hysterical psychedelic fervor. Gradually, all the other dancers began to fall back to form a circle as Abbey and the hirsute Italian waiter she had lured onto the floor began grinding together like copulating animals amid a volley of piercing wolf whistles, cat calls, and almost deafening applause.

Struggling to maintain her composure in the face of almost insurmountable odds, Roxanne stood regarding the spectacle with a sick, sinking sensation in the pit of her stomach. And probably the last person in the world she wanted to see was Patrick Dodsworth De Witte, who was fast bearing down upon her at that very moment.

"Isn't there anything you can do to put a stop to this?" Kelly wailed. "Your cousin is making a laughingstock out of me, and I'm beginning to wonder if she isn't totally deranged."

Roxanne whipped about to face him with an angry flush rising to her cheeks. "Abbey Randolph is *your* fiancée, in case you've forgotten. If you can't do anything with her, you certainly can't expect me to."

"Not any longer she isn't," Kelly barked. "That girl is an utter disaster. *An accident on its way to happen.* Tonight she told me just as calmly as you please that she'd given her diamond engagement ring to some drifter she'd picked up on the beach. And as far as being a virgin . . . well, you can see for yourself the way she's acting, and I have no intention of marching to the altar with shopworn goods."

With that, he turned on his heel and stalked away, leaving Roxanne with the feeling that she had just lost another round. As the executor of the Randolph estate and Abbey's guardian, she was utterly trapped, and something would definitely have to be done about it.

\* \* \*

Ian McVane was at precisely the right point of inebriation to balance off the seething resentment burning inside him against a brittle outer world that sought to overwhelm his creative artistry with greed.

It had begun to rain heavily around midnight, and the rain was coming down in sheets as he left the party and jogged past the tennis courts at a slow trot. Ian welcomed the rain as a cleansing benediction after the smoke and noise and general social pollution he had been forced to endure inside the house. He despised the absurd pretension and abject phoniness of it all.

Leaving the path that led down toward the bay, Ian cut through the thick and dripping foliage and headed toward the brilliantly lighted swimming pool, which was shimmering aquamarine in the black wetness of the night. It felt good to stretch his legs, and he gave in to the easy loping gait of the habitual jogger, while still retaining a prudent grip on the whiskey bottle he had lifted from the bar.

He was breathing heavily, and up ahead, the ground sloped downward through the English rose garden to the flagstone deck surrounding the pool. It shimmered there between the neat gravel pathways and fragrant hedges of rhododendron, pale and luminescent among the surrounding trees, which were strung with colored Japanese lanterns.

Soaked to the skin, Ian shook himself like a big wet dog when he reached the pool and ducked into the shelter of a thatched cabaña. He slumped down on one of the ornamental wrought iron chairs surrounding a circular glass table and bellowed: "The bastards quickly sicken of the calm, once they have known the storm."

He had no earthly idea where the quote had come from, or even why he felt compelled to shout it back toward the house. All he knew was that it would have been so much easier if there had only been a bullet in the chamber the night he had pulled the trigger in Friendlie's Tavern.

Ian took several quick pulls from the bottle still gripped tightly in his hand and then settled back to brood over the events leading up to his being billy-clubbed senseless at the Watermill Gallery and dragged off to the Bridgehampton police station.

In her Saturday column, Cassandra had gleefully reconstructed the carnage of what was by now being referred to as the "Watermill Massacre." With vividly descriptive phrases, she had described the "mass panic of all those expensively slippered and patent-leather-clad feet stampeding like range cattle for their waiting limos."

Of course, Ian fully realized by now that the entire mad charade had been a stupid and vainglorious gesture, which had availed him nothing beyond some lumps on his skull—although he himself had quickly been forgiven his violent and boorish behavior when, for purposes of investment, the price of his paintings had skyrocketed overnight.

In terms of cold, hard cash, it meant that Ian's performance had earned hundreds of thousands of dollars in tax write-offs for the very people he had terrorized. And absolutely none of the beneficiaries were prepared to let him wallow in an endless mire of legal proceedings, public degradation, and—God forbid—loss of earning potential.

It was now perfectly clear that as long as Ian McVane kept his name up in big bright lights, no matter how wildly erratic his personal behavior, he was to be forgiven everything. The charges were quietly dropped, and everybody made out on the deal. By ten o'clock on the evening following the Watermill Massacre, Ian was back drinking himself into oblivion at Friendlie's Tavern.

Ian didn't really know why he had decided to accept

185

Roxanne's invitation that evening. To all those people partying inside the mansion, he was simply a commodity, an accessory like the Vuitton luggage, Austrian skiing instructors, or beach boys scooped up off the sands of Acapulco.

He was nothing more than a whore who sold himself every time he picked up a paint brush, and the more he thought about it, the deeper Ian's mood descended into morose gloom.

Across the darkening sweep of lawn, the mansion loomed up out of the rain and the night like an ocean liner adrift on a storm-tossed sea. Like the *Titanic,* Ian thought, with the doomsday clock ticking off the seconds at one minute before midnight.

Ian had just lit a cigarette, when the soft, crunching sound of footsteps on the gravel path caused him to swing around and squint off into the darkness.

Then he saw her—the shadowy figure of a woman materializing out of the night, to duck beneath the streaming thatched cabaña, where he sat huddled over his bottle.

"Feel like some company?" she said, shivering slightly in her sopping party dress. Her face was interesting rather than beautiful but it immediately captured his imagination. A pale oval, with classic bone structure and huge hazel eyes that looked as if they had seen more of life than they really wanted to see.

"What the hell are you doing out here in the rain?" Ian demanded, his voice sounding far gruffer than intended. "Don't you know there's a hurricane blowing in off the Atlantic? We could all be dead by morning."

Sarah's smile was entirely enigmatic as she held out her empty champagne glass for him to fill. "I followed you," she admitted candidly.

"Why?" Ian questioned, filling her glass with whiskey.

Sarah, her teeth chattering with the cold, took a sip, brushed her streaming hair back from her face, and then turned to grace him with the most extraordinary smile. "You know, I'm not really sure."

"Do you ordinarily make a habit of following strange men?"

"You're not really a stranger," she responded. "I've always admired your work immensely. There was a time when I wanted to be an artist myself, when I was convinced that I was at least a little bit in love with you."

Something about her so completely disarmed him that Ian just sat there staring into her eyes as if he wanted to lose himself in them.

The whiskey seemed to warm her, even as the smile turned sad and then faded altogether. "Don't worry about it," she said. "I got over it soon enough, and there was no harm done."

"Being a 'little bit in love with me' you mean?"

"No. Wanting to be a painter. I decided to become a fashion illustrator instead."

Ian sent the butt of his cigarette arching out into the night and swigged deeply from his bottle. "Was that the end of it—your painting, I mean?"

Sarah nodded and then lifted her eyes to his. "I think I know what you were feeling the other night at the Watermill Gallery, Ian. But success doesn't have to be the end for you."

"How could you possibly know?" he challenged. "Have you ever been a forty-seven-year-old legend in your own time? I've already painted my best work, and I have nothing left to sell except a lot of third-rate copies. A Xerox machine could do as well."

Sarah rose, and her voice was deadly serious and slightly resentful as she said, "That's a lie, Ian Mc-Vane, and you know it. You already are the best . . . but you could still be the greatest."

Then she was gone, swallowed up by the rain and the wind and the night, as if she had been no more than a figment of his alcohol-laden imagination.

187

# CHAPTER 14

Roxanne's Fourth of July gala was ushered in by a summer hurricane of epic proportions. For on the northeastern tip of Long Island, wind and tide often move with sudden and frightening splendor, as the volatile Atlantic roars in to strike the shore at a perilous 45-degree angle. The waves of an approaching storm front rush in to explode against the beaches like hungry mouths snatching away at the sand dunes.

The hurricane that swept in off the Atlantic to wreak havoc at Ox Pasture Farm that evening was later estimated to have been powered by titanic energy equivalent to 10,000 atomic bombs. Nearby houses were unroofed, barns blown down, and century-old trees torn from the earth by their roots.

The tides rose to an alarming height, and the waves rolled in to strike the Hampton shoreline with such demonic force that great swaths of white sandy beach were literally torn away in the dark of that storm-tossed night.

With the storm still in its early stages, the huge baronial dining hall of Ox Pasture Farm was packed with guests crowded around the long refectory table. A post-midnight supper was being served, with platters of broiled squab, pheasant with *sauce amandine,* chilled lobster, Peconic oysters, smoked salmon, and quantities of Beluga caviar.

Weary servants threaded a steady path from the cavernous kitchens, replenishing the Georgian silver platters and bringing an ever-new assortment of such delicacies as strawberries glacé, fresh raspberries chilled in melon cups, and rhubarb sherbet for anyone who might still be watching calories at three o'clock in the morning.

With her 16mm camera still steadily humming away after more than five hours on the job, Kim Merriweather was cataloging the feeding frenzy of Roxanne's guests, even as the eye of the hurricane made its approach at 150 miles per hour from out of the Bermuda deeps. The remnants of the party had by now become a hurricane watch, with gale force winds howling about the mansion like demented spirits of the dead and sheets of rain flailing against the windows in rushing torrents.

Kim had been persuaded by de Roma to wear a long, formal gown and heels that evening. And in spite of the fact that her feet felt like bloody stumps and her panty-girdle was killing her, she had by now become totally fascinated by the scenario she saw playing itself out before the lens of her camera.

By that point in the proceedings, Franco de Roma had virtually drunk himself into impotence, and Abbey Randolph had finally been heavily sedated after suffering an attack of hysteria during an ugly confrontation with her cousin Roxanne. Helene Von Bismark had finally arrived well after midnight to announce that Jason unfortunately was still suffering complications from an undisclosed virus, and Claire Ryan Spencer had stormed out of the party and driven off alone into the night, after a fearful scene with her husband, Clayton.

During the first four weeks of shooting, Kim had often wondered if she was going to make it through the summer. Talents had clashed, sex had reared its ugly head, and egos had painfully collided.

But now, ever since de Roma's mysterious dressing-down by Darnell Hanlan at the Southampton Bay

Club, all that had changed. Franco's determination to possess her body at any cost had taken a sudden leave of absence in the face of Kim's firm refusal to copulate. De Roma's frenetic energy had become more subdued, and his normally exclamatory voice had become hushed and the mood of their daily shooting schedule tautly controlled.

Pasta wouldn't have melted in his mouth as de Roma praised Kim's work on viewing the daily rushes. And yet in spite of the decidedly improved climate of their working relationship, the filming was falling further and further behind schedule, mostly because the weather had become oddly erratic, which made it difficult to plan each day's shooting in advance.

But there was another reason as well, and although Kim had no idea exactly what had transpired, de Roma announced suddenly that the film had to be completed and ready for cutting by August 10 at the very latest.

"It is . . . how you say . . . imperative, according to my financial backers," de Roma informed her in half apologetic terms. "So from now on, we are all living under the gun. Even you, *La California,* will get just a little crazy like me, perhaps," he had laughed. "For we are all desperate people engaged in a desperate race against time."

He went on to tell her that the film was to have its premiere performance at the annual Gold and Silver Charity Ball. It was always held in late August and was the capstone of the Hampton social season, after which the gilded cast of thousands would scatter to the four corners of the earth, like falling leaves on the first winds of autumn.

In spite of everything that had transpired, Kim had come to believe that the documentary she was filming was important. In a way, she had become a voyeur, meticulously recording the many facets of the jeweled life at the top of the heap, even as the diamond of F. Scott Fitzgerald's talent had shone most brilliantly during the summer season spent among the rich on Long Island's Southeastern Shore.

It was almost as if Kim Merriweather had propped herself up against her camera tripod that summer, speculating upon diamonds both real and false, much the same way that F. Scott had propped himself up against his typewriter to document his own age of gaudy over-consumption.

Out on the terrace, beneath the billowing candy-striped tent, the music thundered on through the night in dramatic counterpoint to the flashing lightning, kettle-drum roll of thunder, and banshee-wail of the wind.

For the most part, only the truly hard-core swingers were still dancing, as the tent itself threatened to be swept out into Gardiner's Bay at any moment. Their bodies were still flailing away out there on the dance floor to the loud and dissonant beat of the music, while makeup melted, party dresses became limp with perspiration, and torsos jerked and jolted beneath the flashing pink and lavender strobe lights.


Claire had left Roxanne's party after having a dreadful row with Clayton. It was a night of endings, of things dying away without the faintest distant glimmer of hope or rebirth.

Claire had fled in a desperate race to outrun the relentless sense of panic that was fast taking possession of her. And now, as she glanced down at the softly illuminated speedometer, she steadily increased her speed to send the heavy Buick Ranch Wagon rocketing ahead into the dismal, rain-wet night.

What would it be like to end it all, she wondered, as the rain streaked crazily against the car windows at 85 miles an hour. Was death simply a descent into black nothingness? Or would it be a liberation from the forces that seemed to have driven her so relentlessly toward that particular moment in time?

191

"Suicide." The word barely escaped her lips, whispered almost fearfully as if Claire were trying it out, testing it on her lips like a powerful mantra.

Until that very moment, the thought of taking her own life had never even crossed her mind. There had always been so much she wanted out of life and so little time.

Claire bit her lip as tears streaked her heavy makeup. She watched the speedometer rise steadily to 95 miles an hour, hover there for a moment, and then continue its ever-upward ascent. Kamal's betrayal lay like ashes in her throat, but a far deeper wound was her own betrayal of herself.

Regret was racing in her blood like fever, and flight had become an end in itself. It was, Claire realized, as if she were trying to outrun the realization that her relationship with Kamal had been entirely self-destructive. Of course, she had been forced to drink herself into oblivion every time they were together. Otherwise, she would never have allowed him to do the terrible things he had done to her body—the burns, the bruises, the beatings, and a thousand other degrading indignities.

He had marked her forever with his cruelty, and there was a fragility in her bones now, a sense of having trespassed upon some other zone of time, where life was lived very close to the margins of death.

She had told Clayton everything that night at Roxanne's—about all the other men she had slept with, about Kamal and the things she had allowed him to do to her. Claire had wanted to hurt and wound him the way she herself had been hurt. But instead she saw something in his eyes that had turned her sick inside with self-loathing.

Clayton had always loved her in spite of everything. He had been her Rock of Gibraltar, her shield against the voracious denizens of the barracuda tank, where systematic deception, treachery, and flesh-peddling

192

were akin to holy writ. It was Claire herself who had driven him into the deadly competitive labyrinth of power and acquisition, which at times had taken on all the horrific aspects of the primal blood frenzy of feeding sharks.

But now Clayton was gone for good, she knew. After what had taken place between them that night, there was no going back. And Claire steeled herself against the sense of loss and emptiness as she flexed her hands against the wheel of the car.

She missed her husband desperately in that moment —the ready openness of his smile, the gentle reassurance of his physical presence, and those strong and capable surgeon's hands that could be so impossibly tender when he touched her hair or her cheek in passing.

Claire strained to see the highway through her flowing tears, refusing to slacken speed for even an instant, although by now visibility had been reduced to no more than a matter of yards. As lightning streaked the darkness and gale force winds buffeted the car, she became possessed of the feeling that all nature had combined in a sudden wild fusion of primitive force— a single, untamable entity raging and swirling about her.

Then, as the highway narrowed suddenly, with a diesel truck bulking up out of the dark, Claire came to a decision. The truck was traveling in the opposite direction, and as her hands turned moist and slippery on the steering wheel, Claire jammed her foot to the floorboard and swerved the station wagon directly into the path of the onrushing diesel.

There was a terrible wailing blare of the diesel's air horn, and the sudden blinding glare of powerful headlamps shining directly into Claire's eyes.

She was utterly terrified. "Dear God, no!" Claire screamed aloud. This couldn't be happening, when she wanted so very much to live. But by then, it was already too late, for even though she managed to avoid hitting the diesel by no more than a matter of feet, the Buick had skidded out of control and crashed through a wooden guard railing. Then she was turning crazily over and over, and the last thing that Claire remembered was the sound of shattering glass, the rending crunch of metal, and the wail of an endlessly blaring horn.

By the time that dawn had begun to streak the eastern horizon with sickly yellow light, the hurricane had swept out to sea, leaving a trail of chaotic destruction in its wake. The wind had fallen sharply, leaving a sudden silence upon the landscape around Ox Pasture Farm, while the water in the bay was ominously still and smooth as pewter.

Roxanne stood on the marble terrace that opened off the dining room through tall French doors. The huge candy-striped tent had partially collapsed during the very peak of the hurricane, sweeping across the terrace and carrying everything away in its path.

Fifty cases of champagne had been toppled during the brief, mad flight of the tent, and the floor was virtually awash in enough Moët Chandon to float a battleship. Three hundred crystal goblets had been smashed in one fell swoop, and 12 dozen delicate caneback chairs had been reduced to kindling.

Roxanne stood there amid the carnage and wondered what she could have possibly done to deserve such a disaster on her night of nights. Absolutely everything that could possibly go wrong had gone wrong, and the throbbing pain of one of her recurrent migraines had begun to increase at an alarming rate.

She turned away from the desolate scene and wearily entered the house on lagging feet. Then, as she reached the foyer, she suddenly caught sight of herself in a tall rococo mirror. She felt as if she were viewing a stranger.

Her face was ashen, strained, and ghostly. And her

194

features appeared as if some inner storm had dislocated all the original elements, leaving a sort of wreckage, with bruised shadows beneath the eyes and tautly drawn mouth.

"Can I be of any assistance?" a voice asked.

Roxanne looked up, staring blankly at the incredibly handsome young man in black dinner clothes seated on the staircase leading to the upper floors of the house. She had thought that all of her guests were gone, and for a moment even speculated that the darkly compelling young stranger might be a figment of her disordered mental state.

"Who are you?" she asked a bit vaguely.

Jaime smiled, rose, and reached out to take her hand. "Just someone left over from last night," he responded. Then they were mounting the stairs together, while from the library below the phone began ringing with shrill, piercing peals.

What does it matter, Roxanne thought, as they reached the top of the stairs and moved across the upper hall toward her bedroom door. For now, all she wanted to do was forget the evening just past. Later, there would be time enough to assess exactly how much damage had really been done and decide what her next move was to be.

# CHAPTER 15

It was dusk by the time Helen reached the dock at Cormorant Point. An attendant had already been alerted to gas up the powerful Von Bismark motor launch, the *Lucky Lady*. And within minutes after stepping from her silver Bentley, the powerful engines were churning the harbor water to a frothy jade green.

After tying a silk scarf about her hair, Helene took the wheel and shot away from the jetty amid towering plumes of salt spray. She had just driven out from Manhattan, and the day had been a scorcher, with sunlight flickering over the city like a fire over a vast grate.

Helene breathed in the pure salt sea air and felt a surge of adrenalin course through her veins, as the launch skimmed across the bay toward where the *Golden Hind* lay at anchor in the distance. It was always a good deal cooler out on the island, and a brief thundershower in the late afternoon had left the surrounding countryside glistening and fresh.

The early-evening air gave the impression of mistiness, thickened and dyed a deeper blue in the gathering dusk. Across Shinnecock Bay, vagrant shafts of sunlight still danced over the hills, flashing and sparkling off the mellow red brick and white colonial facades of Southampton Township.

Henri had been right, Helene thought, as she stared off into the velvet dusk. The vultures were definitely circling. And in spite of Jason's disappearance at a time when she needed him most, Helene had no choice but to move in and take matters into her own hands before everything was lost.

Helene had been forced to act because by now it was perfectly clear that Kamal Ali Reza had decided to deal himself into the game in a big way. She had, of course, recognized him from the very beginning as being the consummate opportunist. But what Helene had not counted on was Andrea being swept off her feet like some silly schoolgirl in the first heady flush of romance.

Helene was the first to admit that she and Kamal were, after all, a couple of high-class hustlers walking the same beat. And for once she had met a man who was very nearly her match. She could see that he was a gambler at heart—a slick opportunist with formidable credentials, whose plans for Treasure Cay were proceeding along a carefully charted course.

By now, a top-flight public relations firm had been called in to handle the necessary promotion. But it was also clear to Helene that Kamal had decided to finesse the various obstacles involved himself, in his own inimitable and very personal style.

What he needed most was a Hampton connection— someone of impeccable social credentials, who could ease him past the rising chorus of public sentiment mounting against the Treasure Cay project. People were talking about little else these days, and Roxanne Ryan Aristos had at first appeared to be the perfect vehicle for his ambitions.

But then, Andrea had appeared on the scene, young, dewy-eyed, vulnerable, and as rich as Kamal himself. It was like waving a red flag at a bull, and since their meeting at Roxanne's Fourth of July party, Andrea and Kamal had become the hottest ticket in town.

Together constantly, they were bathed in public adulation wherever they went. And by now it was perfectly obvious to anyone with the eyes to see, that

197

the "poor little rich girl" had fallen hopelessly in love with her Arabian Nights mystery man. It wasn't in the least difficult for Helene to fathom his attraction for her. After all, to Andrea's way of thinking, Kamal Ali Reza was perhaps the only man alive who was both rich enough and so totally secure in his own power not to be in the least interested in the fact that he was avidly courting over $2 billion on the hoof.

How incredibly naive she was, Helene thought. It was, of course, a total fallacy, since her handsome and dashing lover was nothing if not a shrewd and wily Arab trader who had gotten exactly where he was by playing hard and fast, always to win.

Andrea, for her part, had undergone an unexpected transformation since her arrival in the Hamptons—a complete metamorphosis from grub to butterfly. She had become an attractive and self-assured young woman of affairs, who actually seemed to glow with some kind of inner radiance.

Soli San Lorenzo had, of course, been largely responsible. He was a very clever young man when it came to being in the right place at the right time, and he now was making almost daily excursions out to the *Golden Hind* to become one of Andrea's intimates. He did her hair, her makeup, and had been instrumental, along with Sarah Dane, in helping Andrea select an entire new wardrobe of designer fashions, which had helped to complete her entirely new image.

Meanwhile, Helene herself had not been idle. Her first move had been to seduce Dr. Clayton Spencer, after his wife tried to kill herself on the night of Roxanne's party. Both he and his Golden Portals Sanitarium were central to Helene's plan. But the first order of business was getting rid of Sarah Dane.

Kamal Ali Reza would be far more difficult to eliminate, of course. But Helene had already started the ball rolling by contacting a highly placed State Department official, who had long been involved in Middle Eastern affairs. They had once spent a weekend together in Bermuda, and he had promised her a full report on Ali Reza by the end of the week.

Then, as if Helene didn't already have enough problems, there was Jason. For the past three weeks, she had managed to convince Andrea that he was still weak from his recent illness, but that story wasn't going to hold water for much longer. He simply had to be found and brought to heel by any means necessary—although according to Dillon's latest report, the trail had ended after Jason had been seen getting on the ferry for Fire Island Pines.

Helene by now was convinced that Stavros Aristos must have somehow discovered that his son was a switch-hitter and disinherited him because of it. Jason had never said, and Helene's own feelings for her handsome younger husband at that moment bordered on contempt.

It was true that their sex life had long been in decline, but what Helene could simply not understand or tolerate was the fact that Jason could prefer another man to herself in bed. For that she was determined to make him pay, and pay dearly, even though she still needed him to gain control of Aristos Shipping.

The truth had been difficult for her to face. But now that she knew of Jason's homosexual tendencies beyond any shadow of a doubt, Helene fully intended to use that knowledge very much to her own advantage.

By now, the *Golden Hind* lay dead ahead, with all her portholes alight in the purpling dusk. Helene eased back on the throttle and then reversed the engines as the launch swung abreast of the gangway that had been lowered in advance of her arrival.

The Aristos yacht was a magnificent 250-foot floating palazzo, with highly polished teakwood decks and a dazzling white superstructure that gleamed in the twilight like Chinese porcelain. It was equipped with extensive electronic communications equipment and was used by Andrea, even as her father before her, as a highly mobile command center from which she guided the fortunes of the worldwide Aristos Shipping empire.

One of the Greek crewmen bounded down the gangway to help Helene aboard. She already knew that Andrea was dining ashore with Kamal Ali Reza while her friend Sarah Dane was attending a movie alone in Easthampton. Helene had spoken with her sister-in-law earlier and expressed her concern over the series of spectacular jewel robberies that had taken place in spite of maximum security precautions, trained guard dogs, and even electrified fences.

Only recently Helene had acquired a diamond and emerald necklace that had once belonged to the Empress Alexandra, and she had asked Andrea if she might leave it in the ship's safe, at least until the jewel thieves were apprehended. The fabulous acquisition had been widely heralded in the New York papers and, according to Helene, she wouldn't have a moment's peace until she knew it was safely stowed away aboard the *Golden Hind*.

It was all a pretext, of course, but then Helene had a very good reason for everything she did.

The first officer welcomed her aboard and then led her down below deck, where the yacht's communication center was located and maintained under the strictest security measures.

The walls and ceiling were as white and clinically depersonalized as an operating theater, while the room itself was fairly small, windowless, and illuminated by banks of flashing multicolored lights. As Helene was ushered inside, she immediately became aware of the constant background sounds of radar blips and garbled voices emanating from the screens, which were programmed to receive satellite transmissions from around the globe.

Captain Metaxis was relieving the regular radio man that evening. He sat in a swivel chair before the electronic console that put Andrea in direct contact with the vast and varied Aristos enterprises around the world. Metaxis was a handsome Greek with a thick, black mustache, rugged features, and melting brown bedroom eyes.

"Welcome aboard the *Golden Hind*," he smiled. "Signorina Aristos informed me that you would be coming aboard this evening to put some valuable jewelry in the ship's safe."

From the way he looked at her, Helene was convinced that her luck was holding. "I hope I'm not disturbing your work," Helene said in her most seductive voice. "I can see that you must be a very busy man."

Metaxis bowed low over her hand, brushing it slightly with his lips. "I am never too busy to be of service to a beautiful woman," he pronounced in a deep, rich, and highly accented voice. "If you will excuse me for only one moment, I will open the safe."

He crossed the room to twirl the various dials on a large chromium wall safe with a variety of separate compartments inside. Then, he returned to where Helene awaited him and placed a leather case on the table before her. More dials were turned, and finally the case sprung open to display a dazzling assortment of diamonds, emeralds, sapphires, and rubies as large as pigeons' eggs.

By this point, Helene had removed the necklace from her purse, and she held it up for the captain's inspection. "Isn't it beautiful?" she breathed, carefully manipulating the diamonds and emeralds until they rode serenely over the swell of her breasts. "It's very old, very famous, and worth a great deal of money."

201

By this time, Captain Metaxis's eyes were hungrily devouring both the glittering jewels and the well of Helene's cleavage, into which they dipped with tantalizing mystery. "They are most beautiful indeed," he uttered in a hushed voice.

"Perhaps you would like to touch them," Helene purred, taking his strong, bronzed hand and pressing it against her pale flesh, which was literally ablaze with shimmering stones.

Metaxis was, she noticed, breathing rather more heavily than before and the touch of his fingers running over the jewels seemed to scald her flesh with burning intimacy. "Perhaps you would like to see the rest of my collection sometime soon," she purred. "In fact, why don't you come out to Miramar on your next evening off? My husband's away at present, so we'd have the whole house to ourselves."

Georgios Metaxis swallowed hard and nodded, even as Helene allowed the clasp to slip from her fingers and the necklace to fall to the floor with a brittle clatter. With a shocked gasp, Georgios bent quickly to retrieve it, and in that instant, Helene deftly removed a diamond and ruby ring from the case and dropped it immediately into the well of her breasts.

"Fortunately, your beautiful necklace seems to be intact," Georgios informed her as he carefully placed it in a velvet pouch and then closed the lid of Andrea's jewel case. "And you need have absolutely no fear, Baroness. Your treasure will be safe here. This room is under the strictest security at all times."

"You're very kind," Helene breathed. "And while you're putting that back in the safe, I'll write down my private telephone number so you can give me a call when you're free. I'm sure there's a great deal we have in common."

Returning to the main salon, Helene ordered coffee from Marko, the cabin steward, and then pretended to occupy herself with browsing around.

Helene was greatly impressed by Andrea's opulent and highly private little world aboard the *Golden Hind*. She was also convinced that Georgios Metaxis would make a valuable ally, and she was more than willing to make it worth his while.

The luxurious main salon of the yacht was sumptuously appointed with priceless Renaissance antiques, light ash paneling, and deep Persian carpets. As she moved about, sipping her coffee from a Spode china cup, Helene mentally catalogued the changes she intended to make once she herself was mistress of the *Golden Hind*.

More than anything else, the bookcases were revealing of Andrea's personality. A quick scan showed them to contain the works of Balzac, Thackeray, Nietzche, and Proust, as well as all the major classics. There were also books on shipping, economics, and finance, many of which had notes written in the margins in Andrea's own neat hand.

Her sister-in-law had quite obviously spent the last year boning up on her education and had previously informed Helene that Sarah Dane had proven to be an invaluable tutor, confidant, and advisor in the affairs of Aristos Shipping. During another conversation, she had also mentioned in passing that only she and Sarah had access to the safe aboard the *Golden Hind*.

There were simply no two ways about it. If Helene herself were to prevail, Sarah Dane had to be thoroughly discredited, which was precisely the reason that Helene had chosen to come aboard the yacht that evening.

Once she had made reasonably sure that she would not be interrupted, Helene left the main salon and made her way down a circular staircase to the cabin deck below. Earlier, she had casually inquired which of the cabins Sarah was lodged in, and now she had no difficulty whatsoever in locating it.

All the cabins were named after figures from Greek

203

mythology. And upon reaching a teakwood door inscribed with "Aphrodite," in gold leaf lettering, Helene quickly slipped inside and closed the door behind her. Searching Sarah's quarters was a fairly safe maneuver, Helene had decided, since she had a clear view through the portholes of any approaching boats, and in case of discovery by a member of the crew, she would simply say she had come downstairs in search of the powder room and somehow gotten into Sarah's cabin by mistake.

The stateroom was furnished with priceless eighteenth-century Venetian antiques, while the adjoining bath and dressing room were done in Sienna marble, with a floor of delicately inlaid mosaic tile patterned with dolphins and flying fish.

There was a bottle of Rose-Geranium bath salts sitting next to the sunken tub, and after slipping Andrea's ruby ring from her cleavage, Helene quickly dropped it into the glass container and turned the bottle upside down several times, until the ring was totally hidden from view.

With that task completed and the stage set, she then returned to Sarah's bedroom. Helene was not exactly sure just what it was that she expected to find among Sarah's personal effects. But she began by going through her bureau drawers, making sure not to disturb the arrangement of things.

She had already traced Sarah's background and suspected she knew a good deal more about the young woman's past than Andrea herself did—for instance, the fact that Sarah's mother ran a seafood restaurant out in Montauk and was not even aware that her daughter had returned to America after a year-long sojourn in the Greek Isles. In fact, it appeared to Helene that Sarah was even somewhat ashamed of her background.

After discovering that Sarah's birth-control pills were being consumed on a regular up-to-date basis, Helene

204

began to prowl the cabin in search of some indication of who her paramour might be. First she rifled through the drawers of the escritoire, but finding nothing of interest, she moved on to ferret around in both closets, without discovering anything of note.

Helene thumbed through several glossy fashion magazines that Sarah obviously had been reading, and after becoming a bit desperate, she even ran her hand underneath the edge of the blue and gold Bokhara carpeting covering the floor. Then, just as she was about to give up her search in disgust, Helene happened to reach beneath the pillows massed at the head of Sarah's bed, to withdraw a small, locked, leather-bound diary.

A nail file was quickly dispatched to break open the clasp, and moments later, Helene was avidly skimming over several of the most recent entries, realizing that she had struck pure gold.

## June 18

Day hazes into night. The flesh trap yawns once again, and I fall beneath Marko's body. He grunts that he will tear me open with his penis, and I halfway believe him.

The passion in his voice heats my blood and makes me obey his every command, even as I hate myself for doing so. When, I wonder, will this monstrous passion come to an end? The sexual ecstasy derived from allowing him to take me like some kind of she-animal in estrus is all wrong, and I despise my own weakness. He's nothing but a primitive chauvinist brute, and never before in my life have I gone so against my natural inclinations. Why do I continue to submit myself to a man who is so far beneath me in so many ways?

## June 19

I'm exhausted and grow thinner every day. All this

mindless fornicating is draining me, and yet nothing else seems to be any good. Only with Marko planted inside me can I stop my mind from thinking and my emotions from feeling. It is pure lust between us. I don't sleep anymore, even with the pills, since my dreams have become no more than terrifying reminders that I have no other recourse but to seek my own degradation.

### June 20

I worry constantly that Andrea will somehow discover that Marko and I have been fucking like rabbits all these months, while she sleeps alone in her virgin bed. It is, without question, a thoroughly degrading passion, and I sometimes wish that he would fall overboard or simply cease to exist, even while his wiry, hairy body excites me in ways that I never before dreamed of. The truth, I am beginning to fear, is that I need this constant sense of humiliation in order to feel anything at all. Only the crisis of self-hatred and fear of discovery is left to provoke me. Beyond that, there is nothing. I am empty and totally bereft of feeling. God help me—if there is a God.

Helene Von Bismark was smiling as she slipped the diary into her purse and quietly left the stateroom. So much for Sarah Dane, she thought to herself. Fucking the help was something that pure and pristine little Andrea, with her convent upbringing, could simply never forgive. Especially since she had already confessed to Helene that she had refused to sleep with Kamal until after they were married, and she loathed the very idea of promiscuity.

Marriage to Kamal Ali Reza, however, was exactly what Helene had every intention of preventing, no matter what steps she might have to take in order to destroy Andrea's illusion of romantic bliss.

* * *

206

Abbey climbed the stairs to her bedroom, closed the door behind her, and leaned back against the panels, as limp as a rag doll. She squeezed her eyes tightly shut as slow tears ran down her cheeks. At first she cried silently, with only an occasional shivery spasm, like a child not really wanting to cry.

Then came the racking sobs—shuddering and anguished, with her whole body shaking, as her mouth opened and closed with dry, rasping convulsions.

Dizzy with loss and despair, Abbey finally staggered across the room and collapsed on the bed, staring up at the ceiling. Her wide, unblinking eyes moved slowly as she traced the rococo cornice surmounted by sweetly smiling cherubs as it made its way around the ceiling. There were pieces missing in places, and the paint was chipped and peeling.

Like chunks torn out of people's lives, Abbey thought to herself—never to be reassembled.

She had accosted Jaime that afternoon on the street. And now, any shred of hope she still might have had was entirely gone. "Look, you have to quit following me," he had told her. "I don't know what it is you expect from me, but it's just no good. Every time I turn around, you're spying on me. I see you at the beach almost every day—hanging around my house—following me in your car when I go out. Shit, Abbey, you are driving me nuts. And I'm getting good and sick of having you haunt my life like some fucking spook."

"I only want to talk to you," she pleaded. "Please, Jaime . . . it's important. There's something we have to discuss."

"We've got nothing to say to each other," he grunted. "Now just fuck off and stay the hell out of my life." With that, Jaime had turned away and started for his car, which was parked in the next block.

It was very hot, and she was perspiring, but Abbey simply couldn't let him go. Her body remembered only too well the eddies and waves of ecstasy he had brought her. Jaime Rodriquez had become her single, compelling obsession. And throwing all caution to the winds, she ran after him all the way to the corner, where she tugged hard on his arm, trying to make him stop.

Jaime spun around and for a moment she thought that he was going to strike her. His eyes flashed angrily and he jerked away. "I'm gonna give it to you straight just one more time, bitch—and then that's the end of it.

"You deliberately picked me up and did everything short of begging me to fuck you, and so I did. I don't know why, but I got the feeling you wanted your old lady to catch us in the act that day. I think you're responsible for your mother's heart attack, and as far as I'm concerned you got exactly what you wanted from me. A big dick up that tight cherry cunt of yours, and Old Lady Randolph six feet underground."

Abbey hauled off and slapped him as hard as she could. Then she turned and ran back to where she had parked the car. For at least 15 minutes, she just sat there shaking, until finally she recovered enough to drive home.

Now Jaime would never know about the baby, she thought—his baby growing inside her womb like a malignant tumor.

Abbey was drawn from sleep some hours later by the sound of music. It was very warm and still inside the house, and she lay there listening. There was something disquieting about it as it drifted up through her open windows from the beach. The blaring rhythms were sensuous and febrile in the summer night.

Abbey rose from her crinoline-canopied bed and, moving like a sleepwalker, she crossed to stand before the windows. There was a beach party in progress among the dunes below the house. Youthful bodies ran across the sand and tore off their clothes, rolling down the dunes into the eager embrace of a dozen reaching arms, as Abbey watched, enthralled. The naked, wildly prancing bodies glinted golden in the flickering firelight of a driftwood bonfire.

As Abbey stood silhouetted in the faint light, a low sharp whistle came from below in the garden. She looked down to see the figure of a young man in sailor whites urinating into the hedge below her bedroom window.

His body was slim and muscular with narrow hips, and a sizable erection protruded from the front of his pants. A cigarette was dangling from his lips, and there was a languid, suggestive smile on his face, which was illuminated by the light spilling out from the windows along the lower floor.

There was absolutely no question about what he had in mind, as he began to stroke himself with an aching suggestion of sexual need. "Rapunzel, Rapunzel, let down your hair," he laughed. "We're all out here on the beach, and you're all alone up there with a whole big house to yourself. How about sharing the wealth?"

"I'm so lonely," Abbey heard herself whimper plaintively, in a soft, scarcely audible voice. For an instant, doubt and fear played across her features, but for an instant only. These were the summer people that Annabel had always warned her about, Abbey realized. Now at least she was free to join them. Her mother was dead, Jaime had abandoned her, and there was nothing to stop her now.

# ═══CHAPTER 16═══

Roxanne had been having the dream for years, but of late it had begun to recur with alarming frequency. It was always winter and very cold, and invariably she found herself running down Fifth Avenue without a stitch on, clutching her jewels to her breast in a brown paper bag. Someone was chasing her, but Roxanne never looked back to find out who it was.

She was having the dream when she was awakened by a telephone call at three o'clock in the morning. It was from Simmons, the Randolph butler, who informed her in a quavering voice that after 50 years of service at Bramwell Acres, he was tendering his notice.

Miss Abbey, according to Simmons, had completely taken leave of her senses and at that very moment, the house at the end of Lily Pad Lane was being overrun by "a horde of drug-crazed hippies and degenerates."

Utterly stunned by this revelation, Roxanne immediately put in a call to Bramwell Acres and sat drumming her nails impatiently as the phone continued to ring and ring and ring. Finally, after 15 rings, a man's voice answered, although the response was anything but what Roxanne had expected.

"Hot stuff on the line . . . it's your dime, so shoot."

Aghast at the implied familiarity and totally puzzled by the thick Southern drawl, Roxanne scarcely knew what to say next. "I'd like to speak to Miss Randolph," she pronounced. "Please call her to the phone immediately."

"You're gonna have to talk louder, lady. I can hardly hear you." It was true—the din coming over the line was deafening, and by now thoroughly annoyed, Roxanne raised her voice to a tone of imperious command. "Look here, whoever you are, I insist on speaking to my cousin, Abbey Randolph. Now do as I tell you, and call her to the phone."

"Hey, Abbey," the voice rose above the background noise. "Some broad who says she's your cousin wants you on the horn."

There was a burst of raucous laughter, and then the voice came back on the line to demand, "She wants to know which cousin you are . . . the lush or the wicked witch of the East?"

Trying desperately to control her rising indignation, Roxanne carefully framed her words. "You may inform Abbey that her cousin Roxanne is on the phone, and that I demand to speak with her immediately."

Silence. A hand clasped over the mouthpiece. Then came a loud burst of music and a cacophony of voices, even louder than before. "Sorry, Roxy, Abbey says she doesn't want to talk to you. But I kind of like the sound of your voice, so why don't you just buzz on over here and join the party? The fleet's in, sweet chops. When you hit the gangplank, just ask for Spike Yankowski, the number one stud in this man's navy."

Roxanne slammed down the receiver on her pink princess phone and sat on the edge of the bed, shaking with righteous indignation. How dare Abbey refuse to speak with her? What in the name of God could be going on out there, and just who the hell was Spike Yankowski?

With a glass of white wine in one hand, a cigarette in the other, and a distant smile on her brightly painted lips, Abbey drifted through the house as if

211

she were in a dream world of her own creation. All about her, the wildest party of the season ebbed and flowed. Grass was smoked, acid dropped, pills were popped, and booze swilled. There were more people than she could possibly count, floating high and low. They were dancing, smoking pot, snorting coke, and ingesting a variety of other drugs, while crashing, freaking out, and generally having the time of their lives.

Abbey was undisputed queen of the night, and all about her the old mansion was populated by subjects of every possible persuasion. Word of her impromptu party had spread quickly along the shore, and the several hundred people who had flocked to Bramwell Acres in the hours after midnight were not in the least an unusual mix for the Hamptons at three o'clock in the morning.

There was an exotic sprinkling of ghastly beautiful Manhattan models sporting the latest far-out faddish designs and hairstyles; gaunt youths with the haunted, hungry look of off-Broadway actors; a half-dozen sailors from a ship anchored off Hampton Bays; some weekend trippers who just happened to tag along; and the usual Hampton summer crowd of scions, debutantes, and well-dressed swingers, with significantly empty faces beneath perfect tennis tans.

The Randolph mansion was ablaze with lights. Cacophonous music was provided by an itinerant band of hard-rock musicians, and the house was generally filled with laughter, voices, and a drifting haze of pot smoke, through which the dancers moved like ghostly manifestations.

A disembodied hand reached out to proffer a joint, and Abbey took it automatically, drawing the reefer to her lips and dragging deeply to inhale a lungful of dreams. The music was loud and blaring out through powerhouse speakers. The lead guitarist was a burly local youth, wearing nothing but a jockstrap and an incandescent smile beneath his sweeping Zapata mustache.

"What a fantastic party," someone said.

"Yeah, man . . . far out . . . and then some."

Their words were music to Abbey's ears, and she moved easily among them, savoring the sense of belonging at last. Finally, she looked up to see a tall, stunning black woman moving gracefully toward her through the crowd. She was a brazen black beauty, feline and sensuous in her silver lamé disco skirt, which shimmered with layers of beaded fringe.

The girl's hair was a dark, lustrous Afro sprinkled with flecks of glitter, while her ashen face had been painted dead matte-white, in a bizarre reversal of the traditional minstrel's blackface. Then, she and Abbey were dancing together, and a low, velvety chuckle reverberated deep in the girl's throat.

"You really know how to turn on the action and rattle everybody's cage, Abbey, my girl. I wanna show how much I appreciate the hospitality."

In the next moment, she cupped Abbey's face in surprisingly strong black hands and kissed her hard on the mouth. "Here's a little present to remember the Acid Queen by," she said huskily, placing a small lavender pill on the tip of Abbey's tongue, like a communion wafer. "Bon voyage, *chère amie,* and I'll see you on the dark side of the moon."

Then she drifted away on high platform heels, turning slowly through the smoky haze with the effortless glide of a black swan on a mist-covered lake.

Roxanne didn't even bother to dress. She simply threw a silk scarf over her hair and belted a full-length sable coat over her black negligée before starting out.

It took no more than 20 minutes for her to drive over to Bramwell Acres, where she found the drive leading up to the house bumper to bumper with everything from Alfa Romeos to dune buggies and garishly painted vans.

Only moments after ringing the bell, the front door of the mansion swung open, and Roxanne was engulfed by a solid wall of noise, laughter, music, and voices screaming to be heard above the general tumult.

Roxanne, however, could only imagine the identity of the revelers, since her view was largely blocked by a husky six-footer in Navy whites, who filled the doorway with his broadly muscular frame. "Hey sweet cakes," he said, grinning. "Where you been all my life, and what's your handle?"

It was the same thick Southern drawl that Roxanne had heard over the phone earlier. "Unfortunately, I already know who you are," Roxanne articulated in scathing tones. "Any further introduction would be needlessly redundant and totally pointless. Now get out of my way, or I'll have you slapped in jail so fast, it'll make your head spin."

"Well, I'll be damned." Spike's grin widened as he grabbed her by the arm and pulled her roughly inside the house. "If it ain't cousin Roxy, in the flesh. I like a broad with grit, so how about you and me gettin' real well acquainted?"

Before Roxanne could even begin to protest, he had pulled her hard against him and was swinging her dizzily about. "Please . . . you're hurting me," she gasped, twisting her face away as Spike tried to kiss her hard on the mouth.

He smelled of cheap wine, cheap cologne, and stale perspiration. His blunt-featured face was glistening with droplets of sweat, and his white T-shirt was plastered to his muscular torso. They were by now surrounded by a crush of other dancers. And as Spike called out to someone over his shoulder, Roxanne took the opportunity to duck beneath his arm and escape into the flowing, twisting crush of happily perspiring bodies.

Even though it was well past four o'clock in the morning, the lower floors of the mansion seemed like some mad nightmare of overpopulation. There seemed to be people everywhere, and it was clear that the party had been in progress for some time. The portable bar set up by caterers in the lower hall was littered with empty liquor bottles, and cast-off canapé trays had been emptied of all but a few bits of wilting parsley and curling slices of cheese.

Roxanne couldn't seem to locate Abbey anywhere, but it was clear that she had spared no expense. Roxanne could only imagine the ultimate cost in food and liquor, not to mention the damage done to the antique furniture and priceless Persian carpets.

Ever since her mother's death, Abbey had been on a mad spending spree, and already Roxanne had received thousands of dollars in unpaid bills and overdue dunning notices.

Roxanne had visions of Annabel Randolph turning over in her white coffin, as portraits of Abbey's Randolph and Ryan forebears peered down with dour and disapproving faces from the other side of time. Watching like medieval inquisitors as the drums rolled, the lights dimmed, and a spotlight suddenly hit the middle of the dance floor, with a circular cone of hard white brilliance.

"And now," the lead guitar player announced into the microphone. "We have the wild and woolly pleasure of presenting one of the hottest night club acts in the Hamptons. Di-rect from the Pink Pussy Cat in Bridgehampton, I most ecstatically present . . . the one and only . . . Acid Queen!"

Amid thunderous applause, a tall and elegantly feline woman moved out into the cone of light as the crowd fell back to form a circle about her. Her skin was the texture of black velvet, and her features appeared to have been carved out of ebony. A brazenly savage beauty, she stood there for a moment in her

215

glittering sequined G-string, as wave after wave of applause, shouts, and piercing wolf whistles filled the hot and smoky air.

Then the band began to play, and the Acid Queen started to move with the music, clapping her hands and picking up the beat with her wildly undulating hips. A long feather boa was wrapped snakelike about her arms, and she reached out slowly, with palms outstretched, drawing her audience to her with long, crimson-taloned fingers.

By the time that the Acid Queen had begun to sing in a low, throaty baritone, Roxanne had managed to slip through the throng and make her way up the staircase, which was crowded with onlookers. She reached the upper landing, just as the singer sprang into the air, cracking her feather boa like a whip between her legs.

Wildly rocking her torso from side to side, and riding the shimmering black feathers with a savage animal motion, she quickly sent the fever chart zig-zagging upward into an explosion of deafening applause.

The sound followed Roxanne down the upper hall and into Abbey's sitting room, where she closed the door behind her. She took a deep breath. Then, with a frown clouding her features, Roxanne allowed her gaze to follow a trail of casually discarded clothing, which finally terminated at the partially closed bedroom door.

The music was still pounding and throbbing from down below, and the Acid Queen's voice had risen to a shrieking wail. Roxanne tiptoed quietly to the door and bent to listen.

From inside, there was a banging sound and the creak of innersprings, as the bed heaved up and down with a playful, erratic motion. She heard a shrill cry, a bump, and a hoarse male voice. Then the agitation settled down to a distinctly recognizable rhythm—a steadily mounting beat that brought Roxanne even closer to the door, with her muscles taut as she strained to listen.

Then she pushed open the door and peered inside. The room was bathed with a soft, diffused light, and a gauzy pink scarf had been thrown over the shade of the single lighted lamp. Abbey was lying nude on the bed, and a muscular black man with a wiry Afro was buried between her straining thighs. Their bodies were plunging together in the dimness, and their movements were punctuated by rasping, heavy breathing.

They were both completely nude, and Abbey's pale body had been lavishly adorned from head to foot with crazy swirls of color: bright psychedelic streaks, exploding suns, garish flowers, and free-form geometric patterns.

Her cries started with low whimpering sounds and rose steadily until they finally spiraled off into hysterical sobbing, which continued to gain in tempo as she bucked and wallowed beneath her partner.

As she stood watching and listening, unseen in the doorway, Roxanne found that her palms had grown clammy and moist as the steadily mounting sexual beat of flesh slapping on flesh grew ever more fevered and insistent.

She remained rooted to the spot, listening to Abbey's voice, high-pitched and climbing. "Now, now . . . oh, yes, Jaime . . . give it to me now. . . ."

By the time Roxanne reached the downstairs library, she was in the grip of a deadly calm. She knew now what she had to do, and Abbey had only herself to blame for the consequences.

Fortunately, the room was empty, even though dirty glasses and overflowing ashtrays were clearly in evidence. There were burned places where cigarettes had been ground out on the richly patterned Oriental carpets, and hundreds of leather-bound volumes had been tumbled from the floor-to-ceiling bookcases.

Roxanne needed a drink badly and after locking the

door behind her, she went immediately to the tall Chinese lacquer cabinet, where Annabel had always kept a bottle of the very finest Dominique sherry. The crystal decanter rattled against the glass as she poured herself a generous portion and gulped it down in two quick swallows.

Quickly, Roxanne refilled her glass and began to pace the room slowly, formulating a plan of action. Behind her, the great grandfather clock struck the hour of five in solemn, ponderous tones, while from the wall above the mantelpiece, a life-size portrait of Annabel Randolph stared down at her with accusing and icy hauteur.

Roxanne felt better now. The sherry had worked effectively to level out her thoughts, even though the shock and indignation remained. She would not soon forget the humiliation she had been forced to endure that evening, and there was a look of firm resolution on her features as she finally stepped to the desk and picked up the phone.

"This is an emergency," she said after dialing the operator. "I want you to connect me with Dr. Seymour Jacobsen, the director of the Broadmoor State Mental Hospital in Riverhead. This is Mrs. Roxanne Ryan Aristos calling."

# =====CHAPTER 17=====

Jason felt as if he were emerging from a long tunnel of darkness. Vague fingers of nausea probed his stomach, and his head throbbed with a heavy, dull insistence. He didn't know where he was, or even how he had gotten there. But since his car keys were in his coat pocket, he had to assume that he had probably driven there under his own volition and that the Lotus was parked somewhere nearby.

He sat up and looked about him. The air was close and warm, redolent of the sickly sweet smell of burning hashish. There had obviously been a party, which was still in progress, although most of those remaining appeared strung out and lethargic—vague forms drifting off into the limbo of the morning after, against a background soundtrack of soft music from the radio, murmuring voices, and the sound of someone sobbing in another room.

With the room spinning around him, Jason rose unsteadily to his feet. Somehow, he managed to make his way to the bathroom, and once inside, he stood bracing himself over the toilet. He thought he was going to be sick, but nothing came.

Finally, after letting the cold water run from the tap, he bathed his face, dried it on a soiled towel, and then stood staring at his own stubbled reflection, trying to rearrange the shattered mirrors of his mind.

According to his calendar watch, it was 5:15 in the morning on July 22. That meant that he had been spaced out on booze and drugs for over two weeks, drifting aimlessly on a psychedelic sea, without conscious direction or remorse. His clothes hung on his frame, and he had obviously lost weight, while his eyes were haunted and badly bloodshot.

How many of them had there been, he wondered? Fragments of the past two weeks began to emerge in his consciousness, like dark and turbulent currents rising to the surface of a still pond. There seemed to have been numerous hands coming out of the darkness to submerge him with tactile sensations, hands that passed him from one to another as if his body no longer belonged to him but was simply an instrument upon which others played. Time somehow had been suspended. His heavily drugged emotions trod a wild, uncharted path as he churned within a writhing coil of arms, legs, and naked male torsos.

An anguished cry came from somewhere deep within him, and Jason shut his eyes against the gaunt and haggard face staring back at him from the mirror. Then the bathroom door banged open, and Jason spun around to find a tall black woman framed in the doorway, her face painted like a garish white mask.

"So you finally slept it off," she said, closing the door behind her. She swigged deeply from the bottle of Mountain Cherry wine that she held in her hand. Then she regarded him quizzically from beneath thick false eyelashes. "You ain't forgotten me, have you honey child? Like the song says . . . 'After all, we was more than friends.'"

"Look," Jason said, squinting against the harsh fluorescent light. "I need a fix bad . . . have you got anything?"

The girl laughed, producing a chromium inhaler and waving it beneath his nostrils. "The Acid Queen always has *something,* pretty baby. But there ain't nothing in this life for free. It's gonna cost you."

Jason fumbled in his pocket, only to discover that

220

he hadn't a cent on him. The popper, however, had by now taken effect and his brain ballooned, pulsing with blood. The room whirled about him, as his vision alternately faded and then refocused with brilliant clarity and changing color. Everything suddenly seemed to be slightly bigger than life, wavering and distorted.

He swayed and would have fallen, had the woman not stepped forward to catch him in her arms. Then she was pressing him up against the wall with her body, and her snakelike tongue was invading his mouth.

It all seemed to be happening to someone else. Jason was still too strung out and disoriented to respond, and he simply clung there, his arms draped over the towel rack, as the girl dropped down to her knees, deftly unzipped his pants, and began going down on him.

He felt dizzy and nauseous as her scent rose, cloying and musky, to fill his nostrils. Jason pushed her away. "I'm sick," he grunted. "I need something bad . . . some meth or speed, anything you got."

The girl rose reluctantly, her thick lips pursed into a pout as she tugged futilely at his limp organ. A faint patina of perspiration was beading the white pancake by now, and her deep voice had turned slightly hostile. "So you still don't remember me," she accused. "Well, sweet cakes, this may go a long way to jog your memory."

With that, the Acid Queen unzipped her skirt, let it fall around her platform heels, and kicked it away from her. Then she stood there, posing in a sequined G-string, long black mesh stockings, and a feathered black boa.

Staring hard, Jason realized that the legs were far too muscular to be a woman's legs. Then she peeled off her sequined G-string to expose a man's genitals, hanging full and loose like dark primeval fruit, from a black thicket of curling hair.

Jason swayed dizzily, shaking his head as if to

221

clear it of the specter of other legs and other men. Then he dragged his hand across his mouth and spit on the floor, as the drag queen laughed with a low, throaty purr. "That's right, white boy. I'm a grade-A prime cut all-American male."

He grasped Jason's cock and jerked it several times, until it became tumescent. "Does that do anything to jog your memory? Like maybe last weekend in the meat rack at Fire Island Pines?"

Jason gave a choking, strangled cry and lunged forward. Then he began beating the drag queen to the tiles with his bare fists, as the queen shrieked and clawed at his face with long, raking nails.

It felt good to hear the screams echoing somewhere off on the edge of consciousness, to see the terror in the bulging eyes as one of Jason's hands closed about the sinewy black throat. There was a shatter of glass as Jason broke the wine bottle against the side of the tub. "You lying faggot bastard," he grunted as the drag queen twisted and struggled beneath him. Then the broken bottle descended with lightning speed, slashing and stabbing until there seemed to be blood everywhere.

Jason sucked in his breath as his eye caught the speedometer. It rested on 95 for a moment and then began rising steadily to 100. Then it rose to 105 miles an hour, rocketing the twin-cam Lotus through the gray dawn.

The siren shrieking in full pursuit was dropping away now, although the flashing red light atop the highway patrol car was still clearly visible in the rearview mirror. Jason's face was a gaunt mask, while his eyes were feverishly glazed with the speed and the adrenalin shooting through his veins.

Bearing down even harder on the accelerator, Jason increased his speed to 110, propelling the Lotus faster

222

and faster, until the wail of the pursuing police car had diminished to a distant shriek.

The horror of what had taken place at Bramwell Acres was behind him now, and Jason concentrated on handling the wheel with the precise skill he had always exercised as a top-flight racing car driver.

Going fast had always been a basic need for Jason. Ever since his youth, he had always been possessed by the belief that if he could somehow go fast enough, someday he would be able to break through some phantom psychological barrier and know liberation for the first time in his life.

Jason tried not to think. He simply allowed the car to absorb his reflexes as well as the maelstrom of emotions that had come to govern his very existence. He was afraid—afraid of what he had done, and what the consequences might be if he were caught.

Up ahead, the dark, bulky shape of a large diesel presented an obstacle that had to be overcome if he was to retain his freedom. Its red taillights blinked a sharp warning as the truck banked into a blind curve and began mounting a steep incline on the narrow two-lane highway leading out to Montauk.

A slow smile traced Jason's lips as he shifted through the gears and hunched up low over the wheel, even as he caught sight of a long, snaking military convoy coming in the opposite direction. He saw his chance to put the highway patrol and the events of the past two weeks behind him forever—one way or another. It would be a test of his own courage as a man and his inborn instinct for survival.

The speedometer was fluctuating wildly at 115 miles per hour now, and the supercharger screamed as Jason jammed the gas pedal to the floor. He pulled the wheel hard to the left, hung on tightly as he passed the truck in the oncoming lane, and then let out an exuberant whoop as he missed the first jeep in the military convoy by no more than a matter of feet.

Jason's laughter was brimming with hysteria as, several miles further on, he skidded off the Montauk State Parkway onto East Lake Drive, heading hell-bent-for-leather toward the secluded marshy woodlands around Shagwong Point.

Finally, after leaving the two-lane road to bump along for several more miles on a muddy, rutted track, he secreted the Lotus among the dense undergrowth and set out running on foot, slipping and slogging through the tall marsh grass until he got in sight of Oyster Pond near Montauk Point.

By then, the dawn was breaking with a dull, leaden overcast, and the pond shimmered up ahead through the trees, looking hazy and unspoiled. By the time Jason finally managed to reach the secluded far side, he was breathing in short, rasping gasps, and his legs would barely support him any longer.

He finally stumbled into a small clearing surrounded by tall reeds and a thicket of wild blackberry vines. From there, he could look out across the smooth, unruffled expanse of water in the direction from which he had come. And a quick scan of the area convinced him that he had not been followed.

By now, Jason's clothes were torn and splattered with mud. But it wasn't until he sank gasping to the spongy groundcover that he realized his shirt was splattered with dried blood as well. He didn't want to remember what had taken place earlier that morning, for the past two weeks gaped like a black abyss, and to allow any single event to surface was to risk tumbling backward into the void.

No one need ever know, he promised himself. He would simply shut it all away behind a door in his mind, the same way he had shut out the accident that had taken the lives of 16 innocent bystanders—16 men, women, and children needlessly slaughtered in one of the worst car-racing catastrophes on record.

There had been a time when Baron Jason Von Bismark had come very close to having achieved his ambition of becoming the fastest man in the world. His ego had demanded the speed, the adulation of the cheering crowds, and the vindication that came only with winning—at least as far as his father was concerned.

Then it had all ended abruptly at the Grand Prix in Monte Carlo in 1974. Jason had been lagging no more than a few seconds behind the lead car on that brilliant sunlit day, and he had known that he was going to lose.

Trying the impossible from behind the wheel of a powerful Mach II, he had been cut off on a steeply graded inside curve. The car had somersaulted once, burst through a retaining wall into a cluster of onlookers, and ended up as little more than a pile of twisted, smoking metal.

Jason himself had been an integral part of that wreckage, and after being miraculously pulled from the flames, he had spent almost a year in a Swiss sanitarium. His body had been at least partially reassembled by a team of world-famous surgeons. Yet there was scarcely a part of him that had not been broken, crushed, or fractured.

Never once, during all that time, did he hear one single word from his father, Stavros Aristos. Yet Jason had survived the pain and remorse, even though the agonies endured had led to a dependence on drugs that had never been broken.

The scars had gone far deeper than what was actually visible on the surface, and shortly after his release from the hospital, he had fallen easy prey to a she-bitch like Helene—a castrating predator who by her very nature fed upon the wreckage of human lives.

Dazed, strung out, and exhausted, Jason fell into a stupor, until he was suddenly brought back to the moment by the startled flight of quail from the nearby thicket. Then someone was standing over him. Raising his head from the pillow of his arms, he looked up into the deadly muzzle of a double-barreled shotgun, clasped firmly in the hands of a uniformed highway patrolman.

"Okay, sicko . . . on your feet," the man barked. "You're going to have a lot of explaining to do in front of a federal judge."

Just under 24 hours later, Jason was quietly released from jail and driven back to Miramar by the lawyer Helene had retained to represent him. She had had him flown down from Boston in her private plane, and while his fees were astronomical, his name alone was enough to make judges sit up and take notice.

It was just after 10:30 in the morning when Jason entered the house, with a bad case of the shakes. He needed a quick fix in the worst way and was scarcely able to stagger up the stairs.

Loretta, the black day maid, was busy emptying the drawers of his bureau when Jason appeared, slumped in the doorway. Clothes were strewn everywhere—torn from hangers, draped across chairs, and piled in heaps as if they had been thrown from their closets, along with a whirlwind assortment of ties, sport shirts, and various accessories overflowing from a large packing case.

"What the hell is this?" Jason demanded.

Loretta turned to regard him, and her eyes widened in shocked surprise at his gaunt and disheveled appearance. "Don't ask me, Mr. Jason. The baroness herself must have tore this place apart sometime last night. It was like a cyclone hit the place when I come to work this morning. All she said to me was pack it up, and have all your belongings moved to the guest bedroom in the east wing."

In the next instant, a chalk-faced Jason bolted past the startled maid and stumbled into the bathroom,

226

slamming the door behind him just as the first wave of nausea hit hard. His body stiffened and he lurched to his knees, retching miserably into the toilet bowl as his belly began to heave.

For the next ten minutes, Jason gagged and vomited until a sour, burning sensation filled his nose and pointless self-pitying tears coursed aimlessly down his cheeks. He felt chopped into fragments, as the bathroom spun about him in a sickening kaleidoscope of gleaming white tile, yellow monogrammed towels, and brilliant porcelain fixtures.

The light was blinding to his eyes, a flood of fluorescence that seemed to bounce off the tile walls, harsh and scorching in its brightness. At last, Jason was able to get to his feet, and he braced himself against the wash basin to keep from falling. He scowled into the mirror, where he was confronted by an ashen-faced, red-eyed stranger, whose tortured features had come to replace his own familiar ones.

Jason opened the medicine cabinet and fumbled frantically with the dial of the safe concealed behind a sliding panel. Then he had it open, and he was swept by a wave of relief as he stood there viewing the rows of small glass ampules filled with clear, colorless fluid. On the shelf below, there were several disposable plastic syringes and more rows of druggists' prescription bottles, containing a variety of pills in every color code imaginable.

Jason felt as if his body no longer belonged to him as he removed one of the ampules and deftly bit off the glass top with his teeth. Then he slipped the cellophane wrapping from a syringe and slowly withdrew the clear liquid with fingers that shook with a palsied tremor.

Scuffing out of his loafers, Jason dropped his suede pants and kicked them off to one side. Then he stripped off his shirt to expose the needle tracks running the length of the veins in both arms. Some had turned to raised sores and appeared purple and angry in the harsh fluorescent light.

His veins were like rubber, but the effects of an intramuscular injection took too long to work. Jason was growing desperate and time was running out. He inserted the needle with practiced fingers, withdrew the clear liquid, and then held the hypodermic needle poised in one hand, as he pumped up his cock with the other.

Then, biting his lip, he stabbed the needle into one of the pulsing veins and stood watching transfixed as the syringe at first filled with blood and then emptied with sickening rapidity.

Helene had sent word for Jason to present himself. And when he reached the pool house some 30 minutes later, Jason appeared to be considerably recovered. His face was clean-shaven, and he had dressed carefully in dark blue slacks, a soft gray cashmere sweater, and Gucci loafers. A pair of rimless tinted glasses managed to conceal the dark hollows around his eyes. His mood was subdued, deeply withdrawn, and apprehensive.

Helene had converted the pool house into a private gym. The decor was strictly Bronx baroque, with indirect lighting, thick pile carpeting, and mirrored walls. Various pieces of expensive chromium exercise equipment gleamed dully in the soft light, and the lush strains of piped-in muzak were muted and almost subliminal.

His wife was just stepping from the sauna as Jason entered. She wore a white terry cloth robe, her hair was drawn up in a towel, and her face was flushed and beaded with moisture. "Well, if it isn't the return of the prodigal," she voiced with deliberate casualness.

Helene was not alone. And as Jason slumped down into a comfortable leather lounger, a man appeared

228

from the adjacent kitchen, carrying a tray bearing a silver coffee service.

"I had Bruno make us some coffee," Helene advised him. "And you look as if you could use it," she said, pouring two cups full of steaming black coffee and handing one across to Jason. "I assume you still take yours black," she added in a voice oozing sarcasm. "It has been a while since you've been home, after all. A wife couldn't really be blamed for forgetting, now could she?"

"Who's the goon?" Jason questioned, nodding toward her burly companion, who remained standing at Helene's side as if somehow rooted to the spot.

The man she had referred to as Bruno was wearing a white starched uniform that contrasted sharply with his swarthy complexion. He was short yet powerfully built with a flat, featureless face and deep-set eyes that remained completely without expression. His head was very smooth and had been shaven clean.

"The new addition to our household is my personal bodyguard," Helene informed him. "Bruno is a man of many talents, who's conveniently both deaf and mute. A perfectly marvelous combination, wouldn't you agree?"

Her laugh was as brittle as breaking glass. "You'd better watch yourself, Jason. Bruno may not be particularly bright, but if I give the word, he's been trained to go straight for the jugular."

"You two should do well together," Jason observed caustically. "But I'm more interested in knowing just how you managed to get me out of jail . . . and what it's going to cost me."

"That, my dear husband, is a saga in itself," Helene informed him brightly, moving toward the massage table. She dropped her robe and stood completely naked for a moment, sipping her coffee and regarding Jason with eyes as coldly distant as far-away stars.

229

Then Bruno helped her up on the padded massage table and draped a towel strategically over her anatomy. There was a look of almost slavish devotion on his features as he rubbed a clear golden oil over her neck and shoulders before setting to work. He slowly massaged the oil into her skin, and Helene went limp beneath his powerful hands.

While he continued to knead her flesh with complete absorption, Helene turned her head to regard Jason beneath lowered lashes. "Now, let me see . . . where were we?" she mused. "Oh yes, I believe the police referred to the matter as 'emasculation.' But I think that's such an ugly word, so we'll just say that you performed a rather crude form of surgery yesterday morning at Bramwall Acres.

"Fortunately for you, Jason, the young man in question had always wanted to be a woman anyway. So the loss of his genitalia was not exactly what you would call a fate worse than death."

Jason swallowed hard, refusing to meet her hard, mocking gaze. "I don't really remember what happened. I guess I must have been pretty strung out when some guy in drag made a pass at me in the john. I must have just lost my head, and when I realized what had happened, all I wanted to do was to get away."

"Carving someone up like a Thanksgiving turkey is not exactly a minor infraction of the law," Helene informed him tartly. "Your victim almost bled to death before they got him to hospital. But as fate would have it, the young man was not in the least unwilling to undergo a complete sex change operation. Although, as you might well imagine, he most likely would have preferred to have the operation done at the hands of a competent surgeon."

"Stop toying with me, Helene. You're like a cat who's captured something she's already decided to kill and eat. You're deliberately prolonging the agony."

"The truth is, Jason, that you've made a very expensive mistake. Fortunately, when I found out what had happened, my lawyer was able to convince the victim that a quarter of a million dollars would go a long way toward making him both the woman of his dreams, as well as financially secure for life.

"I bought you out of this ugly mess, Jason my sweet, and if I hadn't, you could have ended up doing five to ten years in a federal penitentiary, on charges of gross mayhem with intent to commit murder." Her voice dropped to a soft, malicious purr. "That is, of course, if you had been able to convince a jury that you were only doing the manly thing by defending your honor."

"And just what makes you think I wasn't?" Jason demanded.

"Who do you think you're kidding?" Helene drawled. "It wouldn't have taken a really sharp public prosecutor very long to discover that you'd just come from playing with the boys in the sand over on Fire Island. And I don't think they would have had much trouble producing some of your playmates from the St. Mark's Baths, who would have sworn under oath that you were as gay as Chinese pajamas. You see, Jason, I've had a private detective following you for the past two weeks. I know everything there is to know."

Jason suddenly felt as if he were suffocating. He jerked abruptly to his feet and turned away from her, crossing to stand and look out the window. The children were playing on the lawn outside, beneath the watchful gaze of their Irish nanny. Running and laughing in the sunlight, they were totally unaware and untouched by the stark drama playing itself out in the pool house.

They're like perfect strangers to me, Jason thought. My own children, and I don't even know them at all. The three of us are merely hostages to Helene's ambitions . . . and there's going to be no end to it, unless someone does something to stop her.

"All right," he said, turning slowly to face her. "What do you intend to do?"

Helene smiled and stretched like an opulent animal, as Bruno's hands moved down to massage the soft flesh of her buttocks. "As the first order of business, I'm going to blast Mr. Kamal Ali Reza out of the water with the hottest political sex scandal of the decade. Then you and I and Dr. Clayton Spencer are going to pay sister Andrea a visit aboard the *Golden Hind,* where you're going to say and do exactly as I instruct you to."

# CHAPTER 18

During the first 12 hours following the accident, Claire remained in a semicoma—merely an observer, an inner witness, watching a procession of fractured images move across the shattered mirrors of her mind, like an endlessly running slide projector.

She saw it all—her entire life—and was almost reluctant to return to the present. She retreated instead down the corridors of memory, from the failure of her marriage to Clayton and the prospect of an uncertain future now that she knew the truth about herself.

When she finally did awaken from her long sleep, Claire was informed by her doctor that she had miraculously escaped death with little more than a rather serious concussion and a variety of minor injuries that would heal in time of their own accord. "You're a very fortunate woman to be alive at all," the doctor told her, since the car had been almost totally demolished.

When she was informed that her husband was waiting to see her, Claire refused to have any visitors. More than anything else, she wanted Clayton to take her in his arms and say that everything was going to be all right. But Claire knew in her heart that her own personal battle was yet to be waged and won.

For slightly over two weeks, she lay there in the dazzling clinical whiteness of her hospital room, feeling as if her very being had been displaced into a different continuum of existence. In some ways she was no longer part of the world she had left behind, while in others, Claire had never been more acutely aware of living in the present moment.

Roxanne was waiting in front of the hospital for her when Claire was finally released. And as she watched her sister bid the nurses a fond farewell and move briskly down the walk toward the car, Roxanne realized that Claire had changed.

She was wearing a tightly belted trenchcoat, and her hair had been cropped short and styled simply. There was a sprinkling of gray evident for the first time. And without benefit of cosmetic artifice her features appeared reserved almost to the point of severity.

"I appreciate your offer to pick me up," Claire said as she slid into the back seat of the car and the chauffeur closed the door behind her. "I feel as if I'm making a re-entry from outer space."

"Why did you refuse to see me after the accident?" Roxanne questioned. "You must have known I would be frantic with concern."

Claire turned to regard her with a clear, questioning gaze. "Have you ever really been frantic about anything, Roxanne? Other than your clothes, your jewels, and your bank balance?"

It was more a statement of fact than an accusation, and there was no malice in Claire's tone. "Well, I certainly didn't come all the way out here to be insulted," Roxanne said. "I simply thought you might need a little moral support after your . . . ordeal."

"I'm sorry," Claire expressed with genuine regret. "I didn't mean to be unkind. But you see, Roxanne, I'm through living with lies. That's why I refused to see you in the hospital. Our relationship has been a lie ever since we were children together. I always wanted so much to be just like you. But now I see that I've lived my life for all the wrong reasons."

By now the car was pulling away from the curb and starting off along the tree-lined street. "You know that

234

Clayton's moved out of the house, of course," Roxanne informed her a bit apprehensively.

Claire nodded, averting her eyes to look out the window. "I know," she said. "His lawyer contacted me in the hospital to say that Clayton was filing for a divorce."

There was a long moment of silence, then Roxanne squeezed her sister's hand and said brightly, "I have a simply marvelous idea. Why don't we have lunch at the Maidstone Club? It's a heavenly day, and you've got a lot of catching up to do. I'm sure lots of your friends will be there, and it will do you good to get back into the swing of things as quickly as possible."

"I'd appreciate your dropping me at home," Claire responded. "That life's behind me now . . . and I guess I'm going to have to find out on my own just where I go from here. There seems to be some kind of chasm left in my life with nothing to fill it."

Her voice was without the slightest taint of self-pity. It was simply an admission of fact, stated calmly by a woman who seemed to have found her own center of gravity at last. More than anything else, Claire needed to explore that factor in her life, to look out upon the world with new eyes and nurture the growing hope that it was still not too late.

She lit a cigarette and turned to look into her sister's face. "There's something I think I had better tell you for your own good," Claire said. "It's about Kamal Ali Reza. He's not the man he appears to be. If you let him, he's going to destroy you. I saw the way you looked at him the night of your party . . . and I feel it's only fair to warn you."

"What exactly do you mean by that?"

"I was having an affair with him," Claire confessed.

"You?"

"Yes, amusing isn't it? Little sister Claire, who was always a second stringer, having an affair with a man I knew you would move heaven and earth to bag on

235

your own. In fact, I was so carried away with the whole idea that I had to get falling-down drunk every time we went to bed together."

"Quite obviously you've been out of touch for far too long," Roxanne observed. "But this ought to set you straight at least as far as Ali Reza is concerned."

Roxanne leaned forward to retrieve a copy of the *Hampton Reporter* from a pocket on the back of the driver's seat. Then she carefully folded it to the Cassandra column and handed the paper to Claire:

### "THE INCREDIBLE LOVE AFFAIR OF ANDREA AND KAMAL."

Everybody's talking about it, and why shouldn't they be, since it is, after all, *the* match of the season. The word is out. Andrea Aristos has fallen head over heels in love with swinging petro-dollar tycoon Kamal Ali Reza.

The gold-dust duo have been setting Manhattan ablaze with a round of partying that has cost a fortune and triggered the vitriolic anger of the Hampton Historical Society. That venerable Old Guard institution claims that while Ali Reza romances Miss Megabucks into the wee hours in the Big Apple's tonier bistros, his minions are actively involved in dismembering one of our most valuable natural resources—namely, Treasure Cay.

The Society has been joined in its cries of outrage by prominent environmentalists around the nation, who are vowing to oppose the project all the way to the Supreme Court, if necessary.

Absolutely everyone seems to be up in arms, and not just over Treasure Cay. When Andrea wears that 43-carat Grand Mogul diamond that Kamal presented her with the other night, it does more than "kill" every other piece of jewelry between Easthampton and Palm Beach. Its impact is felt south to Washington, D.C. and north to

236

Albany, where a bill is currently before the state legislature legalizing gambling on what used to be known as Hanlan's Island.

The Aristos-Ali Reza romance was kicked off in super style with a madcap week of sumptuous parties and being seen in all the right places. "Kamal is a very charming, intelligent, and extremely attractive man," Andrea has been quoted as confiding to intimates. "He's rich enough in his own right to be totally indifferent to my money, and he's taught me what happiness is for the first time in my life."

Rumor has it that one of the ways in which Ali Reza makes people happy is by giving them envelopes full of crisp green U.S. dollars in large denominations. In fact, there are a good many Congressmen and Senators in the nation's capital who will tell you right off that Kamal Ali Reza is a superb, elegant, and extremely generous host who doesn't like to see anyone go home empty-handed.

People are even saying that Kamal spends money as if its a disease, and if that's true, then Andrea's caught it. In fact, on a recent visit to Manhattan, she must have established a record in speed of buying, as she swept like a whirlwind through several east side boutiques and more than a score of smart Fifth Avenue shops.

In her wake, all was chaos. Stores looked more or less like a battlefield after a mortar attack. Open boxes, tissue paper, and order blanks were strewn all over the counters, while exhausted sales personnel racked up a series of stunning commissions.

In most cases, the store's manager broke out a bottle of champagne to celebrate the windfall. When Andrea blitzes a store it's almost the same as having a "By special appointment to the Queen," tacked in the window.

One unofficial tally of the damages added up to over $80,000, and that was before Kamal joined her at Cartier's, where he whimsically purchased her a pair of ruby pendant earrings as big as strawberries.

Claire's eyes fell away from the column. She didn't need to read any more to realize that Kamal was using Andrea to gain his own ends. God help her, she thought. Somebody really ought to warn the poor kid about what she's getting into, before it's too late.

Then she chanced to see a public notice toward the bottom of the page, announcing that Bramwell Acres was being sold at auction along with all its furnishings.

"What's this all about?" Claire demanded, turning to confront Roxanne.

"I'm sorry to have to tell you about it so soon after your release from the hospital," Roxanne sighed. "I simply had no choice but to have Abbey committed to Broadmoor State Mental Hospital. Kelly De Witte has broken off the engagement, and the things going on out at Bramwell Acres simply had to be seen to be believed. The mansion had become nothing but a pit stop for drugs, sex, and all manner of wild goings-on."

Claire could scarcely believe her ears. "Good Lord, Roxanne. Abbey Randolph is a very confused and frightened young woman. But she's not insane. How could you possibly have done such a thing? Why, the poor child must be utterly terrified in that place."

"Abbey is not a child," Roxanne informed her sharply. "She was bound to self-destruct. Psychosis was as natural to her as breathing. She's a desperately ill twenty-eight-year-old woman who needs help—the kind of help Dr. Jacobsen can give her at Broadmoor—and that's all there is to it. I do not wish to discuss the matter further."

"Well that's just not good enough. I want to know

238

exactly how all this came about, and I'm not going to be satisfied until I get the right answers."

"Oh, it's all very well for you to carry on," Roxanne said in icy tones. "When Bramwell Acres was literally being sacked of everything of value, and Abbey was upstairs fucking half the U.S. fleet, where were you?"

"Conveniently for you, I was in the hospital, or this never would have happened."

"Indeed you were—after trying to kill yourself over some wretched Arab who simply used you and then tossed you away when he got good and bored. Don't get too precious with me, sister Claire. Not after the kind of spectacle you've made of yourself, sleeping around and drinking yourself into oblivion with a lot of flash trash social climbers. To tell you the truth, I don't blame Clayton one bit for walking out on you. The man's a saint to have put up with you for as long as he has. All those tawdry little affairs of yours with any man who gave you a second glance."

"I'm not at all proud of what I've become," Claire said quietly. "A desperate middle-aged woman aging without grace and trying frantically to become a carbon copy of a sister I don't even like very well. But that doesn't change anything. I think what you've done to Abbey is utterly despicable, and I don't intend to let you get away with it."

With that, Claire leaned forward and rapped on the glass window closing off the driver's seat. "You can let me out at the next corner," she said. "Suddenly I have the need to breathe some fresh air. Something about this whole thing smells very fishy to me."

# ═══CHAPTER 19═══

Andrea sat in the dimness of the master's cabin with one of Kamal's Soubranie Oval cigarettes burning to ashes between her fingers. She was sitting perfectly still in her father's chair behind a gleaming mahogany desk, and there was a leopardskin coat draped about her shoulders.

Kamal had flown to Washington that morning to appear before a Congressional committee, and the headlines of the *Hampton Reporter* lying on the desk before her read: "ALI REZA SUBPOENAED IN SEX AND INFLUENCE-PEDDLING SCANDAL."

Just 24 hours before, Andrea had considered herself to be the happiest and perhaps the luckiest young woman in the world. It had nothing to do with being the richest, and everything to do with being gloriously in love with Kamal Ali Reza.

Her happiness had begun to disintegrate, however, as Kamal's helicopter touched down at Easthampton Airport the evening before. They had attended the theater in Manhattan, dined at Regine's, and then returned to Long Island, arriving just before midnight.

Much to their amazement, they had stepped from Kamal's helicopter to find a hostile throng straining against the chain-link fences surrounding the field. The entire scene had been bathed in the bright glare of television arc lights, and when they reached the terminal, they were literally mobbed by reporters and photographers.

The demonstration had been sparked, Andrea was to learn later, by a speech Roxanne had given that evening before a meeting of the Hampton Historical Society. The auditorium had been packed, and in the course of her delivery, Roxanne had accused Kamal of being a carpetbagging megalomaniac, whose greed and plans for exploitation posed a grave and growing threat not only to the ecology of Treasure Cay, but to the social and economic stability of the Hamptons as well.

Her statement had immediately gone out over all the wire services, adding fuel to the growing controversy over the Offshore Gambling Bill being debated by the legislature in Albany. During their short flight out from Manhattan, a federal judge had been persuaded to place a restraining order on any further development of the Treasure Cay project, and the scene that awaited them at the Easthampton Airport came as a complete surprise.

Crowded relentlessly by the press and surrounded by a smothering blanket of maximum security prompted by anonymous bomb threats, the two of them had been swept into the heaving, shoving crush, with flashbulbs exploding on every side. And the photographs appearing in newspapers around the globe the following day showed Andrea clutching tightly to Kamal's hand, while the leopardskin coat was half falling from her shoulders, and only emphasized the desperate set of her features.

But that was only the beginning. Moments later, as they were ushered into Kamal's limousine, a demonstration organized by various local environmental groups suddenly spilled across the wooden police barricades and surrounded the car with a sea of angry, chanting voices.

Rudely lettered placards denouncing the Treasure Cay project were waving by the hundreds, and a montage of jeering, hate-filled faces pressed up close against

241

the windows as the car was pelted with rotten fruit and rocked crazily back and forth.

In the end, the police had been forced to wade in with clubs and tear gas canisters, while a motorcycle escort had cleared a path through the general melee with screaming sirens. It had all proven to be a shattering experience for Andrea, and throughout the day, she had virtually been held prisoner aboard the yacht by a flotilla of small craft jammed to the gunwales with journalists, all demanding that she make a statement.

Andrea glanced at the clock on her father's desk and saw that it was time for the six o'clock news. She pressed the remote control to switch on the television screen against the far wall. Somehow, she was almost afraid of what she might see, and yet she had to know the latest developments.

"This is the Mutual Television Network bringing you a televised on-the-spot report of the fastest breaking story of the day."

The camera zeroed in to focus on the figure of a television newsman broadcasting from the steps of the U.S. House of Representatives in Washington. "Things are happening fast and furiously here in Washington, where a Congressional hearing has just convened, investigating charges of bribery and corruption in high places.

"One of the principal figures in the investigation arrived only minutes ago after being subpoenaed to answer questions regarding his relationships with certain members of both the House and Senate. His name is Kamal Ali Reza, and the influence-peddling investigation has come about even as the Albany Legislature debates an offshore gambling proposition that would literally create a private gambling fiefdom for the Middle Eastern oil magnate.

"Rumors are flying here in Washington in regard to a mystery witness, who is said to be Mr. Ali Reza's

242

mistress as well as the reputed madam of a local brothel. Her name is Barbara Van Patten, and she surfaced just after copies of a confidential State Department report detailing Ali Reza's alleged illegal activities was mailed anonymously to the *Washington Globe*.

"Now that the report has been made public and Miss Van Patten has agreed to become a voluntary witness under oath before the committee, congressmen and senators are said to be scrambling for cover. There are unconfirmed reports of 'a little black book' said to contain some of the most important political names in Washington, and according to Miss Van Patten's lawyers, their client is prepared to tell everything she knows, if granted immunity from prosecution."

The camera panned around to zero in on the shapely figure of a young woman emerging from a car flanked by a squad of lawyers. Her long, willowy legs were booted to the knee in soft sable leather. Flashbulbs exploded as she started up the steps of the building, and the press closed in to thrust bouquets of microphones in her face.

"Can you tell us, Miss Van Patten, if the allegations are true that you arranged sexual favors for important politicians at the express request of Mr. Kamal Ali Reza?"

The girl, wearing a scarf and oversize dark glasses, was tight-lipped and unsmiling as she nodded. "Yes, that's true."

"Did Mr. Ali Reza also induce you to give some of these men envelopes of money in order to influence legislation favorable to the Middle Eastern oil-producing countries represented by Mr. Ali Reza?"

Once again the girl nodded, as her lawyers hovered at her side with bulging briefcases.

"Is it true that you were Mr. Ali Reza's mistress, Miss Van Patten?"

She pulled off her scarf at this point and ran her

fingers back through her long, lustrous blonde hair. "I was one of them," she said. "We've had a long-standing relationship that was both financial and sexual."

At this point, one of her lawyers stepped in and suggested that his client was not really at liberty to discuss the matter further until after her appearance before the committee.

"One more question, please, Miss Van Patten. As Mr. Ali Reza's mistress . . . or at least one of them —why have you come forth to give evidence before this committee that could result in an indictment naming Mr. Ali Reza being handed down?"

In response, the girl threw back her head and whipped off her dark glasses to expose her battered face. Both eyes had been blackened and one was almost swollen shut, while puffy swellings had distorted her beautiful features into a grotesque mask.

Andrea pressed the remote control and watched the screen go blank. Then she pressed another button, and a mahogany panel noiselessly slid into place to cover the set entirely. She felt chilled and pulled the leopard-skin coat that Kamal had given her more closely about her shoulders. Her hands gently caressed the sleeves as if there was something vaguely reassuring about the rich feel of the pelts against her flesh—almost, she thought, as if the opulent and feline power of the leopards themselves might be mysteriously transmitted to her, giving her strength and making her invulnerable to the ugly and relentless forces that seemed suddenly to be closing in upon her.

"Kamal," she said, whispering his name as she lifted a silver-framed photograph in her hands. She had taken the picture herself aboard the *Golden Hind*, and Kamal had been standing at the railing, with Southampton yacht harbor in the background.

His smiling, handsome features were almost boyishly beguiling, and the sky and sea had been a brilliant postcard blue. Kamal was wearing trunks, and between his long, straddling legs, which were planted as firmly as oaks, the masts of yachts were plainly visible, as though he bestrode the harbor like a colossus.

No, Andrea simply refused to believe it. Kamal was too kind and considerate—always the perfect gentleman. He wasn't a monster.

A knock on the door caused Andrea to replace the picture on the desk and call, "Come in."

The door swung open and the first mate poked his head inside to announce that the Baron and Baroness Von Bismark had come aboard with a Dr. Clayton Spencer and were asking to see her on a matter they said was of the utmost importance.

Andrea had insisted on remaining in total seclusion throughout the day. But after Jason's long illness she felt she couldn't very well refuse to see him, even though she preferred to be alone with her thoughts. She needed time to think things out and pull herself together for the ordeal ahead.

Jason was far thinner than he had been when Andrea had seen him last, and there was something haunted and reticent about his eyes.

"I'm afraid I've been terribly preoccupied," Andrea apologized after being introduced to Dr. Spencer. "I really should have gotten in to see you while you were ill."

"I wouldn't let anyone near that virus of his," Helene interjected. "I'm sure it's the same one that half the population dropped dead from in 1924. It's a wonder I didn't get it myself."

"It has been going around," Dr. Spencer put in a bit nervously. Andrea had liked the doctor at once. He was immaculately groomed, and his dazzling white hair gave his tanned features a comfortable TV doctor look coupled with a pleasing bedside manner.

"I asked Dr. Spencer to come here with us today, Andrea, because I have only your best interests at heart. I know how terribly upset you must be with all that's happened, but this just wasn't something that could wait."

Andrea rose and crossed the deep pile rug to draw open the drapes over one of the ports. Then she stood there in profile with the sun washing through the windows to emphasize her huge, thick-lashed eyes. She looked haunted and apprehensive, and Jason's heart went out to her.

My God, he thought, she's blossomed into a lovely and very desirable young woman. Now they're going to eat her alive, and there's absolutely nothing I can do to stop it.

Andrea ran her fingers back through her hair and then turned, clasping her hands together so the huge diamond she wore caught and reflected the light. "Whatever it is you've come to say, I might as well tell you that I've decided to stick by Kamal. He at least deserves the chance to prove his innocence, and I can't help but feel that there's some kind of vendetta behind this whole thing. I can't prove anything, but I'd be willing to bet that somehow Roxanne's behind it all."

"There could be something in what you say," Helene said. "After all, Roxanne is going to Albany next week to try and convince the legislature not to pass the Offshore Gambling bill." Helene shook her head. "Forget it, Andrea, you're grasping at straws. I know it's difficult for you to accept that Kamal is not the man you chose to think he is, but you simply have to face the facts."

Andrea drew herself up. "I'm afraid you'll have to excuse me now. I'm going up on deck to make a statement to the press giving Kamal my full support. I simply won't believe he's guilty unless I hear it from his own lips."

"I wouldn't be too hasty about involving myself further in this if I were you, Andrea." Helene spoke in an imperious voice. It was a "take charge" voice that spoke in well-defined capital letters.

"Dr. Spencer came to me this morning with a story that I insist you hear. It won't be pleasant listening, I can assure you. But since he was kind enough to come here today, the least you can do is listen to what he has to say."

Clayton cleared his throat and leaned slightly forward in his chair. "It's about my wife, Claire," he began. "Perhaps you read in the paper that she recently attempted to commit suicide in a car crash."

Andrea nodded with a puzzled expression. "I've met your wife on several occasions, Dr. Spencer, but what can this possibly have to do with me?"

"The night of Roxanne's party," Clayton went on to relate, "my wife confessed to me that she had been having an affair with Kamal. It was the same night that she tried to take her own life."

Andrea stiffened. "Whoever Kamal may have been involved with before we met is of no concern to me. Your wife's infidelity is your problem, Dr. Spencer, not mine."

"I'm afraid there's more to it than that," he said. Clayton rose and removed a batch of 8 x 10 glossy photographs from a manila folder. Then he moved to the desk where Andrea stood and fanned them out before her eyes.

"These pictures were taken by the medical staff when my wife was admitted to the hospital. Certainly, some of the bruises and abrasions shown were incurred in her accident. But according to Claire's own admission, the numerous cigarette burns on her breasts, thighs, and genitals were inflicted upon her at the hands of Kamal Ali Reza.

"Aside from the fact that it is my wife involved, I came here today because, as a doctor, I have seen such cases of sadistic sexual abuse before. And in my professional opinion, you'd be taking your life into your own hands if you chose to continue your relationship with this man."

"I can't see you anymore," Sarah said. "And I want you to stop coming to my cabin."

Marko's narrow saturnine features turned sullen and mean, and in the next instant, Sarah was gasping for breath as his strong fingers dug into the soft flesh of her throat.

Muttering a guttural obscenity, he bent her hard against his tautly muscled body, and his lips came down to bruise her mouth until Sarah stopped struggling and became as limp and pliant as a doll beneath his hands.

"All right," she gasped. "But this has to be the last time. You've got to give me your word that you won't bother me again."

Marko laughed as he lifted her in his arms and crossed the cabin to lay her down on her bed. His breath was coming in short, harsh rasps by now, and with a single violent motion, he tore off her dress and stripped the gauzy wisp of bikini panties down over her legs.

Sarah lay back and closed her eyes as his hands began to move over her body like strong, punishing weapons. Then suddenly there was the sound of a key being inserted in the door, and seconds later it crashed open as they both remained frozen on the bed.

Helene Von Bismark was the first one to enter the cabin. Behind her was a short but powerfully built man with the mashed-in face of an ex-prize fighter. His naked skull gleamed dully in the light.

"I hope we're not breaking anything up," Helene announced in a deceptively smooth and silky voice. Her eyes were like ice picks and there was a sulphurous smile upon her lips.

"How dare you break in here like this!" Sarah stormed. She slid from the bed and wrapped herself in a silk sheet as Marko stood fumbling with his zipper and a sorely depleted erection. *"Bastardos,"* he grunted, reeling off a string of additional obscenities in his native Greek.

"I might as well warn you, Mrs. Dane, my companion is a professional bodyguard. If your Greek friend here makes one move, Bruno will break him in half."

Sarah, trying desperately to control the wild beating of her heart, didn't doubt for a moment that what Helene said was true. "Just what are you doing coming to my cabin like this?" she demanded. "You have no right, and I simply won't tolerate this invasion of my privacy."

"You have little choice in the matter," Helene informed her, tossing Sarah's missing diary on the bed. "My sister-in-law has already had a look at your intimate jottings . . . and she has given me the distinct pleasure of ordering you off the yacht."

"I have no intention of leaving until I've explained this situation to Andrea," Sarah countered.

Helene's laugh was low and mirthless. "Unfortunately, this has been poor Andrea's day for bad news," she informed her. "At this moment, the poor child is under heavy sedation and in the care of Dr. Spencer. He's given orders that she's not to be disturbed under any circumstances."

"You . . ." Helene said, turning to Marko. "Get out of here, and get back to your quarters, and you're to keep your mouth shut about this entire affair. Those orders come directly from Andrea Aristos, and if you choose not to follow them, you're going to find yourself aboard the next cattle boat heading back for Greece."

"As for you," Helene said to Sarah, as Marko scuffed into his shoes and scurried from the cabin, buttoning his white steward's jacket without a backward glance, "I want you to pack your things within the next twenty minutes, after which you'll be taken ashore in my launch. Needless to say, my sister-in-law is extremely

249

distressed to discover that you've insulted her hospitality by carrying on a tawdry little affair with a member of the crew. She's asked me to inform you that she has absolutely no desire to either see or hear from you again."

Sarah sighed deeply and nodded her head. She felt totally humiliated and almost on the verge of tears. "You've made yourself perfectly clear," she said. "Now if you would be good enough to leave me alone, I'll pack my things and be on deck as quickly as possible."

# ══════CHAPTER 20══════

After being unceremoniously dumped on the South-ampton public pier, with all her worldly belongings, Sarah called a cab and asked the driver to take her to a car rental agency. She simply didn't know what else to do, and she spent the next several hours driving aimlessly around in a Chevy Nova.

Sarah was angry, stunned, and hurt at the way she had been thrown off the *Golden Hind* by Helene Von Bismark. How dare Andrea simply dismiss her with-out at least allowing her friend to state her case? She was wrong ever to have gotten involved with Marko in the first place, and she knew it. But she and Andrea had been the closest of friends for over a year, and the least Sarah felt she deserved was a face-to-face meeting.

No question about it, Sarah thought darkly. Andrea Aristos had changed since their arrival in the Hamp-tons. The rich had flattered and beguiled her, telling her all the things any naive young thing would simply be dying to hear. But she had given Andrea credit for being smarter than that.

Ultimately, Andrea had looked into the mirror that the Hampton social scene presented to all outsiders, and she had seen only what she wanted to see. Andrea had become a star. She was bathed in public adulation wherever she went, while her handsome and dashing lover showered her with expensive gifts and a vision of the future that appeared limitlessly bright with promise.

Only the day before, when Sarah had expressed concern over her relationship with Kamal, Andrea had accused her of being nothing but a professional crepe hanger, a jealous harpy trying to discredit the man she loved because Sarah herself was totally incapable of loving anything beyond a dead man's memory.

Andrea had, of course, apologized later when she found Sarah sobbing in her cabin. But there was some truth in what she had said. Sarah had indeed become obsessed with death and dying. She read everything she could get her hands on regarding the Vietnam war, and she often spent her afternoons in the periodicals section of the Southampton public library, where she read back issues of magazines and played the entire gruesome Vietnam saga over again and again in her head, like an endlessly running slide projector.

By early evening, Sarah found herself in Montauk, and she parked the car across the street from Mama Rosa's Restaurant. Then she got out and began walking along the fishing wharf, with the collar of her trenchcoat turned up high and a floppy-brimmed hat pulled low over her features.

She tried to lose herself in the ceaseless activity going on all about her, and she quickly discovered, much to her amazement, that very little had changed since the days of her childhood, when little Seraphina Bambaccio had known them all: the shaggy-maned baymen with faces and forearms kilned by the sun, the wizened and ancient clammers with the salty tang of the marshlands in their voices and hands as gnarled and darkened as old roots.

It was a cool and breezy evening beneath a crisp slice of moon. The fishing fleet had only just returned with the day's catch, and the market vendors were busily stocking their stalls with fresh cod and halibut, displayed in boxes filled with crushed ice.

How well Sarah remembered the sounds and smells of the fishing wharf! She feasted her eyes on showcases filled with fresh water shrimp, Montauk clams, and slow-eyed sea bass. And while no one seemed to recognize her, she had grown up with the Salerno brothers, whom she stood watching unload their fishing ketch.

Sarah smiled for the first time that day. At the age of 13, she had thought herself hopelessly in love with handsome Tony Salerno. He had been a Marlon Brando look-alike who now was paunchy, middle-aged, and nearly bald.

Sarah had spent most of her childhood under the distinct impression that she had somehow been picked up by the wrong family in the hospital after she was born. As the only girl, her five brothers had both smothered her with familial affection and yet treated her with the customary disdain that only Sicilian men seemed capable of expressing for their women-folk.

For as long as Sarah could remember, she had wanted to get away. It was the finer things in life that she had always aspired to, and her very best instincts had always been in response to beauty and artistry.

The dinner hour at Mama Rosa's was well under way when Sarah finally crossed the street from the waterfront and stood peering in through the windows of the family restaurant. It was by then fully dark outside, and she felt desperately homesick as she watched her brothers waiting on tables and rushing back and forth to the kitchen beneath the watchful eye of Mama Rosa behind the cash register.

Mama Rosa's Restaurant was in many ways, much like the Montauk fish market across the way—bustling, throbbing with life, and totally chaotic. Her younger brother, Rick, and his band alternated between hard rock music for dining and Neapolitan love songs, while his older siblings waited upon the crowded tables, spilled cappuccino with abandon, and all the while argued vehemently about sports, politics, and the size and quality of the day's catch.

Sarah finally got as far as the door before she lost her nerve. She simply had been away for too long, she realized. Then she turned and hurried back across the street toward her car. The outside world had changed her into someone they probably would not even be able to recognize, any more than she was able to recognize herself.

Sarah had no real idea how she ended up at Friendlie's Tavern. She just found herself there around ten o'clock, turning into the parking lot of the garishly illuminated roadhouse with shiny silver siding.

There was a neon "Vacancy" sign blinking on and off in the window of the motel office next door. And in spite of the unappealing nature of the shabby clapboard bungalows, Sarah quickly decided that her wisest course would be to rent a room, at least for the night.

She was in no condition to continue driving. Her nerves were badly frayed, her emotions in turmoil, and the thought of having no place to sleep was suddenly more than she could bear. What she needed most, Sarah decided, was something to eat, a couple of good stiff drinks, at least two Valium, and a long night's rest.

Ten minutes later, Sarah had checked in at the Shady Rest Motel and, clutching the key to bungalow number 12, she hurried toward the brightly lit roadhouse and diner.

The windows were steamy with moisture, and as Sarah stepped through the door, a brash and raucous wash of laughter, hearty male voices, and blaring country-and-western music seemed to submerge her totally. Heads turned as she stood there uncertainly in her trenchcoat with the collar upturned, the floppy felt hat, and a pain of amber-tinted sunglasses covering her eyes. But Sarah kept her eyes fixed straight ahead, as she crossed the worn linoleum flooring to take a seat at the only vacant table.

"I'd like a double vodka on the rocks," Sarah said to the waitress, who approached her table with a slovenly twitch of her behind. "And . . . a steak sandwich, rare."

For a moment, the girl regarded her sullenly, her sallow, pockmarked face stony with indifference. "Aren't you kind of off your beat, honey? The animals get kind of restless about this time of night."

Sarah glanced around, realizing for the first time that there were very few women present. "Just bring my order," she said wearily. "And if you could direct me to the ladies' room, I'd like to freshen up a bit."

The girl's laughter was coarse and grating. "The can's at the far end of the bar," she announced. "We don't get much call for a ladies' room around here."

By the time Sarah returned to her table, the steak sandwich she had ordered had appeared, greasy and unappealing between slices of burnt toast. Even though she had not had anything to eat all day, she pushed it aside, and by the time she had finished her drink, the two Valiums she had taken in the rest room had begun to work on her empty stomach, and she was feeling decidedly better.

Almost magically, the tension in her muscles began to evaporate. And the desperation and fear that had been gnawing at her throughout the day drained slowly away to be replaced by an almost eerie sense of euphoria.

Friendlie's Tavern was, beyond any question, a very different sort of world than the one she had left behind her that afternoon. The men standing along the bar and milling about the jukebox appeared, for the most part, to be truckers or construction workers. The few women present were a decidedly motley and unappealing lot.

Sarah, however, was really beyond caring. She simply sat there, allowing the music to swirl around her as the men cast hungry canine smiles in her direction and the bubbles continued to climb through the brightly lit neon coils of the Schlitz beer sign behind the bar.

The bar continued to get noisier and more crowded until about 11:30, when Ian McVane walked through the door and up to the bar. A drink immediately was placed before him. It was the third time that Sarah had seen him that summer, and he looked to be about three sheets to the wind.

Leaning against the bar as if he needed it for support, Ian simply stood there staring. He didn't move or even touch his drink, and it took Sarah several minutes before she realized that he was staring directly at her. Then he made his way unsteadily toward her table, his drink clutched tightly in his hand.

"You're the girl in the rain at the party," he said in a muffled boozy voice. "I'm sorry, but I'm afraid I've forgotten your name. Do you mind if I join you?"

Sarah motioned him toward a vacant chair. "I'm not sure that I gave you my name," she said. "But anyway . . . it's Sarah. Mrs. Sarah Dane."

Ian just sat there smiling a bit shyly at her. He was like a huge, lovable animal or a big kid, Sarah thought —without pretense of any kind. All his nerve endings seemed to be exposed, and she had the feeling that he might either laugh or cry at any moment.

They talked sporadically about nothing much in particular—the erratic summer weather, and how nice it was to walk in the rain. He was a Leo and she was an Aries, which shouldn't have worked at all, but somehow it did—a fact that made them both laugh.

People kept coming over and sponging drinks, demanding Ian's attention. They were so condescending and ass-kissing that it made Sarah increasingly resentful of the intrusion. The denizens of Friendlies were parasites who fed off Ian, just like the rich who bought his paintings for fabulous sums because they just happened to go with the decor.

By midnight, it had become increasingly clear to Sarah that Ian needed all the attention; he played directly into the hands of his audience. He needed it the way he needed the booze to let go, to implode and make contact with that inner space that was so deeply locked inside him, as it was in every truly great artist.

He had a tremendous physical as well as intellectual appeal. He was a great bear of a man with powerful shoulders, rugged Anglo-Saxon features, and big, strong journeyman's hands. His blunt fingers were stained from chain smoking Pall Mall cigarettes, and his eyes were perhaps his best feature—full of blue sky and anguish and fixed somewhere beyond that particular time and place.

Sarah didn't mind. It was enough just to sit there and know his genius and his warmth. "What's a classy uptown lady like you doing in a dump like this?" he finally asked. Ian took her hand and turned it over to study the palm like a fortuneteller. "I see at least one marriage here—a very strong career drive, and a tall, light-haired man who loves you very much but doesn't seem to be very much in the picture right at the moment."

"A perfect score," Sarah said without smiling. "My husband was lost over Vietnam. He was a bomber pilot flying his last mission when his plane went down. After three years, he's still listed as an M.I.A., which kind of puts an uptown sort of lady like me in limbo. Sometimes it reminds me of how they used to bury wives along with their dead husbands in ancient times."

"It must be utter hell to live without knowing."

"It hasn't been easy," Sarah said, trying very hard not to sound self-pitying. "But I've survived this long. Although, I must admit, there have been times when I felt that if I ever once started screaming, I wouldn't be able to stop."

"I know the feeling," he whispered, enclosing her small hand in his big one and squeezing tightly. "That's what happened that night at the Watermill. But you already knew that . . . didn't you?"

"It's getting late," Sarah said, glancing down at her watch. "And I'm very tired—it's been a long and difficult day for me."

"Please," Ian said, tightly clutching her hand. His voice carried an edge of depression. "I promise not to be any trouble. I know I'm pretty drunk . . . but I don't want to be alone tonight. I'm afraid."

Sara rose and reached into her purse, glancing down at the key to her motel room. "I'm afraid, too," she said. "I'll be staying in bungalow number twelve at the Shady Rest Motel next door. Give me about twenty minutes . . . and then come over."

The misty dawns of late summer in the Hamptons were as much a part of the season as the daisies and goldenrod—a filmy gauze of whiteness that settled over the valleys, ponds, and fields like a pall of smoke just before sunrise.

It was the shimmer and glow of the changing seasons that came well before the autumn haze began to turn the leaves to a riot of autumn colors—the heavy morning dew that festooned the summer foliage and kept the eastern tip of Long Island lush and green well into the month of September. It was, in fact, the very breath of autumn itself, curling and weathing the lush landscape long before the leaves began to fall with the first hint of frost.

On the morning following her chance meeting with Ian at Friendlie's, Sarah checked out of the Shady Rest Motel and returned with him to Grassy Hollow Farm in his jeep. It was the first morning of what in the beginning promised to be an entirely new life together for both of them.

Everything seemed to sparkle with the dewy freshness found only in the country on a brilliantly sunlit summer morning. Together they raced barefoot across the meadow behind the house, and later they rode bareback on Ian's horses.

Sarah reveled in the feel of the sweet meadow clover beneath her bare feet and after an exhilarating gallop through the nearby woods, with Ian's dogs romping along in hot pursuit, they returned to the farmhouse for a big country breakfast.

Sarah had almost forgotten how much she loved to cook for someone, and she really put out a spread with buttermilk flapjacks, a rasher of Canadian bacon, scrambled eggs, and fresh-baked blueberry muffins fairly dripping with clover honey from Ian's own hives. Somehow, she felt that she had come home at last, and after drinking steaming mugs of hot coffee, Ian and Sarah went upstairs to the bedroom and made love for the first time.

For the next two weeks, they remained totally isolated from the outside world, spending most of their time in the big, comfortable kitchen of Ian's century-old farmhouse. He had restored it as close to the original as possible, and Sarah immediately fell in love with Grassy Hollow Farm.

The main house was a small, cozy saltbox structure with open-beamed ceilings of rough-hewn cedar logs and a minimum of comfortable old furniture. There was a huge fieldstone fireplace, which they always lit in the evening. There was no phone, no electricity and, once Ian had locked the gate, no visitors either.

It was several days, however, before Ian would consent to giving Sarah a tour of his studio, which was in an old converted barn some distance behind the house. Sunlight filtered down through a huge overhead skylight, and Sarah's very first visit was almost like a religious experience.

After Ian had taken the padlock off the door, she walked inside to find herself in a tabernacle of light and energy, surrounded by Ian's genius on every side. The studio itself was a square room with a high ceiling and a wide expanse of windows looking out across the meadow. The whole place was casually untidy, with his easel standing before the windows and a widely scattered assortment of paints, palettes, and jars full of brushes.

Dust stood thick upon everything, and the stale, closed air of the studio was heavy with the resiny, aromatic smell of paints and turps. Then, there were his paintings—at least a half a dozen canvases in one stage or another of completion, either hanging on the walls or standing propped about in haphazard fashion.

"I haven't been able to finish any of them," he confessed. "I guess I just lost the touch."

His voice was scarcely audible, and in that moment Sarah felt his pain, and it wrenched her heart as nothing else could. There had, of course, been a time when Sarah herself had been determined to paint. But after years of bartering her talents and her creative energies in the rag trade, the dream had ended stillborn.

Too much had happened in too short a space of time, and Sarah had seen firsthand exactly what people were capable of doing to one another. Somehow, during the years of not knowing whether Brian was dead or alive, the ability to envision a future bright with color and promise had simply vanished.

The dream was dead for Sarah, but Ian McVane was an entirely different matter. The genius with which he had been gifted might be temporarily flawed and raging out of control. But at least it was still alive and burning brightly within him. Both his life and his talent, Sarah was convinced, could still be saved.

It wasn't love—at least not yet, but it was something very close to it. Ian hadn't touched a drop of alcohol since the night they met at Friendlie's, and they continued to be very peaceful and happy together until the day of their picnic at the Shinnecock Indian Reservation.

Ian had become fascinated by the Indians, and he often went there to sketch. In fact, all of the unfinished paintings that were locked up in his studio had been done from those sketches, and Sarah recognized immediately that they were by far his best work to date. Yet they remained unfinished, a vivid rush of images spilling across canvas rich with the color and tribal rhythms of the ancient Indian culture. There was an incredible intimacy to Ian's Indian paintings, and they seemed almost to have been executed by an ethereal hand. They transmitted a sense of timeless serenity and peace against a panoramic background of solitary sea and sky.

Sarah simply had to see the reservation for herself, and she finally prevailed upon Ian to take her there one Sunday afternoon in the middle of August.

On the way, they stopped and bought food for a picnic: a large oval of reshly baked brown bread, thick sausages, cheese, fruit, and a bottle of dry red wine. The reservation was only a few miles from Southampton, and after traveling along a dusty road beneath a canopy of tall poplar trees, they parked the car near the old Indian graveyard and spread their picnic things in the shade.

It was an idyllic spot, with a stream rushing wildly through rich pastureland, a scattering of fruit trees, and thickets of wild berries. In their annual migration to the south, golden monarch butterflies dipped and fluttered over the tall grass, and the air was vibrant with the lazy hum of bees.

As soon as they were settled, Sarah kicked off her tennis shoes and wiggled her toes in the grass. It felt cool and alive against her bare feet, while the air was fragrant with the smell of wild honeysuckle.

Ian poured them each a glass of wine. Then Sarah

lay back on the blanket while he gave her a brief history of the reservation and the remnants of the ancient Indian tribe that lived there still.

Originally, the reservation was set up by an exchange of deeds between the colonists and the local inhabitants of what was eventually to become the Hamptons. Before the coming of the white man, the Shinnecocks had lived in wigwams made from saplings and grass tied with thongs of rushes.

In the lovely Shinnecock Hills, they raised great flocks of sheep, and all their hunting was done with bows and arrows. It was in 1640 that the chief of the Shinnecocks welcomed a sloop containing nine English families that were looking for a place to settle. They were fed and taught survival, for at that time, Long Island was a virgin wilderness, and only the Indians themselves had been bred to endure its hardships.

The Indians also taught those first settlers to fish, to spear for eels, to dig clams, and in time to plant corn and the other mainstays of life among the Indian people—crops that could be stored and kept for the long, bitter winters so common to that long finger of land shaped like a fish with two flukes, sticking far out into the Atlantic.

Eventually, a strong bond of friendship was established between the white people and the Indians. The Shinnecocks gave the new settlers an area of land to dwell upon in peace. And that land ultimately became the beautifully preserved village of Southampton and its lovely environs.

Sarah and Ian ate their picnic lunch in silence, putting away large quantities of bread, cheese, fruit, and wine. Sarah wasn't worried, however, as they sat there eating and glancing intimately at one another from time to time, sharing a new closeness. They had never once mentioned his drinking during the course of their relationship, and she simply didn't want to spoil the day by broaching the subject.

When Sarah's appetite was finally satisfied, she lay back in the grass, thinking how good it felt. The sun was warm on her face, and the hard, cool earth made her feel as if it was the best possible place to be at that moment in time.

She had almost dozed off when Ian kissed her tentatively, questioningly. "Do you still love him?" Ian asked. "Are you still in love with Brian?"

There was something so strange about Ian's voice and the distance it put between them that Sarah opened her eyes and sat up to stare into his face with haunted eyes. "How could I possibly know the answer to that," she said, "since I don't even know if he's dead or alive? All I know is that once upon a time Brian Dane was the most important man in the world to me."

Ian got very drunk that afternoon, finishing off the half-gallon of wine as if he were trying to punish someone. Himself? Sarah? The world? She didn't know, and she was afraid to ask, fearing to question his brooding silence.

On the way home, he began speeding very fast, and Sarah started to plead with him to slow down. "It's too late for both of us," Ian kept repeating with stubborn insistence. Then he began to laugh in a way that chilled her to the bone.

"Please, stop the car and let me drive," she cried. But by then it was already too late. Bearing down even harder on the accelerator, Ian took a curve much too fast, and Sarah watched with horrified eyes as the next curve came much too soon.

Seconds later, the jeep went into a deadly heart-stopping skid. Then the white guard railing loomed up before her eyes with a splintering crash of wood, and they lurched up over the shoulder of the road.

With the wheel spinning wildly in Ian's hands, Sarah screamed and threw her hands up before her face, just as they plunged out into emptiness. Landing hard, the car went crashing down over a rocky incline for several hundred yards, jolting and lurching along over loose boulders, until it finally came to rest at the bottom of a shallow ravine.

It all ended there with a rending crunch of metal, a shatter of breaking glass, and then silence—eerie, utter, and absolute silence.

# =======CHAPTER 21=======

On the day immediately following her release from the hospital, Claire drove out to Broadmoor. It was located near Sag Harbor and was said to number among its several hundred patients people with some of the foremost surnames in America. It was a mental mausoleum, housing the descendants of vast wealth in whose minds madness had bloomed like malodorous flowers.

Claire was stopped at the outer gates, where she was greeted by a uniformed guard with a cheerful, bulldog countenance. Upon learning that she had come without previously making an appointment, he entered a stone-block guardhouse and put in a call to the administration building. A brief conversation ensued, and afterward she was issued a special visitor's pass.

Finally, she was waved on through the gates in her rented Volkswagen, while a closed-circuit television camera hidden among the foliage slowly panned around to follow her passage up the long, winding gravel drive.

In a previous incarnation, Broadmoor had once been the palatial estate of the Brandon family, several descendants of which were said still to be among the present inmates of the reportedly model institution.

Clare proceeded slowly up the drive beneath a canopy of stately trees. They were very old, with wide, spreading branches that seemed to shake the early afternoon sunlight from their leaves and deposit it in pools of light and shadow on the roadway below.

The surrounding grounds were a thickly wooded mosaic of leafy summer foliage, and cornering a bend in the road, Claire could see the old Brandon mansion cresting a knoll in the distance. It had been converted into the present-day administration building, and it was a sprawling Tudor mansion built of time-mellowed brick and wreathed in creeping vines.

Everything looked incredibly peaceful and serene. And yet from the first moment that she had driven through the gates, she had felt a sense of strangeness about the place. There was a pool but no one swimming in it. Nor were any of the patients visible about the grounds, even though the day was warm and redolent with the smell of new-mown grass and the carefully tended flowerbeds along the drive were bright with late-blooming annuals.

Claire parked the car in front of the mansion and simply sat there for several minutes, listening to the buzz of insects and scattered snatches of bird song. Surrounding the administration building like space-age satellites orbiting an ancient mother ship were a series of concrete-block dormitories surrounded by chain-link fences.

The eerie sense of premonition Claire had been experiencing ever since entering the grounds was further compounded when she stepped from the car. Startled by a sudden fierce barking, she noticed for the first time a half-dozen Doberman guard dogs with bared teeth and low, threatening growls rattling deep in their throats prowling the fence.

Dr. Jacobsen, the director of the institution, received Claire in his office. The room was reminiscent of a large baronial hall. It was furnished with richly patterned Oriental rugs and art objects of obvious worth. One wall was entirely covered by bookcases, while portraits of the various members of the board of directors were prominently displayed along the paneled walls.

Rather surprisingly, Roxanne's picture was among them.

Dr. Jacobsen was seated behind a carved refectory table. Across from him were two straight-backed chairs upholstered in old Pullman-car green. "Good afternoon, Mrs. Spencer," he said, rising from his chair to take her hand in greeting. "Your sister called to inform me that I might very well be receiving a visit from you."

It sounded like some kind of warning, and for several moments Claire simply stared at the thin, bespectacled man with his pale poker face and bland expression. He looked like an undertaker, she thought to herself. And seemed to be made up of indeterminate grays and browns. Even his handshake was lukewarm and limply apologetic.

Claire was motioned toward an uncomfortable straight-backed chair across the desk from him. Dr. Jacobsen sat back and surveyed her, his pale eyes glinting shrewdly through his silver wire-frame spectacles.

"If you had called ahead," Jacobsen informed her, "I would have been glad to arrange a tour of the grounds. It's very lovely at this time of year, as you can see, and no expense has been spared to give our resident patients every possible accommodation. We here at Broadmoor like to think of ourselves as a conservative but up-to-date model institution."

"I've already seen the grounds," Claire informed him shortly. "To be specific, I came here today to see my cousin Abbey, and I would appreciate your making the necessary arrangements for me to do so. From the looks of those dogs out there, I can only assume that one needs a proper escort. Are they there to keep people in, Doctor . . . or out?"

Dr. Jacobsen simply sat there smiling while his long, pale fingers were busily engaged, filling and tamping a pipeful of custom-blended tobacco from an ebony humidor. "Like the relatives of so many of our . . . shall we say, mentally disturbed patients, you seem, Mrs. Spencer, to have a slightly hostile attitude. I want to assure you that I perfectly understand your concern."

"Don't condescend to me, Doctor," Claire retorted sharply. "Just arrange for me to see my cousin Abbey, and tell me what I have to do to get her out of this place as quickly as possible."

After engaging in a slightly frantic search for matches, Dr. Jacobsen puffed his briar into life. Then he leaned slightly forward and shook his head. "I'm afraid that is quite out of the question, Mrs. Spencer. Miss Randolph is in the process of therapy and cannot be disturbed."

"Then I'll wait until she can be . . . disturbed."

Jacobsen appeared to be momentarily flustered, but he hurried his face into a smile, like a benign old clergyman deploring a parishioner's minor lapse. "That, too, I'm afraid would simply be a waste of your valuable time. You see, we have a policy here at Broadmoor. New patients are kept in total seclusion for a certain period of time. It helps them to adjust to their new life here, without the conflicting emotions engendered by seeing well-meaning friends and relatives."

"My cousin is not a mental case, Doctor. She is a very confused and very unhappy young woman, whose recently deceased mother was perhaps the arch-bitch of all time. Abbey simply doesn't belong in a place like this, and I'm prepared to take full responsibility for her welfare."

Choosing his words with care, Dr. Jacobsen observed, "Unless I'm entirely mistaken, Mrs. Spencer, you yourself were released from the hospital only yesterday, after failing in an attempt at suicide. It would seem rather obvious to me that a woman with your . . . shall we say, emotional problems, is in no way prepared to care for herself, much less someone in Miss Randolph's precarious mental condition."

Dr. Jacobsen rose. "According to your sister, Mrs. Spencer, you are a confirmed alcoholic given to suicidal tendencies, sexual delusions, and excessive romantic fantasies with no possible basis in reality. Need I say more?"

Claire left the administration building in a state of frustration and near despair. Something was terribly wrong. She could feel it in her bones, and Jacobsen had quite obviously been stalling for some reason.

Claire slid in behind the wheel, slammed the door of the Volkswagen behind her, and then glanced down to see a small envelope tucked partially beneath the seat. Her name was scrawled across the face, and there was something ominous and strange about the discovery. Claire responded to it immediately with a sharp intake of breath.

Her hand trembled slightly as she reached to retrieve the envelope, and she slid out some Polaroid pictures that were tucked inside. They were of Abbey, and for as long as she lived Claire would never forget the absolute horror she experienced as she looked at them.

Abbey was all curled up in a fetal position, just staring blankly into space. Her head had been shaved clean, and she was surrounded by machines, with tubes and needles sticking out all over her severely emaciated body.

"Oh my God, no!" Claire gasped. "What have they done to her?" Then, on the back of the envelope she saw that a telephone number had been written along with the message: "Please call. Terrible things are going on here, and someone has to do something to put a stop to it."

# CHAPTER 22

Soft, silken womanly flesh was sleeping warm and close beside him. Still half asleep, Jaime slipped his hand into the soft nest between Kim's thighs and snuggled closer.

She sighed in her sleep, turning in his arms and burrowing against his chest like a nursing animal. Jaime must have dozed again, grinding his teeth together as he dreamed, while some deep interior voice told him it was all wrong.

Suddenly Jaime was wide awake, with his heart thumping wildly against his ribs. He was nude in bed, and stark awareness stabbed at him. The woman in bed with him was not Kim. Instinctively, Jaime drew away from the sleeping pink and white torso, only to turn into the embrace of another sleeping body. This one was a man, snoring faintly and equally nude, his handsome features gone slack and decadent in the faint light that sifted in through the draperies drawn across the bedroom windows.

The man murmured something in his sleep, and Jaime quickly slid from bed, fearing he might awaken. Several empty wine bottles littered the floor, and the ashtrays beside the huge circular bed were overflowing with cigarette butts. The woman's perfume seemed to hang on the still, warm air, as a reminder of all that had transpired the night before. And as he stood there staring vacantly about him, hatred for Darnell Hanlan turned in Jaime's belly like a knife.

The Count and Countess de Bressier were just a couple more of Darnell's victims. Marie was the very social slaughterhouse heiress, with a preference for European titles and threesomes. With the help of $50 million and the best minds in the medical profession, the Countess Marie de Bressier had conquered the aging process at approximately 35 years of age. And although she was now well into her fiftieth year, there had been few inroads upon her appearance that cosmetic surgery, silicone implants, and Main Chance Beauty Farm had not been able to rectify.

Grabbing his bathrobe, Jaime staggered into the bathroom and locked the door behind him. Well, at least it was almost over, he thought, avoiding his own reflection in the mirror. The de Bressiers were the last two names on Darnell's Hampton black list. Jaime had balled them all at $500 a head and had by now earned close to $10,000 for the summer's efforts.

Darnell had promised him an additional $10,000 as an inducement to stay the course, and now Jaime was ready to collect. Many of his contacts had, of course, wanted to see more of Jaime. But he had made it a rule to drop them cold as soon as the conquest had been made and duly recorded as conclusive evidence.

Jaime stood for a long time in the hot shower as the steam clouded up around him and his taut muscles began to relax.

The things he had been forced to do in order to survive had never bothered him before meeting Kim. But all that had changed now.

Jaime stood for a long time, drying himself off and staring at his own reflection in the mirror. Then he reached into his shaving kit to produce a switchblade knife.

The long razor-sharp blade shimmered in the light as Jaime flipped it open and ran his thumb along the edge. Those poor fucking bastards on Darnell's black list were not the enemy, he told himself. It was Hanlan himself who had to be destroyed.

For Kim, the fast-fading days of summer had begun to float away like so many gaily colored balloons. She and Jaime had been spending every possible free moment together, and the beachhouse near Montauk had become their own private sanctuary. A secret lovers' lair, safe and very far away from their other, very separate lives.

There were long walks along the beach by moonlight and lazy stolen mornings, with Irish coffee and jelly omelets in front of a crackling fire. They surfed together every chance they got, and Sundays were always set aside for visits to an amusement park near Cedar Point.

After buying a handful of tickets, they rode everything that moved, armed with cotton candy, teddy bears, candied apples and kewpie dolls that Jaime had won for her in a shooting gallery. Each Sunday was like an empty canvas upon which they painted joyful, happy scenes of life and loving. Kim had never been happier.

Then, inevitably, Jaime would withdraw from her, and Kim's heart ached at the sudden distance he would put between them for no apparent reason, retreating always into some private, brooding world where she was never allowed to follow.

He seldom spoke of his past, but Kim was only too aware that the wounds had gone deep, and some of them continued to bleed somewhere inside him. Kim often wondered what was going through his head when Jaime seemed a million miles away, but she deliberately didn't ask questions.

They never spoke of what Jaime did, or why he got all dressed up in the evenings and dropped her at her motel before going off to the Hamptons' very best bars, restaurants, and discos. She simply preferred not to know. Neither did she want to face up to the true nature of Franco de Roma's mission in the Hamptons.

By now, Kim had seen enough to know that all was not what it might appear to be on the surface. Yet even so, the film they were making together had come to involve her completely. It was like a bad B-movie without a plot, for which Kim felt some kind of ghastly fascination.

Kim was in love with Jaime, but she was not entirely blind to the razor's edge of violence that ran like quicksilver just beneath the cool macho facade. Having sex together was never the same twice, but then neither was Jaime himself. There were always other dimensions —dark shadows and shimmering, diamond-bright facets that flashed brightly and then were gone in an instant, as if he were continually exchanging one mask for another.

Kim was totally excluded from that other part of his life. Of course, she knew that he was involved in something for which he was being paid a great deal of money. Kim was anything but naive, and she had realized ever since that night at the Southampton Bay Club that Jaime was playing the role of a highly paid hustler. But who it was who arranged the sexual assignations in which he participated, and why, remained a complete mystery.

All Kim knew for certain was that their own all-consuming sexual union was as close as she had ever come to having a religious experience.

Jaime had never been able to discover a record of his own birth and had admitted to Kim that he had never yet celebrated a birthday. And so it was on August 27, after completing her last day of shooting with Franco de Roma, she decided to throw Jaime a surprise birthday party.

Jaime's yellow Ferrari was not parked in front of the house as Kim turned into the drive that sloped down through heavy foliage and ended in an open parking area. But she knew that the sliding glass doors at the back of the house were always left unlocked, and she had no trouble in gaining entry.

First, she transported two big brown paper bags of groceries into the kitchen and returned to the car to get Jaime's birthday presents out of the trunk. Kim had bought him an expensive red velvet robe and monogrammed silk pajamas at a men's boutique in town.

They were individually wrapped with silver paper, blue ribbon, and big bows. Upon returning to the house, Kim decided to hide them in Jaime's bedroom at the far end of a long hall. The door was always kept closed, and Kim had never even been inside since they always ate and made love before the living room fireplace. Like so many things about Jaime, the bedroom had always remained a mystery.

As soon as she opened the door, Kim realized that she had made a mistake. By any standards, Jaime's bedroom had about it a quality of sensuous abandon, with a mirrored ceiling over the huge circular bed, which was draped with an expensive fur coverlet. It stood on a raised platform, and as Kim touched the light switch, the bed was suddenly bathed in soft pink spotlights.

Feeling as if she had intruded into an unknown realm, Kim hurriedly moved to the closets and swung open one of the louvered doors. Then she stepped back and gasped aloud.

An extremely sophisticated videotaping machine had been installed and was geared to go into operation when a switch beside the bed was flicked. The length of one entire wall was composed of closets, and the louvered doors had been adjusted to allow the camera full range of the room, on a soundlessly revolving tripod.

Jaime's presents fell from Kim's hands as she knelt beside the videotape machine and pressed the switch for "Playback." Kim didn't really want to know what was on that reel of film even as she set the machine into motion. Yet something compelled her, and suddenly she had to know the truth.

The video was audiovisual in black and white. Slowly, the camera panned the bedroom as Kim literally held her breath. Then the bed gradually came into focus, and there was a man lying face down upon the mattress. He was bound hand and foot, and he lay in a pool of blinding white light that plunged the rest of the room into inky obscurity.

Kim experienced a sick, sinking sensation as she watched the man's bare buttocks writhing rhythmically to the steady slap-slapping of a knotted lash being evenly applied by an anonymous hand.

As the man twisted and moaned on the bed, Kim could see that his face was contorted into some kind of agonizing ecstasy. Sweat ran down his back as the lash continued to strike with regularity. He was moving his hips with an automatic pumping motion, accompanied by gasps and heavy breathing spooling out of the audio playback.

Then, at the foot of the bed, a shadowy form became visible as the camera slowly panned around. It was Jaime. Kim recognized him immediately, even though he was wearing a black leather mask, jackboots, and leather pants. The mask covered his face entirely, and there were studded leather straps running across his bare chest.

Standing very still with his feet spread wide apart, Jaime was methodically applying the whips to the man whom Kim suddenly recognized as Darrell Hanlan—the same man she had seen with Franco de Roma at the Southampton Bay Club earlier in the summer.

Jaime simply stood there like a medieval executioner, his chest bare and heaving with the exertion as sweat glistened among the dark hair matting his straining pectorals. The eyes peering out through slits in the leather mask glittered like obsidian arrowheads. The

275

hand clutching the whip he wielded with such obvious precision was gloved in a studded leather gauntlet.

Kim left the bedroom without even bothering to turn off the videotape machine. She simply rose, walked through the house, and out onto the terrace overlooking the sea. It was just past sunset, and already shadows were beginning to lengthen across the beach.

She had always known that there was something tragically flawed about Jaime's character. But more than anything else, Kim had insisted on believing that her love was strong enough to save him from the abyss.

Now, however, as she stood clutching the terrace railing and listening to the wind chimes playing softly on the early evening breeze, she had no choice but to admit the truth.

Jaime was two people—both the man of gentle sweetness she adored and the leather-clad satyr wielding his sex and his whip with equal dispassion.

She had fallen in love with a changeling who could never really love anyone because of the emotional vacuum inside him. The wounds of his vagrant past had gone far too deep.

# ═══CHAPTER 23═══

TERROR BARED AT EXCLUSIVE MENTAL HOSPITAL

The 300 patients at the posh Broadmoor State Mental Hospital live under constant threat of rape, assault, and various forms of medical and psychiatric abuse. Patients of the institution, many of whom are from prominent local families, were said to be suffering from lack of treatment, malnutrition, drug abuse, and random attacks from violent patients quartered amongst them in the overcrowded wards.

These and other serious charges were leveled at the institution and its director, Dr. Seymour Jacobsen, following a surprise raid by police and mental-health authorities last Friday evening. "It's like something out of the Dark Ages," according to Claire Ryan Spencer, who was able to obtain a search warrant after being alerted by a Broadmoor staff nurse to the deplorable conditions existing inside the maximum-security facility.

During a televised interview Saturday morning on *The Hamptons Live,* Mrs. Spencer went on to say that wards designed to house 10 to 15 people at most were severely overcrowded, with between 30 to 60 patients. She also reported shortages of nurses, therapy aides, and maintenance personnel. Both medical care and rehabilitation programs for patients were virtually nonexistent.

In a massive malpractice suit, Mrs. Spencer further charged doctors at the institution with gross negligence in subjecting her cousin Abigale

Randolph to electroshock therapy without running a routine pregnancy test. The young woman, who is a member of a prominent Easthampton family, ultimately suffered a miscarriage during the treatments and nearly lost her life as a result.

According to lawyers retained by Mrs. Spencer in her cousin's behalf, the 28-year-old local woman had been in a deep coma ever since receiving electroshock and is presently being treated in the intensive-care unit of the Westport Medical Center.

Mrs. Spencer, a prominent local socialite, has also sought an injunction against her sister, Mrs. Roxanne Ryan Aristos, who became the executrix of the Randolph estate following the death of Annabel Randolph earlier this summer. In a brief presented yesterday to a federal court judge sitting in special session, lawyers for Mrs. Spencer asked for a court order preventing Mrs. Aristos from liquidating the estate in a public auction which was to be held this week in Easthampton.

The Sunday papers were full of the Broadmoor scandal, but Sarah was in no mood to be more depressed than she already was. It had been a week since Ian smashed up the jeep, and while they both miraculously escaped with only minor injuries, Sarah had walked out on him and returned to the Shady Rest Motel.

Since then, she had come every afternoon to the Shinnecock Indian reservation. Sarah wasn't sure why she continued to come, but there was a peaceful desolation about that place that appealed to her sense of being somehow suspended in time.

On that particular day, Sarah had brought the Sunday paper to read in the shade of the trees surrounding the old Indian burial ground. It was there amidst crumbling sandstone rectangles that the Shinnecock had been burying their dead for over 300 years, pressed and crowded in death. Most of the gravestones were moss-green and lichen covered, while the family burial plots were overgrown with grass and strewn with mouldering wreaths.

It was a brilliant summer day, and it was cool in the shade of the trees. From where Sarah sat, there was a fine view of Shinnecock Bay, with the *Golden Hind* riding serenely at anchor farther out in the harbor.

Sarah still felt that she had been deeply betrayed by Andrea, who clearly had succumbed to the glittering and frenetic Hampton social scene. By Sarah's own estimation, her friend had become just another one of the "beautiful glass people." She deserved whatever fate befell her at the hands of Helene Von Bismark, who clearly had stepped in and taken charge after the downfall of Kamal Ali Reza.

As for Ian McVane, Sarah still cared deeply. She wanted to help him, but she didn't know how to go about it, since she clearly wasn't even able to help herself. There just didn't seem to be anyplace for her to go from there.

Sarah had returned to America only to discover that she was totally unable to blend in with the landscape. The Hamptons and all they had come to stand for appalled her. Nor was she willing to re-establish her links with the family who had nurtured and cherished her until, many years before, Sarah had turned her back on them.

Leaning back against the trunk of a spreading poplar tree, Sarah's gaze fell to the front page of the Sunday paper, lying before her on the grass. Scattered patches of sunlight filtered through the leafy branches overhead. A light breeze had sprung up to send the spangled sunshade dancing, until it finally illuminated the boldface type near the bottom of the front page.

BODY OF M.I.A. PILOT MAKING FINAL TRIP HOME, it read.

The words seemed to leap off the page at her, and Sarah's heart began to race as she recognized a photograph of Brian accompanying the two-column article. Yet even so, she was almost afraid to read further, and it took an act of will to focus her sight through eyes brimming with tears.

279

Air Force Captain Brian Dane, missing since his plane was shot down over North Vietnam, is coming home for the last time.

It was just one week before his twenty-sixth birthday when the Harvard graduate and former Olympic decathlon champion took off on what was supposed to be his last combat mission before being shipped home.

The fate of the highly decorated Captain Dane has remained a mystery up until two weeks ago, when he was identified as one of 11 American pilots whose remains were being returned by the North Vietnamese.

Captain Dane is survived by his wife, Sarah, a former fashion illustrator working in New York City. Thus far, however, government officials have been unable to locate the wife of Captain Dane since her departure for Europe over a year ago. She is believed to be living in the Greek Isles.

Captain Dane's ashes are being flown home aboard an Air Force jet for memorial services at Arlington National Cemetery on Tuesday. The ultimate disposition of his remains is still uncertain, however, until his next of kin can be located by government authorities.

Sarah sat perfectly still as the breeze sifted the leaves above her head. At first she tried to keep back the tears, biting her lip hard and concentrating on little things of no real importance: a fat brown lizard basking in the sun on a nearby rock, a stunted fig tree throwing its shadow upon the grass, while a procession of large black ants marched up the trunk to seek sustenance from the ripe and bursting purple fruit.

The sun glinted and shimmered off the bay, and Sarah blinked as the tears welled up, spilled over, and began to course down her cheeks. Then she was crying as she had never before cried in her life—crying for Brian as well as herself and Ian McVane.

Her long vigil was over. And somehow, from somewhere deep inside her, Sarah had to find the strength to pick up the shattered pieces of her life and begin again.

For Sarah Dane, the memorial services at Arlington were a tangle of confused impressions. She was too emotionally exhausted to really comprehend what was taking place. Only bits and pieces came through, ultimately forming a mosaic that would always be with her, even though the ceremony itself had a dim and hazy quality to it.

Floral tributes to Brian and his departed comrades were spread out over the grassy hillside at Arlington, to create a blanket of brilliant color. From the nation's capital, church bells rang in honor of the fallen airmen, while flags throughout Washington had been lowered to half-mast.

It was mostly political theater, and yet Sarah stood very erect with the other MIA wives, as Air Force jets screamed across the sky and dipped their wings in final tribute. The breeze rippled the folds of her dark mourning veil as a 21-gun salute was fired. There were simply no more tears left to cry.

Following the ceremony that morning, Sarah had flown back to Easthampton aboard an Air Force plane that had been placed at her disposal. How terribly anticlimactic it all seemed, Sarah thought, as a taxi deposited her back at the Shady Rest Motel. She had loved only two men in her life. One of them was dead, and the other was determined to drink himself to death, rather than face the truth about his own will to fail.

Still, Sarah reasoned, it wasn't yet too late. Ian could still be saved, and after changing out of her widow's weeds, she started out for Grassy Hollow Farm in a rental car, with Brian's ashes resting beside her in a burial urn. In an almost prophetic letter from Vietnam shortly before his death, Brian had instructed her that if anything should happen to him, he wanted his body to be cremated and scattered to the winds over the north Atlantic.

By the time Sarah reached the farm, fog had begun to billow in from the Sound and waft through the venerable white oaks surrounding the house. It seemed to come in wave after wave, rolling inland over the landscape, enveloping the house, the barn, and the surrounding fields with a ghostly, vaporous mist.

Sarah discovered Ian in an alcoholic stupor. He was seated at the kitchen table, his head lolling on his arms and a half-empty whisky bottle at his elbow. He was nearly incoherent as Sarah moved about the kitchen, bathing his face with cold towels and tidying up the dishes piled unwashed in the sink.

Finally, she placed a mug of steaming hot black coffee in Ian's hands and sat down across the table from him. "Why did you come back?" he asked in a hollow, slurred voice.

Sarah looked him directly in the eyes, and her voice was very cool and steady as she said, "I came to tell you what I felt the first time I saw one of your paintings exhibited in a gallery. I was so moved by your work that I guess even back then I knew that I was in love with you.

"Somehow, your paintings transferred something of what you are to me—your genius and greatness as an artist. I felt your pain, your violence, and your rage. But I also felt your compassion, gentleness, and strength."

Ian's heavy fist smashed down on the table with a crash that made the crockery rattle in the cupboards. "Stop talking like that," he shouted at her. "Can't you see that I'm a human wreck? I'm a drunk, Sarah, and worse than that, I'm a painter whose gift has deserted him. Can't you get it through your head? I just can't hack it anymore."

"No," she stated firmly. "That's simply not true. I've seen your Indian paintings, and I know that your best work is still ahead of you."

"You're as fucked up in the head as I am if you really believe that, Sarah. Don't you realize I almost killed you last week when I got drunk and ran the jeep

282

off the road? Now get smart and get your ass out of here, or I'll destroy you along with myself."

His voice dropped to an anguished plea. "Please . . . get out while you can. You don't need another living dead man on your hands."

"Brian is dead," Sarah informed him in a tightly controlled voice. "And the time has come for me to lay him to rest, once and for all."

Ian had not wanted to take her up that day. His pilot's license had, in fact, been suspended for over a year. Ever since that momentous Fourth of July afternoon when he had dive-bombed the Easthampton City Hall and ended up by nearly taking off the steeple high atop the United Presbyterian Church.

Once they were airborne, Ian radioed ahead to the control tower on Fisher's Island for a routine weather check. He was sober now, but sullen and withdrawn. Sarah listened with a terrible sense of déjà vu, as the tower radioed back that due to the fog, all flights had been grounded. Was this the way it was always meant to end? she wondered.

"Well, Seraphina, it's all your show. You got us up here, and to tell you the truth, it'll take an act of God to get us down alive. It's a suicide mission, pure and simple."

Ian was clearly testing her nerve in a contest of wills, but Sarah's pale, strained visage gave absolutely nothing away. "How much fuel have you got in the fuel tanks?" she questioned.

He checked the gauges and shrugged. "Two hours flying time at the very most."

Sarah glanced at her watch and made a quick calculation. "It's now a little after two P.M." she said as Montauk Point fell away beneath them, into the mushrooming sea of white mist. "I want you to keep flying straight out over the Atlantic until three o'clock."

"You realize, of course, that there's a very good chance we'll never make it back from that far out.

And even if we did, there isn't going to be any place to land in this fog."

"I know that," Sarah said without looking at him. "It only means that you have exactly one hour to decide whether you want to live or die. I'm with you either way, Ian. There's no turning back for either of us now."

For the next hour, Ian remained wholly absorbed in his own thoughts as the fog thickened and played along the fuselage, like a ghostly white winding sheet. His face was entirely without expression, while Sarah herself remained in a state of trancelike calm. They sat there in the glow of the faint red light illuminating the instrument panel and surrounded by a sea of billowing white mist.

It seemed as if Sarah's whole life had been leading her toward that blind, fathomless destination 200 miles out at sea. Yet whatever the outcome, she was no longer afraid, for she had placed her life squarely in the hands of the man she loved, and she was willing to accept stoically whatever fate awaited her.

It was 3:55 when Ian radioed the Montauk airforce station that they were running out of fuel. Any possibility of landing at Easthampton Airport was by now totally out of the question. And there was a desperate edge to his voice as he requested permission to be brought in by instruments on the military installation's small landing strip.

"We're almost completely out of fuel," Ian announced. "I have barely enough to reach you."

For a moment the radio was silent. Then suddenly it exploded into life. "We are completely fogged in here. Visibility zero. Repeat—visibility zero. But we'll do the best we can to bring you in. Please follow my instructions exactly. We have you on our radar now. Turn five degrees west and maintain your present altitude until further instructions. At your present air speed, you should be ready to land in approximately twelve minutes."

The voice coming over the radio sounded extremely tense. And not without good reason, Ian thought grimly. One slight error or miscalculation, and they would crash into the cliffs at Montauk Point. The airstrip was narrow, short, and extremely hazardous even under the best of conditions. Yet they had no other choice than to place themselves directly in the hands of the disembodied voice that was now their sole link to survival.

Ian flew the plane as though it were a part of himself, flying it as much with his heart and soul as with his hands and his mind. He was extremely aware of Sarah sitting quietly beside him, her face tense and unsmiling. The fog was a ghostly enemy now, blinding and seducing him into making that one fatal mistake that would end it all for both of them.

For the first time in his life, Ian McVane felt utterly helpless. He was totally at the mercy of instruments that could go wrong and men on the ground who were unable to see their own hands in front of their faces. Ian didn't want to die. Not now.

Once again there was a crackle of static from the radio. "Montauk Tower to Piper Apache 901. We have just been notified by the Civil Air Patrol that you are flying without a license." The tower operator's grim, gallows laugh was drowned out by bursts of static. "But I guess that really isn't going to make much difference now, McVane."

Sarah placed her hand over Ian's at the controls. "We're going to make it," she said with quiet certainty. "We have to make it now."

He had tried to break her nerve that afternoon. But Sarah had discovered that the ordeal of Brian's death and Andrea's betrayal had put steel into her soul, as well as a deep, aching sadness. Yet it wasn't until they passed the point of no return and Sarah had scattered Brian's ashes to the winds, that she realized how very much she wanted to live.

Ian, however, had continued flying straight out over the Atlantic, glassy-eyed and seemingly frozen at the controls as he swigged deeply from a flask of whisky he had produced from beneath the seat of the plane.

For several minutes neither of them spoke. Then suddenly a dam seemed to break inside Sarah, with all the pent-up anger and bitter resentment flowing out in a hysterical torrent of abuse.

Raving, ranting, and cursing, Sarah told Ian McVane the truth about himself. Way up there in the midst of a killer fog, she told him about the contempt she felt for all that he had betrayed and went on to describe scathingly the grotesque caricature of a man that he had become.

"You have always had the will to fail," she snarled, pounding her fists against his chest. "You even make me ashamed of ever having fallen in love with you. You're nothing but a man obsessed with failure and wallowing in self-pity. I despise you for what you're doing to yourself," she shrieked. "And I hope you burn in hell for what you're doing to me."

Ian remained silent and totally withdrawn, like a man who had lost the ability to feel anything. He simply stared straight ahead into the fog, and his hands appeared to be frozen at the controls.

Finally, after emotionally exhausting herself, Sarah dried her eyes, ran a comb through her hair, and put on fresh lipstick. Then, very coolly and calmly, she reached over and switched off the ignition, sending the Piper Apache into a heart-stopping stall 200 miles out over the Atlantic.

"Jesus," Ian breathed, his voice sounding loud against the silence that suddenly surrounded them. His eyes fell to the altimeter, which was falling precipitously, and then he turned to look at Sarah as if he were seeing her for the first time.

"Sarah?" his voice questioned.

She turned to search his face, and in that moment, something passed between them. Suddenly, Ian was cursing, huddled over the controls and trying desperately to start the engine, which proceeded to cough and wheeze several times before finally coming back to life.

"Where do we go from here?" he had asked while banking the plane into a steep turn.

"Back to the real world," Sarah had responded, slipping her hand into his, their fingers clutching each other's tightly.

Once again, the disembodied voice of the tower operator came over the speaker against a sputter of static. "Montauk Tower to Piper-Apache flight 109. This is to notify you that you are now coming into your landing pattern. Begin lowering your wind flaps and start your descent."

Ian was aware that the voice of the tower control operator had a new and sharper edge of tension to it now. "Descending . . . two thousand feet . . . fifteen hundred feet . . . one thousand feet . . ."

Still there was no sign of the airfield lights below them. They could have been on the moon for all Ian was able to tell. And yet there was a terrible chill of apprehension that came with knowing that good old terra firma was rushing up to meet them at 200 miles an hour.

"Tower to Piper Apache . . . decrease your airspeed to one hundred twenty. You're now at four hundred feet."

Sarah had by now buried her face against his shoulder, and there was still no sign of the field lights so desperately necessary to bring them in. They would be even with the cliffs now at 300 feet, and there was absolutely no possible margin for error.

Ian's forehead gleamed with perspiration, and he stole another quick glance at the altimeter. The needle was edging swiftly downward to 100 feet, and he knew then that something had gone wrong. Desperately, Ian strained to see through the dense mist, but there was only the treacherous, blinding white sea closing in about them, smothering and blinding them.

Where was the ground? he agonized. It had to be there somewhere, rushing up to meet them.

287

"There . . . look." Sarah's voice was sharp with relief as a row of electric arrows suddenly blazed up out of the fog, directly on course and straight ahead. Then, ten seconds later, they had bumped down at the edge of the runway and were taxiing smoothly across the field.

Figures came running out of the mist toward them as Ian brought the plane to a halt and switched off the engine. "Well, Seraphina," he said, pulling her into his arms. "You're doing pretty good calling the shots, so why don't I just let you take it from here?"

Sarah nuzzled against his chest, feeling safe and warm and good. "I think I'm finally ready to go home," she said. "I've been so very far away for such a very long time."

Later that evening, Sarah and Ian drove out to Mama Rosa's Restaurant for an exuberantly warm and happy family reunion. In spite of her long absence, there was no rancor or recrimination. They were all thrilled to have her back, and for the first time in her life, Seraphina Bambaccio saw her family with very different eyes.

She saw their warmth, their openness, and their simplicity. They were good, decent people who took life's disappointments in stride and lived every moment for all it was worth. There was lots of love and laughter, as well as an incredible number of nieces and nephews that Sarah had not even known existed.

Suddenly it all seemed to come together—Aunt Sarah and Uncle Ian, with a *bambino* on each knee, stuffing themselves to the teeth with her mother's fantastic Italian cooking. It was a night for a lot of good-natured ribbing from her brothers, for endless toasts with Dago Red, and a wonderful sense of belonging—belonging to people and to a place.

Sarah honestly could not remember ever having been happier in her life.

The family Bambaccio immediately took Ian to their

hearts, and he responded warmly, almost as if he too had somehow come home after a long and difficult journey. Ian argued sports with her brothers, danced an exuberant polka with her mother, and was in every way gallant, considerate, ardent, and very much a part of Sarah's happiest of homecomings.

The tables were all full that evening at Mama Rosa's, mostly with Hampton summer people laughing, drinking the homemade wine, and looking out over romantic vistas of the Montauk fishing harbor.

There were candles and bouquets of flowers on all the tables, and the restaurant had a charming old square-rigger atmosphere, with driftwood paneling, barnacle-encrusted anchors, and lavishly strung fishing nets from her father's old trawler.

Both her father and his boat, *The Westwind,* were now no more than childhood memories, and yet Sarah experienced a strong sense of continuity as she sat close to Ian and looked out over the bustling quayside. It had been her playground as a child: the fish market, the bait and tackle shops, and the boiling lobster vats along the wharf, where her father's fishing sloop had been moored.

Her deepest roots were there in that place, Sarah realized. And in spite of everything that had happened to her, they had been strong enough to carry her out into the world to weather many a storm before finally calling her home once again.

Sarah had come back to stay, and Mama Rosa shed copious tears of happiness when her only daughter took her aside and told her she would be living with Ian at Grassy Hollow Farm. Marriage, Sarah confessed, was still a long way off. They both had a lot of work to do, straightening out their lives, and first on the list for Sarah herself was a visit to the *Golden Hind* for some plain talk with her friend, Andrea.

Mama Rosa blanched at the mention of Andrea's name and threw up her hands. "I almost completely forgot," she exclaimed. "There was a young man who came here looking for you, Seraphina. His name was Jason, and he left a letter for you that he said was urgent."

Mama Rosa hastily produced the letter from beneath the cash drawer in the register, and as Sarah took it in her hand, she immediately recognized the Von Bismark baronial crest emblazoned on the envelope.

The letter itself was very brief and to the point, although Jason's handwriting was little more than an almost illegible scrawl.

"Dear Sarah," it read. "I am writing this because Andrea desperately needs your help. She is presently being kept under constant guard and heavy sedation in room 212 at a beauty spa called the Golden Portals.

"Make no mistake about it," Jason went on. "Unless you do something to stop her, Helene will destroy my sister and seize control of Aristos Shipping. Please don't desert Andrea now that she needs you so very much."

The letter was signed simply, "Jason Von B."

# CHAPTER 24

At eight o'clock the following morning, Sarah checked into the Golden Portals under an assumed name. Dr. Clayton Spencer's rejuvenation center was located near Riverhead, on the shores of Wildwood Lake. The architecture was Spanish modern, and the interior decor, according to Sarah's own estimation, could only be described as "Fag Futuristic."

As she filled out the necessary forms, Sarah could look through glass walls into a garden court, with a Roman pool shimmering in the morning sunlight. A muscular, bronzed god of a young man with "Golden Portals" emblazoned across his pectorals was giving a yoga class to a clutch of overweight matrons trying desperately to get into the cobra posture while wearing their gold stretch-nylon sweatsuits and Puma jogging shoes.

Then a six-foot amazon named Helga came striding into the reception lounge to inform Sarah that she was going to have "the poisonous toxins eliminated from her system, the excess fat burnt off, and the muscle-tone-factor redistributed until she would feel, at the end of her two-week stay, absolutely reborn."

Not wanting to arouse the slightest suspicion that she was not a legitimate patient, Sarah endured the various humiliations of a complete physical before the fun and games began. Finally, after Helga had pranced off bearing blood and urine samples for further analysis, she was left to bake in the Herbal Wrap Room.

During the course of the morning, Sarah enjoyed the

sybaritic pleasure of a pedicure, followed by the sweet agony of having a 95-pound Japanese girl walk across her back, massaging each and every vertebra with her toes. Then it was on to the Siesta Room. There she lay under artificial stars winking from a midnight-blue ceiling, while a space-age torture rack rolled, vibrated and stretched her into several directions at once.

The end result was that by lunchtime, Sarah had already lost three pounds that she could ill afford, and she was absolutely ravenous.

Entering the dining room, Sarah found the guests bent over their menus like accountants, busily subtracting a prune yogurt here (40 calories) and adding an eggplant julienne there (36 calories). Bubbly champagne was served from big icy bottles with popping corks. And as her luncheon companions chatted away about "bulging adipose tissue" and "draining their metabolic pools," Sarah was hardly reassured to find that she was sipping only carbonated water with grape flavoring, when what she needed more than anything else was a good stiff belt.

She was finally sent off to her room for a nap, carrying a "people bag," with a rosy red apple inside as a fix for mid-afternoon hunger pangs.

By this point, Sarah had become so apprehensive about Andrea that she could scarcely wait until the premises had settled down for the obligatory afternoon siesta. She waited 20 minutes and then slipped outside into the hall.

Her room was on the first floor, and as she made her way along the dimly lit corridor, Sarah began to feel more than a little unsure about her undertaking. What if she should run into Helene or Dr. Spencer? And what of Andrea? Jason had said that she was being kept under heavy sedation, which could make it extremely difficult to get her off the premises without detection.

Ian had agreed to return at three o'clock that afternoon to pick them up which gave Sarah little more than half an hour to do what she had to do. On reaching the end of the hall, Sarah made her way up a flight of stairs to the second floor. It was dimly lit, and there were numbered, enameled plaques at the side of each door she passed.

The atmosphere seemed to thicken with intrigue wtih each step she took. And as she began to draw closer to room 212, Sarah became convinced that the faint scent of Vol de Nuit, which she detected on the still air, confirmed that Helene Von Bismark had passed down that very corridor not too many minutes before.

It was not a pleasant thought, since Helene was probably the last person in the world that Sarah wished to encounter. She had not forgotten the humiliation she had been forced to endure at the hands of the baroness, and she recognized her to be a shrewd and dangerous adversary, who made it a practice to remain one step ahead of the game.

The room in which Sarah finally found herself was narrow, cool, and clinically austere, with a single white-sheeted bed and no adornment whatsoever beyond Andrea's familiar icon, with its flickering votive lights.

Andrea was seated in front of a small black and white television set, and she did not even turn around as Sarah entered the room and closed the door behind her. There was no sound, and she sat perfectly immobile as if totally mesmerized, pale, still, and wraith-like in her white hospital gown.

Faintly subliminal sounds could be heard from the TV but overall, the entire premises seemed to remain shrouded beneath a spell of conspiratorial silence.

"Andrea?" Sarah questioned in a low, almost whispered voice.

Slowly Andrea turned in her chair to stare with glazed and vacant eyes. For a moment, nothing seemed to register. Her face was puffy from the massive doses of Thorazine, and there was a drugged lack of resolution in her simplest movements, almost as if she were moving and even thinking in slow motion.

293

"Sarah," she said finally. "Is it you?"

After pausing to listen for a moment at the door, Sarah hurried forward to embrace her friend, as tears shimmered in her eyes. "Oh, Andrea . . . what have they done to you?"

There was no expression on Andrea's features as she rose unsteadily to her feet and crossed the room to stand staring out the barred windows. "It's very peaceful here," Andrea said slowly. "There are no pressures . . . no decisions to be made affecting the lives of others."

Her voice fell away, and Andrea shook her head, a sad and hopeless gesture of futility. "It was very hard for me after Kamal, Sarah. I'm just not sure I want to go back to being the richest girl in the world." She sighed. "I guess it just wasn't that easy being my father's daughter."

Sarah moved swiftly to grip Andrea by the shoulders. "Listen to me," she commanded in a low and urgent voice. "Can't you see what's happening? You're willing to throw away everything your father worked to build. Helene is your enemy, Andrea. She's a dangerous adversary, and you have to fight her with everything you've got in you. If you can win this one, you'll never have to be afraid of anything again."

"I'm so tired," Andrea whimpered. "My life will be so much easier if I just give in and do whatever Helene asks. I never realized before coming to the Hamptons that having a lot of money can do terrible things to the people around you. Suddenly I feel as if I were totally isolated, without a friend in the world. There's no one I can really trust anymore."

"Whether you choose to realize it or not, I'm still your friend, Andrea. I'm sorry you had to find out about what was going on between me and Marko. But can't you see that I was desperately confused? I'm only human, Andrea. Can't you find it in your heart to forgive me for making such a terrible mistake?"

Andrea turned to regard her with a vaguely puzzled

expression. "Marko?" she repeated. "Do you mean Marko, the cabin steward aboard the *Golden Hind*? There's nothing to forgive. I can't even blame you for running out on me when I needed you most. After meeting Kamal, I know that I began to turn into someone else entirely. You had every right to want to be quit of me, Sarah."

Sarah searched her friend's face, and then suddenly, she realized what had happened. Andrea had never even seen her diary. Helene Von Bismark had simply blackmailed her into leaving the yacht, while allowing Andrea to believe that Sarah had deserted her in her hour of desperate need.

"Oh, Andrea," Sarah cried, throwing her arms around her and drawing Andrea close in a grateful embrace. "I didn't just walk out on you. Helene came to my cabin and ordered me to leave the *Golden Hind*. She made a lot of lurid accusations and said that you refused even to speak to me . . . to hear my side of the story. She tricked us, Andrea. Helene tricked both of us in order to destroy our friendship."

For several moments Andrea simply stood there, gently fingering the folds of her white hospital gown. Then in the next instant the vacant mask had fallen away, and she was clinging tightly, with her arms around Sarah's neck. "Please help me. I'm so frightened, and Helene will stop at absolutely nothing to gain control of my father's fortune. She's already destroyed poor Jason. I know he hates the life he's leading, but he just isn't strong enough to resist her. Helene is holding us both hostage in order to get what she wants."

"Helene may have control over Jason's emotions," Sarah related grimly, "but not his soul. It was Jason who sent me here to help you. He does care, Andrea, and he needs you desperately if he's going to survive. You have to be strong and come back to the world of the living. To just give up without a fight is not what your father would have expected of you."

295

"My father chose to live in a world very different from the one I was raised in. He belonged among these people—among the Roxannes, the Helenes, and the Kamal Ali Rezas. I'll always be a stranger here. I'll never belong, because I just don't have any instinct for the jugular."

"Listen to me," Sarah said. "Remember all those things I told you about the Hamptons? Well, as you've discovered for yourself, I wasn't entirely wrong, but it wasn't the whole truth either. The Hamptons can be a hard, cold, and superficial place, with all the sham and pretense, but it's really no different than the world outside. There are decent people here who really do care—generous and loving individuals who don't give a good goddamn whether you're rich or poor, pretty or ugly."

Sarah reached out to gently brush the tears from Andrea's cheeks. "You're not alone," she said. "This doesn't have to be the end . . . if you're willing to fight. It can be the beginning—the discovery of that part of yourself that your father always knew was there. The strong, courageous part."

Sarah turned and moved quickly to the closet to remove Andrea's clothes and her single, small suitcase. "Now splash some cold water on your face and get dressed. I'm going to get you out of here. Just trust me, and do exactly as I say."

Even as Andrea slipped her dress over her head and stepped into her shoes, Sarah stiffened. Then, raising a finger to her lips for silence, she tiptoed to the door and stood listening. Then they both heard it—the sound of approaching footsteps.

For a moment they remained as still as figures in some forgotten painting, listening intently as the sharp, staccato sound of a woman's heels approached along the outer corridor. "It's Helene," Andrea whispered. Her voice was an anguished plea. "She'll never let me go, Sarah. And there's nothing you or anyone else can do to help me."

\* \* \*

Less than 30 minutes after Helene Von Bismark had ordered Sarah's ejection from Golden Portals, Sarah and Ian McVane marched into the Riverhead Police Station and demanded to see the chief of criminal investigations.

The lieutenant on duty at the booking desk looked up sharply as Sarah gave her name, and moments later, she discovered, much to her amazement, that a warrant had been issued for her arrest. The charges were "Malicious trespass," and the theft of a very expensive piece of Andrea's jewelry, which had been found hidden in her stateroom aboard the *Golden Hind*.

Everything happened very fast. A police officer appeared and announced that he was taking Sarah into custody, but Ian had other ideas.

"Get the hell out of here," he yelled to Sarah as he landed a solid, damaging blow squarely on the police officer's jaw. Then, as the man doubled over with a gasp and Sarah remained frozen in her tracks, he grabbed her by the arm and they ran out of the police station.

Fortunately, the jeep was parked directly in front of the station house. After ordering Sarah into the driver's seat, Ian spun around just in time to duck a wildly swinging night stick. Bells were ringing inside the station house by now, and after decking the police officer who had pursued them out to the street, Ian suddenly found himself surrounded, as reinforcements began pouring out of the front door.

Sarah realized that it was entirely up to her, and she acted by reflex. There was a screaming grind of gears as she jammed the jeep into reverse. Then she pressed the accelerator to the floor and drove backward over the curb and into the throng of uniformed police, who by now had Ian cornered.

Her move took them completely by surprise, and as Ian vaulted into the jeep beside her, the police were still scattering in all directions. "Let's get the hell out of here," Ian shouted. And with that they were off, spewing a hail of loose gravel in their wake as they careened out into the street and rocketed away from the station.

# CHAPTER 25

## THE SHINY SHEET SET
### by
### Cassandra

Well, *mes enfants,* the end of the season is almost upon us, and as all you cognoscenti already know, for the fifth year in a row, Roxanne Ryan Aristos has been named chairperson of the Gold and Silver Ball.

Meanwhile, the Hampton grapevine has been kept buzzing with each and every new and lurid revelation about Kamal Ali Reza and his Treasure Cay project. Ever since all those scandalous stories about the handsome Middle Eastern magnate's wheeling and dealing in Washington, Andrea Aristos has remained in seclusion at the Golden Portals Spa.

My best informants tell me that poor little Andrea began to get cold feet once the allegations against her Arab paramour began flying like foul balls at a triple-header. It's even being whispered around by those types orbiting Baroness Helene Von Bismark that her sister-in-law has suffered a complete mental breakdown and is in no way able to handle her own affairs.

Then there's the stepmother of the piece. And as most of you already must have guessed, Roxanne Ryan Aristos is a lady who simply never ever gets cold feet. Her campaign to save Treasure Cay has met with such overwhelming public response that the Hampton Historical Society has unan-

299

imously elected her president to serve out the remainder of her aunt Annabel Randolph's term in office.

With all work now halted on the project by a federal court order, the fortunes of Kamal Ali Reza himself seem to have fallen into sharp decline. It of course started with all those lurid tales out of Washington about call girls, bribery, and various and sundry shady dealings, in which the dashing Ali Reza was said to be involved.

Most of us do, after all, watch the evening news at least occasionally, and what has begun to emerge is a picture of a very ambitious Arab profiteer and self-serving propagandist, who hands out money the way other people hand out calling cards. The very charming Kamal appears to be one very smooth operator, Middle Eastern-style, who has achieved his unprecedented success largely by virtue of having political connections in all the right places.

What Mr. Ali Reza seems to have overlooked is the fact that as the former wife of the British ambassador to Washington, who ultimately became president of the United Nations General Assembly, Roxanne Aristos has a few important political connections of her own.

"The Treasure Cay project is an affront to all that we hope to preserve of our national heritage in this country," Roxanne has been quoted as saying. "And if we permit Third-World carpetbaggers like Kamal Ali Reza to just walk in and buy up anything that takes their fancy, we are going to end up being overrun by just anyone with money."

The lady may have a point. There is, after all, such a thing as overexposing a lifestyle already in danger of being accused of wretched excess. The Hamptons is not Palm Beach. There, the smart money maintains a respectably high profile only by virtue of the fact that they can simply pull up their drawbridges if the rabble begin getting overly restless.

The bottom line, folks, is that the unsinkable Roxanne has once again proven herself a force to be reckoned with, in spite of all those ugly rumors. Oh, surely you've heard them. That particularly nasty story, for instance, about how Roxanne had her cousin Abbey Randolph committed to Broadmoor and then got caught trying to auction off the entire Randolph estate, with herself as the immediate beneficiary.

Or perhaps that other story that has so many loose tongues wagging, about how she decided to go after Mr. Ali Reza's scalp, after he showed a decided preference for her ex-stepdaughter, Andrea.

But then that's just a lot of loose party talk, *mes amis*. There's still bound to be lots of surprises in store. You would all do well to remember that the summer season isn't officially over until after the Gold and Silver Ball. Stay tuned for the next thrilling episode of what's going on between the shiny sheets. This reporter is willing to bet her next paycheck that the best is yet to come.


Although the sun was riding high in the sky when Roxanne arrived at Dulles Airport outside Washington, there was a hint of autumn in the air. Surprising her not in the least, an impressive retinue of Ali Reza's lawyers was on hand to meet her, along with a slew of public relations people.

It had all been surprisingly simple, Roxanne thought to herself, as she was escorted across the field to where Kamal's private Boeing 707 awaited her arrival. And thus far, everything seemed to be working out exactly as she had planned.

Roxanne had been in Washington to attend a charity gala at the Kennedy Arts Center, when she was called from her box to take an urgent call from Mr. Kamal Ali Reza himself.

He was calling her personally, he said, in response to a widely circulating report that Roxanne was planning an appearance in Albany to testify against the Treasure Cay project. He went on to suggest that she would be far better informed on all the pertinent data if she were to make a personal tour of the island, for a first-hand view.

Roxanne had agreed, and Kamal had promptly dispatched his private plane to pick her up in Washington and fly her to Orient Point—a sleepy seaside community that almost overnight had become the major staging area for shipments of both men, machinery and materials out to Treasure Cay.

As the big Boeing 707 took off over Washington, Roxanne once again experienced the heady sense of power that had led her into wedlock with three very rich and powerful men. It was the closest thing to sexual fulfillment that she had ever known. Roxanne fully realized that she held all the trump cards at that particular time, and she was prepared to make Kamal Ali Reza pay dearly for the acceptance he so desperately needed. He was on her turf now, and Roxanne determined to drive a very hard bargain indeed.

After a one-hour flight, the pilot set the plane down at Orient Point, directly across the sound from Treasure Cay. There was a black Lincoln limousine waiting for her on the field. And as soon as Roxanne stepped from the plane, she was whisked away to a nearby wharf, where she was to embark on the final leg of her journey.

There was a Silver Streak hydrofoil waiting at the dock, its powerful engines churning the harbor water to a froth. Then, much to Roxanne's surprise, Kamal himself leaped to the dock with almost feline agility and welcomed her aboard with his own, well-remembered brand of highly personal charm.

With Kamal at the wheel, the hydrofoil shot off amidst towering plumes of salt spray. He was dressed casually in white shorts and tennis sneakers and a dark blue turtleneck sweater. Ali Reza appeared very tanned and fit, and there was something compellingly masculine about the way he moved and handled the boat. It was a quality of self-assurance, Roxanne decided, that defied easy accessability or confinement.

While only of medium height, Kamal was strongly

302

built and physically vital. At 48 years of age, he looked very good indeed in the role of youngest billionaire in the world, and he carried himself like a man many years his junior.

Certainly, Roxanne thought, her sister Claire must have been wildly hallucinating to have actually claimed to have had an affair with him. The whole story was utterly ludicrous.

As they skimmed across the water, Treasure Cay swam up out of the sea, looking lush and lovely in the bright afternoon sunlight. There was an austere magnificence to the island. It was shaped like a star, with forested hills, plunging cliffs, and flat ribbons of white sandy beach interspersed with rocky limestone cliffs.

As they drew closer, the island looked incredibly green and infinitely inviting to Roxanne—a veritable Eden with numerous saltwater ponds, virgin marshes, and freshwater springs surrounded by expanses of rolling meadow land. The mansion itself was clearly visible by now, crowning the island's highest promontory. It was an old French chateau, with turrets and towers and myriad banks of leaded-glass windows staring out across the water like vacant eyes.

There were times when the island was visible from the terrace at Ox Pasture Farm—like a mirage, a green haven lifting up above the distant horizon on clear and cloudless summer days.

Whether the island was actually visible or not, Roxanne was always aware of its presence. Enveloped in banks of fog and mist, it was a myth like Atlantis, that one might only half imagine to exist. It was always out there somewhere.

The new yacht harbor had been completed before work had been stopped on the Treasure Cay project by order of a federal court judge. It was an engineering masterpiece that had cost Kamal over $1 million to construct. As they skimmed across the water and Kamal lowered speed upon entering the harbor entrance, Roxanne could easily imagine spectacular yachts from all over the world riding serenely at anchor, with Treasure Cay rising verdant and magnificent in the background.

Roxanne had planned carefully for her meeting with Kamal, and she had dressed with a deliberately casual air, in a loosely flowing peasant-style skirt, ruffled blouse, and gold thong sandals. She had a fringed gypsy shawl wrapped about her shoulders and had tied a silk scarf, *babushka*-style, about her head. She wore an amusing array of turquoise and silver jewelry.

The outfit amused her, and as Kamal helped her ashore, she was reminded of Marie Antoinette playing milkmaid at Versailles.

After a brief tour of the new yacht facility, Roxanne and Kamal climbed into a pink jeep with a candy-striped awning and started off around the island. "Did you know that my Aunt Rebecca Ryan was Darnell Hanlan's mother?" Roxanne questioned, slipping a pair of large amber-tinted sunglasses over her face.

Roxanne pointed toward a peaceful, pastoral hillside, where the Hanlans had been burying their dead for over 400 years. "She's buried there," Roxanne said softly. "I was always very fond of my aunt, although I don't suppose anyone in the family or even the Hamptons ever really forgave her for marrying a Hanlan. They have always been outsiders to us, even after four hundred years."

"Perhaps you never forgave the Hanlans for having something that all the rest of you wanted. After all, they ruled like feudal kings and queens on this island, and during the slave-holding days, they even had the power of life and death over all who lived here. There's nothing new, after all, about man's ultimate dream of power and dominion. Perhaps your Aunt Rebecca simply wanted to be queen of all she surveyed."

He made a wide, sweeping gesture toward the north shore of Long Island, only barely visible on the horizon. "It's possible that she was a woman who wanted to hold the rest of the world at bay . . . out there somewhere, just off on the edge of the horizon."

It was an interesting thought to Roxanne. But in fact she remembered Aunt Rebecca Hanlan as a simple, plump, and genial woman, whose prettiness had faded quickly after coming to Hanlan's Island. Not yet 35 years of age, she became an old woman almost overnight, with hair of the palest spun silver and hands so fragile as to appear almost waxen.

By the time she reached 40, Rebecca Hanlan had gone quite mad, they said, and she had spent her final years locked up in the old stone windmill, which turned slowly against the sky. She was alone, an outcast from her own family, and totally forgotten by the outside world. She had married badly and paid the price.

As they rode along, it was plain to see that Treasure Cay was still a virtual primeval paradise. Herds of deer scattered at their approach, and flocks of wild turkey took ponderous flight from roadside thickets at the sound of the jeep's engine. Strung along the island's 23 miles were mossy stone walls, built centuries before. The air was filled with bird songs, and there were many rare and beautiful species of both flora and fauna native to nowhere else in the world.

They drove around the island for over an hour, with Kamal carefully outlining his overall plans for the future of Treasure Cay. He pointed out where the hotel, casino complex, and 18-hole golf course were to be located. Then, as they emerged from the cool, resin-scented shade of the white oak forest, Roxanne looked up to see the windmill that had become her Aunt Rebecca's prison and asylum during the last years of her life.

The windmill crested the top of a hill, with the chimneys and turrets of the old chateau clearly visible just beyond. Ever since her arrival on the island, Roxanne had been totally caught up in the spell of the place, even as she had been as a child.

"Did you know that this island was once used by pirates to bury their treasure?" Roxanne questioned. "Legend has it that in the old days, the Hanlans were in league with the worst rogues on the high seas, and they used the sails of that mill to signal them when it was safe to land. My Aunt Annabel Randolph used to say that the Hanlans would have gone into league with Satan himself if it would have served their purpose."

Kamal laughed low and deep in his throat, although Roxanne wasn't exactly sure why. "No matter how much things may appear to change," he said, "they always remain the same."

The road they had been traveling eventually wound upward to the chateau, where exotically robed and turbaned servants with faces that appeared to have been carved out of ebony were setting a table for luncheon on the wide flagstone terrace. The view was spectacular, a breathtaking sweep of sea, sky, and the distant green Hampton shoreline, with colored sails skimming across the water of Shelter Island Sound before a steady afternoon breeze.

"This is my favorite view," Kamal informed her as they strolled to the edge of the terrace, to stand looking out. "All my life I've dreamed of owning an island like this."

"It's very beautiful," Roxanne agreed. She turned to face him, deliberately holding his dark, almost mesmerizing gaze. "And I fully intend to see that it stays that way. You see, Mr. Ali Reza, in spite of your most impressive promotional tour, I've already made up my mind to defeat your project. I only accepted your invitation to come here today so that I might tell you that to your face. There are just some things that money simply can't buy."

"An interesting but naive theory," he smiled, still acting far too sure of himself as far as Roxanne was concerned. "Surely a woman of your intelligence and sophistication can do better than that, my dear Roxanne."

Something in his closeness, his voice, and the way that he said her name caused Roxanne's heart to quicken its beat, even though her features gave absolutely nothing away. Kamal turned to accept two balloon glasses half full of brandy from a hovering servant who deftly salaamed and then backed away like a shadow melting into water.

"You're a very beautiful and desirable woman," Kamal went on to say, "and I suspect you're not in the least naive."

"And you are very direct, Mr. Ali Reza. I always thought that Arabs dealt only in veiled subtleties."

Kamal's smile flashed white in his handsome dark face. "Dealing in stereotypes is often deceiving," he suggested with the faintest hint of sarcasm. "One should never take anything for granted. I imagine that you also believe I keep a harem full of beautiful and mysteriously veiled wives."

"Don't you?" she challenged.

"I've never married. You see, I've always been looking for a woman . . . let us say, worthy, of becoming my wife. A very special kind of woman."

In spite of herself, Roxanne was growing more and more intrigued by the moment. She liked his deep, vibrant voice with its Oxford accents, and the way Kamal exuded a sense of power like a pungent musk. His dark eyes were staring directly into hers now. Roxanne almost had the feeling that she was deliberately being hypnotized.

"I'll have to be getting back to Easthampton immediately after lunch," she announced abruptly, seeking to break the spell. "The Hampton Historical Society is meeting later this afternoon, and you just happen to be foremost on the agenda."

"And what if I refused to take you back? I can't very well be condemned, after all, without a presiding judge."

"I am not the Grand Inquisitor, Mr. Ali Reza— merely a concerned citizen intent on performing my civic duty." Roxanne was baiting him now, although Kamal remained totally unruffled.

"I wasn't referring to the vendetta both you and the Hampton Historical Society seem intent on carrying out," Kamal informed her. "Rather, I was thinking that nothing could be more romantically appealing than a warm summer night, an isolated island, and a beautiful woman. There are some men unscrupulous enough to take advantage of such a situation."

"Would you just happen to be one of those men, Mr. Ali Reza?"

"I insist that you call me Kamal. And yes, I might very well be."

"In that case," Roxanne said, smiling, "I shall have to watch my step." Her eyes were full upon him now, pools of deep shadow with but a single bright spark. "You're a very attractive man, after all. I can see how it would be very easy for a woman to become . . . let's say, romantically involved."

"I'm very particular about my women," he said, reaching out to brush her cheek lightly with his finger-tips.

"And I am very particular as well," Roxanne replied, terribly aware of his sexuality, his closeness, and the irreverent male confidence he exuded. "I can't afford to be otherwise. You see, Kamal, you're on my home ground now. My ancestors came here from Europe when yours were still herding goats on the deserts of Saudi Arabia. I have a very important stake in both the past and the future of the Hamptons, as well as Hanlan's Island."

Kamal laughed. "I know all about your illustrious forebears, Roxanne. They acquired great wealth in the slave trade, did they not? Although I believe you've always preferred to refer to it as the spice trade. If my history is correct, the first woman in America ever tried and convicted of witchcraft was hung by some of your ancestors. From all reports, they were a motley lot of adventurers who also kept slaves, bred them like prize livestock, and were known to hang them on occasion."

"You seem to be very well-informed," Roxanne responded coolly. "But even if it were true, that's all ancient history now. As far as I'm concerned, you're nothing but an adventurer yourself—not in the least different from the pirates, slave traders, and gun runners who came here in the past."

"There is one important difference," Kamal asserted. "I'm very rich and very powerful. Within five years I can turn this island into the most exclusive resort in the world—a beautiful and uniquely exclusive paradise reserved for only the very rich."

"Why is this so important to you?" Roxanne questioned. "Aren't you already rich enough? Why do you need more millions?"

"There is no such thing as rich enough, my dear Roxanne. And by the way, it's not more millions I'm interested in . . . it's billions."

"And what has all this to do with me?"

"You have the power to grant me exactly what I want," he informed her. "Treasure Cay has the potential of becoming Monte Carlo, Biarritz, and Acapulco all rolled into one. I intend to rule here as a king, Roxanne, and if kings are to rule over royal courts, they must have queens."

"You're very sure of yourself," she said.

"I can afford to be," he responded.

Kamal turned and lifted the two balloon glasses from where he had set them on the stone balustrade, and their fingers touched as he pressed one into Roxanne's hand. "I'd like to propose a toast," he said. "To the future of Treasure Cay."

Roxanne smiled and lifted her glass to his. "To the future," she toasted.

It was an act of mutual ravishment.

# CHAPTER 26

Roxanne's widely heralded appearance at the committee hearing in Albany the following week was pure political theater. And there was no question left in anyone's mind but that the Treasure Cay project and its attendant gambling legislation now received her full support.

It was a stunning switch, and no less impressive was her subsequent press conference. It was the occasion on which she chose to announce that, in order to preserve the island's natural heritage, she had accepted the position of consultant to the newly formed Treasure Cay Corporation, of which she had been named to the board of directors.

The news had scarcely hit the front pages of the afternoon papers, when Claire Ryan Spencer appeared on a local Easthampton TV show to decry the entire spectacle as "a gross manipulation of public trust."

Claire's exposure of the appalling conditions at Broadmoor had earned her a host of admirers. Almost overnight, Claire Ryan Spencer had been transformed into a woman fired with a mission. And she had found a very compelling issue in the "suffocating, corrupt, squalid and inhuman conditions" that she had discovered to prevail behind the vine-covered walls of the so-called "model institution."

In fact, her sister Roxanne's highly touted press conference, at which she announced her "full and unswerving support" for the Treasure Cay project, was given short shrift that evening on the six o'clock news.

Instead, all of Long Island, most of Connecticut, and

at least the eastern half of New Jersey was treated to a virtual chamber of horrors tour of Broadmoor, with Claire Spencer undeniably running the entire show.

Claire was without question the woman of the hour. Shortly thereafter, a high-level investigation into the administrative affairs of the hospital was launched, and Dr. Jacobsen found himself under indictment by a grand jury on a variety of charges.

Little was made in the press or media coverage in general, however, of the fact that Roxanne Ryan Aristos was found to be a member of the board of trustees. Nor was any action taken on Claire's charges that her sister was guilty of "overt collusion" in having Abbey Randolph committed to the institution against her will.

There simply wasn't any legal evidence to support such a charge, and Abbey herself remained in a deep coma in the intensive-care unit of the Westport Medical Center. She had never regained consciousness following the electroshock therapy to which she was subjected, and her doctors conceded that she would "most likely remain a vegetable for life, as a result of extensive brain damage."

It was clear to everyone who saw the televised exposure of the inhumane conditions at Broadmoor that Claire Spencer had become a totally different person. Perhaps equally surprising was the fact that she publicly declared herself to have been a pill-popping alcoholic who had lived her life for totally selfish reasons.

The Hampton party circuit was talking about little else besides how one of the social scene's foremost swingers had been virtually "born again." Offers began coming in from all over the area, requesting Claire to speak before various prestigious women's groups, and that was precisely what she did.

Claire was utterly convinced that she had experienced a miracle in her own life, and she publicly vowed to devote her time and energies to championing causes important to women like herself—those victims of urban fallout who were trapped between middle-class con-

311

formity and the newly risen female consciousness.

Following her first week of speaking engagements to enthusiastic audiences everywhere she appeared, the state chairman of the Independent Party announced that they were backing Claire Spencer as their candidate in the forthcoming Congressional primary. That was the beginning of Claire's run for public office, and everywhere she went, her message was a basically simple one: the exurban Good Life was finished, and the pressures outside the barricades were growing. Inside the fortress walls, resistance to change was feverish, but spirit and vigor were waning. Exurbia was dying because its life sources were drying up, and its organic defenses were eroding with alarming swiftness.

The inhabitants of the affluent enclaves from Westport to Pasadena constituted an elite within American society that had previously set standards, embodied a way of life to be emulated, and determined goals to be strived for. But now all that was changing, and it was the urban woman who was ultimately the victim, through isolation and insulation from problems, cities, neighborhoods, and even the members of her own family.

The "good life" was clearly crumbling, and Claire Spencer was the first to carry the message that it hadn't really been all that good in the first place.

Then came the *real* bombshell. The Gold and Silver Ball, currently being orchestrated beneath the baton of Roxanne Ryan Aristos, was going to be held on Treasure Cay. Ali Reza had agreed to absorb the entire cost, which meant that all the proceeds would then be available for a variety of local charities.

No one was ever really sure whether it had been his idea or hers. But it was generally conceded by those in the know about such matters that they were a perfectly matched pair, who couldn't have deserved each other more. Within a matter of days after her visit to Treasure Cay, Roxanne and Kamal Ali Reza were the hottest new twosome around.

Cassandra started out in her column on the day before the Congressional primary:

Well, *mes enfants,* the end of the season is almost upon us, and the Gold and Silver Ball appears to be shaping up as the most spectacular event ever. But then why shouldn't it be? After all, my lovelies, the indestructible Roxanne and her Arabian knight have just got to be *the* power match of the decade.

You can take it from me that there are a lot of people who may think they're getting a very fast shuffle, but mum's the word. I mean that nobody who's anybody has the slightest intention of raking over a lot of old garbage only to find themselves left sitting on the dock when Kamal's Silver Streak hydrofoils begin plying the waters between the Hamptons and what is fast stacking up to be the most exclusive and glamorous resort of its kind in the world.

It's no secret that queens deprived of court need kings with clout or must make do with tacky half-measures. And quite frankly, my dears, there just haven't been all that many honest-to-God kings running around here of late. At least not until the dynamic and oh-so-terribly-rich Mr. Megabucks Ali Reza.

As almost anyone will tell you straight out, all that really counts these days is cold hard *dinero,* so let's tell it like it is. The Hamptons' very own Roxanne has shown herself to be a very practical *Hausfrau* indeed when it comes to putting two nickels together, and there are even those who claim that she's down to her last million.

I mean, let's face it, my pretties. With Lady Got-Rocks throwing her prestige on the line to ensure the success of Treasure Cay, all opposition to the project has magically melted away like ice sculptures on a hot summer day. Kamal Ali Reza has gone legit in a big way, and its no longer considered amusing dinner table talk to do more than hint at his past indiscretions.

After all, the Congressmen that promised to nail

313

him to the wall suddenly discovered they were hanging onto the tail of a greased eel. It wasn't long afterwards that the Congressional investigation quickly disintegrated into petty squabbles and unauthorized news leaks about who got what from whom, and soon after came the amazing *pirouette en point* of the investigating committee's star witness.

In case you haven't yet heard, Barbara Van Patten, the play-for-pay blonde bombshell, with her little black book full of important names has suddenly decamped. She was last seen, however, wearing a red wig and being spirited off to a secluded Acapulco villa in one of Mr. Ali Reza's private jets. If this happens to sound like a very intriguing scenario, she'll no doubt turn up some day to write a book and do the talk shows. (Maybe she'll even give us the details on how she got all those bruises in the course of her dealings with the mysterious Mr. Ali Reza.)

Anyway, it all just goes to show you that Congressional committees aren't all that enthusiastic about investigating themselves when it comes to matters like sex, influence-peddling, and political chicanery. Now that the New York State Legislature has made Offshore Gambling a *fait accompli,* it looks as if the Treasure Cay project is afloat at last.

Let's face it, all you society groupies. In the land of illusion, fantasy is king—which just about brings me to today's hottest, just-off-the-grapevine item.

A little bird with brilliant plumage just whispered in my ear that the Gold and Silver Ball is going to be a *bal masque.* That means get out all your fancy drag, folks, for one last end-of-the-season rocket to the moon. Everyone who's anyone is going to be blasting off for Treasure Cay this coming Friday night. And I'll just bet you'd rather lose an arm or a leg than miss out on a single, solitary minute of what promises to be the season's biggest and most prestigious *affaire sans pareil.*

# =CHAPTER 27=

From far out at sea, the waves came thundering in bigger than she had ever seen them before. Yet from where Kim stood high on the cliffs near Montauk Point, they had a deceptively blue and innocuous look as they mounted up in the distance.

Yet as each wave reached the shallow water feeding into the deadly pipeline at Suicide Alley, it rose suddenly to unexpected heights and then turned green and concave as it started its rush toward the beach. It was sleek and smooth and massive, right up until the instant when the wave finally came crashing down in a seething, frothing wall of white water, roaring in toward shore.

It was the third day in a row that Kim had surfed Suicide Alley, and yet there was a hollow strangeness in the pit of her stomach as she removed her fiberglass surfboard from the rack atop her car. Jaime called the place the "meat grinder," and he had consistently refused to take her surfing there because he said it was simply too dangerous. Even on relatively calm days, the surf barreled in out of the Atlantic like an onrushing freight train and broke with explosive force on the submerged rocks about 200 yards from shore.

On that particular afternoon, the place was deserted, the beach below empty and strewn with driftwood and mounds of seaweed washed up by the morning tide. Kim shielded her eyes against the glare and watched the waves pile in from out at sea without break or pause.

Jaime had taught her a lot about surfing during their

all-too-brief summer together. Kim realized immediately that what she was looking at was merely the vanguard of a storm that was most likely still thousands of miles away—huge and roiling juggernauts, twisted by the deadly undertow, and streaked with clouds of seaweed and sand.

The waves had already narrowed the beach, and by the time Kim reached the bottom of the narrow path leading down from the cliffs above, she was already breathing hard.

Still staring off toward the horizon with an apprehensive and far-away look in her eyes, Kim stripped off her jeans and sweatshirt. The sand beneath her feet was still warm as she wiggled her toes, but just below the surface it grew chilly and slightly damp. The sun, climbing the arch of the sky, was pale and diffused with a hazy corona blocking its warmth.

She shivered involuntarily, realizing that summer was over—just so many days circled on a calendar, now past and gone forever. A solitary gull came winging in from the sea, *kaaing* with sharp and piercing cries, as if warning of the storm to come.

For a moment, Kim watched its flight. Then she bent to wax the surface of her board and tried desperately not to think of Jaime.

He had been standing there beside the highway, hitchhiking a ride north on that first day, smiling, youthful, and golden in the sunlight as she pulled over to the side of the road and stopped the car. She had watched him run toward her in the rearview mirror, a duffel bag slung over one of his shoulders and a surfboard clutched beneath his arm.

It had been the beginning of a dream that had now clotted and curdled in the summer sunlight, turning finally into a twisted and distorted nightmare from which Kim wondered if she would ever be able to extricate herself, without leaving large chunks of her innermost being strewn along the way.

Kim heard a voice calling her name and turned to

see Jaime staring down at her from the top of the cliffs. His eyes were masked behind mirrored sunglasses. For several moments, they stared at one another, with the seconds stretching into an eternity of pain.

Then she ran down the beach to throw her board into the water, leaping on top of it while the board was still in motion, she paddled away from shore with short, powerful strokes.

Kim paddled hard, with her cheek pressed against the board. Her weight slid back as the nose of the board hit each successive wave and sent mountains of water rushing over her body, filling her eyes and her nose. She blinked hard and continued paddling until she was well beyond the surfline.

Then she swung her board around and slid into a sitting position. The power and force of the waves had frightened her on the way out. But here, the surface of the sea appeared deceptively flat and glassy smooth.

Her teeth began to chatter and Kim shivered. She watched Jaime's distant figure running across the beach. Then he threw his board into the water and started paddling out toward her. His head was down and his shoulders moved powerfully, the muscles rippling and glinting in the sun with each stroke he took.

Oh dear God, she thought. Don't let me have to face him. Somehow, please . . . just let me die or disappear.

"Just what the hell do you think you're doing?" he called out, as his board drew near. "You've gotta be crazy to come out here on a day like this."

Kim said nothing as he paddled close. She simply sat there, refusing to meet Jaime's eyes as he swung his board around and slid into a sitting position no more than four or five feet away. "I'm sorry about what you saw, Kim," he said finally. "But it wasn't what you think. I was just an actor . . . playing a role. That's what I get paid for, and that's what I do."

The wind was sharper now, whipping across the tops of the waves that swept beneath them, rose up about

50 yards farther on, and then crashed down in the shallows to thunder toward shore. Still Kim didn't speak, nor would she even look his way.

"Come on," Jaime urged. "Talk to me. Don't just shut me out like this."

"You're not the same," she said finally. "You're different. Someone I don't know at all."

Kim didn't know where the words came from. She didn't think them with her mind or try and phrase her feelings. They were simply there—cast to the winds.

"You're wrong," Jaime said. "I haven't changed. What you saw on that videotape was someone else entirely. An actor. You've got to believe that."

She shook her head and bit her lower lip, trying hard to keep back the tears. "I've had a few days to think it over, Jaime, out here with the waves, the wind, and the sky. The summer's over, and I've got to be getting back to the real world."

His face and his voice were anguished. "Come away with me, Kim. We can leave this place behind us. I've got money now, and it isn't too late. Look, I got myself into something that I just couldn't handle. The whole sick, stinking scene makes me want to puke, and I'm sorry that I ever got involved." -

"Me too," she shot back. "Boy, am I sorry that I ever got involved!"

Even as she spoke, Kim felt something prickle along her spine, like an early warning signal. She looked back over her shoulder even as Jaime swung around, as if he had felt it too.

Then suddenly, there it was—the biggest wave she had ever seen, humping up in the distance, entirely blotting out the horizon. Kim sat there frozen as the monster wave continued to rise, with the chilling offshore wind whipping sea spume from its crest.

Jaime gave a low, appraising whistle and began frantically backing water. "I've never seen anything like it," he cried above the wind. "It's a killer, and we've got to get farther out before it breaks."

He turned his board and began paddling directly toward the approaching wave, which seemed to be sweeping down on them in slow motion. It looked like a ten-story nightmare to Kim, and she appeared utterly mesmerized, watching as the color of the wave changed from blue to translucent green.

By now, the roar was deafening as the wave heaved up to display a delicate filigree of seaweed, reaching out like ghostly, skeletal arms. For an instant, a huge stingray seemed to remain frozen in time, its massive batlike wings spread wide, as if for flight.

Then, almost without any volition of her own, Kim began to paddle, lining herself up to ride the wave. She heard Jaime's shout of warning from somewhere behind her. But by then the primal mass of water had already swept her up to the crest, and Kim was taken by the feeling that she was about to step off of the edge of the world.

It was like suddenly finding oneself on the peak of a great mountain, and the abyss gaping beneath her board was simply too awesome, too staggering and unbelievable to even begin to contemplate.

In the very next instant, Kim was hurtled forward with a massive thrust of power that took her breath away. Her board dropped down the face of the wave, and suddenly she was on her feet, clutching desperately with her toes for balance, leaning her body backward into the wave, and then sliding gracefully into the curl at speeds beyond imagining.

In the very last instant before the wave swept her away, Jaime had paddled hard to catch the peak. He saw Kim rise to straddle her board and then cut sharply left as she hurtled down the concave face of the massive, green comber.

Jaime knew the rocks were just ahead of her, and as he pressed down hard and hunched his body sideways, angling across the face of the wave, he knew exactly what he had to do.

Slicing down upon her from above amid a massive

convulsion of sound and sea, he dove suddenly for Kim's knees. And in the very next instant, they were both hurtled into the sea, with the giant wave breaking above them, and snatching eagerly at their closely entwined bodies.

It felt as if the entire Atlantic Ocean had them in its grip, as they were thrown hard against the sandy bottom and then swept through a patch of slime-covered sea grass that whipped about their bodies like coiling tentacles.

Suddenly, the massive pressure was miraculously lifted, and they were being swirled over and over amid raging clouds of sand and twisting ropes of kelp. Their bodies clung tightly, desperately, together, as they were swept upward, almost to the surface, only to be thrown once again, down to the floor of the sea.

The wave seemed somehow to have come to possess them, and Kim opened her eyes at one point, to find Jaime's distorted features close to hers. The two of them were suspended in time and space, as he gripped her fiercely in the vise of his strong arms. They were swept across a shoal of barnacles, with Jaime angling his body around, until the razored edges sliced across his flesh like hundreds of tiny knives.

Kim's lungs were bursting by now, and she was beginning to black out, even as she saw the sunlit surface far overhead. Then, the next thing she knew, Jaime had pushed her up toward the light and the air with a mighty thrust of his arms.

Air. All she wanted was air and life, and yet it seemed to be so very far away. But Kim was no longer afraid, for there on the bottom of the sea, she had come to know that Jaime loved her. And she felt almost a peaceful euphoria as the world tilted up suddenly to spin crazily away into black, black infinity.

The next thing she knew, Kim found herself on the sand, with Jaime bending anxiously over her. She coughed and vomited up saltwater as he pulled her hard against his chest. Then he held her like a child in his arms, drawing the sand-matted hair back from her face. "I love you, Kim," he whispered. "You've simply got to believe that."

For a moment, Kim remained very still. Then she lifted her head to kiss his salty lips with childlike innocence. "Oh, Jaime," she sighed, clinging tightly, "take me away from here . . . before this place destroys us both. It doesn't matter where . . . just as long as we're together."

# CHAPTER 28

For the first 12 days following her removal from Broadmoor, Abbey had remained in a deep coma. She was merely an observer, an inner witness, watching a procession of fractured images move across the shattered mirrors of her mind, like an endlessly running slide projector.

It was a dreamlike and surrealistic landscape, where memories swirled about her like poisonous, suffocating cobwebs, and the sense of impending doom was as sharp as pain. It was a slow descent into an oblivion of nothingness, through a kaleidoscopic reverie of half-formed images.

Again and again, Abbey relived the horror of what had happened to her at Broadmoor. But she relived it as a child playing alone at Bramwell Acres, a child humming softly to herself in an upper bedroom, as a Dresden music box tinkled lightly in the simmering hush of a long summer's afternoon.

There had been no foreshadowing of the horror that was to come, nothing more sinister than the sound of soft footsteps outside in the hall and the sound of whispered voices. Then a key was turning in the lock and the door was slowly opening.

Even the sudden and quite unexpected appearance of a strange man dressed in what looked to be a hospital orderly's uniform had caused no more than a momentary sense of curious wonderment. It was only a man, the child thought, with one of her mother's silk stockings drawn down over his face like a sadly pathetic clown.

The child laughed as the intruder signaled for silence, holding his finger to his lips, as if they were playing a game. Then the man wearing the clown mask was moving across the room to stand looking down at her with oddly slush-colored eyes. "Who are you?" the child asked as another white-garbed figure appeared behind him in the doorway. It was a young boy in his teens, with a thin face, long, stringy hair and feverishly darting eyes. He giggled obscenely as he closed the door behind him and then began stroking himself in front with a grubby hand.

"Mother . . ." Abbey cried out, suddenly frightened. Then abruptly, the clown face wasn't smiling anymore. The man seemed suddenly angry, looming over her and cursing beneath his breath while muttering something about not calling the matron.

He was carrying a brown paper bag, and his hand shook spasmodically as he reached inside to pull out a large kitchen knife. It was sharp and very shiny as the man bent over and held it to the child's throat. Then the fear began, running through Abbey's veins like ice water, even as the Dresden music box continued to chime out its precise and pristine notes, tinkling merrily on the silence.

Abbey wasn't sure just when she realized that the room in which she found herself was not her own familiar bedroom at Bramwell Acres. It was small, narrow, clinically white, and there were bars at the windows.

The two men in white were hovering over her now, and Abbey was totally helpless. Once again, the man with the silk stocking pulled down over his face reached into his brown paper bag, this time pulling out a pair of rawhide laces. Then he tied her wrists tightly together behind her back, stuffed a dirty handkerchief into her mouth, and tore the white hospital smock from her body.

323

After that, everything that happened began running together, like watercolors spreading on a wet canvas. Abbey struggled beneath the weight of the man's body and choked against the gag. The man's hands were rough and calloused, and his breathing grew labored. Then he was stabbing at her . . . somewhere down there, hurting her terribly, as Abbey squeezed her eyes tightly shut against the hideously distorted face.

It all ended with the sound of distant, excited voices and footsteps running along the outer corridor. Then the door crashed open, and the room quickly filled with people.

By then, the Dresden music box with its tiny, twirling figure had completely run down, and Abbey had gone limp and silent, retreating from the horror and the pain into some secret hiding place deep within herself.

Abbey finally awakened at the Westport Medical Center, with her own screams echoing in her ears. Her eyes shuttered open, and she tried to raise her head from the pillow, only to fall back with a gasp of pain.

She ached everywhere. Her throat was dry and parched, and Abbey had no coherent idea of where she was or even what had happened to her.

All Abbey knew was that she seemed to be emerging from a long, twisting tunnel of blackness, with her vital energies drained and her emotions weighted with fatigue. Her head was throbbing with a heavy, dull insistence, and she blinked against the light, through eyelids that were scarcely open.

The perspiration was wiped from her forehead with a damp cloth, and a voice seemed to come out of nowhere. "I think she's finally coming out of it, Doctor."

Abbey managed to turn her head slightly, looking up into the gently smiling face of a nurse wearing a crisply starched uniform and white cap. Her vision was blurry and lacking focus. And for several moments, the man standing next to her bed seemed to be part of the dazzling whiteness, except for two very piercing bright blue eyes.

The doctor smiled to reassure her and placed a cool palm upon her forehead, while the nurse lifted a glass of water to Abbey's lips. "Well, Miss Randolph, how are you feeling, now that you've decided to come back to the world?"

Abbey heard the words, but their meaning was only vaguely understood, as she reached up to feel the bandage drawn tightly about her head. The pain was intense. There was a loud buzzing going on somewhere in her head, and she was swept by wave after wave of dizziness and nausea.

When she failed to respond to further questioning, the doctor checked Abbey's pulse, and then shone a small flashlight into the pupils of her eyes. He frowned and cleared his throat. "I doubt if the police will ever be able to discover exactly what happened to her," he said. "The effects of the electroshock therapy might very well have caused an undetermined degree of amnesia."

"What about the young man?" the nurse whispered. "The one who comes every day with flowers." At her words, Abbey realized for the first time that the room was filled with roses. And for a moment, she even thought she smelled their delicate scent upon the air. She was literally surrounded by vases of long-stemmed red roses.

The doctor moved to the foot of the bed and began making a series of notes on her medical chart. "Does the name Jaime Rodriquez mean anything to you, Miss Randolph? He's come every day to see you, and he seems to be extremely anxious about your recovery."

Returning to stand beside her, the doctor lifted a hypodermic needle from a tray presented by the nurse. He held it poised for a moment, allowing a single crystalline drop of morphine to run down the shining steel shaft. "Do you remember this Jaime Rodriquez?"

he asked. "Try to think. Try to remember his face."

Abbey turned away as the needle pierced her flesh. "Jaime," she whispered in a softly muffled voice.

There was a soft and distant roaring in her ears now, like surf breaking on some far shore, as the bright mercurial river of morphine began to pulse and surge through her veins.

"Jaime," she whispered again, but the name conjured up absolutely nothing. Then, feeling light as a feather cast to the winds, Abbey began to experience a lovely, languid, peaceful feeling. It was so pleasant not having to think or be or do anything.

Perhaps this was what death was really like, she thought a bit vaguely. No longer caring about anyone or anything. Just letting the welcome darkness close in on every side as you slowly drift away.

# CHAPTER 29

Kim and Jaime decided to leave for Rio de Janeiro on the night of the Gold and Silver Ball. But there was yet much that had to be accomplished before their departure.

Jaime instructed Kim to take the $10,000 he stuffed into her bag and drive into Manhattan early that morning. Before she left, he gave her a set of passport photos he had had taken, along with the address of a place on Fourteenth Street known to execute falsified documents for a fee.

Her next assignment was to sell her car at a used-car lot somewhere in Queens and then take a taxi to Kennedy, where she was to purchase two first-class tickets to Rio, on a flight leaving sometime after midnight. Jaime kised her good-bye and instructed Kim to wait for him at the airport, where he promised to join her after taking care of what he termed a "personal matter."

Darnell's 65-foot cabin cruiser, the *El Diablo,* rode the light swell at the end of the Three-Mile Harbor jetty. It was a sleekly rakish vessel, powered by twin diesel marine engines that could outrun anything short of the U.S. Navy.

The eggshall-white hull reflected upon the harbor water like glazed Chinese porcelain. And as Jaime made his way along the dock, he thought how peaceful and serene it all looked. A beautiful summer afternoon, a lovely pastoral setting, and a rendezvous with a man he wanted very much to kill.

Hanlan was a fanatic about keeping his boat in perfect, ship-shape condition. As Jaime swung aboard the cruiser, the teakwood decks were brightly varnished, and the brasswork gleamed and flashed in the afternoon sunlight.

"I've come to settle accounts," Jaime said.

Darnell, who had been tinkering with the engine in the wheelhouse, turned and squinted toward Jaime. Then he pulled out a soiled red bandana and mopped his brow. "I was rather expecting that you'd be showing up today, Jaime. And I guess you're right . . . your work here is finished. Now I suppose you'll be running off with that tall, skinny broad you've been screwing all summer."

It was the first time that Darnell had ever even acknowledged Kim's existence. Jaime, however, was not surprised. Hanlan made it his business to know everything.

"We had a deal, Darnell. I fulfilled my end of it, and I came here today to get what I have coming. I came to collect my ten thousand dollars."

Darnell smiled that strange, mocking smile of his. "Patience, Jaime my boy. Don't you even want to hear about my travel plans? I was sure that you'd be interested."

After wiping the grease from his hands and replacing the cover over the engine, Darnell pulled out a map and spread it on the bulkhead. "There's Bermuda," he said, stabbing at the map with his finger. "I'm leaving for there later this afternoon. Then, after a couple of weeks, I plan to head for the Gulf of Mexico and the Yucatan. It should be quite a trip, Jaime—just traveling down the coast of Central America, going from port to port with all the women, drugs, and booze you could ever want. How does it sound?"

Jaime's laugh was a short, harsh bark of derision. "Three months ago, Darnell, you might have hooked me on all that crap. But I'm a little older and a lot wiser now. I know I've been living on borrowed time, always on the run. I never gave a shit for anybody in my life, and all I wanted was to get mine while the getting was good."

"And now?" Darnell baited him.

"Now I don't give a good shit what you do or where you go. I'm no longer for sale. I want you to be very straight on that, Darnell. The simple truth is that I hate your guts."

"What a pity," Darnell drawled, his tone fairly oozing sarcasm. "And I had hoped that you might at least feel the faintest twinge of gratitude, considering what I've done for you. Why, just look at yourself, dear boy. I've made you a star. Thanks to me, you've spent the summer fucking some of the most expensive pussy in the good old U. S. of A. Why, you've practically fucked your way through *Who's Who.*"

"I also did a lot of things I'm not very proud of," Jaime said. "Tell me something up front, Darnell. Just what the hell do you get out of all this?"

Suddenly there it was. The question that had remained unasked throughout their relationship. The question that Jaime had never really been sure that he wanted answered.

There was something sinister and deranged in Darnell's laugh. "The truth is always stranger than fiction, my dear boy. Most simply put, I want to be remembered as the man who put the Hamptons on the map as the Sodom and Gomorrah of the nuclear age. Revenge is the name of the game, Jaime my lad. An eye for an eye and all that sort of thing."

Suddenly Jaime didn't want to hear any more. He just wanted to get away from there, away from Darnell and all that he had come to represent. He wanted to be free of his malign influence and the pure, visceral hatred he felt for the man.

"I haven't got much time," Jaime informed him

329

abruptly. "Let's get this over with. There's something about you that makes me feel dirty all over."

"Ah, youth," Darnell laughed. "Always so impatient to get on with things. You really must learn to take yourself a little less seriously, Jaime. All this smoldering anger and brooding resentment are becoming rather tedious to me. I must insist that we have one final drink together before parting and going our separate ways."

As Darnell led the way down the steps into the spacious cabin, Jaime paused and drew the switchblade knife from his pocket. He flicked it open, holding the weapon in his hand for a moment as it glinted wickedly in the sun. Then, with a shrug, Jaime tossed the knife overboard and followed Darnell down the stairs.

Kim would be waiting for him at Kennedy, and that was all that really mattered now. Not Darnell, nor the revenge Jaime so badly wanted to exact. The past was behind him now, Jaime realized, and for the first time in his life, it looked as if he was going to have a future.

Once inside the handsomely appointed teakwood cabin, Darnell poured each of them a shot of Pernod at the bar. "Chin chin," he toasted, clinking his glass against Jaime's. "Bottoms up, and all that rubbish."

As he drank the sickly sweet Pernod, Jaime's eyes were drawn to the heavily weighted bullwhip hanging coiled against the bulkhead. There were jagged chunks of lead fastened along the tip. Darnell had once informed him that the whip had been used originally by his forebears, on runaway slaves.

"An interesting piece of equipment, is it not? Quite lethal and certainly one of the most hideous weapons of torture ever invented. It belonged to the original Darnell Hanlan, who settled here in the seventeenth century. According to the family scuttlebutt he used to quite regularly flail the flesh from the body of any slave who had displeased him."

"I wish you'd asked me to use it on you just once, Darnell. Just to even the score."

"I may be into bondage, Jaime, but I'm not suicidal. At least not yet. I've known all along that you are quite capable of killing me if I were to provoke you enough." Darnell's laughter was brimming with obscenity, as Jamie just stood there staring at him blankly.

"But don't you see, my boy? That's why sex was so exciting with you. You're like a bomb that might go off at any time."

"You're sick, Darnell . . . and the only way you can get off is by dragging a lot of others down into that slimy gutter you exist in. Now let's get going. I want to put you and this place behind me as fast as possible."

Darnell cackled with amusement. "Patience, patience, my boy." He circled the cabin, pulling the drapes, and Jaime had the distinct impression that for some reason he was stalling. Then he removed an oversized moroccan leather briefcase from a brass-bound captain's trunk and laid it on one of the built-in bunks.

"I'm a very rich man, you know, Jaime. Not that five million dollars was nearly enough money to compensate me for what I've lost." Once again he laughed that odd, braying laugh. "But then, I fully expect to be more than compensated in ways that you couldn't possibly be able to comprehend."

Jaime paid little attention, since Darnell's love of intrigue often led him to talk in veiled terms, with all kinds of subterranean meanings important only to himself. Jaime swayed slightly, feeling a little queasy as a wave of dizziness swept over him.

"Now then," Darnell said, twirling the dials on the combination lock and then springing open the lid. "Feast your eyes, Jaime my lad, on more money than you will ever see again in your lifetime. An impressive sight, is it not?"

Jaime's eyes widened at the sight of all those crisp new bills in large denominations, and he reached out to steady himself against the bar. "I couldn't care less," he said huskily, in a voice that sounded thick and slightly slurred. "Just give me what you owe me, so I can get the hell out of here. This place is beginning to suffocate me."

Darnell's eyes licked over him, and he was smiling a narrow, wolfish smile. Then he removed a banded stack of thousand-dollar bills from the case and counted off 15 of them. "Here you are, my boy." He handed them to Jaime. "You've earned your money, and I've even decided to toss in a five-thousand-dollar bonus for good measure. I must say, you never failed to provide a stimulating performance."

Clutching the money in his hand, Jaime suddenly staggered backwards as the room seemed to spin about him. His vision was blurred and wavering, with double images and changing hues and colors.

"You sick faggot bastard," he gasped. "You put something in my drink, didn't you?"

Darnell's voice was smooth, silky, and deceptively ingratiating. "Surely you didn't really think that I spent all summer creating a masterpiece, just to let you wander off with the first cheap little slut that caught your eye. Thanks to me, Jaime, you've become quite a valuable piece of property."

Darnell laughed as Jaime struggled to retain his balance on legs that would no longer support him. "Don't fight the feeling, baby. I put enough chloral hydrate in your drink to send you off to bye-bye land for some time to come. By the time you start to come out of it, we'll be halfway to Mexico."

More than anything else in the world, Jaime regretted throwing away the knife he had brought with him that day. He was by now very close to losing consciousness, and with a guttural curse, Jaime flung out his arm to throw the money in Darnell's face. Then he was sprawling on the floor of the cabin, amid the sound of shattering glass and the sickly sweet smell of Pernod rising up to fill his nostrils from the broken bottle.

The last thing that Jaime saw as the roaring blackness began rushing in to enclose him was Darnell's face leaning very close. His features were smiling and grotesquely distorted, like a diabolical and obscene countenance peering down at him through a swirling mist of rushing seawater.

It was the steady throb of the diesel engines that finally awakened him. Jaime opened his eyes, moved a little, and tried to raise his head from the pillow. Fatigue clung like a ghostly residue to his bones, and when he tried to lift himself up, Jaime fell back with a soft groan.

From somewhere up above came a trace of light. Was it morning? Afternoon? Evening? Jaime couldn't be sure. He had totally lost all sense of time, and the heavy drapes drawn across the portholes succeeded in sealing the cabin in semigloom.

What he did know for certain was that the powerful marine engines of Darnell's sleek cruiser were humming beneath him. Jaime was lying on one of the bunks in the cabin, and as full consciousness returned, he reached up to draw back the draperies covering the porthole above his head.

He experienced a cold, numbing sensation that seemed to penetrate the farthest extremities of his body. And for several long, dizzying moments, Jaime felt as if he were staring up from a deep well of blackness, with a circular space of stars glimmering high overhead. The heavens appeared to be terribly distant, shimmering with star-heavy galaxies, as cold and far away as some future century he would never live to see.

Then he remembered that Kim was waiting for him at the airport, and the thought immediately galvanized Jaime into action. If only he could manage to get to her, he knew that everything would be all right.

Darnell was standing at the wheel, and as Jaime staggered up the steps from the cabin below, he turned to see the heavily weighted leather bullwhip clutched tightly in Jaime's hand. His handsome face was contorted into a mask of pure hatred, and his pale green eyes were fixed and staring with a look that Darnell had never seen before.

As Jaime lurched up the stairs, Darnell slipped his hand inside the light blue nylon windbreaker he wore and withdrew a German Luger. Clicking off the safety, he waved the nose of the gun in Jaime's direction. "A rather formidable weapon, wouldn't you agree, Jaime boy? The Germans have always impressed me greatly with their mechanical genius in warfare."

Darnell laughed, and his voice had a high-pitched, almost hysterical, quality that grated on Jaime's ragged nerves like fingernails being drawn across a chalkboard. "This is a war I've been waging. You know that, don't you. Just me . . . Darnell Hanlan. The last of an ancient bloodline that has been at war against society for over four hundred years."

"You're insane," Jaime grunted, bracing himself against the recurring waves of dizziness that continued to sweep over him.

"Perhaps. I shouldn't be the first of the Hanlans to go stark raving mad, although I shall certainly be the last. Now I must warn you, Jaime, that if you take one more step, I'm going to stop you dead in your tracks. It would be so easy, you know—so easy just to kill you and throw your body overboard. I mean, who would know . . . or even care? You're nothing but a sexual robot. A cheap little hustler who sold himself for nickels and dimes all his life. You're nothing without me, Jaime. Nothing at all. I created you . . . and I'll never let you go. Not ever."

Jaime stood at the top of the gangway now, leaning heavily against the bulkhead and staring into the muzzle of Darnell's Luger as if he were staring into the deadly basilisk eyes of a venomous cobra. His vision was hazy and distorted, while there was but a single thought in his mind.

"Not one more step," Darnell shrilled. "I'm warning you."

Jaime staggered slightly and tried to focus his senses. The night was brightly moonlit, with a pale moon rising on the eastern horizon. Off to their left, Jaime could see the lights of Orient Point. In the other direction lay Treasure Cay, with a flotilla of yachts, hydrofoils, and power launches ferrying hundreds of colorfully costumed guests across the sound for the Gold and Silver Ball.

The strains of music came drifting across the water to them, and in the very next instant, an incredible display of fireworks erupted from atop the island's highest point.

Darnell was thrown momentarily offguard as sunbursts of red, green, and yellow pinwheels spiraled high into the sky, to explode into galaxies of brightly colored stars. He appeared to be momentarily captivated by the spectacle, while Jaime was suddenly provided with exactly the opportunity he had been looking for.

In an instant, he had unleashed the long, snaking bullwhip, sending it curling out to slither around Darnell's wrist. The Luger fell to the deck with a metallic clatter. Then Jaime struck again, lashing out this time to curl the whip about Darnell's face and throat.

Darnell screamed, as the sheer force of the blow threw him against the throttle and sent the cruiser shooting ahead. Then, as the whip unspooled from about his antagonist's face, Jaime saw that Darnell's upper lip had been almost completely severed, and the disdainful high-bridged nose had been reduced to mangled pulp.

It all happened so fast that Hanlan had been taken completely by surprise. "Aaarggh," he cried. One of Darnell's eyes was blinking wildly now, and the other appeared to be little more than a bloody socket. The leaded weights along the tip of the whip had wreaked a swift and terrible vengeance. Darnell's mouth hung open like a gaping wound, with broken stumps of teeth protruding, as he stumbled blindly about.

Jaime lunged for him, and seconds later they were

335

struggling together on the deck, with the Luger no more than inches away from Darnell's clawing fingers.

The *El Diablo* was ploughing the water now, in gradually widening circles, and the wheel was spinning wildly out of control. Jaime didn't see Darnell's hand close over the gun. All he heard was a loud *thunk,* as if he had suddenly been struck by lightning.

Stumbling to his feet, he managed to kick the Luger from Darnell's fingers and then dragged him to the railing, grunting and heaving with every step.

"No . . . Jaime . . . please . . . no . . . don't . . ." Darnell Hanlan's cries were sharp and piercing like those of a woman in terror, and the sound seemed to penetrate Jaime's brain like a sharp knife. There was an ugly gushing wound in his belly, and blood was pumping out with every breath he took.

With an almost superhuman effort, he lifted Darnell halfway over the railing, and his hands closed tightly about his throat. For a moment, Jaime stared into the bulging, horror-stricken eye, and then he heaved him over the side and into the sea.

Darnell's cries were quickly drowned out, while from across the water, Jaime heard the music, the laughter, and saw the lights. Kim was waiting for him, and somehow he had to get to her, Jaime realized. Darnell was gone now, and none of the rest of it seemed to matter.

Jaime turned from the railing and lurched heavily toward the wildly spinning wheel, only to have the deck rise up suddenly to meet him.

His vision was blurring badly now, and bright shafts of pain were tearing at his guts. With a moan, Jaime doubled up and vomited a warm, rushing flow of blood, shuddering and holding himself very tightly. His lips moved as he whispered Kim's name, but no sound came.

Then, with one hand draped limply over the wheel, Jaime Rodriquez stiffened and lay perfectly still. His eyes were wide and staring, vacant as the windows of an empty house, as skyrockets rose screaming into the night sky to explode into convulsions of brilliant color.

# =======CHAPTER 30=======

It was a night for heroines.

Several hundred people strained against the wooden police barricades in front of the Old American Hotel. Most of them were women well over 30, but there were also youthful girls with incredibly fresh and hopeful faces.

They were only part of the volunteer army that had marched across northern Long Island to bring Claire Spencer victory in the Congressional primary. It had been a stunning upset. These were now Claire's people, and they had come to her campaign headquarters that night to claim her as their own.

Inside the main ballroom, on the lobby floor, the party regulars, with their CLAIRE FOR CONGRESS buttons, moved excitedly among the instruments that had played such an important part in winning the election primary: the TV cameras, the unwinding tape recorders, and banks of computers that had been estimating the voting potential of each district.

A corner suite, well-insulated against easy intrusion, had been reserved for the candidate, but Claire had opened the doors and let everybody in. That was the way she had won—by being accessible and concerned. It was also the way, Claire insisted, that she was going to Washington.

By eleven o'clock, 78 percent of the vote was in, giving Claire a clear margin of victory. In the living room of her suite, Claire was sitting on a folding chair beneath a very bad Van Gogh print. She was without question the center of all attention, and gathered about her was a delegation of highly placed politicians, led by the lieutenant governor of the state.

They were talking in low, confidential tones, even as their eyes moved back and forth among the four TV sets, all going at the same time. About them, all was chaos. People were wandering in and out of the room, and whisky flowed freely at a portable bar, even though Claire herself was sipping from a can of diet Fresca. Canapé trays with an unappetizing assortment of leavings were scattered about the room. The Cheeze Whiz was beginning to turn brown at the edges, and the chopped liver had a sickly cast to it.

The noise level in the suite was high but at the same time slightly subdued and still expectant, a low, vibrant hum, interspersed with the clinking of ice cubes and bursts of nervous laughter, spiraling off to die abruptly.

The wave of excitement had not yet crested. That would come later, with Claire's scheduled appearance in the ballroom downstairs.

The woman of the hour was a very different Claire Ryan Spencer than the woman who had started out on the grueling primary trail some weeks earlier. She wore an absolute minimum of makeup now, and there was an obvious sprinkling of gray in her short, curly hair cut in a do-it-yourself style.

Perhaps most apparent was the fact that Claire had lost that certain distance. The cool arrogance that had once stamped her personality with a brittle facade had vanished completely. She seemed somehow to have discovered her own sense of self during the short but grueling campaign. She had matured in many ways, and now Claire knew how many different threads of hard work, luck, and perseverance were needed to put together a winning ticket with all the right ingredients.

"It's going to be a tough election," she was saying to the lieutenant governor, who was herself the first woman to have been elected to high state office. "I'm going to need all the help I can get, but I have no intention of compromising the real issues that have brought me this far."

As they went on to discuss the voting patterns among women in various districts, Claire happened to glance up and see Clayton standing in the doorway. She was shocked by his appearance, for although he was, as always, immaculately groomed, from his dazzling platinum hair to his expensively tailored sport coat and Gucci loafers, his face was gaunt and strained.

Clayton just stood there, staring across the room at her with eyes that held the look of a man condemned to live with some terrible inner pain for the rest of his life. He looked ill, tired, and defeated.

"I'm afraid you'll have to excuse me," Claire said to the lieutenant governor. She rose and quickly crossed the crowded room to take Clayton's arm, drawing him aside. "Hello, Clay," she said softly. "Thank you for coming. I had hoped very much that you would."

Clayton nodded slowly. "Well, this time you've really done it, Claire. You're going to make it all the way now . . . and I can't tell you how proud I am. I know that you're going to do a lot of good for a lot of people."

Something in his voice revealed the depth of his own unhappiness. And as Claire kissed him on the cheek, tears welled up, and Clayton was forced to turn his face away. "I'm sorry," he stammered. "I had no intention of falling apart tonight. It's just that seeing you again . . . well, I've missed you a lot, Claire."

"Come with me," Claire said. "I think we should talk privately."

After Claire had left instructions that she was not to be disturbed under any circumstances, they retired to one of the suite's bedrooms. Clayton was sitting on the edge of the bed by the time she finally shut the door behind her and crossed the room to sit down at his side. "What is it, Clay?" she asked. "What's happened to make you so terribly unhappy?"

He made a grieving sound deep in his throat, and then he dropped his face into his hands. He cried silently, but his shoulders were heaving convulsively as Claire slipped her arms around him and pulled his head against her breasts. Holding him tightly and rocking back and forth, Claire said, "I think you'd better tell me all about it, Clay. I've never seen you like this before. I know it will do you a lot of good to just get it off your chest."

For the first time in their lives together, Clayton had dropped the patient, slightly stuffy, and clinical facade to reveal a totally different side of himself. All the barriers seemed to have fallen away between them, and he was crying out to be pacified, comforted, forgiven, and loved. For a long time, Claire simply held him close against her, stroking his hair and murmuring words of reassurance. Never before had she seen him cry, Claire realized. It was she who had always been the emotional basket-case, running around like an accident on its way to happen.

Finally, Clayton got up and went into the bathroom, still without speaking a word. When he returned, some minutes later, he had splashed cold water on his face and was obviously making a supreme effort to pull himself together. His surgeon's hands trembled as if they were palsied, as he tried to light a cigarette. And finally, Claire had to do it for him, after which they both laughed a little.

Then Clayton told her everything—about his affair with Helene Von Bismark and how she had seduced him into going against all professional ethics by keeping Andrea Aristos a virtual prisoner at Golden Portals.

"May God forgive me, I helped her gain control of that poor girl's mind," he confessed. "I've broken every ethical code a doctor lives by. I was blinded by my desire for Helene, even though I knew it was wrong from the very beginning. She simply used me, Claire, and when I was of no further use to her, she tossed me aside. She threatened to expose me for the charlatan I was if I ever breathed a word about what had taken place."

He shook his head with a weary, dogged motion and

sighed deeply. "I have no choice but to give up the practice of medicine now. I'm not a doctor anymore. Anyone capable of doing what I've done has no right to pretend he's interested in helping people. I've sold out . . . and I just don't know where to go from here."

When Claire spoke, her voice was very low and serious, and her words carried the clear ring of truth. "When I first met you, Clay, you wanted more than anything else to be a country doctor with a general practice, wife, kids, and probably even a white picket fence and your shingle tacked up beside the front door.

"When you fell in love with me, I deliberately set out to change all that. Because of my own neurotic ambitions, I turned you into something else, Clay. Don't you see that you were simply never cut out to be a convenient Dr. Feelgood to all those rich people I wanted so desperately to emulate?

"I can see it all so clearly now," she said. "By playing the game, I never had the time to face the truth about myself. But once you've started, you can't ever stop even for a minute. You just keep moving very fast from one drink, pill, party, and love affair to the next, even though you know that none of it will ever be enough.

"My sole function in life was to try and keep the empty spaces in between small enough, so I didn't fall through into the pit that was always there—like a cliff I was ready to fall over at any given moment. Then, when the spaces began to get wider and the fall scarier, I started to panic. I saw my body decaying from day to day, and I knew that I had nothing at all to fall back on."

She clutched his arm, beseeching him with her eyes. "I was frightened too, Clay. Too frightened to see the warning signs that you saw only too clearly and tried to warn me about, even though I wouldn't listen."

Claire slipped from the edge of the bed and dropped to her knees before him. She clasped both his hands in hers and bent to kiss them, each in turn. "It isn't too late for us," she whispered, her eyes welling with tears.

Then she was smiling and holding very tightly to his hands. "Don't you see? The very fact that you came to me tonight is all that really matters. We can put the past behind us and go on from here. Sure, we've made mistakes, and two-thirds of our lives are behind us. But what the hell? I know now that I married a man I happen to be very much in love with. We can start again and do it right this time."

"Do you really want that, Claire . . . do you really want . . . me?"

She blinked back the tears, smiling, nodding, and pressing herself close against him. "I not only want you, Dr. Spencer, but I also need you very, very much."

"Of course, one can't say for certain in these matters," Dr. Robinson said, puffing on his pipe and flicking a trace of ash from the lapel of his dark blue blazer. "But it is my professional opinion that Miss Randolph will never recover sufficiently to become a . . . shall we say, productive member of society. In other words, Dr. and Mrs. Spencer, Abbey will very likely be unable to care for herself at any time in the forseeable future."

Claire and Clayton stood staring in at Abbey through the glass wall of the Intensive-Care Unit at Westport Hospital. She was lying upon a white-sheeted bed, being fed intravenously. Her face was very white and gaunt, with great bruise circles surrounding her eyes.

Abbey had finally regained consciousness after two weeks in deep coma, but there was not the slightest sign of recognition. Rather, she simply lay there staring up into the light of a ceiling fixture shining directly above her head, curled up like a child, with her hands knotted into tight fists against her breasts.

"We've done absolutely everything possible for her here," the doctor went on to say. "But I really can't hold out much hope." There was a pretty blonde nurse standing at his elbow, and after exchanging glances, Dr.

Robinson pointedly looked at his watch and cleared his throat.

"The bottom line, Mrs. Spencer, is that your cousin Abbey will need custodial care for the rest of her life. We can only keep her here another two weeks. After that, the hospital will recommend permanent institutionalization. I've already discussed the matter with Mrs. Aristos, and she's agreed with our conclusion that the case is utterly hopeless."

"My wife and I intend to institute legal proceedings to be named as Abbey's legal guardians," Clayton informed him. "I don't think that Mrs. Aristos will be willing to go to court over the matter, so we can safely assume that she has no further say in the case. As soon as Abbey is discharged from this hospital, we intend to have her moved to my sanitarium, where I fully intend to see that she has the kind of care she needs in order to make the best recovery possible."

Dr. Robinson raised one bushy eyebrow, then shrugged and removed his pipe from between his teeth. "That's entirely up to you and the courts," he said. "But quite frankly, Doctor, I must repeat that I can't offer you much hope. As you can see, Miss Randolph has regressed to an almost infantile stage of behavior, and we really have no way of knowing exactly how much damage has been done to the brain."

"You've rather put your finger on the reason we want to have Abbey placed in my husband's care," Claire informed him. "Because hope is the one thing that we do have to offer her. You see, Dr. Spencer and I are determined to bring my cousin Abbey back to the world."

"If you can manage to do that," Dr. Robinson said with a condescending air, "it will most assuredly be a first-rate miracle."

Claire slipped her arm through Clayton's and looked up into his face with all the love she felt shining in her eyes. "But you see Doctor, I happen to believe in miracles," she said. "In fact, whether you know it or not, you're looking at one right now."

*"We want Claire, we want Claire."* Over and over the crowd kept chanting the refrain as the temperature continued to rise among all those closely packed bodies in the ballroom of the Old American Hotel.

Then, just after midnight, Claire appeared on stage by way of a back entrance, and the entire room ripped into a loud tumult of screams, cheers, and almost deafening applause. She was smiling radiantly, with all the tiredness gone from her face. More than anything else, she looked like a winner.

Clayton was standing slightly behind her among the coterie of important political supporters who had come there that night to share her victory. There was a look of intense pride illuminating his handsome features.

Finally, after the rousing ovation had begun to subside, Claire signaled for silence and took the microphone in her hand. "I am not a woman who practices any formalized religion," she said, with her voice ringing out loud and clear over the speakers. "But over two thousand years ago, a very wise man by the name of Jesus was quoted as saying, 'Lay not up your treasures where moth and rust doth corrupt and thieves break in.' I stand here before you tonight for many reasons. But foremost among them is a man who has been my treasure, my Rock of Gibraltar and my devoted husband for over twenty years . . . most of which must have been pure hell.

"I want to thank all of you for coming here tonight. But most of all, I want to thank him for being here and for seeing something in me that I didn't even know was there." Claire reached to clasp Clayton's hand and drew him up beside her on the podium. "Ladies and gentlemen, it is my very great pleasure to introduce you to my partner, friend, and most ardent supporter through all the dark days. My husband, Dr. Clayton Spencer."

# =====CHAPTER 31=====

For over two weeks, a veritable army of landscape gardeners, construction workers, caterers, and interior decorators had been at work transforming Treasure Cay into a Disneyland fantasy version of Versailles. And on the night of the Gold and Silver Ball, the entire island luxuriated beneath the crystalline radiance of a full moon.

Pale and immense, the moon scattered its silvery brilliance over the sound, while the long drive leading up to the chateau was illuminated by flaming torches. From inside the mansion, the melodic strains of a full orchestra mingled with laughter and voices. Outside, on the newly sodded acres of perfectly manicured lawns, wandering minstrels serenaded clusters of resplendently attired guests as they strolled about the formal gardens, beneath stately white oak trees strung with thousands of brightly colored lanterns.

Since early that evening, horse-drawn fiacres had been carrying the lavishly costumed guests up to the chateau from the newly constructed marina. The carriages were festooned with flowers. The horses trotted smartly up the drive beneath cockades of feathered plumes, while their manes and tails were plaited with brightly colored ribbons that streamed out behind them in the light evening breeze.

When they reached the chateau, the celebrants stepped from their carriages to mount the marble staircase, between ranks of liverymen. A flurry of famous and celebrated faces had skimmed in from the sea on

345

a flotilla of yachts or arrived at the island's new airstrip aboard a steady stream of private planes.

They had come to Treasure Cay that evening, as if drawn by some primal, tribal urge to gather en masse and reaffirm their species. Masked and costumed, they would dance away the evening hours, while parading the colors of their own special breed. Once again they would prove to themselves and to each other that it didn't matter what you did as long as it was done with style and flair.

The grand ballroom took up one entire wing of the chateau and was done in red plush and gold, with garlands of imported flowers decorating the fluted marble columns. Elaborate costumes embroidered with jewels and plumes shimmered beneath glittering crystal chandeliers. And while the orchestra played for dancing, liveried servants moved among the guests bearing trays of gourmet delicacies.

For Roxanne and Kamal, the Gold and Silver Ball had climaxed a week that was straight out of the *Arabian Nights,* with all the beautiful people in attendance. It had all started on the previous Sunday, with a lavish luncheon given by Ali Reza at the Maidstone Club. The press was excluded, but one of the invited guests excitedly informed the waiting crush of reporters that Kamal would scarcely allow Roxanne out of his sight and had playfully spoon-fed her Caspian caviar.

Later that same evening, a curtained limousine whisked the loving couple off to Shazam, the Hamptons' swingingest disco, where they danced until dawn. Roxanne had never looked more radiantly happy, and on Wednesday they had flown off to Manhattan in Kamal's helicopter, to attend a star-studded gala at the Waldorf Astoria.

That was the evening they announced their engagement, and Roxanne proudly displayed the huge square-cut diamond Kamal had given her, as they smiled happily and obliged the photographers with intimate poses. The stone was said to be worth over $3 million.

On Thursday, Kamal's new yacht sailed into South-ampton Harbor and was duly christened the *Roxanne,* with its namesake dutifully swinging a bottle of cham-pagne against the hull. It was a new, magnificent vessel, carrying a seaplane, a crew of 24, and two power launches, and it came equipped with a freshwater swim-ming pool. There were 12 beautifully appointed guest suites and a large apartment for the newly engaged couple, crammed with priceless paintings and antiques.

Roxanne and Kamal were feted like royalty wherever they appeared. By the end of the week, it was an-nounced that they planned to honeymoon in Saudi Arabia following their wedding, as guests of the Saudi royal family. Perhaps the only unpleasant note during the entire incredible week was the mention in Cassan-dra's column that the magnificent 44-carat Grand Mogul diamond with which Kamal had pledged his troth was the same stone he had earlier presented An-drea Aristos, reset in a new platinum setting.

That was a fact of which Roxanne herself was only too aware, although she preferred simply not to think about it. Diamonds, after all, were her stock in trade, and any really important stones had belonged to a host of previous owners in any case, she reasoned.

The receiving line that night at the ball was posted at the top of a Florentine marble staircase, leading down into the ballroom. A powdered and bewigged major domo with a silver staff announced the name of each of the arriving guests. Then they made their way down the grand staircase, flanked by more liverymen. It was an impressive parade that went on for over two hours, with the light from the crystal chandeliers catch-ing and sparkling the incredible array of jewels, to send emerald, diamond, and sapphire reflections dancing off across the frescoed walls and muraled ceilings.

At the head of the receiving line, Roxanne looked radiant as Marie Antoinette, in a powdered wig, dia-mond choker, and voluminous gown of billowing white silk. At her side, Kamal appeared darkly handsome as

Napoleon Bonaparte. He seemed to wear his triumph with an easy grace, accepting the plaudits that were his due as 500 rich and famous guests moved by like compliant courtiers.

Finally, with every eye in the room upon them, Kamal took Roxanne in his arms, and they began to waltz across the dance floor as the music swelled about them. Almost immediately, the floor began to clear, and there was no question in anyone's mind but that the evening belonged to them alone—to Roxanne and Kamal, sweeping around and around before the glittering assemblage who had come there that evening to pay homage and fealty to the new king and queen.

The stroke of midnight brought the surprise announcement that they had been married that afternoon in a private civil ceremony, before a local judge. Then everyone moved outside onto the wide flagstone terrace to take part in the official groundbreaking ceremony of the Treasure Cay project, which was held in conjunction with a spectacular fireworks display.

Afterward, there would be dancing until dawn, the premiere showing of Franco de Roma's Hampton documentary, and casino gambling inside the chateau, for all those wishing to try their luck. It had turned out to be an evening in which almost everybody on the guest list felt lucky and very select. The night had a mystical quality about it, and all the very best people were there, among their own kind, gathered together to celebrate themselves and the rarified world in which they seemed to live charmed lives.

The Gold and Silver Ball was, without question, an enormous success. And yet for Roxanne herself, her triumph at presiding over the elaborate spectacle as Mrs. Kamal Ali Reza was marred by an incident that took place around two o'clock in the morning.

Gambling tables had been set up at one end of the ballroom, with all of the proceeds going to charity. While posing for pictures at the roulette table, one of the reporters asked Roxanne to take the place of the

348

croupier, spinning the wheel of fortune and then raking in the losing chips across the green baize table as flash-bulbs popped on every side.

At first, Roxanne appeared only too willing to comply, until Kamal suddenly appeared on the scene and leaned close to whisper something into her ear as their hands intertwined. Then, turning to the photographers, he announced in no uncertain terms that he preferred not to have his wife expose herself to "cheap publicity shots of that kind."

The photographers were ordered to expose the film that had already been shot. Those that refused, had their cameras quickly confiscated by Kamal's body-guards, who seemed to appear out of nowhere.

"But I really don't mind at all," Roxanne countered, looking flustered and confused. "I mean, after all, darling, it is for a worthy cause."

Ali Reza's voice took on a razor's edge, and his dark eyes went hard as stone. "I said that I don't want you to do it, Roxanne. There's simply nothing more to be said about the matter."

As Roxanne flushed and continued to remonstrate with him, his hand closed over hers, and she felt the huge 44-carat diamond pressing into her flesh. Then, with everyone looking on, her features blanched, although none of those present actually saw what was taking place.

Holding her hand behind his back, Kamal had bent one of Roxanne's fingers back from her hand, smiling into her eyes as he increased the pressure until the bone snapped and the pain sped up her arm to explode into her brain.

Then he was leading her out onto the dance floor once again, and Roxanne's features had assumed a smiling, glazed mask in order to hide her pain and confusion. It hadn't really happened, she kept telling herself, as an aching numbness began to dull the pain. It had merely been an accident, spawned in the heat of their first disagreement. She had absolutely no reason in the world to feel afraid of the smiling, handsome stranger who held her in his arms, like a very expensive possession.

After all, Roxanne thought a bit wildly as they whirled about the dance floor, she was now Mrs. Kamal Ali Reza, and their lives together had only just begun. Their marriage was the most brilliant match of the decade. There was simply no going back now, in spite of the pain, the humiliation, and the uncertainty of whatever it was that lay ahead of her as the wife of a man she scarcely knew.

While the celebrants gathered for a post-midnight supper beneath the softly muted radiance of giant silver candelabra, two of the masked guests slipped away from the chateau. There were standing warrants out for both Ian's and Sarah's arrest, but they had managed to elude the police for over a week. When the night of the ball arrived, they had joined the gaily costumed throng aboard a hydrofoil and were transported, unrecognized, to Treasure Cay.

Since most of the guests had chosen costumes from the period during which Versailles was the *centre du monde,* Sarah had come gowned as Charlotte Corday, while Ian had assumed the cowled robes of a humble Jesuit friar.

There was by now a slight chill to the night air as they left the chateau and hurried across the grounds to disappear into the pine forest sloping downward to where the cliffs fell away to the sea below. The pine needles underfoot were soft and spongy, while the luminous wash of moonlight scarcely penetrated the dark green canopy high overhead.

Without exchanging a word, they followed a narrow path through the trees, breathing in the resin-scented air. Sarah was extremely apprehensive about what they might find once they reached the *Golden Hind,* which was anchored offshore, and the champagne she had consumed throughout the evening had made her feel slightly lightheaded.

After walking for about ten minutes at a very brisk pace, they were both breathing heavily by the time they reached the path winding tortuously down the side of the cliffs to a small sheltered cover below. The night was very still and quiet except for the slight wind rustling the treetops and the sound of the surf rushing in to crash upon the beach with a low, thundering roar.

Finally they emerged from the trees to see the *Golden Hind* riding serenely at anchor, about 300 yards offshore. The hull of the yacht appeared white and ghostly in the moonlight, and the portholes were brightly lit from bow to stern.

Ian had made an earlier reconaissance, and discovered that there was a skiff kept on the beach below. It had been drawn up above the tide line, and after paddling out across the gently lapping waters of the cove, they were able to clamber aboard the *Golden Hind* without incident.

That was, at least until they reached the top of the gangway, where they encountered the dour and disapproving figure of the first mate blocking their way. "I'm sorry," he said in heavily accented English. "But no one is permitted to come aboard."

"It's all right," Sarah said, taking off her mask. "It's me . . . Andrea's friend, Sarah Dane."

The first mate did not appear surprised to see her, and his response was almost surly. "The baroness has given strict orders that no one is allowed aboard. We sail for the Mediterranean tomorrow at dawn. I'm going to be very frank with you, Mrs. Dane. The baroness has given the captain instructions that if you should try to come aboard or disturb Miss Andrea in any way, the harbor patrol is to be called, and you are to be arrested."

"Why don't we try assault and battery for starters?" Ian said, landing a right hook squarely in the man's gut. Seconds later, they were running through the main salon and down the spiral staircase to the cabin deck below.

By now there were angry shouts from above. As they turned the corner of the thickly carpeted passageway leading to Andrea's quarters, an enormous figure loomed up suddenly to block their path. He was built like a *sumo* wrestler, and the flesh of his bare arms seemed to be all bulging muscle.

"Get out of my way," Ian barked. He planted himself squarely in the center of the dimly lit passageway, as Bruno's small, close-set eyes glittered menacingly beneath his prominent brow.

"Be careful," Sarah cautioned from behind him. "It's Helene's bodyguard, and he's dangerous."

There was a smile curling on Bruno's lips, and every inch of his massive frame seemed poised, like some huge Hyperborean animal ready to pounce.

Moving very slowly and never taking his eyes from Ian's face, he bent to produce a long stiletto from his boot and then began moving toward them in a low crouch.

Shoving Sarah securely behind him, Ian lifted his hands in a fighter's stance. His muscles were taut and ready for action, as adrenalin pulsed through his veins and his breath came in short, harsh rasps.

"I'm not afraid of you or that knife," he snarled. "Whether you like it or not . . . we're going right straight through that door."

"Ian . . . please," Sarah cautioned. "Don't do anything foolish."

"You've got to be kidding," Ian laughed back over his shoulder. "That's all I've done since I met you, Seraphina, my girl. So why let a slab of beef like our friend here break a winning streak? I'm sorta getting to like playing at being James Bond."

Sarah saw the barest flicker of something in Bruno's eyes, just before he leaped forward to slash at Ian with a wide, cutting arc of the flashing blade. Footsteps could be heard clattering down the stairs from the deck

352

above, along with a babble of voices speaking in rapid-fire Greek.

Sarah screamed as Ian dodged to one side. But he wasn't quick enough. And while Bruno's savage thrust only narrowly missed its target, the razor-sharp edge of the blade sliced through the heavy homespun material of Ian's robe, and blood began to soak through the white wool material. With a riot of angry voices exploding behind her in the passageway, Sarah was beginning to panic.

"Why don't you help him?" she shouted at the tight little cluster of uniformed officers who had come to a halt, staring in disbelief. Sarah could hear fists pounding against a door at the end of the hall, and Andrea's voice screaming to be heard.

Weaving wildly from side to side, Bruno moved in swiftly and then darted suddenly forward, swinging his knife wide. Then, changing directions sharply and unexpectedly, he plunged it at Ian's throat.

He missed, but Sarah's scream had a shrill, hysterical quality about it, even as she remained pressed against the wall with the ship's officers stacked up behind her like chessmen momentarily frozen in play. All of them were staring at the startling scene playing itself out before their eyes.

Once again Ian managed to avoid the blade, and with a quick sidestep, he brought his hand down hard, with a lightning karate chop to Bruno's stiffened wrist. Bruno's face was pale and taut, and beads of perspiration sprouted on his forehead, as the knife clattered against the bulkhead and fell to the floor.

With the ragged snarl of an enraged beast, Bruno charged head on, swinging his fists wildly. A direct blow to the stomach finally sent Ian crumpling to his knees, while a left jab caught him squarely on the jaw with a sickening crunch.

By this point, Ian was only too aware that he had underestimated his adversary and was in serious trouble. He found himself pinned flat on his back, with

Bruno's knees wedged squarely between his thighs. Bruno's fists were raining down with alarming rapidity, dealing blows to his head and his face and his stomach.

They were hard, damaging blows, falling one upon another, and Ian realized that he was very close to passing out. Then, in his final flickering moments of consciousness, he saw Sarah descending upon his assailant from behind, like an avenging angel. There was something fiercely protective sparking her eyes, as she flung herself bodily on Bruno's broad back, clawing blindly at his face and gouging at his eyes with long, raking talons.

The cries escaping her lips were almost inhuman, and as if in answer, Ian heard Andrea calling to her from the other side of the door. Then, with Ian's own blood smearing her hands and face, Sarah snatched off her spike-heel pump, and brandished it overhead, bringing it down like an ice pick against Bruno's skull, with each blow ripping away at his bare scalp.

Within seconds, blood was spurting from a half-dozen puncture wounds. And to Ian's glazed and staring eyes, as Bruno's hands clutched his throat, choking him, the heel of Sarah's shoe was like a dagger descending with incredible force and rapidity, to pierce and tear at the flesh.

"Sarah . . . help me," Andrea screamed from behind the locked door of her cabin. "Please . . . help me."

A sudden stream of Sicilian obscenities escaped Sarah's lips, curses she wasn't even aware that she knew. She kept battering and clawing and shrieking out until Bruno released his hold on Ian's throat and tumbled over backward to writhe and twist upon the floor, clutching at his face with both hands, as blood streamed between his fingers.

But by this time, Sarah was far beyond any kind of rational thought or behavior, and as Bruno tried to crawl blindly away, she leaped after him, vaulting over Ian's prostrate form to plant one stockinged foot squarely in his crotch.

"Aaraagh," he bellowed, doubling up in a fetal position, vomiting and moaning in sheer agony.

"Andrea . . . I'm coming," Sarah cried, rushing back to help Ian to his feet. Then they both ran down the corridor.

Ian threw all his weight against the teakwood panels, with a splintering crash that carried both of them staggering inside.

"Thank God you've come." Andrea was almost beside herself, as she and and Sarah fell into one another's arms. Then they both were laughing and crying together as Ian gathered them both in a big bearlike embrace.

Between midnight and three o'clock in the morning, flight after flight of exploding rockets rose screaming into the summer sky over Treasure Cay. The music played, the champagne bubbled, and dancing couples became vivid splashes of color against the white marble floor of the grand ballroom.

For the Von Bismarks, it was a bon voyage party as well, for they planned to sail aboard the *Golden Hind* for Europe, directly after the ball. Helene had been in exuberant spirits all evening and had attended the ball costumed as Madame de Pompadour, from the Court of Louis XIV.

She was exchanging champagne toasts with a Milanese industrial magnate when someone came up and whispered in her ear that the *Golden Hind* was sailing out to sea. Her bodyguard, Bruno—battered, beaten, and dazed—had been set adrift in a small skiff, only to be picked up by the Coast Guard just off the harbor entrance.

Helene simply could not believe her ears, and yet the view from the terrace of the chateau quickly confirmed the truth. The yacht was indeed sailing away, and as she stood watching all her carefully laid plans melting away into the night, Jason came out to join her, standing at the stone balustrade.

"Well, Helene," he said, "There it goes. Two billion

dollars, sailing away forever. Funny how things work out, isn't it?"

Helene turned slowly to face him. Her eyes were like chips of ice, matching the sparkling green-fire of her dancing emerald pendant earings. "It was you who arranged this, wasn't it?"

Jason, costumed as the Prince de Conti, smiled and slowly sipped his champagne. "I only wish I could take full credit," he said. "Actually, it was Sarah Dane who pulled the rug out from under you. She wasn't afraid to bite the bullet, and Andrea's lucky to have her as a friend. Sarah and Ian McVane are aboard the yacht with Andrea. I should imagine that by the time they arrive in Monaco, there're going to be a few heads rolling."

Helene's features had the hard, glazed look of a Dresden china doll. "The game isn't over yet, Jason my love. Don't forget I still hold at least a few trump cards."

"If you're talking about Andrea's godchildren, you might as well forget it. You're no longer holding hostages, Helene. Our perfect pair of matched *his* and *her* twins are at this moment aboard a flight to Vienna, in the care of their nanny. My mother's family has agreed to take them in, and if you try in any way to interfere, I'm perfectly willing to expose you for the kind of mother you are . . . in court."

"I give you my word, Jason. I'm going to destroy you if it's the last thing I do."

Jason dragged deeply on his cigarette and then sent the glowing butt arcing out into the night. "You'll have to find me first, Helene. I've already arranged to have myself committed to a sanitarium. After I get myself straightened out, I'll be joining Andrea in Monte Carlo. She knows everything—including the truth about you and Henri."

There was a breaking sound as Helene's champagne glass shattered in her clenched hand. She stood there

356

staring at Jason's back as he walked across the terrace and disappeared inside the chateau.

It was at that very moment that Franco de Roma's Hampton documentary began to flash across a huge screen at the far end of the ballroom. It was the moment of ultimate truth for many of those present.

Suddenly, there they were in all their sybaritic glory —the Hampton summer people, playing out their golden games against a lush and extravagant background, for all the world to see.

In cutting, splicing and editing the film, de Roma had proven himself a master. The composition was faceted with prismatic brilliance, and the initial impact had all those present absolutely riveted to the screen, fascinated, like the narcissists they were, with the way they looked and moved and acted.

The ravishing technicolor spectacle playing upon the screen had managed to fully capture and encompass one entire summer of their lives: polite party laughter, snatches of conversation, on-the-spot interviews, and the hard, pounding beat of the disco music that had carried them from dusk to dawn throughout the long summer nights.

Then, almost imperceptably at first, the camera began to speed up, racing ahead with sexually explicit scenes interspersed with gracious homes, palatial gardens, lush scenery, and a variety of cameo walkons from a hundred parties they had all attended that summer.

Faster and faster the film ran, wildly out of sync now, as the various scenes began to blur and interlace into a kaleidoscopic collage of well-known faces and bodies conjoining in a variety of sexual positions and perversions. It was a veritable fountain of spurting orgasms, writhing limbs, and voices raised in a mounting crescendo of ecstatic cries, gasps, moans, and shrieks.

"Can't someone stop it?" a woman screamed. But by then it was already too late.

# ═══CHAPTER 32═══

It was four in the morning and the human maelstrom that flowed perpetually through airports all over the world had dwindled and ceased during the long dark hours just before dawn.

The plane for Rio had left at two A.M. And by now, whatever final threads of hope Kim continued to hold had finally come unstrung. She felt like a marionette whose strings had been suddenly and irrevocably released.

It had been a dream far too fragile to survive, and Kim now realized with a terrible sense of déjà vu that she had known all along she would never see Jaime again.

Reaching into her purse, she removed a small gift-wrapped package he had given her during their final, poignant moments together. Inside she found a blue-velvet jeweler's case and a spectacular yellow diamond ring. The setting was new and had an elegant simplicity about it. Inside the band was the engraved inscription: "From Jaime to Kim with love," followed by the date of their meeting and two words that, more than anything else, had come to sum up her life. "The Hamptons."

Kim sat mute, staring down at the shimmering multi-faceted stone as she slipped it over her finger. She felt empty and bereft, totally unable to take whatever steps were necessary to set her in motion once again. The summer was at an end, and Kim knew that somehow she was going to have to begin putting the pieces of her life back together again.

She and Jaime had been drawn together that summer like characters in a Greek tragedy, with some inexplicable destiny animating them in ways unknown. Kim had never believed in predestination. And she wasn't even sure what she believed about the purpose of human life, beyond the knowledge that you took your chances, learned from your failures, and somehow continued to pick yourself up and survive—no matter what.

As Kim sat there, dreading the inevitable decisions she was going to have to make, Franco de Roma came breezing into the terminal through the electronically operated glass doors. Accompanied by a tired-looking PR man from Alitalia Airlines and a flurry of baggage attendants, he swept up to her, wreathed in smiles and exuding a plethora of good cheer.

Franco de Roma was $250,000 richer, he grandly announced, although things had ended *'molto terribile'* for Darnell Hanlan, his erstwhile employer.

Their joint film-making venture had caused a virtual stampede at the Gold and Silver Ball, de Roma informed her, although Darnell himself had apparently not lived long enough to share the full bitter fruits of their mutual endeavor.

His body had been found by the Coast Guard shortly after midnight, floating in the sea off Treasure Cay. He had been beaten into a bloody, broken, and scarcely recognizable corpse. According to de Roma's account, a drifter by the name of Jaime Rodriquez had been found in the wreckage of Darnell's cabin cruiser after it had run aground on the rocks off Orient Point.

From what the police had been able to piece together, Darnell had been involved with him in some kind of depraved and symbiotic relationship that had ended in death for both of them. Also found aboard the *El Diablo* was a suitcase full of crisp, new $50,000 bills of undetermined origin.

As de Roma dramatically expounded on the climactic

events that had taken place on the last night of the Hampton summer season, Kim's face remained a blank mask behind her oversize sunglasses. There was just so much pain that it was hard to tell where she hurt the most. Even so, she managed to keep her voice from betraying her emotions as she politely refused de Roma's offer to accompany him to Italy, with bed and board for as long as she cared to stay.

After Franco embraced her warmly and dashed off like a minor whirlwind to catch his waiting plane, Kim remained sitting exactly where she was. The terminal was nearly empty now, and there was a terrible vacancy inside her.

Jaime was gone, lost to her forever for reasons that Kim could not even begin to comprehend. With all the good and all the bad, that summer season in the Hamptons was behind her now, and Jaime's dream of escaping to Rio had died stillborn. Kim had nowhere to go and no one to run to. Once again, she was utterly alone.

*There are only diamonds in all the world. Diamonds —and perhaps the gift of disillusionment.* Fitzgerald's words came back to haunt her now, as she lifted her eyes from the diamond ring that Jaime had given her to the closed-circuit TV screen, continually printing out the chronology of arriving and departing flights.

Blinking rapidly in order to see through her tears, Kim saw that there was a plane leaving for Los Angeles at seven o'clock the following morning. It seemed a very long time to have to wait, and yet somehow, the first decision had been made. Now she had two seemingly endless hours stretching ahead of her like an eternity. The minutes slowly ticked away, like mourners passing slowly in a funeral procession.

Kim didn't want to cry. At least not yet, not there in that vast, empty, impersonal airline terminal, at five o'clock in the morning. For the moment, she was simply too drained, too stunned, and too dazed to feel very much of anything beyond a terrible sense of loss.

To keep herself from breaking down altogether, Kim opened her flight bag and took out a spiral notebook with the inscription "SCENARIO—The Gold Coast" printed across the front, along with the words "A screenplay by Kimberly Merriweather."

Sniffing and dabbing at her reddened eyes with a crumpled Kleenex, Kim ferreted around in her purse until she found a leaky ballpoint pen that immediately smudged her fingers with ink.

Then she began to write in a firm, neat, tightly controlled hand.

*The Gold Coast* starts out with two people meeting on their way to a destination previously unknown to either of them.

The roles of these two characters (a darkly handsome young man and a pretty, young Malibu blonde with too-knowing eyes), while very different, have previously been determined by the levels and caste systems of the society in which they live. Each in his own way is a loner. Yet they both refuse to accept the stifling conformity of the predetermined roles into which life has cast them.

Although poles apart, they are both looking desperately for a way out . . . for an escape.

Kim paused for a moment, nibbled the end of her plastic ballpoint pen in a thoughtful concentrated manner, and then continued writing, as tears began spilling slowly down her cheeks.

Someone once wrote (a Russian no doubt) that a bird defends its own cage because of territorial imperative, for that is the only thing that it can do if it belongs to the ancient blood-race of caged birds.

For in the reality of the caged bird's life and experience, the open door is not the exit to freedom but rather the entrance to approaching catastrophe.

Yet the caged bird sings, even though it knows

that the hungry cat awaits in the darkness outside.

That is the reality of the caged bird. But its dream is of freedom and flight, to a world beyond the bars that surround it. Thus, in the opening scene of *The Gold Coast,* two people meet on the highway one sunlit June day. It is a day bright with the promise of a long and endless golden summer, stretching away into a limitless future like a yellow brick road.

# EPILOGUE

From far out at sea, the lights of Treasure Cay were still visible to the two people standing at the railing of the *Golden Hind*. Already the tangy salt-sea air was tinged with the faintest hint of cooler climes, as the spectacular white vessel sailed steadily eastward across a sea as smooth and simmering as green bottle-glass.

From moment to moment, the powerful Atlantic currents seemed to be sweeping them steadily away from the shores of the North American continent—away from the Hamptons and the shoreline that by now had become little more than a distant scrim of twinkling lights, gradually merging with an infinity of stars shining brightly overhead.

Ian's hand closed over Sarah's on the smooth teak railing, and he bent to gently kiss her cheek. "Andrea's going to be all right," he said. "You don't have to worry about her, Sarah. We'll stick around as long as she needs us, but eventually she's going to have to make it on her own."

"I know," Sarah whispered, as tears brimmed and spilled. She accepted the handkerchief Ian pressed into her hands and then looked up at him with all the love and sadness and hope she felt shining in her eyes. "I was just thinking about all the things that got broken this summer . . . the lives that were shattered. There wasn't enough money in all the Hamptons to put them back together again. Not really."

Ian smiled and nodded sadly. He was battered, gray-faced, and utterly exhausted, yet somehow peaceful and very content as he drew Sarah into his arms. "Some of us survived," he said. "And that's all that really matters. Now dry your eyes, my little Seraphina. It's almost dawn."

Sarah turned and slipped her arms around his neck, clinging tightly. "I want you to take me to bed," she whispered. "Take me to bed . . . and hold me. I'm so very tired that all I want to do is wrap myself around you and fall asleep in your arms."

"I'll hold you very tightly," Ian said gruffly. "And tomorrow we'll begin again."

Dear Reader:

The Pinnacle Books editors strive to select and produce books that are exciting, entertaining and readable . . . no matter what the category. From time to time we will attempt to discover what you, the reader, think about a particular book.

Now that you've finished reading *The Hamptons*, Book I, we'd like to find out what you liked, or didn't like, about this story. We'll share your opinions with the author and discuss them as we plan future books. This will result in books that you will find more to your liking. As in fine art and good cooking a matter of taste is involved; and for you, of course, it is *your* taste that is most important to you. For Charles Rigdon, and the Pinnacle editors, it is not the critics' reviews and awards that have been most rewarding, it is the unending stream of readers' mail. Here is where we discover what readers like, what they *feel* about a story, and what they find memorable. So, do help us in becoming a little better in providing you with the kind of stories you like. Here's how . . .

## WIN BOOKS . . . AND $200!

Please fill out the following pages and mail them as indicated. Every week, for twelve weeks following publication, the editors will choose, at random, a reader's name from all the questionnaires received. The twelve lucky readers will receive $25 worth of paperbacks *and* become an official entry in our 1979 Pinnacle

Books Reader Sweepstakes. The winner of this sweepstakes drawing will receive a Grand Prize of $200, the inclusion of their name in a forthcoming Pinnacle Book (as a special acknowledgment, possibly even as a character!), and several other local prizes to be announced to each initial winner. As a further inducement to send in your questionnaire *now*, we will also send the first 25 replies received a free book by return mail! Here's a chance to talk to the author and editor, voice your opinions, and win some great prizes, too!

—The Editors

# READER SURVEY

*NOTE: Please feel free to expand on any of these questions on a separate page, or to express yourself on any aspect of your thoughts on reading . . . but do be sure to include this entire questionnaire with any such letters.*

1. Are you glad you bought this book, and did it live up to your expectations?

2. What was it about this book that induced you to buy it?

   (A. The title_____)  (B. The author's name_____)

   (C. A friend's recommendation_____)

   (D. The cover art_____)

   (E. The cover description_____)

   (F. Subject matter_____)  (G. Advertisement_____)

   (H. Heard author on TV or radio_____)

   (I. Read a previous book by author_____ . . . which one? _____)

   (J. Bookstore display_____)

   (K. Other? _____)

3. What is the book you read just before this one?

   And how would you rate it with *The Hamptons?*

4. What is the very next book you plan to read?

   How did you decide on that? _____

5.  Where did you buy *The Hamptons?* _____
    _____
    (Name and address of store, please):
    _____
    _____

6.  Where do you buy the majority of your paper-
    backs? _____

7.  What seems to be the major factor that persuades
    you to buy a certain book?
    _____

8.  How many books do you buy each month?
    _____

9.  Do you ever write letters to the author or pub-
    lisher . . . and why? _____
    _____

10. About how many hours a week do you spend
    reading books? _____ How many hours a week
    watching television? _____

11. What other spare-time activity do you enjoy
    most? _____ For how many hours
    a week? _____

12. Which magazines do you read regularly? . . .
    in order of your preference _____,
    _____, _____,

13. Of your favorite magazine, what is it that you
    like best about it? _____
    _____

14. What is your favorite television show of the past
    year or so? _____

15. What is your favorite motion picture of the past year or so? _____

16. What is the most disappointing television show you've seen lately? _____

17. What is the most disappointing motion picture you've seen lately? _____

18. What is the most disappointing book you've read lately? _____

19. Are there authors that you like so well that you read *all* their books? _____
    Who are they? _____

20. And can you explain *why* you like their books so much? _____
    _____
    _____

21. Which particular books by these authors do you like best? _____
    _____

22. Did you read Taylor Caldwell's *Captains and Kings*?_____ Did you watch it on television?_____
    Which did you do first? _____

23. Did you read John Jakes' *The Bastard?* _____
    Did you watch it on TV?_____ Which first?_____
    Have you read any of the other books in John Jakes' Bicentennial Series? _____
    What do you think of them? _____

24. Did you read James Michener's *Centennial*?_____
    Did you watch it on TV?_____ Which first?_____

25. Did you read Irwin Shaw's *Rich Man, Poor Man*? _____ Did you watch it on TV? _____ Which first? _____

26. Of all the recent books you've read, or films you've seen, are there any that you would compare in any way to *The Hamptons*? _____

27. Have you read any other books by Charles Rigdon? _____ Which ones? _____

28. Have you read any books by Burt Hirschfeld? _____ Which ones? _____

29. Have you read any books by Harold Robbins? _____ Which ones? _____

30. Have you read any books by Rosemary Rogers? _____ Which ones? _____

31. In *The Hamptons*, which character did you find most fascinating? _____
Most likeable? _____ Most exciting? _____ Least interesting? _____ Which one did you identify with most? _____

32. Do you think any of Charles Rigdon's characters were based on real people? If so, who reminded you of whom? _____
_____
_____
_____
_____

33. Rank the following descriptions of *The Hamptons* as you feel they are best defined:

|  | Excellent | Okay | Poor |
|---|---|---|---|
| A. A sense of reality | _____ | _____ | _____ |
| B. Suspense | _____ | _____ | _____ |

C. Intrigue    \_\_\_\_    \_\_\_\_    \_\_\_\_

D. Sexuality    \_\_\_\_    \_\_\_\_    \_\_\_\_

E. Violence    \_\_\_\_    \_\_\_\_    \_\_\_\_

F. Romance    \_\_\_\_    \_\_\_\_    \_\_\_\_

G. History    \_\_\_\_    \_\_\_\_    \_\_\_\_

H. Characterization    \_\_\_\_    \_\_\_\_    \_\_\_\_

I. Scenes, events    \_\_\_\_    \_\_\_\_    \_\_\_\_

J. Pace, readability    \_\_\_\_    \_\_\_\_    \_\_\_\_

K. Dialogue    \_\_\_\_    \_\_\_\_    \_\_\_\_

L. Style    \_\_\_\_    \_\_\_\_    \_\_\_\_

34. Do you have any thoughts regarding the length of this book?\_\_\_\_ Would you have liked it to be longer? \_\_\_\_ Shorter? \_\_\_\_

35. Would you be interested in a sequel to *The Hamptons*? _____

36. Would you be interested in reading a similar story, but in a different locale? \_\_\_\_ Where, for example? _____ _____

37. Do you like to read about people involved in international finance?\_\_\_\_ Government and politics?\_\_\_\_ The "jet-set"?\_\_\_\_ Show business?\_\_\_\_

38. What, in your opinion, is the best or most vivid scene in *The Hamptons?* _____ _____

39. Did you find any errors or other upsetting things in this book? _____ _____

40. What do you do with your paperbacks after you've read them? _____
_____

41. Do you buy paperbacks in any of the following categories, and approximately how many do you buy in a year?

   A. Contemporary fiction (like *this* book) _____
   B. Historical romance                   _____
   C. Family saga                          _____
   D. Romance (like Harlequin)             _____
   E. Romantic suspense                    _____
   F. Gothic romance                       _____
   G. Occult novels                        _____
   H. War novels                           _____
   I. Action/adventure novels              _____
   J. "Bestsellers"                        _____
   K. Science fiction                      _____
   L. Mystery                              _____
   M. Westerns                             _____
   N. Nonfiction                           _____
   O. Biography                            _____
   P. How-To books                         _____
   Q. Other _____

42. And, lastly, some profile data on *you* the reader . . .

   A. Age: 12–16_____  17–20_____  21–30_____
           31–40_____  41–50_____  51–60_____
           61 or over_____

   B. Occupation: _____

C. Education level; check last grade completed:
10_____ 11_____ 12_____ Freshman_____
Sophomore_____ Junior_____ Senior_____
Graduate School_____, plus any specialized
schooling _____

D. Your average annual gross income: Under
$10,000_____ $10,000–$15,000_____
$15,000–$20,000_____ $20,000–
$30,000_____ $30,000–$50,000_____
Above $50,000_____

E. Did you read a lot as a child?_____ Do you
recall your favorite childhood novel? _____
_____

F. Do you find yourself reading more or less
than you did five years ago?_____

G. Do you read hardcover books?_____ How
often?_____ If so, are they books that you
buy?_____ borrow?_____ or trade?_____ Or
other?_____

H. Does the imprint (Pinnacle, Avon, Bantam,
etc.) make any difference to you when considering a paperback purchase? _____

I. Have you ever bought paperbacks by mail
directly from the publisher?_____ And do you
like to buy books that way? _____

J. Would you be interested in buying paperbacks via a book club or subscription program?_____ And, in your opinion, what would
be the best reasons for doing so? _____
_____ . . . the problems in
doing so? _____

K. Is there something that you'd like to see writers or publishers do for you as a reader of paperbacks? _____

_____

*THANK YOU FOR TAKING THE TIME TO REPLY TO THIS, THE FIRST PUBLIC READER SURVEY IN PAPERBACK HISTORY!*

NAME _____ PHONE_____
ADDRESS _____
CITY _____ STATE _____ ZIP _____

Please return this questionnaire to:

The Editors; Survey Dept. TH
Pinnacle Books, Inc.
2029 Century Park East
Los Angeles, CA 90067